FIRST KILL

FIRST KILL

Copyright © 2019 by David Hagberg

A Forge Book
Published by Tom Doherty Associates
175 Fifth Avenue
New York, NY 10010

www.tor-forge.com

Forge® is a registered trademark of Macmillan Publishing Group, LLC.

The Library of Congress Cataloging-in-Publication Data is available upon request.

ISBN 978-0-7653-3733-7 (hardcover)
ISBN 978-1-4668-3438-5 (ebook)

Our books may be purchased in bulk for promotional, educational, or business use.
Please contact your local bookseller or the Macmillan Corporate and Premium
Sales Department at 1-800-221-7945, extension 5442, or by email at
MacmillanSpecialMarkets@macmillan.com.

First Edition: May 2019

Printed in the United States of America

0 9 8 7 6 5 4 3 2 1

FIRST KILL

DAVID HAGBERG

A TOM DOHERTY ASSOCIATES BOOK

NEW YORK

one hundred kilometers from Santiago, but the president had not been to Valparaíso in at least one year. Arm's length enough.

Only one man, Varga mused. Coming alone from Washington. Or, perhaps he was already here.

He had stayed at his office in the military academy very late, attending with his staff to the results of the interrogations of eighteen more prisoners who had been rounded up last week in a dingy warehouse on the north side of Santiago's industrial district. The thirteen men and five women had been working on an anti-Pinochet demonstration that was supposed to have taken place this weekend. The trouble was they'd told too many people about their plans and word had gotten back to someone attached to the Army Intelligence Directorate and therefore to Varga.

"They'd admitted to much more than a simple demonstration," Varga told his people. "In fact they were planning to execute the president. We found a sniper rifle."

One of his lieutenants had actually smiled. "A Russian sniper rifle?"

"Of course not. An American weapon."

The others had laughed, because just now anti-American sentiment was growing. He did not, however, share what Torres had told him.

It was midnight by the time he got off the nearly deserted highway and headed south along the narrow paved road that led through the hills, roughly parallel to the coast. Five kilometers farther a branch of the road turned east, deeper into the hills, finally dropping into a narrow valley in which his compound had been constructed in the midst of boulders, scrub brush and hardscrabble soil five years ago—about the same time his extrajudicial executions had begun in earnest.

Roving spotlights illuminated the razor-wire coils that ran along the top of the twelve-foot reinforced-concrete walls. Motion sensors and even the newly acquired American infrared detector ringed the four-acre compound. No one could get close without silent alarms sounding, which would call to arms a lieutenant and eight men on duty each twelve-hour shift, 24/7. Their orders had been simple from the beginning: Shoot to kill any person or persons unknown to the officer on duty. No warning shots; no attempts to wound or capture would be made against the assailants.

A strong light atop the steel gates brightly illuminated the interior of the car as he pulled up. A moment later the light went out and the gates swung open for him.

No one came to greet him as he parked in front of the rambling one-story ranch-style house. But the gates swung shut and someone would come to put away his car.

Before he went in, he cocked an ear to listen for sounds, any sounds other than the highly muffled noise of the electrical generator in its shed off to the far left. But there was nothing. A half-dozen other buildings were scattered here and there, including the barracks for the troops and bungalows for the three officers. A mess hall was on the other side of a small parade ground, beyond which was a small-arms-training range, and the shells of three buildings, one of them two stories, that were used for urban incursion and hand-to-hand-combat training.

Three years ago, at Karina's insistence, they had constructed a well-lighted studio where she could work on her paintings without disturbing the house staff. And she'd also insisted that he build a putting green complete with a difficult sand trap.

"The officers must not only indulge in the opera and ballet, but mark my words, Mati, the time will come when the president will take up the game, and those of his officers who play, and play well, will gain his ear."

Who has time for stupid games? he'd thought then, but Karina had been right. A few months later Pinochet had begun taking lessons and Varga had been at his side. His position in the army and the government was more secure than ever.

Cook had made them a nice dinner of roast beef, potatoes and salad and Karina had laid out a bottle of de Jerez, their favorite Spanish brandy, in the dining room. A movie screen was set up beyond the end of the long table, and on the left an easel held her latest painting, covered by a cloth.

He set his briefcase on the floor next to the 16mm projector and she came into his arms, her thin nightgown falling open, her nude body for-ever exciting him like no other woman's ever had. Not even the women he'd tortured to death, some of them as young as twelve or thirteen and quite pretty at the start, moved him like Karina.

FOR LORREL, AS ALWAYS

We must know what we are talking about—and the only way to know is to have lived and loved and cursed and floundered and enjoyed and suffered. I think I don't regret a single "excess" of my responsive youth—I only regret in my chilled age, certain occasions and possibilities I didn't embrace.

—HENRY JAMES

INTRODUCTION

Kirk McGarvey first appeared in *Without Honor*, published in 1989. In that novel and in several others, I alluded to his first kill. The first assignment in which he carried out an assassination. *Mokrie dela*—"wet work," the spilling of blood, as the KGB called such actions; or black ops, the CIA's term.

I've been asked a number of times to go back to when McGarvey was just starting out with the Company, and tell the story of his first black op. How it developed, how it turned out, and how it deeply affected the rest of his life—and ultimately, the price just about everyone close to him paid.

In this story Mac is young and inexperienced, so cut him a little slack; after all, it was his *First Kill*.

FIRST KILL

PROLOGUE

□

Driving through the night from Santiago, Chile, to the coast, Army Brigadier General Matias Varga was not worried nor was he in any particular hurry, though he'd been warned that someone from the CIA would be coming to assassinate him. For operating outside what were considered the norms of decent human behavior. For crimes against humanity. For executions without trials. For torture, hangings, beheadings, whippings, even the burnings of those still alive.

Sometimes he would wake in the night hearing the screams in his dreams. But there'd never been regrets, only a sense of enjoyment that neither he nor his wife, Karina, ever found odd.

At forty-three, Varga was a lean man with thick black hair, an angular face and thin lips that never smiled. It was said that his wide black eyes could bore into a soul of a man where the truth of crimes against the state existed. If the accused denied the charges, Varga would find them guilty just for the pleasure of knowing that they would be executed.

One of Pinochet's bright boys, Felipe Torres, who was the deputy director of DINA, the Directorate of National Intelligence, had called him at noon for lunch at the military academy, where the little *puta* had told him that the CIA was sending someone for him.

"How do you know this?" Varga had asked, careful to keep his tone neutral. He'd felt no fear—in his entire life he'd never known the emotion. But Torres was an important man.

"We have our sources."

"Reliable?"

Torres smiled and dabbed his lips and pencil-thin mustache with his napkin. Like a lot of people in the regime, the deputy director had come from humble stock—his father had been a cowboy and his mother had worked in the ranch owner's kitchen, and possibly the man's bed. And like others working for Pinochet he had taken on the manners of a grandee—a man of cultured stock. Even his fingernails were manicured. "Si."

"Why have I been singled out? Perhaps you or even el Presidente would make more enticing targets for the Americans."

"But infinitely more difficult to kill than you," Torres said. "The fact is that you have become the nation's . . ." He searched for an appropriate word. "I was going to say garbageman, because you see to the removal of our rubbish, but perhaps with too much zeal for some."

Varga wasn't impressed. He'd survived the coup d'état that had brought Pinochet into power. And he'd survived several assassination attempts in the past few years, ever since he'd begun mass executions at the soccer stadium in Valparaíso. "If they send an army across our border, they'll be stopped."

"Apparently this will be one man."

"Mano a mano."

"Si," the deputy director said. "And let me be perfectly clear, how you handle this is your business. I've brought you the warning and you understand the reasons they want you eliminated. They believe that with you dead the special program will end."

"It won't," Varga said. "With or without me the need exists."

"Without you, my dear Matias, the necessary work would not proceed so efficiently."

Well away from Santiago's bright lights, the stars were brilliant, sweeping from horizon to horizon, and even in the hills above the coast, above the port city of San Antonio, it seemed as if the Pacific was insignificant in comparison to the heavens.

Torres had promised that their agents in Washington were working around the clock to learn the identity of the assassin, and exactly when he would be coming, but he could offer no promises. Nor could he offer any official assistance. President Pinochet would have to remain at arm's length. For deniability.

The soccer stadium where many of the executions took place was only

"How was it this afternoon?" she asked.

He had married her eight years ago when she was fifteen, a country girl up near the town of Monte Patria where at the time as a light colonel he'd taken part in a mountain defense exercise. She'd waited tables at a small *taberna* on the outskirts and the moment he laid eyes on her he knew that she would become his wife. Her father had no objections; he had seven other daughters and only one son.

"You'll see," Varga told her.

It only took him a minute or so to load the first of the three film reels onto the projector and start the machine. They'd been taken today—two at the stadium and the third in the autopsy and special preparations room—and developed and dried in time for him to bring them home.

Karina poured the brandies and they sat side by side as the film began, with General Varga in combat fatigues, the main star of the drama.

Nine men, seven women and three children—two of them girls around ten and one boy five—came into view, all of them naked, all of them showing signs of abuse. Two of the women had their breasts cut off, the wounds roughly stitched up. All of the men had been castrated, five of them their penises cut off. All of them had been whipped, long bloody stripes along their torsos, some had their teeth chiseled out, almost all had no nails on their fingers or toes, and not one of them could walk without help.

Karina clapped, the nipples of her breasts erect. "My God, Mati, I wish I could have been there," she cried. "From the beginning when they were still fresh."

"This time I have some of that work on film too. But I wanted to save it for next to last."

"I don't know if I can wait that long. I want you now."

On film Varga had his pistol out and he shot the children in the face. They fell back and not one of the adults made any move to stop what was happening.

"They're not fighting back," Karina said.

"They did earlier. My God, it was fabulous. You'll see."

One of the nurses in a white coat handed him a baseball bat and he beat three of the women and one of the men to death, crushing their skulls.

Sitting watching the film, remembering all of it, his eyes flitting to his wife's breasts and her pudenda, her legs spread for him, he got an erection.

"Let me see your painting," he said.

Drink in hand, Karina went to the easel and pulled off the cover. She'd painted a beach scene, huge waves crashing against the shore. It had been painted on the tanned and stretched skin of one of his victims—a woman whose back had been perfect.

"Wonderful," Varga said. "Mengele's wife couldn't have done better."

PART
ONE

Call to Arms

ONE

Kirk Cullough McGarvey, at twenty-eight, was in such superb physical condition that near the end of the eight-mile confidence course he had raised only a light sweat. He had the circuit all to himself this morning, his second go-around for the day.

None of the fourteen recruits midway through their training at the Farm, the CIA's facility along the York River near Williamsburg, had elected to run with him again, and he was secretly glad for the solitude, something hard to come by here.

He had demons riding on his shoulder, whispering scandalous secrets in his ear, not only about Katy, his wife of three years, but about someone coming for him. Someone lying in wait for him to make a mistake, turn the wrong corner, fail to keep up with proper tradecraft; to forget to always mind his six, be forever hyper-aware of his surroundings, any little bits and pieces that seemed to be out of place.

It was the field agent's stuff that done right saved your life, but done wrong—just one mistake that often led to a chain of missteps—would cost you your life, or at the very least end you up in a gulag somewhere.

The last mile wound its way through the woods along a path that was mostly uphill, some of it steep. In the distance to the left, away from the river, the sound of small-arms fire drifted his way on a light breeze. Someone shouted something, the words indistinct, followed by a sharp explosion. Urban incursion exercises.

At the final rise McGarvey stopped. He was a little under six feet with eyes that were sometimes green or sometimes gray depending on his mood or the circumstances, husky without being muscle-bound, and handsome in a rugged sort of way. Most women found him devastatingly masculine.

Spread out below was the Farm's center—the administration buildings, barracks, dining hall and the various classrooms where experienced field agents, some of them who'd worked deep cover in badland as NOCs, No Official Covers, taught the newbies how to survive. It was something that was very often impossible. The stars, no names, on the granite wall in the lobby of the original CIA Headquarters Building at Langley marked the deaths of field officers who could never be publically recognized for their service.

Truth, justice and the American way was their motto, but at times situations became so goddamned lonely that McGarvey had to stop in midstride, like now, to wonder why the hell he, or anyone, for that matter, would opt for this sort of life.

But his answers from the beginning of his three-year career to this point were: *It's what I do. Who I am.*

At one of his annual psych evals a Company shrink pressed him on his motivations. "Are you in it for the money?"

"Not on a GS-13's pay," Mac had shot back.

"But then you're a rich guy, aren't you? You inherited your parents' cattle ranch in Kansas and instead of following the family tradition you sold it. So money has no meaning for you. But maybe it's ego that drives you. You want to prove a point that you're the smartest man in the room. Maybe you get a laugh or two. Or maybe it's something buried in your conscience? The beating you gave the high school players you caught trying to gang-rape a girl? Maybe you regret it."

That eval had been in the late fall, just like now. The day had been gloomy at Langley, a low overcast sky, a light drizzle that was close to snow. It had infected just about everyone on campus, so tempers were short. His included. He was tired of being fucked with.

"MICE, is that what you're talking about, doc?" It was the company's acronym for why people became traitors to their country: Money, Ideology, Conscience or Ego. The shrink was asking him if he'd thought about defecting.

The psychologist had glanced down at McGarvey's file and smiled. "You're married, you have a young child and plenty of money to give them a very good life." He looked up. "So why go through this kind of shit? They

want you for black ops, but of course you know that because you volunteered. So what's the real deep-in-your-gut why of it, Mr. McGarvey?"

"Maybe I want to make a difference."

"Bullshit."

"Maybe I hate bullies and I want to even the score."

"More bullshit," the shrink said. "Your primary evaluator wrote that
you were a man who values the truth above just about everything else.
Sounds good on paper. But why are you here? What do you want, McGarvey? The truth, now."

"Washington is great at solving the big problems," he'd said. "Winning
the space race. Building the biggest nuclear arsenal. Flexing our financial
muscle to bring some dictator into line. Fielding a first-class army. Deploy-
ing more carrier fleets than every other country combined."

"But?"

"We're next to worthless when it comes to the little bits and pieces.
The lone gunman who slips under our radar and manages to put a bullet
into someone's brain. A couple of guys hijacking an airliner. The bomb
maker who decides to take out a football stadium in the middle of a game."

"Extrajudicial sanctions."

"Actions Washington can't take because of our laws."

"Who decides what needs to be done?" the shrink asked. "You?"

"The president. The DCI. The Bureau. Not me."

"You want someone to point you in the right direction and send you
off."

"It worked in the early days of Vietnam. But everything started to go
bad when we put more boots on the ground, and it got even worse when
we started bombing Hanoi. All our nuclear weapons, all our aircraft carrier groups and all our ground troops and economic sanctions could not
win the war."

"You want to be an assassin, is that it?"

McGarvey had nodded, not at all surprised by the look of disappointment, even revulsion, on the psychologist's face. But the need was valid. In
his first three years he'd been sent on a half-dozen deep-cover assignments
in Europe and twice to the Middle East. Brief missions, usually nothing
more than a little fly in the corner, nothing more. Observe and report.

HUMINT—Human Intelligence—operations. He'd seen and reported and had given his recommendations.

He headed down the hill as the hand-to-hand-combat instructor, Marine Sergeant Major Tom Carol, pulled up in a jeep on the dirt road at the bottom of the hill. He was deceptively mild looking, not someone you would expect could teach you how to kill a man with your bare hands in a dozen different ways. His desert camos were crisp as usual. "They said I'd find you out here. How'd it go?"

"Easier the second time. What's up?"

"Someone's down from Langley—wants to have a word with you. Get in."

McGarvey climbed in and they headed to Admin. "Who is it?"

"Didn't say, but I'd bet even money that he's a DO man. Has the look."

The DO was the CIA's Directorate of Operations, which handled clandestine missions. McGarvey's assignments had originated from the DO, and he supposed this would be more of the same. It had been several months since he'd been sent to Moscow to explore setting up an American dollar account at Arvesta Bank. The idea was to funnel hard currency into the country that could be used to directly fund some low-key intel ops. The CIA wanted to test the KGB's reach.

His part was a success. He'd managed to open the account with one hundred thousand cash. The irony and the danger for him was that the hundred dollar bills were counterfeit. But he'd gotten in and back out with no problems.

Between soft assignments like that one, he'd come out here to the Farm to work out with the new recruits so that he could keep his edge. Not only his physical sharpness, but his skills on the various firing ranges and his ability to take care of himself under the sergeant major's tutelage.

"Take care of yourself, Mac," Carol said, pulling up at Admin. "I got a feeling about this one."

"Me too, Sarge," McGarvey said and he almost smiled.

T W O

Bob Connelly, the Farm's director, beckoned McGarvey into his office. Before he'd quit the navy and joined the CIA, he had been a highly decorated SEAL lieutenant commander, the sort of special operations officer who'd never been afraid to get his hands dirty in the field with his boys. And like so many special ops people he was an amiable man, not large, but fit.

"Just a word before you go in," he said.

"Sergeant Carol said someone from Langley was here to talk to me. What's up?"

"Do you know a guy by the name of John Trotter?"

"I've heard the name."

"He's number two in our Special Activities Division and apparently he knows all about you. Spouted the highlights of your service record both with us and the OSI. Thinks that you're a hothead."

Before he'd been recruited into the CIA, McGarvey had worked in the Air Force Office of Special Investigations. His two specialties at Kansas State had been the French philosopher Voltaire and abnormal psychology. His unit CO had told him point blank that philosophy was a total waste of time, especially French philosophy, but he had use for a man who could get inside the head of a nutcase.

McGarvey had made the offhand comment that sometimes ignorance was a dangerous bliss.

"What the hell is that supposed to mean?" the major had asked.

"It can bite you in the ass, sir."

It had been the first of a number of insubordinations, but McGarvey was also commended for excellence and outstanding abilities. When he had quit the service after three years, the same CO, who was now a light colonel, shook his hand. "I don't know whether I'm going to miss you or if I'm glad to get rid of you. But the CIA apparently wants to give you a chance."

Connelly stared at him the way he did at the recruits during their first briefing. It was called the eval look, and if you didn't pass muster you were out, no explanations given.

"Any idea what this guy wants with me?"

"No, but I wanted to give you a heads-up. If you want to continue with the Company, don't fuck with him. I have a feeling he can either make you or break you. He comes across as way-over-the-top serious."

"Aren't we all?" McGarvey said.

Trotter was perched on the edge of the table in the small conference room down the hall from Connelly's office. He was a tall man and exceedingly thin, almost ascetic looking. Bottle-thick glasses were perched on the bridge of his large misshapen nose. His suit and correctly knotted tie looked as if they had just come back from the cleaners.

When McGarvey walked in he jumped up, his face all smiles. "John Lyman Trotter, Junior," he said. "I've heard a lot about you, all of it simply stunning. I mean *stunning*."

They shook hands. "You have me at a disadvantage," McGarvey said.

"We'll soon rectify that. Let's go for a walk; I want to tell you a story."

To McGarvey's way of thinking the man could have stepped directly out of the Sunday comics page, or a twenties silent film. He was a caricature of a real person, all angles with impossible hair that stuck out in every direction as if it had been placed that way on purpose. Even his gait was jerky and he walked in fits and starts, making it almost impossible to keep in stride with him.

They took a path that led down toward the docks on the river a half mile away, but Trotter didn't say a thing until they were well out of sight of the administration compound.

"What's the very worst thing you can think of?" he asked.

"An innocent man convicted of murder."

Trotter laughed. "Voltaire. He'd rather see a guilty man go free, than convict the one innocent. But then you're something of a scholar, aren't you, Kirk?" He pulled up short. "I can call you Kirk, can't I?"

"My friends do."

"I'd like to be your friend," Trotter said. "But perhaps not for all the obvious reasons. I'll never ask you to have a beer with me or a backyard barbecue, go fishing, play a round of golf now and then. Nothing as silly as that. I'm talking about something that could depend on deeper issues." He gestured toward the compound. "Like what some of these people here are training to do. Am I making any sense?"

Strangely, what the man was saying did make sense, but McGarvey shook his head. Trotter was being too earnest. "No, sir."

"I'm talking about trust. Basic, right down to the gut level of two friends unconditionally trusting each other with the keys to the keep."

It was a setup, of course. Trotter wanted something important, and McGarvey didn't want to make it easy. He didn't want the pep talk; he wanted the truth. Besides overearnest men, he'd learned to mistrust people who couldn't or wouldn't come to the point without first dumping a load of horseshit.

"What I'm talking about are life-and-death issues."

"I'm not a team player, Mr. Trotter."

"Good heavens, I know that. We all do. You've already developed a reputation as the lone wolf. Point him in the right direction, Lawrence told me, and then get the hell out of his way."

Lawrence Danielle was an assistant deputy chief of the agency. He was a rising star and would almost certainly run the entire Company one day.

"You've come down from Langley to ask me to do something for you. What is it?"

Trotter was surprised. "Not for me, nothing like that. Heavens."

"For the Company."

"Actually, for humanity."

"Bullshit."

"Anything but," Trotter said earnestly. "But first I want you to listen to someone, nothing more than that. Two of them, actually, and what they have to say is nothing short of stunning."

"Stunning," McGarvey said. "You like that word."

"Have you ever heard the name Josef Mengele?"

"The Nazi doctor."

"Experimented on concentration camp Jews. Dreadful stuff."

"We're using some of it."

"If you mean the results of the hypothermia experiments, you're right," Trotter admitted, and he seemed to regret it.

In the Nazi experiments, a Jewish man was stripped naked and put into a barrel of ice water up to his neck. This was outside during the winter. It didn't take long for him to lose consciousness and die soon after. The idea of the experiments was to find the best way to revive an unconscious man before he died, and before damage to the heart and brain became irreversible.

At first the experiments failed. All the subjects died or had to be executed because they had become cripples or brain dead. The Nazis were trying to come up with something to revive German pilots who'd been shot down over the English Channel or North Sea.

Meticulous records had been kept. Heating blankets, warm showers, rubdowns, sauna baths—nothing worked, until the near-dead subject was put to bed with two naked women who revived him with their body heat. Some of the subjects got erections and had intercourse. That method never failed.

"Chile may have its own mad doctor."

"But you're not sure."

Trotter looked away. "There are other political considerations."

"That shouldn't stop us."

"This time is different."

"What exactly are you asking me to do, Mr. Trotter?"

"For now nothing more than listen to what we have to tell you."

"And afterward?"

Trotter couldn't look him in the eye, and McGarvey got the distinct impression that the DO officer was either afraid or ashamed or both. "Just listen, please."

THREE

□

On the interstate heading north toward Washington, traffic was fairly light until they were well past Richmond and it picked up. Trotter was driving his own anonymous Chevy Impala with Maryland plates, and for the first hour he kept to himself, only making an occasional comment about the weather, which was warm, or that the traffic around D.C. was always terrible.

McGarvey thought again, as he had earlier at the Farm, that something was troubling the man. And he had the instinct to trust his hunch that whatever was bothering Trotter was going to send more than a simple assignment his way.

"You were going to tell me a story," he said.

Trotter glanced over. "Actually I'll leave that to Munoz and Campos. I don't want to affect your judgment with any spin I might put on it. And God knows there's already been plenty of that to go around. At the highest levels, I can say that much."

"Who are they?"

"Dirección de Inteligencia Nacional," Trotter said. "Part of Pinochet's bully boys until it started getting too rough for them."

"Defectors?"

Trotter nodded. "Bearing gifts. I can also tell you that what they brought has been . . ." He hesitated.

"Stunning?"

"I was going to say nearly unbelievable."

As part of his training in the OSI and then the Company, McGarvey had studied the case files on dozens of defectors, most of them from the

Soviet Union. The ones who'd come in with the routine bits and pieces of spycraft or statecraft—the dirty little secrets of one minister or another's affairs, sometimes with boys—were the most easy to swallow. But the superstar wannabes who came over offering the sun and the moon were almost always con artists and opportunists looking for some payoff. One million well-used U.S. hundred dollar bills, nonsequential serial numbers, was the usual starting bid.

"Are you guys worried about making fools of yourselves?"

"Only if we take it to the White House, which no one is suggesting at this point. For the moment it stays on the seventh floor."

The DCI had his office on the seventh floor of the Original Headquarters Building at Langley.

"And the third floor." It was where the Clandestine Service, or DO, the largest of the directorates, was located.

"To this point we're just the middlemen—trust me on at least that much, Kirk. We pump product upstairs and the advice comes down for us to keep our collective mouths shut."

"Do you want me to kill these guys?" McGarvey asked on impulse just to see what Trotter's reaction would be.

"It's been suggested, and from where I sit it might be the easiest course. But no, it won't be that simple."

"What, then?"

"Just listen to them. Tell us what you think."

"Us?" McGarvey asked.

"Me." Trotter was sharp. "And I'm advising you right at this moment that before this goes one step forward you'll agree to sign a Secrets Act agreement. No one outside the op we've designated DKDISTANTMOON-LIGHT will be privy to what you'll learn—even if you don't accept the assignment in the end, or heaven forbid, fail. That means your friends, even your wife. No bragging rights. My God, the Post and Times would crucify us. Emasculate the lot of us."

And that was the rub for McGarvey. Kathleen knew that he worked for the CIA, but she only had a vague idea of what he actually did—an analyst of some sort, she wanted to believe. The type who sat behind a desk thinking big thoughts.

But in the three years of their marriage that image had never squared for her. In the first place, in her estimation her husband was a man's man. He was too physical, his muscles too finely tuned, his gaze and manner too direct, to be desk-bound, though sometimes lately she had complained that he had become distant.

And his disappearances almost always with little or no warning—one minute he was there and the next minute he was gone, and never an explanation when he came back of where he had been or what he had done—bothered her to no end.

After the Moscow trip, which had taken him away for the better part of two weeks, she had accused him of having an affair.

"Who is the bitch?" she shouted.

Upstairs, Elizabeth, their three-year-old daughter, was asleep.

"There's no woman," he'd told her. "And let's not wake Liz."

"I'll give you one mistake, Kirk. But it goes no further than this."

"Sometimes my job takes me away."

"To do what?" Katy screeched, but then turned away to get control of herself.

"I can't tell you that."

"Are you saying that you're a spy? Some fucking sneak thief in the night?"

He had no answer for her.

"You'll end up getting yourself shot to death or put in some prison somewhere, and I'll never be told what happened to you." Tears welled up in her eyes. "My God, Kirk, what am I supposed to tell our daughter? Daddy's off getting himself shot?" She laughed, but it was without humor. "It would be easier to tell her that you were shacked up somewhere and decided to leave us."

He waited for her to calm down a little. "I love you, Katy, but you have to understand that what I'm doing is necessary. It's like I'm a soldier."

"Oh, no. If you were a soldier, I could understand it. You'd be off fighting some war—even like Vietnam—but you'd be serving a purpose. You wouldn't be a dirty little spy."

"It's the same thing."

"No," she'd said. "Soldiers don't shoot each other in the back."

. . .

It was midafternoon by the time they reached the CIA campus outside Langley. Trotter was waved through security at the main gate but drove right past the executive parking lot at the rear of the OHB.

It always struck McGarvey as odd coming here. He wasn't an NOC—the field officer who never showed up on campus—but he detested bureaucracy and all the petty conventions that went with it. No one saluted in the Company, but one's government service rank defined the pecking order. Pay grade was important, though the real people didn't give a damn about the money, or at least pretended not to. Most of them were in the game because, as one Watch officer had told him: "We get to know everything." Working here made you an insider. But the price in petty bullshit was high.

"We're holding them at the Hartley House—too dangerous to put them up someplace along the Beltway," Trotter said.

Honorous Hartley had been a Civil War colonel whose roots went back to before the War of Independence. Like other properties in the Washington environs, the sprawling CIA campus just south of the George Washington Parkway that followed the Potomac once had been civilian, but had been absorbed by the government.

The house was a typical two-story colonial, with white clapboard siding and green shutters. It had not been kept in good repair, and in fact most of the case officers and interrogators who used the place to debrief their johns referred to it as the Slums.

In general the least important defectors were housed here, and McGarvey said something about it.

"Serves its purpose, doesn't it?" Trotter said, pulling up and parking on the gravel driveway at the rear of the place. "We don't want to call any attention to the op."

"What about security?"

"We have a couple of teams from Housekeeping, but believe me, our johns are not runners. They're too goddamned frightened."

Of what or who? McGarvey wanted to ask, but didn't. That question, along with a ton of others, would hold for now.

FOUR

□

McGarvey followed Trotter through the mudroom just off the kitchen, then down a short corridor past the dining room and into the front stair hall, where one of the housekeepers was waiting.

"Any trouble from our boys?" Trotter asked.

"No, sir."

"Paul Reubens, Kirk McGarvey," Trotter said, making the introductions.

Reubens was a solidly built man, a bit over six feet with broad shoulders, thick dark hair, blue eyes and a warm smile. "Heard your Moscow run turned out good," he said, shaking hands.

"I got lucky that no one at the bank realized the money was counterfeit. Could have been dicey. But I'm a little surprised that someone outside the team knows about it."

"Paul works special ops," Trotter said. "He ran the same scam in Beijing eighteen months ago, and we used him as a planning adviser on your gig."

"How'd you end up in housekeeping?" McGarvey asked. It was a rude question. The implication was that Reubens had done something wrong and was demoted. But the man was here backstopping something that was supposedly *stunning*.

"This is special," Trotter said. He and Reubens exchanged a look. "I just want you to listen to these guys, hear them out."

"May I ask a question or two?"

"Of course. This will be a transparent operation—at least this segment of it will be. Afterward we'll just have to see how the chips fall."

It was there again. Trotter was afraid of something—McGarvey was sure of it. The way the man held himself. The way he spoke, stiff, almost too formal, as if he'd practiced the words in front of a mirror. The way his eyes darted, never lighting on anything or anyone for longer than a moment or two.

"Do you want them both down or one at a time?" Reubens asked.

"Both," McGarvey said, and Trotter nodded.

Reubens went upstairs and Trotter led McGarvey into the fairly small and poorly furnished living room. Rough-hewn beams crossed the low ceiling, and only one small window looked out on the woods in the general direction of the OHB. They could have been deep in some colonial-era forest with no living soul for fifty miles in any direction. A pair of wingback chairs had been drawn up in front of a ratty Queen Anne couch, a low table between them.

The room was cold and so quiet that McGarvey could hear the low sounds of a conversation upstairs.

"Would you like something to drink?" Trotter asked. "We have coffee made, or some water."

"How about a beer?"

Trotter went back to the kitchen and returned with a bottle of Heineken as someone came down the stairs. "We want your opinion—we need it."

"Why me especially?" McGarvey asked. He'd always been wary of liars, and especially of their motives. A friend of his in the OSI had said that Mac's bullshit meter was the best he'd ever seen. McGarvey had taken it as a compliment.

"Because there's no shrink on staff who can match your combination of field experience and knowledge of abnormal psychology."

"Are these guys psychos?"

"I don't know. It's up to you to tell me. Do you understand?"

"No. But I'll listen to them, and then we'll talk about whatever you want to talk about. I'll want to know what you want me to do. And I'll take written orders on it."

"Fair enough."

Two men appeared at the stair hall doorway and stopped, Reubens towering behind them. They were short, under five-five, but stout, thick-chested, as many South American mestizos tended to be, with olive complexions, black hair and deep-set eyes. They were dressed alike in jeans, black T-shirts and sandals. The one on the left had a scar on the side of his face, part of that ear gone. He'd been shot some time ago. The one on the right had a six-inch tattoo of a cross from which blood dripped high on his right arm, where his sleeve was rolled up.

McGarvey's first impression was that they were even more frightened than Trotter was, but determined, focused. They wanted something very specific and he thought that it wasn't as simple as a defection.

"Lucas Munoz with the tattoo—we call him the warrior. And Juan Campos, who we call the preacher. Until eight days ago, when they came to our embassy in Mexico City, they were on the run from their own people in the DINA," Trotter said, introducing them.

"Maybe now you finally believe us?" Campos said. His accent was thick, but his English was good. He was educated.

"I want you to tell your story to this gentleman, who'll have some questions. Then we'll see."

"Screw that, Trotter. We gave you the crown jewels and now we want to be turned over to the FBI's WPP." The WPP was the Bureau's Witness Protection Program. But McGarvey was surprised that the Chilean intelligence officer knew Trotter's name. It made no sense. Interrogators never let their subjects learn their real identities.

"You'll have to earn it."

"Fuck it," Munoz said. "And who the fuck is this guy supposed to be?"

McGarvey put his beer on the table, sat in one of the wingback chairs and crossed his legs. "Sit down, please."

"Screw this," Munoz said.

Reubens gently laid a hand on his shoulder. "This is the end of nice."

Munoz looked up at him, but then nodded and he and Campos came the rest of the way in and sat down on the couch facing McGarvey.

Trotter remained where he stood, and Reubens leaned against the doorframe. They had the remainder of the day, or however long it would take. No one was in a hurry.

"I've not been briefed, except that you gentlemen defected from the DINA, which means there's a price on your heads—unless you're just some low-level scumbags," McGarvey began.

"We don't have to take this kind of shit," Campos said. He started to rise, but McGarvey motioned him down, and he complied.

It was bluff and bravado—the message came across loud and clear. But bluffing about what, and why the bravado? Presumably they knew that they were safe here, out of reach of anyone who wanted them dead. But they didn't act as if they believed they were beyond Pinochet's reach.

"It started when the Russian field officer showed up out of the blue. We've already told Mr. Trotter this," Munoz said, but McGarvey interrupted him.

"Take me back to the beginning—your beginning. I want to know where you were recruited, who was your first training supervisor, what were your courses like, your instructors, your classrooms, your field training, hand-to-hand, firearms, explosives, codes, languages, structure."

Munoz looked to Trotter, who turned away.

McGarvey could see that Trotter understood that before the messenger could be believed, his background had to be nailed down. If the two DINA officers told the truth about their early days, their triumphs and perhaps some of their failures, a baseline could be established from which the truth could be separated from the self-serving bullshit that was sure to follow.

They were reluctant at first, but it wasn't long before they were back six years in Munoz's case, a few months earlier for Campos, when they had been recruited from their high schools, both of them in Santiago for the Escuela Militar—the military academy. Munoz studied the history of warfare, while Campos studied international relations.

Good years, they agreed. Hard studies because they were on state-sponsored scholarships that included ROTC training. But good because there had been parties and a lot of city girls who were more than willing to spread their legs for the prospect of marrying a future military officer.

But after four years the day of reckoning came in the late fall, just before graduation, when a man in a civilian suit came to interview them. He told them about an exciting career in the DINA, protecting Chile's freedom.

It was better than going back to farming or ranching. And infinitely better than taking some desk job as an ordinary functionary. Travel, adventure and even more girls, an endless supply of women.

Paradise. At first.

FIVE

☐

It was in the middle of the Pinochet era when el Presidente was at the height of his power. That was a full seven years after the so-called Caravan of Death in October 1973, when seventy-two people were killed by the regime. But those numbers soon rose; at one estimate in the following year more than twenty-one hundred people were murdered, among them ninety children younger than twelve, and thirty thousand were tortured.

"We were just kids, naive, you know," Munoz said. "We had our degrees, but they amounted to little more than book learning and repeating our professors' opinions. Word for word got us the highest grades. We were little yellow parrots."

"Except for the norteamericanos," Campos said.

"Si, a few ROTC cadets from somewhere in Massachusetts, I think, showed up for one semester. And those guys could say anything they wanted to. Arrogant pricks. We thought that they would get all of us in trouble. But no one bothered them, and they went home with good grades."

"It was Señor Ortiz who recruited us," Campos said. "Once we were in we never saw him again, but in the two months it took to check our backgrounds and run us through an endless series of tests, he was there every day. He had us call him Uncle Bastian. Sometimes he took us out for steaks and beers. We were special, he said."

"We were his boys," Munoz agreed. "Told us he had the highest hopes for us. We were destined to do great things—me with my understanding of war, and Juan knowing how diplomacy was supposed to work."

"You knew each other by then?" McGarvey asked.

"We were roommates at school almost from the beginning."

Someone at the DINA had spotted them early on, their professors instructed to make sure they did well. They had been a matched set from the beginning. Groomed first in school and nurtured in the service for some long-range operation. But one-trick ponies. Once they had finished the one op, they were to be discarded.

Tossing away highly educated and well-trained officers wasn't done lightly in any intelligence service. There were those trained for missions in which survival was less than a fifty-fifty shot; that wasn't uncommon even in the CIA. Every NOC understood the risks they were taking; the stars on the granite walls in the OHB lobby attested to it. But there was a class of operatives who worked pretty much in the open. Usually at embassies around the world, or at UN headquarters in New York, where they were expected to come into regular contact with representatives of foreign governments—targeted representatives. And from time to time one of them would be found as a victim of an apparent traffic accident, or drowning in the East River, or suicide.

"When did you suspect that you were being set up for a one-way mission?" McGarvey asked.

Munoz was startled but Campos took the question as if he had expected it.

"We didn't at first, though I began to have my suspicions a few months in," he said. "The other recruits spent several months on the confidence courses, firing ranges, close-order battle drills, explosives, but our drills involved partying until we could pass as someone who had been born wealthy and expected fine service."

Trotter had evidently not heard this part. "The training mustn't have been effective."

McGarvey held him off. "What else?"

"Listening," Campos said. "And understanding what we were hearing. We got to be sympathetic listeners. Even better, we learned to ask the right questions at the right time. When to press, when to back off. Even when to offer a shoulder to cry on, give some advice."

"Love?"

Campos nodded. "That too."

"Sex?" McGarvey asked.

Munoz bridled, but Campos stayed calm, though he was uncomfort-able. "If need be."

"You learned to be actors."

Munoz jumped up. "What the hell do you think we were, you bastard?"

"I don't know," McGarvey said. "What were you?"

But he figured he knew the answer to that question, though he had only a vague notion where it might lead, except that the two of them had been trained for a very special onetime operation that would involve someone likely at the highest levels of government in a compromising situation. One in which some useful flow of intelligence would occur. They had been trained to prospect for a gold seam.

"*Puta.*"

"Oh, sit down," Trotter said as if he had no idea what else to say.

"When did you two go operational?" McGarvey asked.

"Twelve months ago," Campos said. Munoz sat down.

"And when did you learn that you were marked for execution after you completed the mission, whatever it was?"

"Two weeks ago. It was why we ran."

"Take me through it."

"There was so much confusion, so many things going on that it seemed like twenty hours a day, every day," Campos said. "It was so easy to get caught up in it, get lost, that I don't think I can give you any logical order of things, or even their nature." He glanced at Munoz, who had a forlorn expression in his dark eyes.

"Every time we asked our control officer if we were doing the right things, he told us that we were on a mission. Keep up the good work."

"Was Uncle Bastian your control officer?"

"No, a rat-faced little son of a bitch who I think was the one who'd pull the trigger when the time came."

"Do we have a name?"

"Cristobal Peña."

McGarvey glanced at Trotter.

"Almost certainly a work name—we're checking it out."

"What was the first thing you did?"

"Went to a party at the Russian embassy," Campos said.

"What were your legends?"

"I was Eduardo Parra. My father was Daniel Celsi Parra. Lucas was Franco Reyes, my cousin on my mother's side."

"Daniel Parra is the king of copper in Chile," Trotter said. "One of the richest men in the country. Without him Pinochet would never have commanded anything higher than a battalion."

McGarvey knew the name; Parra was an aging jet-setter, a handsome man whose background was Castilian—Spanish nobility. "These two don't fit the mold," McGarvey said to Trotter. "They have the education and might have learned the bearing, but not the look."

"Parra always kept his wife in the background. She's mestizo. I don't see what the trouble is."

Trotter's response was one of McGarvey's first insights into the basic tradecraft principle that people saw, heard and thought what they expected they'd see and hear. His OSI buddy called it the Sheeple Principle: *People are herd animals, Mac. Plain and simple; they follow the flock.*

"If Parra père is as connected as well as we all think he is, he would have known that these guys were masquerading as his son and nephew."

"As a favor to Pinochet."

"As a favor to copper," McGarvey said. "It hasn't been nationalized yet." He turned back to the Chileans. "You cleaned up and took a limo to the embassy?"

"A cab," Munoz said. "We weren't exactly show-offs."

"Who was your mark?"

"A Russian captain by the name of Valentin Illen Baranov," Campos said. "He was new to Santiago, but I think that he or someone like him had been expected even before we were recruited."

Even though the operation had occurred nearly one year ago, it was fresh enough in the Chilean defectors' minds that it was obvious they were reliving it in 3D.

"We were told that he was a party boy, and that he was well connected to our government."

"How well connected?" McGarvey asked.

"Pinochet?" Trotter said.

"I think so, but we had no idea at the time," Campos said.

"How did you approach him?" Trotter asked. He was eager; he had the nervous energy.

But McGarvey held up a hand. "I'm curious about something before we continue. Is he still there?"

Campos shrugged. "So far as we know. He was spearheading something called CESTA del Sur, some sort of a spy network in the hemisphere south of the U.S. border."

SIX

☐

Trotter leaned forward, the bit in his teeth now. "But there was a complication, wasn't there?" he said to the Chileans. "You left that out."

"Still is, last we heard," Munoz responded glumly. "That was the part that really scared the shit out of us, you know. Made us think twice about coming here. It's why we went to Mexico City first. But the place is a madhouse. Damned near as many Russians and Cubans as there were norteamericanos. Not a safe place for us."

No place was safe, McGarvey wanted to tell them. It was another lesson among a growing list he was beginning to learn. There would always be complications. He almost felt that he was in school with these guys.

"From the beginning again," he said. "I'm assuming that this 'complication' happened before your first party at the Russian embassy."

"The same day," Munoz said, and fear was written sharply on his face, especially in his squinting eyes, as if he were a deer caught in a car's headlights.

"Peña picked us up at the SIM, said someone wanted to have a word with us before we went in."

"SIM?" McGarvey asked. He wasn't familiar with the term.

"Simulated environment. It was in the same compound as the urban warfare complex. Anyway, this place was a pretty fair mock-up of the Russian embassy's main reception area—where they held their parties, dinners, VIP receptions, things like that."

"Were there mock-ups of the rest of the embassy and its grounds?"

"That was in another space, but yes, we were required to memorize all of it."

"Did you?"

"Of course," Munoz said. "We were professionals by then." He glanced at his partner. "We hadn't lost all of our naivete, but we were learning."

McGarvey waited.

"Peña had a car and driver and he took us over to the interior ministry. They let us right through the gate without stopping, which was a very big deal. A mob had gathered the day before and did some damage. Bus fares had gone up again and the people were pissed off. They did some damage, not much, but the entire place, including the Presidential Palace, was on lockdown."

"Who was it that wanted to talk to you?"

"Señor Cardenas. A big-shot."

"Mauricio Cardenas, foreign trade minister," Trotter said.

"What the hell was a foreign trade minister doing at Interior?" McGarvey asked. Anomalies bothered him.

"Unknown."

"Did you see him?" McGarvey asked.

"Eventually," Munoz said. "Peña took us up to a conference room on the second floor where we were told to sit down and keep our mouths shut. He went next door, but left the door open a little. We could hear them talking."

"What were they saying?"

"We couldn't hear the words and I didn't think that it was such a good idea to stick our noses in too far," Campos said. "Lucas wanted to listen at the door, but I talked some sense into him."

Again McGarvey held his silence. He had the feeling that something was coming that none of them was going to like very much. Maybe even the real reason—or at least one of them—why he'd been called here.

"You have to understand that this was important. We were about to go over to the Russian embassy to get close to this captain, maybe even turn him, or at the very least find out what the hell he really wanted and how he intended on getting it. But first Señor Cardenas was going to give us a pep talk."

"Doesn't make sense," McGarvey said.

"Didn't to us either," Campos agreed. "But after a couple of minutes Peña came back and told us we'd have to wait a little longer, and then he left."

"Back to Cardenas's office?"

"Yes."

"But the minister's door was still open a little."

"Sí."

"What happened?" McGarvey asked.

"Someone else came to see him."

"They had a conversation?"

"Sí."

"You could hear them talking but not what they were saying, right?"

All of a sudden Campos was nervous, uncomfortable, which didn't make a lot of sense to McGarvey. The men had already told this story to Trotter. Campos was just repeating it.

"For the most part."

"What do you mean by that?"

"How they were talking sounded strange. Different, but I couldn't put my finger on it until whoever it was talking to the minister raised his voice."

"What'd he say?"

"'Don't fuck with me. There's likely to be blowback,'" Campos said. "In English."

McGarvey didn't let his surprise show. It was a setup for the one-way case officers. But he'd expected the Russian to be there. "Did he have an accent at all?"

"Norteamericano."

"Had either of you ever heard that voice before?"

"No."

"Or after? Maybe a guest at the Russian embassy?"

Campos shook his head. "Their meeting didn't last long. And when they were done, Peña came for us and brought us in to meet Cardenas. The minister said he was proud of us, and that he couldn't stress how important our mission was."

"Again, what was your mission?" McGarvey asked.

"To find out about Baranov. Cardenas acted as if he had a lot of respect for the Russian."

"Then what?"

"Sir?"

"After you found out about this captain, you were ordered to try to turn him, but if that became impossible, were you to assassinate him?"

Campos started to answer, but Munoz cut in. "Peña said that there might be something else later. Something even more important."

More important than an American warning a foreign trade minister not to fuck with him? That there would be blowback? It was a CIA term, meaning unintended consequences.

"Let's take a break, shall we?" Trotter said. "Paul, bring our guests something to drink, would you?"

McGarvey went out into the stair hall with Trotter. "The American was CIA, someone from our Santiago station?"

"Dick Beckett swears up and down it was not his operation," Trotter said. Beckett was chief of Santiago Station. "We had them listen to a series of regional voice recognition programs. Pinned it down to a reasonable level of confidence that the speaker was educated somewhere in the Northeast. Maybe Boston or somewhere close. He was likely born elsewhere, but educated at MIT or some smaller school thereabouts."

"Is the DO running any independent op down there?"

"Three, but none involving anyone with that voice."

"What did Beckett say?"

"He's not involved."

"He's the COS; it's his AOR." Area of Responsibility.

"I don't make the rules, Kirk."

Another lesson learned. No one person knew everything, or they were not disposed to talk about it. "What do you want me to do? What's my assignment?"

"There's more," Trotter said.

SEVEN

□

"We were going over as representatives from the Ministry of Culture to meet Baranov, who was posing as the new cultural attaché to the Russian ambassador," Campos said.

"But we were warned that he probably knew or guessed that we were sent to find out what he wanted," Munoz added.

"He knew that he'd been pegged as a spy," McGarvey said. "But were you ever given a hint at what he might be after?"

"No," Munoz said.

"Cardenas seeing them had to have been an oblique hint," Trotter intervened. "The foreign office had sat up and taken notice."

Reubens had brought them beers and they'd already drained the bottles, but they had sense enough not to ask for more.

"Take me through what happened next," McGarvey said. "You showed up at the Russian embassy, presented your credentials and made your way through the crowd—I'm assuming there were a lot of people—looking for Baranov."

"We were on the guest list, and yes, there were maybe seventy-five or a hundred people there."

"From other embassies? Perhaps ours?"

"No, mostly just us and the Russians. A lot of our artists, musicians and practically the entire state ballet company. The directors of the Bolshoi and Kirov were there, along with several of their principal dancers."

"Anyone besides you two from the Ministry of Culture?"

Munoz shook his head. "It would have been awkward. We were briefed on some of the staff, the people we supposedly worked with and answered to, but we'd never actually met them."

"Keeping the ministry out had to have been ordered either by Pino-chet himself or Nunez," Trotter said. General Armando Nunez was the new DINA director. "No one would have questioned their orders."

"We didn't have to look for Baranov—he found us right at the start," Campos said. "Came over, shook our hands, then hugged us like we were all best of friends."

"The bastard was built like what you norteamericanos call a brick shit house," Munoz said. "Solid. I think he might have been a wrestler at one time. I got the feeling that he was telling me that he could crush my body any time he wanted to do it. And I believed it."

"He knew who we were and he wanted to let us know about his power," Campos added. "He was looking for respect."

"Did you get the sense that someone was watching all of this?" Mc-Garvey asked. "Maybe someone from the KGB?"

"We spotted a couple of them, plus a couple of our own guys."

"I wasn't clear how you could tell," Trotter said.

"They were the only four people in the room who weren't drinking," Munoz said.

"But Baranov and you were," McGarvey said.

"Vodka," Munoz said.

"I hated it," Campos said, but Munoz just smiled.

"No one bothered to introduce them around," Trotter said.

"Within ten minutes he asked if we wanted to go to a real party, and we had to say yes. Our brief was to do whatever the man wanted us to do. We were to gain his confidence."

"Were you also briefed to hint that you might want to defect?" McGar-vey asked. He had a fair idea where this was going now.

"Especially that, but only after we found the right time and place to admit who we really were and what our mission was."

"When did that happen?"

"That night," Campos said.

Baranov hadn't been long in the country, and although he had an apart-ment at the embassy his real place was down in San Antonio, on the coast about one hundred kilometers from Santiago. It was a compound that a Russian friend of a friend on Pinochet's staff had found for him. Out of the way but only an hour from the capital. The place came complete with a housekeeper, a cook and an all-around handyman, plus some Russian muscle from time to time.

"It was incredible. Here we were a half hour after meeting him, in his car on the way to his compound, when he told us about his Russian minders. No denials that he was KGB."

"He practically drew them a goddamned picture," Trotter said. "Nothing left to the imagination."

"We were way out of our league," Campos said. "Nothing in our training dealt with the situation we were in."

"Improvise, we were told," Munoz added. "But what the hell are you supposed to do when the fucking ship is sinking right out from under you?"

Something else struck McGarvey at that moment. Both men were using a lot of American slang. Not Spanish or Russian, as he expected would be the case, considering their assignment. And he was getting the uncomfortable feeling that the op Trotter had brought him concerned not the Russian, but the mysterious American who'd gotten tough with the foreign minister. "Where was this place, exactly? And how was it laid out?"

Trotter gave Munoz a pad of paper, and the Chilean drew a sketch of the interior of the main house, and directions to the place. "Not easy to find."

"Who was at the compound when you got there?"

"More people than I could count. The place was lit up like Christmas, cars parked inside the walls and outside—Mercedes, a couple of Rolls, even a Ferrari and a couple of Caddies. An American country-and-western band was playing in the courtyard, and just inside the main room three guys were playing Russian guitars."

"Balalaikas," Trotter said.

"Upstairs on the balcony a woman played a violin, something sad, the entire night."

"The pool was lit up," Munoz said.

"Tables filled with food and booze," Campos added. "Bartenders, waitresses everywhere."

"Don't forget the hospitality table," Munoz said.

"Really big bowls of coke. Just about everyone there was drugged out."

"Stoned," Munoz agreed. "And happy. Everyone was laughing."

"And women. At least two for every man. All of them young and beautiful and naked." Campos shook his head. "I never saw so much tits or pussy in all my life. Never even dreamed about it."

"It must have been great," McGarvey said.

"We were too goddamned scared to enjoy ourselves," Campos said. "At first, anyway."

"But something must have come out of that night. You must have brought product back to your handler. Or didn't you continue? Was that the end of it?"

"Not the end. There were more parties. And yes, we brought back information about their new over-the-horizon radar to counteract the Americans' OTH in northern Greenland somewhere. Got the names of two Russian spies trying to turn one of our cryptanalysts. And the name of one of our people who'd been turned in Moscow."

"Your handler must have been happy."

"Over the moon, but then General Varga and his wife started showing up at the parties, and shit started to get weird," Campos said. "That was about two months ago, when we began to realize that it might be time to get out while we could."

"Who is Varga?" McGarvey asked.

"They call him the Butcher," Munoz said. "Lots of blood on his hands. Chilean blood."

"He and his wife are both crazy," Campos said. "Have to be, considering what they were supposedly doing. But Baranov told us he was going to have them both because with them in his bed he would have the essence of Chile in his soul."

"Did he bed them that night?" McGarvey asked.

"I don't know," Munoz said and Campos shook his head. "We were otherwise occupied trying to figure a way out."

"It was the only time we ever saw them and Baranov together," Campos answered before McGarvey could ask.

"But that wasn't the last time you were at one of Baranov's parties."

EIGHT

□

The story was winding down. Other than Baranov's admission about the Russians' work on OTH radar, the attempt on the cryptanalyst in Santiago, and the Moscow field officer who'd been turned, nothing else of any real value came out of the parties, except that it seemed as if just about everyone who was anybody showed up out there.

"He had spotted us from the beginning, fed us something to keep our handler happy and then turned his back on us," Campos said. "We had served his purpose."

"Did you get the feeling that maybe it was time for you to stop going out there?" McGarvey asked.

"Yes, but Peña insisted we stick with it. Said the bastard was going to make a mistake sooner or later and he wanted to nail him."

"But?" McGarvey asked. He'd heard a slight hesitation in the Chilean's voice.

Campos glanced at Munoz. "There was something else. Peña never said anything specific, but each time we reported to him he asked a lot of questions about who else was at the parties. Who Baranov might be sleeping with. The women were of no interest—it was the men the Russian was fucking that Peña wanted to know about."

"Any names in particular?"

"If you mean the American, no. There were no Americans there."

"And we never mentioned what we heard outside the minister's office," Munoz said. "Self-preservation."

"Maybe insurance," McGarvey suggested.

"Only if we got in deeper, learned something new, came face-to-face with this gringo."

"Which you never did."

"No," Campos said.

Not long after their last night in San Antonio, Baranov announced that he was flying to Mexico City on business. Peña arranged for Campos and Munoz to take the very next flight out. The drill was for them to hang around the Russian embassy until they spotted Baranov and then follow him, see who he met, what he did. It was so loose it was laughable. But they were fixed up with bulletproof passports identifying them as Mexican citizens, and enough cash to wait it out for at least a month. Under no circumstance were they to make contact with their own embassy. And they were to report directly back to Peña only if and when Baranov did something significant.

"Did he tell you what he meant by *significant*?" McGarvey asked. The story was way over the top.

"Said we'd know it if we saw it," Munoz said.

"But you didn't follow him, did you?"

"No. We went to ground in a cheap hotel—the Catedral—in Zócalo and read the newspapers, watched TV at a bar down the street."

"Looking for what?"

"Anything that might involve the Russians." Munoz shook his head. "But there was nothing, so we decided to run. To the American embassy first, but they didn't give a shit about us. If they knew about Baranov, they didn't admit it, just sent us on our way."

"They showed up in Miami a few days ago and called our eight hundred number, said they had a great idea for a movie involving a Russian spy and a norteamericano in Santiago," Trotter said. "Actually quite inventive. They were transferred over to the public affairs office and finally to Carl Thompson, who's our new film industry liaison. Took him about two seconds to realize who these guys were and he bounced them up to me."

There it was again, another anomaly, to McGarvey's way of thinking—this one wide enough to drive a truck through. A couple of Chilean low-level intelligence officers wanting to defect in exchange for some fantastic story about a Russian in San Antonio should not have been believed for all the copper in the country—not without a lot of verification.

Yet Trotter had picked up on it, and had them brought up here for a second telling, and then got McGarvey for the third go-around. But not a team of interrogators—even though the CIA had the best of them just about anywhere.

Trotter motioned for McGarvey to step outside.

"Now what?" Munoz asked.

"We'll check out your story, and then we'll see."

"Goddamnit," Munoz protested, but McGarvey followed Trotter to the stair hall and then outside.

"Smoke?" Trotter asked.

"Sure," McGarvey said. Katy was trying to get him to quit, and he supposed he would sooner or later, if not for her, certainly for himself, for his wind. "What's the op? Digging out the American?"

Trotter was startled. "Heavens no; even if he exists outside their imaginations, we'd need to turn over an entire deck of cards before we could be sure of our position. My guess is that it was an embellishment to their basic story. Something meant to make us sit up and take serious notice. Which we have."

"Sorry, Mr. Trotter, but that's crap."

"Please call me John. I don't want any formality to get in the way of what I think is an extremely important task. And believe me, I'm not alone in that opinion."

"The Russian?" McGarvey said. "Have we established who exactly he is and what he's doing throwing parties down there?"

"No one important at this moment. Tom Barkin, one of our station guys, is keeping an eye out for him. If something develops, we'll see. But I do have a mission for you. An important one."

McGarvey would remember this exact moment for a very long time, because it marked a watershed for him—not only for his career but for his life.

"I'll drive you back to the OHB, we've set up a small office for you, and if need be we can arrange an assistant, though I'd rather keep you isolated as much as possible. You do understand."

"No."

"Good heavens, man, you're going into badland and you need to prepare yourself."

"Chile?"

"Yes, San Antonio."

"You said you weren't interested in Baranov for now."

"General Matias Varga. He has a compound just a few klicks from Baranov's. It's black op. Just the sort you wanted when you signed up." Trotter stopped and looked McGarvey in the eye. "We want you to assassinate him for us."

"Why?"

"He's called the Butcher for a very good reason. Under Pinochet's direction the man has set up an office to clean out Chile's dissidents. Thousands have already been arrested, tortured and then murdered. With more to come. The man supposedly thinks of himself as a Nazi doing a righteous job of cleansing."

"Feed it to the press," McGarvey said. "Expose the bastard. It'll soon stop."

"It would spill over to the Presidential Palace."

"That's the point. Take down the entire regime."

"No." Trotter hesitated. "I'm told that there are other considerations."

"Which you can't discuss with me," McGarvey said.

"They'd simply replace the general."

"They'd know that we know. It'd be a very clear message," McGarvey said. "A warning to stop." Everything was wrong. "I'd need to speak to Danielle or someone on the seventh floor."

"I'm as far as it goes."

"Will I have help?"

"No."

"I'm to be deniable," McGarvey said.

Trotter nodded. "Something like that. Will you do it? Will you take on the job and the responsibility?"

McGarvey had asked for this very thing, though at the moment he couldn't recall exactly why. He'd known that it wouldn't—couldn't—be so neat as he'd hoped. Nothing in the real world ever was. And the world of international espionage was less so.

"I'll need something in writing."

Trotter shook his head. "You're on your own, Kirk. In this business you'll always be on your own."

What to tell Katy? McGarvey wondered, but he nodded. "I'm in."

NINE

□

The Prince of Wales Country Club in Santiago's Metropolitan Region was in restricted-entry mode when Baranov's black Cadillac pulled up at the gate and the driver powered down the window. A guard with a crisp army uniform, a pistol at his hip, came out of the gatehouse.

"The president is expecting us," the Russian driver said.

The guard glanced at Baranov in the backseat, then stepped back a pace, saluted and waved the car through.

Baranov wore khaki slacks with a light sweater against the late spring weather, but no blazer or suit today. The club, which had become fairly exclusive since Pinochet had taken up golf, had nevertheless relaxed its once strict dress code. Away from his official duties, during which he wore his military uniform with medals, the president was informal, and he expected his staff and others around him to dress the same way.

The club was housed in a meticulously maintained Tudor-style building with exposed dark wood beams across white stucco walls, and at the entrance the only cars in sight were military vehicles, several of them troop trucks, empty now. Five helicopters circled overhead. A pair of soldiers in fatigues, automatic rifles at the ready, stood at the front door. When Baranov got out of the car, they came to attention.

"I'm Captain Baranov here at el Presidente's invitation."

"Yes, sir, straight back in the barroom. Are you armed?"

"No."

The club was empty except for Pinochet and a group of men in the bar, all of them dressed in golfing clothes. The president was far less of an imposing man in civilian attire than in his uniforms. And this morning he didn't seem as forceful as normal, possibly even a little sad or worried. He was starting to look his age.

He was seated at the round table with a half-dozen of his advisers, one of whom said something to him as Baranov walked in. He looked up and smiled.

"Ah, my Russian spy come to play golf with me."

Baranov nodded. "Diplomat, Mr. President, and unfortunately, I don't play golf. Not a very practical game in Moscow."

"Too bad—I was hoping to have a long talk with you about your mission, whatever it really is. Certainly not the arts."

"I can caddy for you, sir," Baranov said. At thirty he was on the verge of a promotion if he could pull off what KGB Director General Maxim Leonov was calling a coup. CESTA del Sur was the KGB's operation in the western hemisphere south of the U.S. border. To this point it was stuck gathering intelligence and peddling influence mostly in Mexico and a few of the Latin American countries. Cuba was a completely separate operation, but Chile was high on the list.

"It's the prize we need to take away from the Americans," Leonov had explained. The U.S. had backed Pinochet's coup in September 1973, and still had a huge influence on the government. It was Baranov's mission to bring the country and its intelligence services—especially the DINA—into CESTA del Sur.

The ultimate goal was to burn American intelligence operations all the way up to Mexico, and eventually to Cuba, the biggest prize of all, through the back door. Through Chile.

"You have balls, Captain, I'll give you that much," Leonov had said last night, laughing.

Baranov had reported to him via encrypted telephone about his activities at the San Antonio compound and his invitation to play golf with the president.

"I didn't know you played the game."

"I don't."

"Then be careful, Captain, that you don't lose your head trying to gain the country."

Baranov turned to Pinochet, who said sharply, "I don't need a caddy; what I need is a partner. It's a game you might think about."

General Varga, in golfing clothes, walked in. He seemed to be in a foul mood.

"Matias," Pinochet said, rising. "Unfortunately there will be no golf today." He motioned for Baranov to come with him and they went outside to a line of four golf carts, armed soldiers everywhere, even on the driving range and out on the course.

"The general seems disappointed," Baranov said.

"He's an important officer—I'll make it up to him. You drive."

They got in the lead golf car and headed away from the clubhouse, by-passing the first tee at Pinochet's direction. A golf cart with four presidential guards followed.

"Actually General Varga is a neighbor of yours in San Antonio, you know this. Lovely wife, but they tend to stay to themselves. Unfortunately they've never developed a credible understanding of the real world."

"Which is why I was sent here, Mr. President."

"Did your government send you merely to spy on us, or are you after something else?"

"Copper," Baranov said.

"You have all the minerals you need in Siberia."

"Making a deal with Chile would be easier than opening new mining operations."

"In exchange for what, Captain?"

"Intelligence on American activities. Washington is not your friend."

Pinochet laughed. "Washington's only friend is Washington—didn't they teach you that at School One?" The school was the KGB's main academy outside Moscow.

"It's a fact that could be used against them."

"Without their assistance I would not be president."

"And without our assistance you might not remain president much longer."

Pinochet was instantly angry. He motioned for Baranov to stop. "Talk to me, Captain, but not in riddles."

"The president's advisers want to block Japan's negotiations for exclusivity to your copper exports. At the same time they're worried that your General Varga's activities in Valparaíso might become public. It would be an acute embarrassment to the White House. By supporting your government it might appear that the Americans are also supporting Varga."

Pinochet pursed his lips, trying to control his anger. "What happens in Chile stays in Chile."

"Varga fancies himself another Josef Mengele. You know how that turned out for Germany."

"Don't threaten me, or you might not live to visit Valparaíso yourself."

"I'm trying to help you, Mr. President."

"Like Washington, Moscow's only friend is Moscow. You say you came here for copper—what else? You want me to sever ties with America—ties that I might remind you have completely turned our economy around. It was my Chicago Boys who pulled the magic out of their hats."

The Chicago Boys were a group of Chilean economists who went to the University of Chicago while in exchange a group of professors from Chicago came to the Catholic University of Chile to turn its department of economics around. The program was financed by the U.S. Agency for International Development. Chile owed a large debt to the USAID.

"But Valparaíso is a potential embarrassment that would change everything. The U.S. is sending an assassin to kill the general."

"I know this!"

"I was told that you did," Baranov said. "But I have brought a plan that would turn Varga's murder into a coup for you. An act that would satisfy the White House that you were still a friend to the U.S."

Pinochet laughed. "While buying you time to work here with us—with my intelligence agencies. Giving you an open door to Washington."

"Exactly, Mr. President."

"Tell me."

"They're sending a young CIA officer for the wet work."

"One man?"

"Yes. But I suggest that you wait in ambush until he completes his task then kill him and completely destroy his body so that it could never be found."

"And what would this accomplish? We need Varga's skills."

"You will claim responsibility for the general's death. You will say that when you found out the full details of his grisly work, you had no other choice but to eliminate him, without a public hearing. You wanted the program to end. And as far as Valparaíso and the general's skills, you can move the program and hire someone else for the job. I'm sure there are other men in Chile such as the general."

Pinochet looked away for a moment. "Do you have someone on the inside in Washington who knows the name of this American?"

"His name is Kirk McGarvey, and this would be his first kill."

"Why let it go that far?" Pinochet said. "Why not kill him before he ever comes here? In the meantime I'll have Varga attended to."

"If that's what you wish, Mr. President."

TEN

□

Although McGarvey had been in residence at the Farm for only ten days, his homecoming seemed odd, even a little disjointed. Driving up in his red Mustang convertible, he thought how out of place he sometimes felt in his and Katy's expansive two-story colonial, located on the south side of the Chevy Chase Club. But it was Katy's place. He'd bought it for her, hoping she'd be happy, especially during his absences. It hadn't worked out that way.

He parked in the three-car garage next to her Mercedes and custom-made golf cart, both in powder blue. In less than one year she had been elected to the club's board of directors. It was a singular honor, she'd told him. Something normal people aspire to.

He'd been too tired to argue with her that night in bed, and she'd taken his silence as disapproval.

It was a little after five, Friday, and Katy was in the kitchen drinking a glass of Chablis. When he walked in, she got a beer from the fridge and opened it for him. "Glass?"

"Bottle's fine," McGarvey said.

Katy was tall, just a couple of inches shorter than him, with a long graceful neck and delicate facial lines under high eyebrows. Slender but in perfect shape because of her three-times-a-week visit to the salon, and her personal fitness trainer and dietician, she could have been a movie actress. Blond hair, blue eyes, a flawless complexion and a default attitude that was as often as not haughty.

"Did Liz get off okay?"

"Peggy picked her up and took her to Dulles yesterday morning. They got to your sister's around ten."

McGarvey's sister lived with her husband and two girls in Salt Lake City. She had discussed with Katy about having Liz out for a visit, and Katy had agreed. Mac had just gone out to the Farm and Katy had called him after the fact. Their housekeeper would travel with Liz.

"I'm sorry I missed her," he said.

"She was sorry too."

What was probably the last foursome of the day was playing down the thirteenth fairway. After the round they would have drinks and maybe even dinner with their wives, who had undoubtedly played bridge all afternoon. It was something Katy did from time to time, complaining that Kirk ought to take up golf. It could be a pleasant life, versus dropping everything usually with less than a moment's notice to go off running God only knew where.

That life, and especially this house—with its perfect furnishings, perfect paintings, perfect color schemes, perfect bedspreads, chintz and lace, chaise lounges, Turkish rugs laid down here and there in perfect harmony— wasn't for him.

He'd been a rancher's son in western Kansas where life was plain, sometimes even brutal in winter; job one was saving the cattle from starvation no matter the weather. Whereas Katy was East Coast, refined, the daughter of successful, philanthropic parents; she'd found Mac to be devastatingly handsome, but dangerous.

After Mac's parents had died, his sister had been given their money, and he had inherited the ranch. His parents' Manhattan lawyer—Katy's father by happenstance—had arranged the will and the sale of the property, netting Mac several million dollars, which he had invested.

He and Katy had met outside her father's office and something about him was untamed, she'd admitted to him once. Maybe even untamable. He'd become a project for her and along the way they'd fallen in love.

"Are you back now for a stretch?" Katy asked. "There's a reception for Senator Bitterman at the club. I thought that since we contributed to his last campaign you might want to meet him."

"When?"

"A week from Tuesday. It means that you'd have to stay available for eleven days. Can you do that for me?"

"I might have to go away before then."

Katy turned away. "Christ," she muttered.

"I'll take a shower and change, and we can go out to dinner. We need to talk."

She turned back. "We certainly do. Any place you'd like?"

"Somewhere neutral, if you don't mind."

The Capitol Hill Club, a private enclave for important Republicans, was located two blocks from the Capitol. He and Katy were members because her father was an important contributor to the party. In Mac's estimation it was even more stuffy than their country club, but at least it was neutral.

They were a little early but the club was busy as usual for a Friday night. The main dining room was full but they found a spot in the Grill Room, which didn't accept reservations, and was often used for Washington insider business.

Katy ordered a chicken breast with a simple lemon butter sauce and Mac a six-ounce New York strip, rare, and a Caesar salad. They shared a bottle of Dom Pérignon. It was the wine they'd had on their first date, when Katy learned she was pregnant, at Liz's birth and on just about every other occasion that was significant.

"If you're bearing bad news, this won't soften the blow," she said.

"I'm sorry, Katy—" he started, but she interrupted him, something she only did when she was angry.

"Kathleen."

"I've been given an assignment that I can't turn down. It's important enough that I can't discuss the details with you, but necessary. At least I think it is."

"Can't turn down, or won't?"

"Won't," he said.

She thought for a moment. "Dangerous, I suppose."

McGarvey nodded. "I won't lie to you."

"When do you leave?"

"A few days, maybe a little longer. I have to do a little research."

"Is it the Soviet Union or China or someplace dreadful?"

"I can't say."

"How long will you be gone this time?"

McGarvey had a few ideas but nothing definite had jelled yet. "A few days, maybe a week. I don't know."

"And I sit home alone worried sick about you. Never knowing what dirty little spy mission you're on. Maybe you're off someplace killing someone or getting killed yourself. And still I'll never know."

Their dinners came, but Katy threw down her napkin. "I'm done here, Kirk. And I'm just about done with you. I can't take the uncertainty. Maybe my father was right after all. Maybe I should have insisted that we settle in some godforsaken corner of Kansas. At least I'd know where you were every day."

She got up and headed for the door. Mac paid the waiter, who didn't show he was flustered—this was Washington, after all—and followed his wife.

Katy was at the curb when a taxi slid up as McGarvey got outside.

All of a sudden everything was wrong. A dark-colored car—a Buick—had just turned the corner onto First Street, its passenger-side front and rear windows down, one man driving, one in the shotgun position, the other directly behind him.

McGarvey pulled his Walther PPK from the holster beneath his jacket at the small of his back, thumbing the safety catch off as he raced from under the club's entry canopy.

"Katy!" he shouted.

She turned, a sour look on her pretty face, her left hand up as if she were waving him off.

He got to her, shoving her to the sidewalk with his left hand as he raised his pistol over the roof of the cab at the same moment the Buick was opposite them. The men in front and back opened fire at the same time. Large-caliber pistols, maybe even ten-millimeter—the thought flashed across Mac's head at the speed of light, as he fired one deliberate shot after the other.

As the Buick passed, Mac rose up and followed it, firing until his Walther went dry. He ejected the spent magazine, took the spare from his jacket pocket, seated it in the handle, cycled a round into the chamber and continued firing until the Buick was around the corner.

ELEVEN

□

Baranov had stayed the night at the embassy, and in the morning he was having breakfast with the KGB's chief of station Anatoli Kaplin when an aide came directly to their table.

"Captain, there is a telephone call for you in the *referentura*." The room, or quite often a series of rooms and meeting spaces in every Soviet embassy, was the one area completely secure from any form of electronic or physical bugging.

"The call you were expecting?" Kaplin asked.

"*Da*," Baranov said, putting down his napkin and rising.

"Good news, I hope."

"I'm sure of it."

The windowless strategic-planning office on the third floor was deserted. The single-line phone was off the hook. As soon as the aide had withdrawn and closed the door, Baranov picked it up.

"Yes."

"It's Henry," the man in Washington said. The call, which was being relayed through a re-dialer in Luxembourg, was not encrypted, but was reasonably secure. Nevertheless they used false names and discussed their subject obliquely.

"Anything new?"

"The objective was achieved, though I didn't see the need."

The man spoke with a U.S. East Coast accent. Baranov had turned him in Moscow a number of years ago, mostly out of vanity on the American's part. He was the type who always thought he was the smartest man in the room. He believed he was smarter than Baranov, which was just fine. He thought he was getting away with something no one else could under-stand. It was amusing.

"Just the message, nothing more?"

"Then I assume that you're going to proceed?"

"Of course," Baranov said. "It's a favor to you, actually."

"It'll get us off the hook."

"Quid pro quo, my friend. Nothing more."

"Yes," Henry said, and he hung up.

The attack on the young American CIA officer had failed. He would be coming to Chile after all.

Baranov went across the hall to the well-equipped signals room, about the size of a Pullman car, with banks of electronic equipment manned by operators along both long walls. A supervisor sat at her desk at one end.

"Any word from my SQ surveillance team?" Baranov asked the attrac-tive and bright young woman.

"Yes, sir. As a matter of fact he and his wife just left their dacha and are driving into town."

"Here?"

"San Antonio."

"I'm taking a staff car with a radio; let me know wherever they go. And tell the team that they must not be spotted."

"Yes, sir."

The highway down to San Antonio was broad, modern and well paved. Despite the fairly heavy traffic Baranov made good time in one of the em-bassy's Mercedes sedans. He had planned on inviting Varga to his com-pound after the attempted assassination of McGarvey. But he had figured that wouldn't happen until tomorrow, possibly Sunday.

The general had a source within the DINA who had warned him that an American was coming to kill him. Pinochet knew about it as well. But Baranov had not been able to find out who the source was, nor how he'd gotten his information—presumably from inside the CIA's directorate of operations.

It was a loose end. Bothersome. Yet something had held him back from asking Henry—someone who would know about the leak, and more important, the reason for the leak. Something else just beyond his ken was going on.

For now he wanted to get to Varga with the news before his DINA source did. It would be another opening move in an overture of friendship. Trust building. Basic tradecraft.

Twenty kilometers outside of San Antonio the signals day supervisor radioed him. "They're at the Club Las Brisas de Santo Domingo," she said. "Do you know it? Over."

"Yes, I do. Let me know if they leave."

"Yes, sir."

Las Brisas was actually a golfing club. Such places had become immensely popular ever since the president had taken up the game. General Varga was reportedly pretty good, which had gained him favor. His disposal work—as it was being called by those in the know—was vital to Pinochet and was another plus for Varga. At this moment the general was a very popular man in Chile—in some circles.

Driving up to valet parking, Baranov was struck by how young and smartly dressed everyone seemed to be, whereas he was dressed in khakis, a red polo shirt and a shabby tweed sport coat. It was an image he sometimes projected, of a man who offered absolutely no threat to anyone. The sprawling clubhouse was about as modern as anything in the country and so were the people. Mercedes, Jaguars and a lot of big fancy American cars filled the parking lot. Whatever else might be said about el Presidente he and his Chicago Boys had turned the country around economically. The word miracle was used just about every day in just about every newspaper in Chile. Even the term president for life had taken on a life of its own.

Chile was vital to the Soviet Union's interests in the hemisphere.

On the basis of the diplomatic plates, Baranov was granted entrance to the club, where he told the manager that he had come to speak to General Varga at the president's suggestion.

"I'm very sorry, sir, but the general is presently on the driving range. However, Mrs. Varga is on the patio. Shall I present you?"

"It's not necessary," Baranov said, and he followed the manager to a patio that overlooked the first tee.

Karina sat with her back to the doors. She was drinking what looked like brandy from a small snifter. Her shoulders were narrow, her body slight, but her sleek black hair hung thick and long nearly to the middle of her back. She was dressed in a stunning white sundress, white gloves and black-and-white heels.

Most of the half-dozen or so other tables were occupied with couples or foursomes. But she was alone, and when Baranov walked over, she looked up, a very slight smile playing at the corners of her sensuous mouth.

"Here to see Mati?" she said, lifting a hand for him to take.

He kissed it. "May I join you?"

"Of course, but only if you promise not to drink that dreary vodka."

"A de Jerez would be nice."

She smiled faintly and motioned for the waiter to bring them a drink. "You've done your homework, or was it a lucky guess?"

"While in Rome."

After their drinks came, she came directly to the point. "What is it that you want my husband to do for you, Captain?"

"And you've done your homework, Mrs. Varga," Baranov said, returning her smile. "But it's not what your husband can do for me; it's what I can do for him."

"Which is?"

"Save his life, of course."

This time she laughed out loud. "I think you had best call me Karina," she said. "You're speaking about the assassin the Americans are supposedly sending?"

"His name is Kirk McGarvey. I had friends in Washington try to kill him, at el Presidente's suggestion, but they failed."

"If he comes here, he will certainly die."

"Perhaps, but I would like to help make it so."

"Why?"

"May I explain that to you and your husband?"

"My husband will be at least another hour or two practicing. But perhaps you'll join us for dinner this evening at our compound. This time at eleven?"

"I wouldn't miss it."

TWELVE

□

Mac and Katy had been tied up with the police until nearly midnight. Now as the sun was just coming up, he stood at the bedroom window watching his wife sleeping.

Somewhere along the line things had started to go wrong for them. Their marriage had come to several crises points over the past year or so, about his unexplained absences and his work for the CIA, but last night had been different. After the shooting she'd been calm, even friendly.

"You were quite good, Kirk," she said on the way home. "Even the police officers were impressed."

He didn't know where she was going with this and he was wary. "My training just kicked in. It was automatic."

"But no one came down from Langley to see if you needed help. Isn't that unusual?"

He wanted to tell her no, that it wasn't. The Company expected its field officers to take care of themselves. If they couldn't in their own country, how could they manage in badland?

"It was over too fast, but in the morning I'll have to go out there to make a report and then a couple of interrogators will ask me some tough questions wondering why I had instigated a shootout downtown in front of a lot of innocent bystanders. Didn't I understand collateral damage?"

"But it wasn't your fault," she'd blurted.

"It was, by virtue of my job, what I do," he said, and he regretted opening his mouth the moment the words came out.

She'd turned away, her mood suddenly brittle. "What you do," she said. "What you are. What you've become."

When they got home, she'd taken a shower and had gone straight to bed, leaving him downstairs. When he finally came up around three she was sound asleep, and he didn't have the heart to join her, wondering about their future.

He cleaned his pistol and reloaded the two magazines, then took a shower, got dressed and left the house before Katy woke up. He drove through Bethesda and crossed the river at the American Legion Bridge near Turkey Run Park—the route he normally took to work—but instead of turning south on the parkway he headed out to Dulles International.

Parking his car out of the way in one of the long-term lots, he went to the car rental agencies and got an anonymous gray Ford Sierra. Once he was clear of the airport and reasonably certain that he hadn't picked up a tail, he got on the Beltway.

At one point he suddenly switched lanes and got off at Jefferson, immediately got back on the highway, getting back off again at Annandale. No one was behind him, no one had taken any notice, and unless a Rusian spy satellite had been retasked to track his moves—which he thought highly unlikely—he was in the clear.

At eight-thirty he pulled up and parked in the driveway of a well-maintained split-level ranch, shut off the engine and waited. The garage door opened almost immediately and Janos Plonski came out, his wife, Pat, watching at the kitchen door. She waved uncertainly and Mac waved back.

Janos was a Polish immigrant who worked as a senior archivist for the Company. His mother had been a hero of the resistance against the Soviets, and Pat was a Cockney girl whom he had met while he was studying at Oxford. He'd gone through training at the Farm with Mac and they'd become fast friends. Janos thought Mac was competent and Mac thought Janos was one of the kindest, gentlest and most honest men he'd ever known.

"Christ, you're an ugly son of a bitch," one of the instructors had said. Janos was a large man—six-five—with a wrestler's build, completely bald with a wildly large nose and a heavily pockmarked face from a bad case of childhood chicken pox.

Janos had smiled good-naturedly. "But I have a good heart, Senior Master Sergeant."

Everyone in the class had laughed, and every one of them had become his instant friend and admirer. One of the women recruits had put it best: *Janos has cojones.*

Janos got in beside McGarvey. "I heard about your trouble last night. Is Kathleen okay?"

"A little shook up, but they missed."

"Any idea who they were, why they wanted to take you down?"

"A couple of ideas, but it's why I came out here. I need your help."

Pat was still at the kitchen door. Janos looked at her. "This is a bad business, Kirk. What I'm hearing is that you've gotten yourself into something outside our charter. There're to be repercussions."

"Who said that?"

"No one, everyone. Who knows how these things get started? Word is out that you've stepped over the bounds."

"I need some information from you. About a man with a New England accent. Could be fairly high up in the Company, but maybe not. Definitely a Washington insider."

"Are you listening to me, Kirk? You could be a marked man now. Maybe it is time to get out."

"He was in Chile within the last month."

"Pat wants me to get a regular job here on the Beltway. Consulting, maybe for security work."

"He is someone who carries some weight with at least their foreign ministry."

Janos turned to him. "Computers are the next big thing, Kirk. I shit you not. They'll revolutionize everything. I've been studying. IBM has come out with some very excellent tutorials. If I keep my nose clean, I could head the new department. It's coming."

"This guy could have a connection with a KGB captain by the name of Valentin Baranov."

"CESTA del Sur," Janos said almost automatically in response. His expression suddenly turned sheepish.

"The Soviet's hemisphere network. They want Chile as a back door to Mexico, then Cuba and finally us. I need to know—"

"What?" Janos interrupted. "Be careful what you wish for. More than once you've said that shit could rise up and bite you in the ass. But my ass is on the line too. So is Pat's and Barney's and Elizabeth's."

Barney and the baby Elizabeth were their children. Katy had been god-mother to the baby, whom the Plonskis named after Mac and Katy's daughter.

"Trotter is sending me to Chile to assassinate someone."

"General Varga."

McGarvey was shocked to the core. "How the hell do you know this?"

"Vouchers," he said.

"What?"

"We work on vouchers, Kirk. All of us, all the time. Vouchers for our paychecks. Vouchers for when you need a new typewriter ribbon or ream of paper. Vouchers for food, ammunition, weapons, bedsheets, bath tow-els, at the Farm. Vouchers for a coffin when you die in the line of duty."

"Even for black ops?"

Janos nodded sadly. "*Accountability* is the new key word. 'The days of reck-less spending are over, Janos,' they tell me. 'Keep track.' We need account-ability for someday when Congress decides that the American people need to know. Even for unspecified travel."

"Was my name mentioned specifically?"

"Trotter's was. Chile was. I merely put two and two together just now."

"I need to know the name of the American with an East Coast accent who was there. And why he was there," McGarvey said.

"What's Trotter say?"

"He's lied to me, I think."

"And yet you're going through with it?"

"I don't have a lot of choices," McGarvey said. "So it comes down to the truth. Will you help me?"

THIRTEEN

☐

Baranov came down the long winding dirt road to the Vargas' compound a few minutes before eleven in the evening, the windows in his staff Mercedes down. The night sky was perfectly clear and there was only a hint of a breeze off the ocean. Sounds carried forever, even the rollers breaking on the shore kilometers away.

He had thought long and hard about his role here in Chile before accepting the bigger assignment and switching operations from the embassy in Mexico City.

CESTA del Sur was the key to making inroads from the Americas. Winning Pinochet's trust was the first major step, and finding a way to him was the method that Varga would provide.

He stopped at the entrance, a brilliant spotlight from the top of the wall completely blinding him for several seconds until it was shut off and the gate swung open and he drove inside.

A lieutenant directed him to the main house, where the general himself came out to meet him.

"Promptness is a good thing," Varga said. He was dressed in linen slacks, a yellow guayabera and sandals.

Baranov took a leather satchel out of the backseat and brought it over. "Good evening, sir. I brought some de Jerez and a few bottles of Krug as a peace gesture."

"Peace for what?"

"For interrupting your game of golf with the president."

"I was told that you didn't play."

"Never learned the game. But I wanted to talk to him in an unofficial setting. About you, actually. And the norteamericano the CIA is sending to kill you and how that could work to our advantage."

"Come in, then; we have lobster and sea bass."

"And perhaps some home movies?"

"Of course."

The cook took the satchel of wine and Baranov followed Varga through the house to the swimming pool just off the living room, where Karina was seated in a chaise lounge sipping brandy. She was stunning in a black French bikini, only partially concealed under a sheer pool jacket cinched at the waist.

"Captain Baranov, so good of you to join us. And your offer to help my husband. We're intrigued."

She held up a hand and Baranov went over and kissed it. "So am I by the stories I've been hearing."

"All good, I hope."

"All interesting to Moscow, and possibly to our advantage if we can arrange for the CIA to stumble."

Varga brought fresh brandies for his wife and Baranov and himself, and the two men sat in patio chairs on either side of Karina.

Some mournful guitar music from a stereo played softly in the background, the lights were low, the night soft, isolated, sensuous. Baranov could almost feel the heat radiating off the general and his wife. And something else as well. Anticipation, perhaps.

He smiled and raised his glass. "I would like to do business on behalf of my country by helping save your life. But first I think that we should get to know each other a little better, don't you agree?"

"We have read your dossier," Varga said. "You've done things."

"And I've read yours. Your wife's."

"Please call me Karina."

Baranov nodded. "With pleasure. And I'd like to see your paintings."

Varga was somewhat startled though he tried to hide it, but Karina smiled. "But first a movie, and afterward we can discuss exactly how you mean to help us and why you think that we need you here."

"And why Moscow as opposed to Washington," Varga said.

Baranov laughed out loud as he stood and took off his jacket. "Let's become friends. You have your movies and paintings and I have something to give."

The movie was without sound, which made the black-and-white images on the 16-mm screen seem all the more brutal and surreal. Except that Baranov had seen the real thing in person at a couple of the gulags in the Far East; he'd heard the screams, the pleadings, smelled the blood and excrement and fear.

But the real thing as well as the movies were boring. He preferred his opponents to fight back. He preferred the intelligent operator to the bovine victim being led to slaughter.

It was different for Varga and his wife, who both became visibly aroused within the first minute or so of the first movie.

At one point Baranov chuckled. He got another brandy and came back.

"Do you think this is amusing, these completely helpless people dying like that?" Karina asked.

"Actually, I do," he said. "There are no innocent enemies of the state, didn't you know? If they were so helpless, why did they take part in such a foolish revolution? Why didn't they run away? Or at the least keep their fucking mouths shut!"

An older woman, naked, with large pendulous breasts, came on-screen. Varga strode up beside her and lopped off her left breast with a razor-sharp machete. She fell back, mouth open in a scream, silent on the screen, blood gushing from the massive wound.

The general turned to look directly at the camera, an enigmatic smile on his narrow lips. *La Joconde* at the Louvre, was the first thought to come to Baranov's mind, and he gave voice to it.

For a longish moment Varga and his wife were dead silent, but then Karina clapped her hands and Varga threw his head back and roared with laughter. "You understand," he said, choking between breaths. "You understand."

Everything Baranov had read about them was correct; they were certifiably insane. They killed simply for the pleasure of it. The units of the Gulag Archipelago, on the other hand, served a valuable purpose: they cleansed the state.

But there was a purpose here too: CESTA del Sur.

The thought hung on the air for a long time, until Varga and his wife exchanged a glance.

"Are you hungry?" she asked her husband.

"Not for lobster," he said.

"Valentin?" Karina asked.

"Not for dinner, no," Baranov said. "But friends call me Vasha."

"But you're hungry?"

Baranov turned his attention back to the images on the screen. What he was watching reminded him of the movies he'd seen from the Nazi concentration camps. The victims were just that—victims and not people, at least not in the social sense of the world. No friends, next-door neighbors, fellow workers, lovers, wives, husbands, children. Just objects whose status was less than that of barnyard animals at the slaughterhouse.

He'd supposed then as now that the run-of-the-mill Nazi concentration-camp soldier was able to carry out his gruesome duties because he could separate the identities of the victims from their status as real people.

Looking at Varga and his wife, he had the feeling—chilling even for him—that they had never needed that fiction.

"Never been more hungry in my life," he said, putting down his drink.

Karina and Varga got to their feet, and between them they led Baranov from the lanai and inside the house to the bedroom.

FOURTEEN

□

Janos Plonski had spent the entire day after his unsettling meeting with McGarvey falling behind. He'd gotten to his meager office at the records section in the basement of the OHB on time, and puttered, not getting anything of any real value done.

As he drove back now around midnight, traffic was light, the air damp and still, his windows down. With his head fully extracted from his ass, as he would tell his boss Tony Winston in the morning, he had the feeling that someone was looking over his shoulder. And it was not a friend.

Janos was also unsettled about how he had left it with Pat. She'd always liked Mac, but she'd once admitted that she was frightened of him.

"He's a man with the weight of the world on his shoulders, Janos," she'd said. "If he falls—which he will do someday—he could take us all down with him. You especially."

"Why me especially?" he asked.

She'd looked away for a moment. "Because you're so bloody much like him. You admire him. You'd like to be him."

"He's just a friend."

"Why a friend like him?" she'd screeched. "Can you explain at least that much to me, so that I can understand your fucking fascination?"

Because he'd never had anyone else to trust—other than his wife. Not his parents, who'd been too busy for him. Not his brother, who'd died young; no sisters, all the aunts and uncles and cousins dead. No one out there who gave a damn about whether he lived or died. No one, other than Pat, who would listen to him. And even Pat had never been the total answer for him, simply because he couldn't discuss the details of the most classified operations he dealt with.

She would not understand. Only Mac could. Which made him not only a friend but a refuge.

"He'll kill you one of these days," she'd told him, her voice bleak. "Mark my words, guys like that always leave bodies in their wake."

As Plonski pulled up at the main gate the security guard slid open the window and waved him through. The campus was in full operation 24/7 so it wasn't unusual for officers to show up at all hours of the night or day.

He'd been totally honest with McGarvey about his job in records keeping. The system's attention to detail—a voucher for every aspect of every operation—was its strength against congressional oversight as well as its weakness, a point he made more than once to his superiors.

"Tell that to the folks who control our budget," Larry Danielle, the assistant deputy chief of the Agency, had made it clear.

"Including our Black Budget?" someone had asked. It was during a meeting in the DCI's seventh-floor conference room.

"Especially for those ops. But with care, gentlemen. The record trails need to be handled with exactly the same attention to detail that the actual operations demand." Danielle had looked across the table at them as if he were a god looking down from Mount Olympus. "Lives are at stake. Don't ever forget that you are not simply dealing with bits of paper in a file box somewhere."

Driving up to the seven-story OHB, Janos parked in the front lot and went through security in the main lobby. The first-floor corridor was mostly quiet, only a couple of staffers in the coffee shop to the right, and his footfalls seemed loud to him. Damning, in his mind, marking him as a thief in the night.

Downstairs in Records, Dominique Walters and Patsy Cline were filing the day's bits and pieces, and doing standby duty for anything needed to be pulled by someone in a field office somewhere in another time zone.

It was another of Plonski's suggestions that had gone unheeded: all operations worldwide, including here at Langley, should be on the Zulu clock—Greenwich Mean Time. Everyone would be playing from the same deck.

Patsy was on a rolling ladder just around the corner from Janos's office and she slid over when he walked in. "Came down to find out if we're having a party?" she quipped.

"I've heard stories, but I haven't seen the line item requests yet," he said. "Anything doing in the overnights?"

"Mr. Trotter asked for a clarification on a line item from Station Santiago."

Plonski stopped himself from reacting. "Anything important?"

"They've got one of the new laser surveillance units. Now they're asking for authorization, after the fact."

"Big bucks."

"I'll say. But at least he's not lit a fire."

Plonski's office was in the corner of the exposed basement with a window that used to overlook a sloping wooded area that had been recently cleared for construction of a new building. The CIA was growing by leaps and bounds.

He draped his jacket over his chair and went out to Patsy, who rolled her chair back.

"Pull Santiago's budget requests and voucher summaries for the past ninety days, please. And pull the DO's replies and any special ops orders."

Patsy hesitated. "Those were the same you looked at the other day, weren't they?"

"Just the last thirty days. I want ninety."

"Looking for something specific, boss?"

"No, just curious about why they already got the laser and only now are asking for the pay order."

Janos went back into his office and sat looking out the window for ten minutes until Patsy came in with four large accordion files on a wheeled cart. "These are just the summaries."

"These'll do for now. But I want you to start looking for the same requests for surveillance equipment from some of our other stations. Mexico City, Caracas, Bogotá, Quito, Lima."

The girl, actually a woman in her late thirties, who refused to wear skirts or dresses or makeup, was the picture-perfect librarian. Just about everything she did she took seriously. Plonski had often tried to kid her nto believing that he thought that she was a secret party animal, and sometimes, like earlier, she'd take him up on it. But she was very serious now.

"If you can give me a hint where you want to go, maybe I can help."

He smiled. "Just fishing for now. If I get a bite, I'll let you know."

When she left, he opened the first accordion folder and pulled out a file marked SECRET, STATION SANTIAGO above the subheading *Line Items for the Month of September*—two and a half months ago.

He glanced at the clock on his desk, the Brandenburg Gate from the East Side, a gift from Pat. It was eight minutes after one when he began reading. Robert Stanwick, request for an update on his health insurance policy and a revision to his will. Toby McIntyre, request for transfer to Station Berlin. His wife was German and she wanted to go home for a while. Requisition for one thousand rounds of 9mm pistol ammunition, above the usual monthly resupply of five hundred rounds for proficiency practice.

Curious, Plonski called for an explanatory file, which Patsy found and brought to him, without comment, in under five minutes. A shooting competition had been arranged between the U.S. and British embassy teams, and the Agency had fielded four competitors who needed the practice. Turns out the U.S. won handily.

Ten minutes after two his telephone rang. One hour and two minutes. Actually a bit longer than he'd thought would be the case. It was Trotter.

"Burning the midnight oil, are we, Janos?"

"Couldn't sleep."

"I have the same problem myself. Especially when I have a bee in my bonnet. Do you have a bee?"

Plonski was a little disappointed, but not surprised. "I got behind today—don't know what happened but I sorta went blank."

"Mac has that effect on people. Even me. Anything new for him?"

"Actually it's nothing directly for him, though he's asked me to check around."

"Check for what, exactly?"

"Station ops, routine shit. He's on a mission and he wants to cover his ass. Looking for the anomalies."

Trotter was silent for just a moment. "Have you found any anomalies?"

"Nothing other than the request for laser surveillance equipment that's already been delivered. An expensive item."

"Yes, it is."

"I'm wondering why they need it."

FIFTEEN

□

Cook, who was an old mestizo with no expression on her lined face, served coffee to Baranov on the pool deck just as the sun was rising on a beautiful day. Morning was his favorite time, and being alone was his favorite state of being. After last night he was glad for the moment.

He'd not drunk any of the champagne because it was laced with enough LSD to have an effect on Varga and his wife, but he had reaped the benefits. They were not hooked, but they were vulnerable.

He'd never been married, though once as a young man at Moscow State University and again at the KGB's School One he'd fallen for girls. But they had been girls—especially at the university. And the KGB recruit had been tough, almost emotionless—sex was little more than another physical exercise.

On an early assignment in London he'd made contact with an MI6 cipher clerk at a Turkish bathhouse and over the next months, developing his john, he'd engaged in a homosexual relationship. But it had never seemed odd or unnatural to him, even from the beginning. He was a field officer, working a john for valuable product. It was sex, not love, just like with the college girls and the KGB recruit.

And the Vargas, in exchange for information and position.

Karina, dressed in a bikini bottom and T-shirt, came out and sat down. Her hair was a mess and she wore no makeup. Her eyes were red and puffy but she managed a faint smile. "That was something," she said.

Cook came out with her coffee and a small glass of de Jerez.

"How's Mati?"

"He was just coming around when I got up. He'll be okay—he has a very strong *constitución*," Karina said. She tossed back the brandy and sipped her coffee. "You are a formidable hombre who wants something important, I think. The problem is how what you want will affect us. Or your methods—how destructive will they be?"

"I'm here to help—"

She waved him off. "Save the speech, Captain. I had visions last night, fantasies, and so did my husband. But not you. When I woke up, my head was clear, and I counted the champagne glasses. Only two of them. What was in the wine for us?"

"A stimulant. Nothing harmful, I promise you."

"But why did you think it was necessary to drug us? For the sex? None of what happened was new to either of us, just the chemical. So my question remains: What do you want from us? What does Moscow want?"

"Chile," Baranov said.

She was amused. "Then you must have a very high notion of us. Me, to get to my husband. My husband, to get to who? El Presidente? But you have taken a ride around the golf course with him. If you wanted Chile, why didn't you ask him? Or did he turn you down?"

"We only talked about your husband and the assassin the CIA is sending to kill him. And the why of it."

"Because of the cleansing at Valparaíso."

Baranov almost laughed. "It's become an embarrassment to Washington. At lot of money, time and diplomacy has been spent by them."

"Yes, for copper."

"More than that. For stability in this hemisphere."

"A stability that you have been ordered to interrupt."

"Just to change—from Washington to Moscow."

A light blinked on in Karina's eyes. "Cuba," she said. "If you can get Pinochet to cooperate, the others will—Venezuela, Colombia, Ecuador, Peru, Bolivia. Castro would be contained to the north and the south. But first must come us. And what does my husband have to do with your grand plan?"

Very often at this point in a turning, the issue of truth came out. Sometimes a little truth was more harmful in the end than the entire truth—or at least some version of it. The point was not to be caught in a lie at a later juncture that would puncture the balloon.

"I have a friend in Washington who warned me about the plan to assassinate your husband, and Washington's reason for it. And he is enough of a friend to understand how the news would benefit me."

"And Moscow."

Baranov nodded.

"Who is this guy, another Kim Philby?"

"That, you will never know," Baranov said.

"Maybe my husband will turn it over to his boss. Maybe word will get to el Presidente that you are not so much of a good friend as you present yourself to be. Maybe an assassin will come for you."

"Maybe I'll step aside and let the CIA kill your husband."

Karina's anger spiked. "*Puta*," she said. "Do you think that we are afraid of some cowboy? Look around you—we are prepared here."

"Yes, here. But there are a thousand other places for it to happen. Even if he were to ride around in the middle of armored columns. And even if he were to suddenly stop his work, which of course we don't want to happen, they'd still send someone."

"But you can singlehandedly save my husband," she said, now suddenly amused.

"Yes. Because I know who he is, and I'll be told when he's on his way, and how he intends to do it."

"You have resources in Washington—kill him before he tries to come here."

"We want him to try."

"And of course I'm to be the bait for your little trap," Varga said from the door.

"Exactly," Baranov said, looking up. He'd known for a minute or so that Varga was standing there listening to them. It was the reason he'd stretched out his explanation.

The general came across and sat down next to his wife, who kissed him lightly on the cheek and gave his shoulder a squeeze.

Cook came with his coffee and refills for Karina and Baranov, including more brandy.

"Obviously there is a quid pro quo that you're seeking," Varga said. "And despite what you told my wife there are methods to protect our lives short of staying here and short of surrounding myself with troops. So, the question hangs: What do you want in return for your little favor?"

"You were already warned about the assassin."

Varga nodded.

"Who warned you?"

Varga shrugged.

"Your boss? Someone in the DINA?"

"Why do you need this information?"

Elementary, my dear Watson, Baranov wanted to say. Because whoever warned the DINA about McGarvey's coming could possibly be the same source in Washington that Baranov had relied on for several years now. And if that were the case, it would mean that his contact had his own agenda.

"I'm playing a dangerous game, General. It's not only your life that's at stake. Let's just say that I have a vested interest in keeping you alive, keeping you doing what you do best for Chile."

"And for that you drugged us for your little game?"

"I needed to get your attention."

"You have it."

"I need an introduction to whoever warned you."

"Why?"

"I would like to pool my resources."

"For the good of Moscow."

"Yes, and for the good of Santiago."

Varga exchanged a glance with his wife. "Torres."

Baranov was startled. It wasn't a name he'd expected. "Felipe Torres? The deputy director of the DINA?"

"Yes. And I should have warned you to take care with what you wished for. General Torres is a dangerous man. Maybe the most dangerous friend you might have here."

SIXTEEN

□

The morning shift began arriving around eight. Plonski got up from his desk and went down the hall to the coffeemaker, where Patsy was making a fresh pot before leaving.

"Finally finished?" she asked.

"For all the good it's done me," he said, keeping a straight face. But he'd stumbled on something—at least in the negative sense—a couple of hours ago and he'd kept coming up against dead ends. The anomalies Mac worried about and that Trotter had asked after.

"It's common knowledge that Beckett is a prima donna; what'd you expect, for him to beg for alms?" Pasty said.

The chief of Santiago Station loudly protested that the post was a dead end for his career. After Vietnam the next big trouble spots would be in the Near East, Iran, Iraq, Saudi Arabia—all of those places were set to explode and careers were to be made there. Dick Beckett's downfall was his connections on the Hill, especially in the Senate, where his sister was serving her third term for Massachusetts, and his wife, who had been born in Puerto Rico and understood Hispanic machismo. He'd been put in Chile because it was believed he would do a good job there, well away from Washington, where his sister had sometimes been a vocal critic of the entire U.S. intelligence community, especially the CIA and the National Security Agency.

When he'd been assigned to Santiago, he'd been briefed that Chile was poised to be the bellwether for just about everything happening in the southern hemisphere, especially where it concerned the Russians.

But Beckett never bought it. And in his two years in country his monthlies bore out his opinion that nothing was doing, except for the mass murders that were coming to light in Valparaíso.

His request for the expensive laser equipment had come out of the blue. And he hadn't offered any proposal for an operation where it would be needed.

His station was going after something or someone, but he'd not said what or who it might be. And the most damning bit in Plonski's estimation was that no one in the DO had pressed him.

"It's already there," he said. "But there've been no vouchers."

"If you're done, I'll refile the lot before I leave. And if you ask me, I think that you should go home and get some sleep," Patsy offered.

"I probably will."

Trotter, freshly shaved, his tie knotted correctly, was just coming off the elevator when Plonski headed back to his office with his coffee. He was not surprised to see the man, though he was concerned.

Mac had wanted to know about anomalies, and here was Trotter—a very large anomaly.

"Good morning, Janos. Still have the bit in your teeth?"

"I'm a detail man, sir. Can't help it."

Patsy came out of Plonski's office with the wheeled cart. Trotter stepped in her way and cocked his head to read the legend on the spine of the front file. He smiled and stepped aside to let her pass.

"Coffee?" Plonski asked when Patsy was gone.

"No, I just popped down for a little chin," Trotter said.

Plonski had always thought that Trotter's bon mots were forced. But he'd never tried to figure out why. He motioned Trotter into his office and both men took seats at Plonski's desk. "Santiago's becoming an interesting place."

"Every station has its time," Trotter said. "Good heavens, you're still not concerned with Dick's shopping list, are you? It'll have no effect whatsoever on Mac's mission. Trust me."

Plonski trusted damned few people, and Trotter wasn't one of them. "It's just the coincidence of it."

"Has Mac shared his op with you?"

"No, he wouldn't do that. He just asked me to take a quick run past Santiago's housekeeping budget. The loose items, you know."

"Like the laser?"

"Beckett suddenly mounts a surveillance operation on someone sophisticated enough to realize that he was being watched. I was just wondering a couple of things."

Trotter nodded.

"Who is being watched, and does it have anything at all to do with Mac?"

"A Russian KGB officer—one of the powers in CESTA del Sur."

"Mexico City?"

"Yes. And as far as it concerns Mac, these are two totally separate activities," Trotter said. He hesitated for a beat. "But I thought I may have heard a third question."

The construction crew had come on duty outside, and earthmovers and a crane were powering up, but none of those sounds penetrated. The windows here as elsewhere throughout the campus were double glazed, the spaces between the panes filled with nitrogen gas and continuously bombarded with white noise. Laser surveillance devices wouldn't have a chance.

"I was just wondering who ordered the surveillance of the Russian, and exactly what the Russian is doing in what I assumed has been pretty much our exclusive territory."

"Trying to make inroads, of course. It's how the game has always been played. But as for whose particular project this is, I suppose I'd have to go over to the Russian desk and see what's up."

"Then it's possible Mac could be affected."

"No," Trotter said, a little too sharply, and he immediately smiled. "You and he are friends—I know this. And I hope that you know he and I are close. I want you to believe when I tell you that Mac's operation has been authorized at the very highest of levels, and will rise or fall on its own merits."

"And Mac's abilities with no outside interference."

Trotter got up, closed the door and came back. But he did not sit down.

"I've been told that we need accountability," Plonski said before Trotter could speak. "Nothing more, Mr. Trotter. Who authorized the purchase and against what operation shall I list it as? Simple bookkeeping."

"The operation is classified beyond your level of need-to-know."

It was an extraordinary thing for Trotter to say, because down here in the basement were essentially the keys to the kingdom. "I can accept that. But I need a name—an operational name, or short of that the authorizing signature."

"No operational designator."

"Then just let me jot your name down in the margins so that when the dust settles, we have a source."

"Good heavens, no, Janos," Trotter said as if he were genuinely pained. "What do you think this business is all about?"

Which business? Plonski wanted to ask, but he didn't. He'd struck a nerve, which for now was enough. Something was going on that someone was ashamed of. Or least it was something that wasn't supposed to see the light of day. Not now, perhaps not ever.

"I'll mark the file as open," he said.

"Fine," Trotter said. He went to the door but turned back. "We need more discussions like this, Janos. Believe me, transparency is the only way any of us—this agency—will possibly survive."

Plonski almost laughed out loud, but he just nodded, and Trotter left.

Patsy came in a minute later. "What was that all about?"

"Accountability," Plonski said. "Go home."

When she was gone, he closed the door again, and telephoned Major Leonard Treitman, an old friend of his who was at Ft. McGillis Army Depot outside Lynchburg. Treitman was in charge of the Special Records Section, where just about every scrap of paper the U.S. intelligence community generated finally ended up.

"Good morning, Leonard."

"Janos, good morning. How're Pat and the kids?"

"Just great, thanks for asking. But listen, I'm following up on a request by Santiago Station and I'm coming up empty-handed. I thought I'd drive down this morning and borrow one of your clerks for an hour or so."

"Absolutely. Can you share on this line?"

"Nothing important, believe me. It's just a handful of vouchers in the last thirty days that the operational officer, whoever he is, forgot to sign. And no one upstairs wants to deal with it. Frankly I think someone screwed up and doesn't want to admit it."

"Might be better to let sleeping dogs lie."

"I intend to do just that, which is why I called you personally. All I want is an operational name to tidy the record."

"I'll have Mrs. Goldberg pull the files for you."

SEVENTEEN

□

Plonski signed out, telling the chief clerk that he was going home for some sleep and wouldn't be back till tomorrow, and was on the road a few minutes before nine. He stopped at a Shell station, where he filled up his green Chevy Impala and phoned Pat.

"I'm home sleeping. If anyone calls, tell them I'm not to be bothered until dinnertime."

She was angry. "Are you with Mac?"

"Honest to God, no."

"But you're doing something for him that no one at work is supposed to know about. That's it, isn't it?"

"I'll explain when I get home."

"Goddamnit, Janos, I'm afraid."

"Don't be," he said.

Mac hadn't warned him specifically to be careful who he told, but the implication had been there. And Trotter had been lying through his teeth this morning. The problem was that already too many people apparently knew what Mac had been ordered to do. It was sloppy; more than that, it was incredibly dangerous.

But the thought had struck him even before Trotter had left his office that whoever the East Coast American was who'd been sent down to Santiago was the key to the operation. Perhaps even its architect, and that the laser surveillance equipment had not come out of the blue after all.

"It's the little bits and apparently disconnected threads that make the whole," Howard Vitense, his old mentor in archives, had told him at the beginning a few years ago.

They'd been standing on the balcony in the main warehouse at Ft. Mc-Gillis, looking down at the rows of double-sided shelves, twenty feet tall, that seemed to stretch to the horizon. File clerks driving electric golf carts scurried like mice through a maze looking to retrieve those bits and pieces.

"Everything is there for the asking. Get the right pieces and you'll solve the puzzle."

"The problem is finding out what the right pieces are," Plonski had said.

Vitense was a white-haired, stooped old man who looked at the world through thick glasses. He was on the verge of retiring. "Ideally you need the picture on the box of the jigsaw puzzle first," he said, chuckling.

Plonski had caught the joke. "How often does that happen?"

"Almost never."

"So you start with a few odd pieces and go from there."

He showed his security pass at the gate through the tall razor-wire-topped chain link fence and was admitted to the small post nestled in the hills just east of the city a bit past one-thirty. Almost all of the buildings were constructed of red brick with white wood trim, the millions of feet of records housed in long warehouses.

Driving over to Admin, he was struck as always by the base's air of desertion. A few cars were parked here and there, but no one was out or about.

He'd been told that eventually everything would be computerized, but that these paper records would be transferred to a climate-controlled underground facility at Ft. A.P. Hill, a lot closer to Washington. That was a couple of years off and until then records thirty days old and older were sent here.

Treitman was in the middle of a staff meeting but he'd alerted the front desk that Plonski would be arriving from Langley and that Mrs. Goldberg was to be assigned to give him a hand. The young lieutenant gave him a pass and directed him to 101 Baker.

"It's the incoming-document processing facility," she told him. "Would you like an escort?"

"I know the way."

"I'll let Major Treitman know you're here."

"Sure," Plonski said.

. . .

Ruth Goldberg turned out to be a plump young woman with a vivacious smile and long, delicate piano player's fingers. The processing facility was busy. A dozen clerks were hard at work cataloging and organizing files, scraps of paper, handwritten notes, photographs, maps, and stacks of newspaper and magazine articles in more than a dozen different languages.

The material was delivered by truck at the loading docks in the rear, and carted to the vast sorting area, where it would eventually be transported out to the warehouses.

"No one is brief," Ruth said.

"Mea culpa," Plonski said. "Some of those documents came through me."

"Yes, sir, I know your name. But not to worry—it's job security. So exactly what name are we looking for?"

"That's it—I don't have a name; it's why I'm here. I'm looking at operational expenditures for the past thirty days at our embassy in Santiago, Chile."

"Money spent or requested?"

"Both. Let's start with requests from Dick Beckett. He received the laser surveillance equipment. I want to see who signed off."

Ruth set him up in a small office behind glass windows that looked out at the sorting area. The room was not assigned and was equipped only with a desk and chair, a phone and a four-drawer file cabinet that was empty.

The woman was back in under five minutes with a thick file folder, a half-dozen pencils and a stack of ruled legal pads. "Would you like some coffee?"

"Not yet. For now I'd like to see the visitors' log. Who came and went from the station, what they were doing and under whose signature."

"I see what you're doing," Ruth said. "Somebody paid for the equipment and the travel. Are you trying to connect the laser and the visits?"

That was exactly what he was looking for, but he just smiled. "Just fishing for now, Mrs. Goldberg."

"Ruth," she said.

The laser file consisted of three parts. The first were the technical specs on the gear, the second was its intended use and the third was the operational funds request, signed by Beckett, but not yet signed by anyone in Langley. The order was pending. But what was most interesting to Plonski was that the request had simply been routed to the Science and Technical Directorate. Not to the deputy director, and not to the Directorate of Operations.

Beckett wanted to mount a surveillance operation on a Russian KGB officer by the name of Valentin Baranov, who lived part-time out of the Russian embassy, but who had also set up camp at the compound of a former air force officer in San Antonio.

Trotter had not been lying about the Russian, and Plonski knew enough to understand why the suits on the seventh floor had sat up and taken notice. Chile was America's, had been ever since the U.S. had bankrolled Pinochet's rise to power. No one was letting it go without a fight. Especially not to the Russians.

But nowhere was it mentioned if the laser unit was to be aimed at the windows of the Russian embassy. If that were the plan, it would be a very large deal if it was detected—the largest and most politically dangerous operation against the Russians in years.

Ruth came back with a half-dozen files, these of visitors to the CIA station in the embassy. "The station's operational logs are classified *need-to-know*. I'll have to get someone to countersign under an operational heading before I can show them to you."

"How about budget requests and funds actually expended for the entire embassy?"

"The station's budget is black."

"But it's included in the embassy's bottom line. Mr. Beckett's expenditures would leave holes."

"Devious," Ruth said, grinning. "Be back in a jiff."

Plonski flipped through the visitors' list, but none of the names stuck out in his mind, until he compared the date of the laser request with dates of visitors from Washington. Four days after Beckett's paperwork went through, someone showed up from Washington. The name had been redacted from the log.

The telephone rang at the same moment Ruth appeared at the door. She wasn't carrying any files.

"I believe the call is for you," she said.

It was Trotter. "They said you'd signed out but no one knew where you'd gotten yourself. I was just wondering if I couldn't lure you back. Perhaps we could go to dinner somewhere, maybe have a drink or two."

He had struck a nerve. "I'll give Pat a call, tell her I'll be late."

EIGHTEEN

☐

Torres agreed to meet at a sidewalk café on the Avenida José V. Lastarria just around the corner from the U.S. embassy. It was a joke, of course, because the café was a hangout for norteamericanos.

It was just four in the afternoon when Baranov came around the corner from where he had parked his car, spotted the intelligence officer at a table and joined him. Traffic was heavy and the café was crowded. Four men and a couple of women who were probably American were seated nearby.

"Thanks for being prompt, unusual for a Russian," Torres said. His voice was thin, and still held a hint of his rural background. Aside from Varga and his wife, Torres was possibly the cruelest man in Chile. It was he who routinely ordered the death warrants that his general carried out in Valparaíso.

Karina said that Torres had several of her paintings hanging in a secret room in his house. "He's a big fan, actually."

"Has he ever visited the stadium?"

Karina had smiled. "Never, though I think he would enjoy himself."

Her husband had agreed. "Be very careful with this man," he said at the door as Baranov was leaving. "By comparison el Presidente is a reasonable man."

"I'll keep that in mind."

A waiter came and Baranov ordered a coffee, with a de Jerez on the side.

"You and Señora Varga have apparently hit it off," Torres said. He was dressed in a blazer and open-collar white shirt, but he held himself erect as if he were in uniform attending an official function.

Or signing another death warrant, the thought struck Baranov. "Interesting people, doing a necessary job. But possibly with too much zeal for some."

"That sentiment has never bothered Moscow."

"No, but then we are a very large country, with more than nuclear parity and the means to deliver."

"Mutual assured destruction."

"Keeps the wolves away from our door."

Baranov's coffee and brandy came.

"So, you have come to Chile to do what for us? And are here today to ask me what?"

"Not so complicated, señor. I explained it to your president."

"Si, he warned me that you would probably come to see me. But you've apparently brought nothing but the name of the assassin that Langley is sending us. And your attempt at eliminating the man in Washington was a failure."

"It was meant to fail."

Torres's expression didn't change, though his eyes narrowed a little. "Did you tell el Presidente?"

"No, I thought that you would have done so by now."

"You're not here for copper, of course, or even to keep the Japanese or Americans away from it. This has to do with your Mexican intelligence network, and ultimately with Cuba. We would be a feather in your cap, we understand this. But I'm not clear on what you meant to accomplish for your CESTA del Sur by telling us about the assassin."

"For starters, your goodwill."

"Save it for a believer, señor," Torres said. "If you mean to embarrass the Americans by capturing this assassin and possibly putting him on trial, it wouldn't work. He's coming as a sacrificial lamb. And his coming here is to be an act by Washington to show its solidarity with us. He is a rogue killer with no charter from the CIA."

"I never thought of it that way."

"Of course you did; otherwise, you would not have come here with your story, nor would you have ordered the failure in Washington. You've come here for the same reason Washington is sending the poor bastard on what they know will be a one-way mission. When it is over—whether he succeeds or not, it won't matter—he'll never be able to go home. They're hoping that the KGB will become involved. They know about your network, and they know what Chile means to you. At the very least they want to embarrass you."

"And at the very most?"

"Have us declare you a persona non grata."

Baranov held back a smile. "How do you know this, señor?"

"We have our sources."

"I'm sure that you do. I meant to ask, how did you learn that an assassin was coming for General Varga?"

"As I said, we have very good people in Washington and New York."

"But I would like to know the name of the man who told you about the American."

"Certainly, in exchange for the name of your source."

"His work name is Henry; he's a medium-ranking officer at the CIA's headquarters in Langley."

Torres was startled, and he couldn't hide it. "If you are telling me the truth, which I sincerely doubt, then our sources are not the same."

"It's not likely that two different people would have given up the operation. One to us, one to your government."

"No, but I understand what you're trying to do. The real reason you're here. You don't care about an American assassin; you came to trade information. My source for yours."

Baranov nodded. "You're right, and you were also right about Chile's role in containing the Americans' adventures in Cuba."

"You have further plans."

"Indeed," Baranov said. "Do we have an agreement?"

"I would need to see and evaluate the dossier on your source before I made such an exchange."

"I'll have to get authorization from Moscow."

"Then get it," Torres said. He laid some money on the table and got up as a black Cadillac came down the street and pulled over to the curb. He didn't look back as he climbed in and the car took off.

. . .

Baranov finished his coffee and brandy then walked back to where he'd parked his car. Even with heavy traffic it only took a few minutes to get back to the embassy on Calle Cristobal Colon, where he went up to the *referentura*.

KGB Director Leonov had aides equipped with detailed briefing books standing by 24/7. It was the middle of the night in Moscow when Baranov's call went through to Leonov's private number. Viktor Mendikov answered.

"*Da*."

"I'm calling from Chile. I need an authorization for an exchange of information. An amended file for DKHENRY, but I need it by cable no later than noon my time."

The Washington source was highly placed, a gold seam. Only Jesus Christ Himself showing up in Moscow would be bigger.

"Just a moment, Captain," Mendikov said. He was a very bright man, bright enough to understand the importance of any decision he made on behalf of Leonov in terms of his own survival. The KGB director did not tolerate mistakes by his staff.

Mendikov was back moments later, apparently the briefing book open in front of him. "An exchange of what information, with whom and for what purpose?"

Baranov quickly outlined what he had been doing over the past weeks that had culminated in this afternoon meeting with the deputy director of the DINA.

"He says that he has a source at the Farm that could be vital to my operation here."

"Perhaps he is working you."

"He almost certainly is, which is why I need only a sanitized version of Henry's file. Under no circumstances should we give them the means of direct contact."

"You'll have your answer within eight hours. In the meantime do nothing, Captain. Am I perfectly clear?"

"Perfectly," Baranov said.

NINETEEN

□

Plonski met Trotter a few minutes after six at Clyde's on M Street in Georgetown. It was an older restaurant with leather booths, small tables with white tablecloths and memorabilia on just about every possible surface.

A waiter led him to one of the booths in back where Trotter, his suit, shirt and tie looking as if they had just come from the cleaners, sat drinking a glass of white wine. Plonski ordered a draft Bud.

"I'll get right to the point, Janos," Trotter said. He didn't seem angry, just neutral. "Your zeal for making absolutely certain that our records would hold up to close scrutiny is admirable. I'll be the first to give you that. Believe me, you turn a necessary and vital cog in the wheel of intelligence gathering."

Plonski almost laughed out loud at the man's theatrics, except that this was trouble. Mac trouble, Pat would call it. "Some things were not adding up, sir."

"What things? Specifically, if you please."

"Santiago Station's request for the laser."

"Fully one-third of our stations have made the same request and some have already received the equipment."

"Yes, sir. For primary operations, and many of those have been denied or delayed."

"Your point?"

"All the requisitions were sent to the DO for an authorizing signature. In many instances yours, sir. But not Santiago's. It was sent to Science and Technology, where it was approved. But when I checked, the signature had been redacted."

"That happens in some instances."

"Why?"

"In this case, you're not on the need-to-know list."

"I still need the authorizations for the expenditure. Mr. Danielle made that perfectly clear to me on more than one occasion. I'm just following orders."

"In this case your orders are different."

"Whose orders?"

"Mine."

"Was it your name redacted on the request?"

The waiter came to see if they were ready to place their dinner orders, but Trotter shook his head. "Give us a minute," he said.

"I just wanted to know if it should be charged to S and T or to the DO."

Trotter glanced at the other diners. The place wouldn't be full for another couple of hours, but still, there were a few people within earshot. "But that isn't the real reason you went looking. Is it still McGarvey you're worried about?"

"Too many anomalies for me."

"We've already had this discussion, and I made it perfectly clear that you're not on the need-to-know list."

"I can read vouchers, and I can add the numbers and match the dates. Accountability, sir. For the laser request. For the two Chilean intelligence officers we're putting up here. And for Mac's request for a specific training routine, including a mock-up of some sort being constructed at the Farm. Unspecified purposes, sir, but for a fair sum of money."

"Black Budget funds, I might remind you, are not reportable to Congress."

"Until after the fact."

"Not in all cases."

"But I need the numbers."

Trotter held his silence for several beats, but then nodded, his expression still neutral. "You'll have your numbers, Janos. First thing in the morning. But I'll ask only one thing from you."

"Sir?"

"Stop snooping."

"My job—"

"It's an order."

"Do you want my resignation?"

Trotter was pained. "Good heavens, no. What do you take me for?"

"I don't know," Plonski said. "I'd like to see the vouchers for the laser, for the mock-up and for the American who visited our Santiago Station, but whose name was missing."

"You shall. Now, shall we order?"

"No, sir, I'm not very hungry," Plonski said. He got up and walked out.

He'd parked his car across the street and halfway up the block over a bridge across a narrow canal. Just at the corner McGarvey stepped part of the way out of the shadows. "Janos."

Plonski practically jumped out of his skin. "Jesus, you gave me a fright."

"Hold up a moment."

From where they stood they could see the front of the restaurant. Mc-Garvey had been watching from here.

Plonski turned and looked back at the same moment that Trotter came out and got into the backseat of a Caddy limo that just pulled up. The driver headed back toward the city.

"What the hell are you doing here? Following me?"

"Trotter. He lives out in Arlington, and I wanted to see who might come to visit, but he had his limo bring him here, so I figured he was meeting someone. You came as a surprise."

"He found out that I was down at McGillis."

"Let's walk," McGarvey said. They headed up the hill toward a little bridge. There was no traffic up here, the street mostly in darkness.

"Whoever your American is probably signed off on Beckett's request for the laser gear," Janos said. "But his name was not on the request form, nor did it show up in the visitors' log. When I asked Trotter, he denied that it was him. I think he was telling the truth, about that, at least."

"How'd he seem to you?"

"I'm not sure. Be he's hiding something, and I think it has to be pretty important. Maybe something to do with Baranov and CESTA del Sur."

"Not Varga?"

"He knows that I'm aware of your op, and I told him that things weren't adding up, which is why I went down to McGillis. He told me to stop snooping."

"I'll bet he did."

"Mac, he ordered me to keep out of it. But he did promise to send me the travel vouchers and the vouchers for the mock-up they're building for you at the Farm."

McGarvey stopped him. "What mock-up?"

Plonski was surprised. "I don't know what it is, but for Christ's sake, it's for your operation."

"They're building stuff down there all the time. Are you certain it's for me?"

"Your name was on the request almost four months ago."

"Over whose signature?"

"It was redacted."

"I never knew," McGarvey said.

"Trotter's?"

"I don't know," McGarvey said. He shook his head. "But I think he's the point man; someone else is pulling the strings."

"On the seventh floor?"

"Probably. But listen, I want you to back away from this thing at least for now. Something is going to happen—I don't know what—but there'll be unintended consequences, I'm damned sure of that much."

"Why don't you walk away?"

"Not a chance, Janos. Not a chance in hell."

TWENTY

☐

After Janos was safely away, McGarvey drove out to Dulles, where he returned the rental Sierra and picked up his red Mustang from the long-term lot. He no longer cared if he was being followed; in fact, he hoped Trotter had sent someone to find out what he was up to.

Twenty minutes later he was waved through the main gate at Langley, but instead of going directly to the OHB he drove over to the Hartley House.

One of the beefy minders in shirtsleeves, his hair cropped short in military style, came to the door and McGarvey showed the man his credentials.

"These guys aren't supposed to have any visitors other than Mr. Trotter."

"And me," McGarvey said. "I was out here before, and I just need to ask them another question. Won't take more than a few minutes. Call John if you need authorization."

"Mr. Trotter doesn't like to be disturbed in the evenings."

"Then call Paul Reubens—he knows me."

"I'm sorry, sir."

"I understand," McGarvey said. "John can sometimes be a pain in the ass for details. I'll go down to the OHB and phone him myself. What's your name again?"

"Tom Steed."

"Your call, Tom."

Steed stepped aside. "They're in the kitchen watching TV."

"Anyone else here?"

"Al Cannon in the back.

"You might want to let him know that I showed up."

"He already knows, sir."

The kitchen was at the rear of the house just across from the small dining room. Munoz and Campos were sitting at an old, beat-up wooden table watching what looked like a game show on a small black-and-white television set on a stand with wheels.

They looked up, startled when McGarvey walked in and switched off the TV. "I want to know more about this American in the minister's office. Did you ever get the impression that you were supposed to overhear them talking?"

Munoz shook his head. "I think it was just an accident. Anyway, we didn't hear very much."

"Your control officer left the door open."

Both men shrugged.

"But you guys were frightened. Why's that? No one was threatening you, or did your control officer tell you to keep your mouths shut?"

"We never mentioned it to him," Campos said.

"Why not?"

"It didn't seem significant. Anyway, as I said, the conversation wasn't meant for us."

"Bullshit. It was staged for your benefit, because your mission was to go after the Russian who was in Chile trying to chip away Washington's hold on el Presidente."

"That was way beyond our pay grade," Munoz said. "Baranov, yes, but anything else, no."

"Why did you go to ground in Mexico City?"

"The setup didn't feel right."

"Then why didn't you simply go home and explain it to your control officer? Why defect, unless you were afraid for your lives?" McGarvey asked. A pack of Marlboros and a battered Zippo were lying on the table. He took a cigarette and lit it. "I'm just trying to understand. Were you being threatened? I mean, did your control officer tell you to turn Baranov or you would be handed to General Varga? Was that the real reason you guys jumped at the chance to get out of Dodge? Things were crazy in Mexico City but at least it was away from home, and a lot easier to get to the U.S. from there than from Santiago."

"We weren't thinking about anything like that, at least not until the last minute," Campos said. "At any rate you people were closer to our government than Moscow was."

"It never occurred to you that Washington and Santiago were so close that you might be sent home the minute you made contact?"

"It never occurred to us," Munoz said.

"We'd never been briefed on the connections between the DINA and the CIA," Campos added.

"You're lying, of course, but I just can't put my finger on what your real brief was."

"We've told you the truth—I swear to God," Munoz said.

"Your English is too good. Beyond your pay grade, I think you said. You told Trotter to screw himself, and that you'd already given him the crown jewels. You told me that you were way out of your league dealing with Baranov. And just a minute ago when I asked you why you jumped at the chance to get out of Dodge, you didn't ask what I meant."

Neither of the Chileans said a thing.

"Your assignment was to go after Baranov, but someone did a good job teaching you idiomatic English—American slang, not Russian. Can you explain that, and why you lied about it, and how you knew to get our attention?"

Trotter came to the door. "Could I have a word with you, Kirk?"

"First I want an answer."

"I can give that to you; just come outside with me for a minute."

McGarvey let it hold for a longish moment, then stubbed out his cigarette in the overfull ashtray, and followed Trotter to the stair hall and out the front door.

"Who the hell are these guys and why was I dragged out here to listen to their bullshit story?"

"We think that there is a mole very highly placed in the Company. We think we might have the list narrowed down to eight or ten people. But we're not going to risk tossing out the baby with the bathwater, if you know what I'm saying."

"Are you talking about the American these guys overheard?"

"Yes. It's how we narrowed the list. We think that he's working with Baranov's CESTA del Sur, and the current target is Chile."

"But he also has the ear of at least the foreign minister."

"That came as a complete surprise to us—you can believe me."

McGarvey did. "What's the real reason for my op?"

"You're to assassinate Varga, if for no other reason than simple decency. Humanity."

"What other reason?"

"Varga has become close to Pinochet, and the mass murders are important enough to el Presidente that the White House wants the general to be eliminated. We've practically invented Chile and it would look bad if we turned a blind eye to what's happening in Valparaíso. At the same token we can't afford to lose Chile to the Russians. We're walking a very fine line here."

"It doesn't add up," McGarvey said. "Why would assassinating Varga have anything to do with finding the mole?" But then he had it. "I'm to be bait. Your mole will out me to make points with Pinochet." He looked back at the house. "The scumbags' job was to help recruit me. I was going to Chile to kill Varga, whose compound was practically next door to Baranov's."

Trotter didn't say anything.

"All you had to do was draw me a diagram of Varga's compound, give me some decent intel about the security in place, firepower, detection systems, things like that. You didn't have to build a mock-up at the Farm unless it was to hit your mole over the head with a hammer. Maybe just talking about sending me wasn't enough. It had to be made real. What else?"

"I don't know all of the details, but I was told that we're sending a piece of surveillance equipment—a rather expensive laser, actually—to Chile, to the DINA."

"Whose technicians will install it at Varga's compound to let him know when I'm trying to get over the wall. Microvibrations in the concrete."

"It's possible, though no one seems to be sure," Trotter admitted. "Janos stumbled across it, but of course he believes it went to Beckett. Thing is our mole knows about it too. We made sure of it."

"Couldn't two lasers have been sent—one to Beckett and the other to the DINA?"

"Unknown."

"Why wouldn't the mole, whoever he is, just order the op to be canceled?"

"It's exactly what we're hoping he'll do. Could be he'll tip his hand."

"Me, the mock-up, the laser and now these two DINA guys, and he's not taken your bait."

"No. But he'll have to stop you, or at least try. We'll have to wait him out."

"*Me*, John, not *we*," McGarvey said.

TWENTY-ONE

□

A car, driver and bodyguard picked Baranov up at noon at the Russian embassy for the ride over to La Moneda Palace. The men were silent. The car was a black Cadillac limousine, its rear side windows nearly opaque to anyone on the outside. He'd gotten the heavily redacted dossier on his CIA resource four hours earlier, and had phoned Torres's office at DINA headquarters.

"Shall we compare notes?" he'd asked.

"I'm looking forward to it," Torres said. "Where shall I have you picked up?"

"At the embassy, but I can get to your office on my own."

"We'll be meeting at the Presidential Palace, and you can't imagine the preparations that I would have to make to allow you inside without an escort."

"As you wish," Baranov agreed, hiding his surprise.

Downtown along the broad Alameda, traffic was heavy, and no one seemed to pay attention to the lights or speed limits. Bicycles and pedestrians mixed freely with the cars, trucks and buses, and overall, everyone seemed to be in a hurry and happy. Very much unlike downtown Moscow, with its somber weather, somber government and somber people.

A big problem for the KGB with its agents abroad was defections. All the propaganda and strict training in the raison d'etre of the socialist state, the workers' paradise, the real government of the people, couldn't deny the prosperity and freedom in places like Paris, London, New York, which began to work on the agents the moment they stepped off the plane.

And here, Baranov thought. But for him especially Mexico City, where the biggest game in town was unfolding, Santiago was just a stepping-stone, a small but important chip on the table, that he meant to win before returning to his real love.

The massive palace that had housed the mint until the mid-1800s was now the office of the president as well as the minister of the interior, the General Secretariat of the Presidency and the General Secretariat of the Government. It served roughly the same function as did the Kremlin, only it wasn't behind tall walls.

They pulled up at the main entrance to the building, which stretched for a full city block. The smartly dressed honor guard came to attention as the bodyguard escorted Baranov inside to a large entry hall. A short, pleasant-looking man in an ordinary business suit met them and dismissed the guard.

"Señor Baranov, I am Alex Molina, chief liaison officer with our DINA. Welcome to La Moneda. If you will just follow me, you'll be meeting in the Blue Room."

They headed down a broad marble-floored corridor, busy now, toward the rear of the building

Baranov was startled. "That's where the president meets with visitors."

"You know the history of this building. We have long known that ceremony and a certain amount of pomp are necessary for the proper functioning of a government. Great Britain's monarchy and the changing of the guards at Buckingham and all that lead to a majesty. Wouldn't you agree?"

"We have Lenin's tomb."

Molina smiled faintly. "Indeed," he said.

The ornately draped French doors in the Blue Room looked out on the Orange Trees Yard, a green courtyard on the palace grounds where actual orange trees grew. It was a popular lunch spot in good weather for employees, and the general public was often let inside. An ornate chandelier looked down upon a grouping of antique furniture, to one side of which was the Chilean flag.

Torres stood looking outside and when Baranov was shown in, he turned around. "You've brought the information I asked for."

"It was to be a trade," Baranov said. Torres held nothing in his hands nor was there anything like a file folder or envelope on any of the tables.

"But nothing in writing from me. My part of the trade will be verbal."

"Shall I keep this?" Baranov asked, raising the folder.

"As you wish. I'm sure that it's so heavily censored that it would be of very little use to me, as my report would be to you."

"Then why bother?"

"Your request has created even more issues than your presence here has."

"The Americans know of our meeting?"

"Not yet."

"Don't threaten me, Señor Torres. I'm here at my government's request to offer you help out of what could turn into a rather ugly diplomatic situation. We're offering you a lifeline."

"Then throw it."

Baranov laid the file on the table. "A sign of our good faith. He is an officer in the CIA's Langley headquarters."

"Which directorate does he work in?"

"Clandestine Services."

"Am I to take this on faith?" Torres asked.

"His immediate supervisor is Lawrence Danielle."

Torres thought a moment. "That narrows it to a dozen, perhaps twice as many people. I'll need something more specific."

"Quid pro quo, señor," Baranov said.

"Ours is code-named Leon, and he is a senior instructor at the Farm."

"A simple instructor, not such a valuable resource as mine."

"He is the man who trains operatives for special missions."

"It would put him in a position to know a great many things," Baranov said. "You knew McGarvey's name and his mission even before I came with that information."

"We knew of the mission but the officer wasn't picked until a few days ago."

Baranov knew of the mission and McGarvey's name nearly one month ago. His source was the lead officer, but there was more—he was sure of it. He'd long suspected that what Henry was giving them was disinformation, but so far everything had panned out, including two separate instances of airliner hijackings, and two position papers on rapprochement with Vietnam, and plans for Cuba.

"I learned of the mission and McGarvey's name four days ago. It's why I was sent here, to make a deal."

"Then your source is McGarvey's operations officer."

"And yours is his trainer."

"Si, but as of yesterday Señor McGarvey had not yet begun his training. It is possible that your attempt to have him assassinated has either altered his schedule or has made him rethink accepting the mission."

"I was told this morning that the mission is still on point."

"It's your opinion that McGarvey will come here after all."

"It's what I was told."

Torres came across the room, picked up the file folder and quickly looked over the three pages. "This man is a very important resource for you."

"He is."

"I would like access to him—through you, of course."

"In exchange for what?"

"Access to mine."

"Not an equal exchange."

"We have other resources."

"So do we," Baranov said. "But the real reason I was sent here was to learn about the CIA's activities in Chile, along with the work of other U.S. agencies, especially in the financial sector."

Molina opened the door and stepped aside to let Pinochet enter the room. The president took an earbud from his right ear. He'd been listening to their conversation. "Which would allow you to easily sabotage their efforts, replacing their friendship with Moscow's," he said.

"We have much more to offer, Señor Presidente," Baranov said.

"I would listen to a delegation of senior Kremlin officials, in secret, of course."

"I'll arrange it immediately, sir."

Pinochet turned to Torres. "I want McGarvey eliminated as soon as possible."

"He will begin his training at the Farm soon, Señor Presidente. Accidents do happen there."

"Make it so," Pinochet said. He gave Baranov a look of indifference then left.

TWENTY-TWO

Katy had her Red Cross board meeting at three, and afterward she called and said she was having drinks with several of her friends at the Hay-Adams across from the White House. It was six-thirty when she finally got home, and McGarvey was in their bedroom packing his bags.

"Are you off, then?" she asked. She laid her purse on the dresser and kicked off her shoes. Her mood was brittle, which Mac had thought it would be.

"I don't want to argue with you, Katy."

"Kathleen," she automatically corrected. "Any hint where you're going, or how long you'll be gone? *Into badland* I think is the term you people use, isn't it?"

Whatever he said or didn't say would be the wrong thing. They had been down this path for a year or so now. "I'm going to the Farm first thing in the morning for a couple days of training, maybe a bit longer, and then I'll be off."

"To where?"

"I can't say, but it shouldn't be for more than a week, probably less this time."

"If you come home at all," she said. "I assume you'll be going into harm's way. Someplace where they'll want to shoot you, or at the very least arrest you. But of course you know that even if you do survive this . . . whatever, the White House is very strong in not bargaining with hostage takers. And Tom Friedman agreed with me."

McGarvey held himself in check. "Who's Friedman?"

"He's the executive director for Red Cross overseas disaster relief."

"What'd you tell him?"

"Nothing that he didn't already know."

"Specifically, Katy—it could be important."

"If you're going to press me, I told him about the shooting incident and how you handled it. Of course there was no mention of our names in the media, and Tom picked up on that right away. So I had to tell him that you worked for the CIA, and were off at a drop of the hat for God only knows where."

"Did you tell him that the shooting might have been related to what I do?"

Katy gave him a blank look. She went into her walk-in closet, where she took off her business attire and dressed in jeans and a T-shirt. She went into the bathroom and started taking off her makeup.

McGarvey phoned Trotter, and asked if the name Tom Friedman meant anything to him.

"He's an exec over at the Red Cross. Foreign disaster relief. Why?"

"Does he ever have contact with us?"

"Tony Benz gives him situation reports from time to time." Benz was the deputy director of intelligence. "Have you had an encounter with him?"

"Katy is on the Red Cross board, which met today. She and some others, including Friedman, had drinks this afternoon at the Hay-Adams and somehow the shooting incident came up. Apparently he was curious about why our names weren't mentioned in the media."

"And Kathleen outed you?"

"Yeah, you might want to do some damage control, see how much this guy knows or suspects."

"I'll find out right away."

"I'm going down to the Farm first thing in the morning. Keep me posted, would you?"

"Will do."

Katy was standing at the open bathroom door when he hung up, an ugly expression on her face. "Tom Friedman is a gentleman."

"I'm sure he is. But now that he knows, or guesses that I work for the Clandestine Services, my life could be at risk."

"In the field, Kirk. But not here if you stayed at home."

"The people who tried to kill me the other night didn't seem to mind that I was home."

"Because they probably knew that you were getting set to run off again."

Through all of that, neither of them had raised their voices. Before their daughter, Elizabeth, was born, they'd have the occasional knock-down-drag-'em-out fight at the top of their lungs. Afterward they would go to bed and make love just as noisily. But after the baby came they'd tacitly agreed to tone it down. It didn't matter now because Liz was gone, but their arguments were no longer noisy. Unfortunately, their lovemaking lacked the old passion.

"Did anyone else overhear your conversation or was it just you and Friedman?"

"What the hell is that supposed to mean?"

"Exactly how it sounded. We'll need to do damage control, and I'll need to know who else might have heard you. Maybe they asked questions?"

She went back into the bathroom and brushed her short blond hair in the mirror.

McGarvey followed her in, and she looked at his reflection.

"It was just Tom and me, outside waiting for a cab."

"What about the others?"

"They'd already left."

"The doormen?"

"I don't think so."

"How about the cabbie?"

She turned around. "We took separate cabs. And what are you implying now?"

"Are you sleeping with him?" McGarvey said, and the instant the words left his mouth he was sorry. More than that, he felt incredibly stupid. He took a half step toward her, but the look on her face stopped him.

"No," she said. She turned back to the mirror and continued brushing her hair.

"I'm sorry, Katy," McGarvey said.

"Kathleen."

He went back to the bedroom and finished packing. When he was done he brought both bags out to the garage and put them in his Mustang. In the kitchen he got a beer and went outside to the back patio, which overlooked the fourteenth fairway of the Chevy Chase Club.

They'd bought the colonial at the end of a cul-de-sac in an upscale neighborhood. They'd joined the club, or rather Katy had, but he'd only ever been there a couple of times for parties, at her insistence. He didn't golf, and the chitchat with her friends seemed less than meaningless to him.

He smoked a cigarette, a habit he'd gotten into in the air force, but it tasted lousy to him and he didn't finish it.

The phone rang twice and from where he stood he saw Katy answer it. He watched her awhile talking to someone. He couldn't make out the words but she wasn't animated.

He turned away and finished his beer. The night was cloudy, the breeze cool. It was fall, which meant it was spring in Chile. Getting warmer.

Katy called to him from the patio door. "The phone is for you," she said, and she walked away.

It was Trotter. "I don't think we have anything to worry about. I talked to Friedman, who understood perfectly. Your name or your connection to the Company will never be mentioned."

"What'd you tell Katy?"

"Nothing beyond the fact that you have been assigned to do a mission overseas, and that you would be in absolutely no danger," Trotter said. "She pressed me on it. Smart girl, but she's worried sick that one of these days you'll get yourself arrested in some third world country, or worse yet get yourself killed. I assured her that you weren't that kind of an agent."

"She was standing next to me when those guys took a potshot, and I fired back."

"She said as much, said you were fantastic. But I told her that all of our officers are trained to react in just that fashion. And incidentally there've been no traces of the shooters or the car. But the Bureau is working on it."

"Did she buy it?"

"I honestly don't know, Kirk. But they're expecting you at the Farm in the morning."

"I'll be there."

TWENTY-THREE

☐

McGarvey arrived at the Farm outside Williamsburg a little before eight in the morning. A half-dozen trainees, their desert camos filthy—it had rained here—straggled up the road from the river, where they'd been on an overnight mission. They were beat, but they looked satisfied for having survived one of the toughest courses in the curriculum.

Sergeant Major Tom Carol in the lead—his camos wet but otherwise perfectly clean—came over as McGarvey parked in front of Admin and got out. The trainees split off and headed to the dining hall.

"Got word you were starting today," Carol said. They shook hands. "Bob's already here. He wanted to go over a few things with us before we got started."

They got coffee before they went back to the conference room. Admin was empty; staff wouldn't be showing up until nine. But Bob Connelly was waiting when they returned.

He got straight to the point. "Any word who the shooters were who tried to bag you the other night?"

"The Bureau's working on it," McGarvey said.

"Was it a random shooting or do you think it had something to do with this op?"

"It wasn't random—I'm sure of it. Those guys were waiting for me to come out of the club, which means they had good intel. Probably surveillance, but I didn't notice anything out of the ordinary the past few days."

"They missed," Carol said. "Was it deliberate? A warning, maybe?"

"Unknown, but they weren't amateurs. Maybe just unlucky."

"The problem I'm having is if the incident was related, then it could mean you were supposed to turn around, but if you didn't, they'd be wait-ing for you at the border," Connelly said. "You wouldn't have a chance."

"I thought about that too. But if they weren't meant to succeed, it might mean there're two sets of people or agencies interested in me. One wanting to warn me off, and the other wanting me to carry on no matter what."

Connelly and the sergeant exchanged a look. "That's what we figured," Connelly said. "But it'd have to mean someone here in Washington knew you'd be walking into a trap and it's exactly what they wanted to happen."

"This thing stinks to high heaven, if you ask me," Carol said. "Fucking politics."

"Word is that the Russians are making a run at Pinochet. They want us out. Sending you down to take out this general isn't the real reason. You're supposed to fail, and it's meant to make us look so bad the Russians will have the opening they want," Connelly said.

"Why do you think it's someone in Washington?" McGarvey asked. "Maybe a spy right here?"

"Probably Langley. Someone has fed the KGB the entire op."

"Then why not just back off, let me do my training and jet off to San-tiago, where a couple of suits from the DINA show up and arrest me on the spot?"

"This shit is never that easy, Kirk," Connelly said. "It's something you've yet to learn. This is going to be your first kill, and just as many people want you to succeed as want you to fail. But in either case it'll have to be noth-ing short of spectacular. Both sides want to make their point with you."

McGarvey had never liked bullies. He'd never like seeing someone pushed around, and he was stubborn enough to hit back fast and hard whenever someone tried it with him. It was a streak that had worried his mother and had infuriated his sister. "Just walk away from trouble," they'd told him growing up on the ranch in western Kansas.

Of course he hadn't been able to the day he saw several of the high school's star football players trying to gang-rape a freshman girl. He'd waded in and beat them so badly with his fists that the police, and the entire football-crazy town, were convinced he'd used a baseball bat. He was only fourteen.

When it was proven what had actually happened, he was left completely alone, so that when it was time to go off to college, and later, when he'd inherited the ranch, he never looked back. He graduated from Kansas State and sold the ranch.

"If that's the case—and assuming there is someone working for the KGB either here or at Langley—they might want to eliminate me right here. They'll try to kill me."

"Then back off. Trotter will understand," Connelly said.

"If and when they try to take me out, we'll let them think they succeeded. The advantage will be mine."

"Unless they actually do succeed," Carol said.

McGarvey smiled. "Then I guess I wouldn't be as good as everyone thinks I am."

Carol was troubled. "Be careful of that ego of yours, laddie."

"Right now, Sarge, it's my greatest asset."

By nine McGarvey was outfitted with black sneakers made to look more or less like street shoes, black trousers and a black long-sleeved shirt. The clothes would make him nearly invisible at night, and yet with a light gray blazer he would be nothing more than an anonymous businessman on the streets in Santiago, or with a light tan jacket just another tourist at some border crossing.

He had read James Bond novels as a kid, so his weapon of choice was the Walther PPK but in the .38-caliber version. No range instructors were able to talk him out of what they termed a "girl's gun," but not one could ever fault his marksmanship.

He rode over with Connelly to one of the helicopter hangars where a scale model of General Varga's compound had been set up on a large table supported by trestles. No chopper or maintenance personnel were there.

"His place is in the foothills above San Antonio on the coast about one hundred klicks southwest of Santiago. I have a detailed briefing package for you, which includes a number of travel and insertion scenarios. When you decide how you'll not only get into the country, but how you'll get to the compound, I suggest you keep it to yourself. Everyone assumes that your kickoff point will be Mexico City, but that's up to you."

"San Antonio's a port town, so the locals will be used to seeing for-eigners," McGarvey said.

"But the DINA will be expecting you. So will Varga, who not only has a competent staff of boots on the ground, twenty-four/seven, but he has the latest surveillance and detection systems in place, including acoustic, infrared and motion detectors. Lights all over the place, tall walls, as you can see, topped with double coils of razor wire. If you manage to get in-side the compound, there are dogs on patrol, and the house itself is hard-ened, metal shutters on all the windows and doors that automatically close when a threat is detected. And if that happens, an alarm is automatically sent to the local police as well as to the DINA's security directorate."

"Automatic weapons on the perimeter wall, helicopter surveillance?"

"Not that we know of. But it's anyone's guess."

"Mines?"

"We don't think so. There are probably enough deer, boar and other wildlife roaming around that would make a minefield useless."

A small building just adjacent to the main house had a sloping roof oriented east–west, and studded with broad skylights. "What's this?"

"Mrs. Varga is an artist. It's her studio. Or at least we think it is," Con-nelly said. He pointed out the barracks, dining hall, generator shed and putting green. "All of it protected, of course."

"No place has perfect security," McGarvey said, half to himself. He could think of several entry possibilities, not all of them by stealth. If there was a mole here or at Langley—and it still was a large if in his mind—he wouldn't share his final plans with anyone. Rather he would set up an ap-proach that would seem logical, and would be reported as such. It would leave him free to do something else. What that was he still had no con-crete idea, but staring at the model, scenarios were popping up.

Even Ft. Knox was vulnerable.

TWENTY-FOUR

☐

Baranov sat on the patio of his house, sipping tea in a glass with a silver holder, enjoying the spring morning, waiting for the shoe to drop, as it were. Sometimes like now he felt as if he were a juggler, who once he set the balls in motion had no choice but to follow through with the act. If he simply turned his back, or worse yet missed one of them, all hell would rain down on his head. His promotion would never happen.

He had a cook and a gardener, but their only instruction, other than doing their jobs, was to keep out of his way. Breakfast of toast and cheese and the tea had materialized in the dining room, but the old mestizo who cooked for him was nowhere in sight.

The telephone on the small table beside him rang. It was Torres.

"I just got word that he showed up at the Farm twenty minutes ago. Shall I proceed?"

It was an odd question. "El Presidente wants him eliminated."

"Si, but I know that you had other plans."

"I don't think you have any other choice."

"There always are choices. The trouble is finding the right ones and following them to their logical conclusions."

"Which are?" Baranov asked. The call was almost certainly being recorded, so he chose his words with care.

"Our president is blinded by Washington's money."

"You're not?"

"I think that there could be other options."

"You're an ambitious man," Baranov said. "But the president has agreed to meet with a delegation from Moscow."

"Which he will report to Washington. The CIA will know every word that's said. It'll gain him prestige, enough, he thinks, to ask for money to build a nuclear power station. His standing in South America will be nothing short of stellar."

"It's likely that my government could do the same thing for him."

"Your reactors leak."

"So what?"

Torres was silent for several beats. "We have no other choice but to go ahead."

"Then send the word to your resource."

"It's already been done."

Barnov's grip on the phone tightened. "Then why this call? Are you playing a game with me, señor? Because if you are, I'd advise against it."

"You're in no position to advise for or against anything," Torres said and he hung up.

Baranov sat back. His overall brief was to seriously beef up CESTA del Sur. The Americans felt that this hemisphere was theirs and theirs alone. Moscow wanted that to change along as many fronts as possible. And the only way to accomplish it was through a spot-on intelligence-gathering organization.

Chile was his idea. Leonov wanted him to stick to business in Mexico City, but had reluctantly agreed to the plan in light of the CIA's intention to send an assassin to handle the problem of General Varga.

"But take care, Captain, that we are not included in the likely fallout."

"The benefit will be ours, General," Baranov had promised.

He phoned a pager number in Washington and left the message that Henry's investment adviser wanted to chat about an opportunity at IBM. The CIA followed up on most of these types of calls, but in this case both the investment adviser in New York and the investments were legitimate. The small firm had been created years ago, and only one employee at any time knew that the insider information he was getting came from Moscow. And it was almost always so good—thanks to the KGB—that the company had been a success from the start.

It was nearly one hour before the call was returned. "I was in the middle of a meeting," Henry said.

"Are you at a secure location?"

"Of course, or else I wouldn't have returned your call. What is it?"

"The DINA has an asset at the Farm."

"We've suspected as much. Do you have a name?"

"No. But I learned this morning that they know about McGarvey and his mission and Pinochet has ordered his immediate elimination. I don't want that to happen."

"Christ. I don't know if I can stop it from happening without a name. I can call him back up here for a conference, but sooner or later he'll have to finish his training. And he's already suspicious. This would be like waving a red flag in front of his face."

Baranov was angry. "I don't give a fuck how you do it, just make sure he comes here. Do you understand completely?"

"Of course."

"Are you clear?"

"Yes."

Henry would move heaven and earth to do whatever was asked of him. His own life was on the line.

Baranov had dressed and was on the way out the door to get his car and drive up to the embassy in Santiago. He needed the secure phone in the *referentura* to call in this latest twist with Torres. Karina Varga came up the driveway and through the gate in a silver Mercedes 300-class convertible.

Her long hair was blowing free and when she stopped, she had to push it away from her eyes. She wore a white blouse without a bra and a very short dark skirt that hiked up when she got out of the car, giving him a glimpse that she wasn't wearing panties.

"I was just leaving for Santiago," he said.

"I've come to ask a favor of you, and it can't wait."

"The general isn't with you."

"No, he's up in Valparaíso on business."

"That's the problem, then," Baranov said. "Would you like some coffee?"

"Just a brandy, and some privacy. What I have to ask is for your ears only."

They started back inside but at the door Karina put a hand on his arm and stopped him. "You cannot say no to me, Vasha. It's too important."

"Valentin," Baranov said, and he knew exactly why she had come, what she wanted and what she was willing to offer. And it wasn't about sex. He'd had her and her husband in a ménage à trois twice already. This morning her coming was about intimacy.

He got a bottle of de Jerez and two glasses from the liquor cabinet in the living room and they went back to his bedroom suite, the large French doors open to the mountain breeze. A pair of upholstered wicker chairs and a table were set up just outside on a small patio.

"Would you care to sit down and tell me exactly what favor you want?"

"A drink first," she said.

Baranov poured one for her and put his glass and the bottle aside. He watched her long, delicate throat as she tipped her head back and drank the brandy in one swallow. The nipples of her small breasts pressed against the material of her blouse.

She set the glass down and, never taking her eyes off his, stepped out of her sandals, undid the zipper at the side of her skirt, let it drop to the floor and kicked it aside.

He noticed for the first time the smallness of her feet, the curve of her thighs and the narrow patch of black hair at her pubis that she had shaved since the last time he'd seen her naked.

She took off her blouse and smiled. "Whatever you want, Valentin."

"Did Mati send you?"

"No. This I'm doing for him, not with him."

"What's the favor?"

"You told us the Americans are sending an assassin to kill him. I want you to stop it."

"I don't know if I can," Baranov said. She was a good-looking woman, young, firm, all the right proportions. But she wasn't exciting to him. Sex was merely a tool he was adept at using whenever the need arose. Beyond that he wasn't much interested. A friend once joked that he would fuck a donkey if he thought it would advance his career. He hadn't answered the jibe, of course, but his friend hadn't been too far off the mark.

"I think you do know," Karina said and came into his arms.

"What do you have in trade?" he asked, suppressing a smile.

She looked up at him. "Aren't I enough?"

"*Da*, but only for a down payment this morning."

TWENTY-FIVE

☐

McGarvey stood on the slight rise looking down at the full-scale mock-up of Varga's compound. Sergeant Major Carol got out of the jeep and joined him. At this point they were about a mile inland from the York River. Admin was well off to the west, beyond a broad swath of trees, and beyond it were the firing ranges, urban warfare settings and one of the confidence courses. This side of the Farm was mostly used for specific operations training. Not too far away was a Boeing 707 passenger aircraft, its fuselage pitted with bullet holes, one of its wings and both the starboard engines in pieces.

"Won't be able to simply waltz in," Carol said. "Means you'll most likely have to either blow the gate, or come up over the wall and blanket the razor wire."

"They'll invite me in," McGarvey said.

"How do you see that?"

"I don't know yet. Maybe I'll come from our embassy with a personal message from the president, that he knows about Valparaíso and he'll offer a very large reward for the general and his wife to disappear. Maybe Switzerland."

"Do you think that the ambassador or our station chief will go along with you?"

"I'll be in and out before they'll know I was there."

"You'll have to get into the country first. I assume you'll be flying in from Mexico City under false papers."

"I'll be coming from the sea," McGarvey said.

Carol shook his head. "I'm not going to ask how you plan on pulling that off, but it's six klicks from town to the compound, so you'll have to steal a car."

"Or take a taxi."

"Something could go wrong. Lots of complications, laddie. You'll have to whack the general, then get out without rousing the guards. That alone will be something. But I suppose that you have a plan."

"That'll be the easy part. But getting back out might be tougher. I want to set something up down at the dock. Maybe a mock-up of one of the loading berths. And I'll need four one-kilo blocks of Semtex and acid fuses."

"We can't detonate anything that large so close to the river."

"I'll only need a few ounces here for the mock-up. Just to get a feel for the timing."

"But you'll be taking four kilos with you, plus weapons, civilian clothes and whatever gear you'll be needing to jump ship once it reaches port. And after the hit and the diversionary explosion, then what?"

"I'm working on it, Sarge," McGarvey said. "How soon can you set something up on the river?"

"How accurate do you want it? A commercial loading dock is a fairly large structure."

"I'll need the base of the crane, maybe up to ten feet tall, and a fifty-foot section of the seawall. In wood, not concrete."

"You won't be going out the same way you came in."

"That part I might have to play by ear. But I figure everyone's attention will be on the docks long enough to give me a break."

Carol was skeptical, but he nodded. "I'll get Connelly's authorization, but I think we can get something knocked together by tonight. You're planning a night op?"

"Yeah," McGarvey said.

McGarvey left the facility shortly after five and drove directly down to the Greyhound bus depot in Norfolk, where he stashed his go-to-hell kit and the leather bag with his extra clothes in one of the lockers, then bought a round-trip ticket to Washington on the 8:00 A.M. bus under the name Larson.

He called Janos from a pay phone. Pat answered.

"I don't know what the hell you and Janos have got cooked up, but he's been walking on eggshells for the past twenty-four hours," she practically shouted. "This stops now, Kirk. I mean it."

"It ends tonight—I promise you. May I talk to him?"

"Aren't you listening to me?" she screeched, but she was cut off.

"Hello, Kirk," Janos said. "Has it started?"

"Tonight. But I'll need your help, and no one, not even Pat, can know about it."

"Can't keep something like this from her—you know how it is."

"You can tell her that you're helping me, but she can't know the details. I need your word on that."

Janos hesitated for a long beat. "You have my word. What do you have in mind?"

McGarvey told him.

It was after seven when McGarvey stopped for gas just west of downtown. He paid cash inside then got the addresses of the two Red Cross offices in town, one just off Southampton Avenue and the other on Providence Road. On the front of the Yellow Pages was a street map of the city, which he tore out.

The Southampton office was closed for the night, but he picked the rear door lock and quickly searched the building, without finding what he was looking for. He got lucky at the other office, behind which a bloodmobile bus was parked. No one was around as he picked the lock in under ten seconds and let himself in.

Enough light came through the windows for him to find a blood bag, a needle and tubing set, disinfectant, gauze and a roll of tape.

He set up the bag at the side of a reclining chair, rolled up his sleeve, disinfected the inside of his arm beneath the elbow and stuck the needle in a vein. As he released the clamp his AB negative blood began slowly draining into the bag.

A rough mock-up of one of the San Antonio loading docks had been knocked together. When McGarvey, dressed in black, a rucksack over his right shoulder, showed up in one of the jeeps, the last of the construction crew was driving off.

It was past ten and Sergeant Major Carol came over with a small brick of Semtex and the fuse set. "I didn't know where you wanted to place this, so it's up to you."

"I don't want any observers, at least not for this. We'll do a walk-through of the compound in the morning, and I'll go through the gate afterward. You can tell me what I did wrong."

"But not this?"

"No."

"Any particular reason I should know about?"

"I'll tell you over a beer when it's over," McGarvey said. "Go back up to the dining hall and have a cup of coffee. When you hear the explosion, come on down."

"You'll be waiting here?"

McGarvey shrugged.

Carol gave him a skeptical look but got into his jeep and drove off.

For a full minute McGarvey listened to the night sounds. A night op was in full swing on the other side of the hill, the gunshots just audible on the light breeze. In the distance the horn of a small boat sounded twice.

He went to the base of the loading crane, where he taped the Semtex to one of the legs. From his rucksack he pulled out the bag of his blood, still a little warm, slashed the top of it with his knife, then splashed it across the dock to the river.

The fuse could be crimped from six minutes at one end to ten seconds at the short. He stuck it in the brick then crimped the long end. The fuse went immediately active, and he had just a second to throw himself off the dock into the river when the plastique blew with an impressive bang. Without looking back he managed to get the rucksack over his shoulder then swam with the current toward the opposite bank.

Janos, at the wheel of his eighteen-foot ski boat moving just above idle, appeared out of the darkness and McGarvey clambered aboard. Janos, throttling up slightly, let the river current do most of the work of getting them away.

"I have dry clothes for you in the truck at the boat launch by the Yorktown park. Only a few campers tonight, but no one paid any attention to me. You were cutting it awfully close back there."

"Not a word to Pat?" McGarvey asked. He didn't know what to say, but he wasn't going to tell Janos that the fuse had been sabotaged to blow early. To kill him.

"Someday I'll have to tell her, but only when you're back safe and sound. Deal?"

"Deal."

"Where to now?"

"The Greyhound bus depot in town, and then a motel just down the block from it," McGarvey said. He looked over his shoulder the way they had come, but they were far enough from the Farm that nothing was to be seen.

"They'll come looking for you," Janos said.

"They certainly will."

And in a day or two, someone would drive out to the house to tell Katy that her husband was missing, presumed dead in a terrible training accident. He would make it up to her, or at least try, but thinking about her now, he knew it would probably be the end for them.

The most immediate problem was Sergeant Major Carol. McGarvey couldn't bring himself to believe the man was the saboteur.

PART

TWO

The Mole

TWENTY-SIX

□

Janos showed up at the Farm's main gate around nine in the morning and his hand shook as he held out his CIA identification wallet to the guard, who looked at the photograph.

"They're expecting you at river dock B, sir," the guard said, handing the wallet back. "Do you need an escort?"

"I can find my way, unless the layout's changed since I went through the course a few years ago."

"No, sir."

Janos drove slowly through the gate. A quarter of a mile through the woods the road split and he took the dirt track that went up on a low hill to the east. His nerves were jumping all over the place, Pat's warning before he left coming back at him over and over.

He's going to get you killed!

He'd just hung up from talking with Trotter, who wanted him to come down to the Farm immediately. The expression on his face had been bad enough that it had frightened her. "Kirk's dead."

"What?"

"Some sort of a training accident last night at the Farm. Mr. Trotter wants to see me right away."

Pat had realized in one piece what was going on. "You were there last night, helping him, goddamnit. You got yourself involved and now they want to know what the hell you were doing." She turned away for a moment. The kids were upstairs, hopefully still asleep despite the racket she was making. "Maybe they'll just fire you. It'd probably be for the best in the long run."

"I have to go."

"Are they going to put you in jail, is that it? Did you and Kirk do something illegal last night, something that got him killed?"

"He's not dead." Janos let it slip.

Pat looked at the phone. "But you just said Trotter told you he was dead."

"Shut your mouth and just listen to me for a minute."

She reacted almost as if she'd been slapped. They'd never talked to each other that way, and it shocked her.

"He's on a difficult assignment and there's probably a spy inside the Company who wants to stop him. He was faking his own death last night, but something went wrong and he was almost killed for real. He thinks the explosives he was using were sabotaged to blow prematurely."

"And now you'll have to lie for him."

"He's a friend."

The morning was pretty, the air crisp, the leaves turning. He and Kirk had gone through the course together at this time of the year, and he remembered their sneaking off base on some nights to have a burger and beer in Williamsburg. They'd been co-conspirators then, watching each other's six.

And it had been fun. He remembered that part, but cresting the hill and starting down to training dock B on the river, he couldn't bring back the feeling of fun they'd had. A darkness had settled over him. Not only had he gotten himself involved, but he'd inadvertently sucked Pat into it.

A half-dozen students in battle fatigues, plus several men in blue windbreakers—housekeepers from Langley, he figured—were sifting through the wreckage of the commercial berth mock-up at the river's edge. An FBI forensics truck was parked nearby, several technicians busy at work. They would find the blood and Kirk's jacket, which he said he hadn't had time to grab. Out in the middle of the river and for several hundred yards downstream, four York County Sheriff's boats were working a zigzag pattern, dragging for Kirk's body.

Trotter, dressed as usual in a three-piece suit, broke off from talking to one of his people and came over as Janos pulled up and got out of his car.

"Have you found anything yet?" Janos asked. He was working hard to keep his head straight. He wasn't used to lying, especially not on a scale this large.

"Some blood. The Bureau's already typed it. Same as Kirk's."

Janos looked out at the sheriff's boats. "A body?"

"No. But if he's out there, we'll find him," Trotter said, and his tone brought Janos around.

"Sir?"

"You were working on something for him that had to do with his Chile assignment. Did he contact you last night? Maybe a phone call just to check up on a fact or two? You were running down the laser requisition. Anything new that you might have passed on to him?"

"Not last night. But he told me that he was coming down here to train."

"Train for what?"

"He said he had orders to kill a general in San Antonio. The Butcher."

Trotter was genuinely surprised. "Good heavens, he told you that? How extraordinary."

"Yes, sir, I thought so. He was worried about it."

"In what way? Worried how?"

Janos and Kirk had talked for more than an hour last night about just this conversation. "John is a suspicious man by nature."

"I'm not a very good liar, Kirk."

"I know. Which is why I want you to tell him the truth. What you'll have to say will feed so directly into his doubts that he'll have to believe you."

"And what's that truth?" Janos had asked.

"That I was worried about there being a mole at the Farm and possibly even one up at Langley."

Janos had been taken aback. "They'll put me in jail."

"For repeating what I told you?" McGarvey said. "I want you to pay very close attention to his response."

"Maybe he won't say anything," Janos said. He was in over his head.

"He will. But I want you to look at his mouth and his eyes. Whenever he's worried, he smiles at the same time he squints."

"Christ."

"Yeah," McGarvey said. "But some son of a bitch tried to kill me, and I need to know who it was before I go any further."

"Who brought you the Semtex?"

"Sergeant Carol, but I can't believe it was him."

"You don't want to believe."

"No."

Trotter was looking at him. "Worried how?"

"He told me that he thought there was a mole here at the Farm, and maybe even one at Langley. He thought his ass would be on the line if he didn't find out who it was before he left."

Trotter squinted against the morning sun, and his smile when it came was thin, just lips, no teeth.

Janos had to catch his breath without making it obvious. He glanced again out at the sheriff's boats. "Seems like he might have been right."

"Who else have you told about this?"

"No one."

"Pat?"

"No, sir."

"Then don't," Trotter said.

"Why?"

"He might be right," Totter said. "And Janos?"

"Sir?"

"Soon as you hear from him, have him call me."

☐

TWENTY-SEVEN

Baranov was having one of his house parties at the compound in the hills above San Antonio. It had started around ten and was roaring strong a half hour later. By then most of the young women he'd brought in from the city were in the pool naked, or were draped around some general or another, sometimes two women to a man. But by two the house had already settled down, most of the pairs off to find a place to be alone, some in the house, others in the long narrow cabana with its eight changing rooms.

The Vargas, both of them naked, sat at the pool drinking brandy, as the sun came up their feet dangling in the water when Baranov came out of the kitchen with a glass of hot tea. He was dressed in swim trunks and a pool jacket. The morning was gloriously cool without being cold, the cloudless sky high and deep blue, the scent of wildflowers mingling with that of the sea five kilometers away. In the distance a ship's horn sounded one long blast as it backed out of its loading berth.

"You two don't look any the worse for wear," he said.

They looked back, grinning. "A little tame for our tastes, actually," Karina said.

"No movies?"

"Exactly," Matias said. "Maybe you would like to see another?"

"I can hardly wait," Baranov said. His stomach did a slow roll, not so much at the gruesome sights they'd captured on film—he'd seen stuff like that from the gulags—but rather their reactions. No revulsion there, not even indifference, no turning away at the worse parts, but as before, genuine pleasure, arousal. They were like American kids watching cartoons, especially the Road Runner. *Beep beep.* He smiled.

Karina smiled back, telling him with a shrug and a look that their secret liaison was still a secret and would remain so.

The poolside telephone rang. It was Torres calling from Santiago. "Good morning, Captain."

"Good morning," Baranov said. "Is this an official call or are you in the blind?"

"Actually I'm in my office. The deed has been done. It was a training accident, just as you wished. I found out an hour ago."

"Do they have a body?"

"Some blood, a piece of clothing. Apparently an explosive went off prematurely."

"Have you told el Presidente?"

"Not yet. I was waiting for your reaction."

"It's good news. Now Moscow is willing to send a small diplomatic group to open a dialogue."

"In secret."

"Of course," Baranov said.

"One curious aspect, though," Torres said before he rang off. "They'd built him a mock-up of a commercial berthing dock of the type we have at San Antonio. The explosion was apparently to be used as a diversion. He was either coming by sea or leaving that way."

"Or both," Baranov said.

"Si."

Or neither, Baranov said to himself after he hung up.

He put his tea aside, took off his pool jacket and swim trunks, got an empty glass and sat down beside the Vargas, his feet in the pleasantly warm water. He held out his glass and Karina poured some brandy for him.

"Pretty morning," she said.

"Indeed it is," Baranov said. He took a drink. Harsh, filthy stuff compared to vodka. Even champagne—a good vintage—was better. But while in Rome. "Good news, you two."

Matias glanced at the phone. "Who was it?"

"Torres. He said that your would-be assassin is dead."

The general nodded, but Karina raised her glass in salute. "That's good, Vasha. Very good. We need to celebrate."

"My bedroom?" Baranov asked.

The general nodded again, a faint smile on his thin lips. "Too bad we don't have any films."

"Yes, too bad," Baranov said, rising. "Bring the bottle."

It was nearly noon before the Vargas left, neither of them bothering to take a shower, which bothered Baranov to no end. He'd never liked dirty people. After he'd cleaned up and got dressed in light linen slacks and a loose cotton shirt, he went out to the pool, where the cook laid out a lobster salad, croissant, butter and a bottle of Chopin, his favorite Polish vodka.

"Have the others gone?" he asked in Spanish.

"Si." She nodded and left.

She'd acted as if she were frightened of him from the first day he'd hired her. But he was almost 100 percent certain that she was a spy for Torres. A lot of what he said and did out here was for her benefit, except for his phone calls. He swept the lines and the entire house every day, and always made certain that when he was talking to someone important it was out of earshot of her and the gardener.

He left a message at Henry's number. While he waited for the call back he ate his lunch, the salad fantastic—spy or not, the cook was very good—the croissant fresh and the vodka so cold it almost hurt his throat.

Henry must have been out of his office and away from his safe location, because it was twenty minutes later before he called. "You've heard by now."

"Yes. Is it true?"

"I'm not sure. They found his blood and a jacket on-site, but the Bureau came up with something else. There apparently was a break-in and robbery overnight at a Red Cross bloodmobile in Norfolk. But nothing was taken except for a collection bag and a needle set."

"I can't imagine that he'd be that sloppy."

"It was the fifteenth of the month, the day they take inventory. It's the only way they discovered it so soon; otherwise, it would have been next month before they noticed the discrepancy."

Baranov wanted to believe that it was a coincidence, and he said so.

"There's more. One of the records supervisors on campus is a friend of McGarvey's. He knew about the assignment. He knew about the laser. And he admitted that McGarvey told him there was a mole at the Farm and probably one on campus."

The news shook Baranov. By all accounts McGarvey was some kid just out of the Air Force OSI, and so far had only been on a couple of soft assignments. It was the main reason he'd not been overly concerned. McGarvey was to have been a sacrificial lamb. A very small pawn in a very large game of geopolitical chess.

"How do you know all this?" he demanded.

Henry chuckled. "I feed you information, but I won't give away my methods or especially my resources any more than you would. Not yet at least."

"*Yeb vas*. Is he reliable?"

"Very," Henry said. "I think that McGarvey's still alive, and I think that he's going to try to out me. But I think you better adjust your thinking down there, just in case I'm right."

"*Da*," Baranov said, and he hung up.

For a long time he drank his vodka and stared at nothing as he tried to calm down. If he had been there, he would have put a bullet into Henry's brain. One shot with a 9mm Makarov to the back of his head.

But the first principle in dealing with informants was to make their lives as simple as possible.

"Coddle them, make them feel loved, necessary, useful, comforted," an instructor in field tactics at the KGB's School One had lectured. "Hell, even fuck them, man, woman or child, if it will help the cause."

At two he phoned his control officer, where it was seven in the evening. "There may be complications that would delay the delegation."

"Tell me."

Baranov told him. "I'll take care of it," he said.

"See that you do."

TWENTY-EIGHT

□

McGarvey's bus hadn't reached Washington's downtown terminal until nearly three. From there he took a cab over to the Marriott just across from the Pentagon. He registered under the work name Michael Larson, one of three IDs in his go-to-hell kit. It wasn't until four before he was downstairs in the bar having a beer and a ham sandwich.

The hotel was old and nearing the downside of shabby, but it suited his purpose of anonymity just fine for the moment. He was going to Chile to finish the op he had been given, but first he was going to cover his back by finding the mole or moles. And the only way to do that, he decided, was to paint a very large, very visible target on his back, and sit back and wait for whoever it was to come out of the woodwork.

But he needed Janos's help one last time, and Pat was the problem. Putting himself under the gun was one thing, but engaging it was something else.

When he was finished at the bar, he got a couple of dollars in quarters, and walked down the block to the PDQ, where he used a pay phone to call Sergeant Major Carol in his quarters at the Farm.

Carol answered on the second ring. "Yes."

"Are you alone?"

The line was silent for a long time. "Yes."

"There's a McDonald's at one-oh-four. It'll take me four hours to get there. Let's say nine-thirty."

"I'll be there," Carol said and hung up.

One-oh-four was the exit off I-95 about twenty miles north of Richmond.

McGarvey called for a taxi to take him over to Washington National, and when it came, he instructed the driver to drop him off at the arrivals terminal for Pan Am. "I'm meeting a friend," he explained.

It took only a few minutes for the short ride, and McGarvey tipped the driver reasonably, but not so well that the man would remember his face. It took him less than fifteen minutes to arrange for a Chevy at Hertz, paying for five days with a Diners Club card, and fifteen minutes later he was on I-395 heading south to I-95, less than an hour from the 104.

McGarvey sat drinking a coffee in one of the booths from where he could see the frontage road. He had spent the better part of an hour and a half cruising back and forth on the interstate between routes 110 and 98, just at the outskirts of Richmond, looking for anything out of the ordinary. He drove with the windows open and the radio off to listen for the sounds of circling helicopters, or even a spotter plane flying low enough to effectively surveil the McDonald's.

Satisfied no one was coming, he went to the restaurant, which was moderately busy at this hour. He was on his second cup of coffee when an old D-series Volvo pulled up and Carol, dressed in khaki slacks and a light yellow V-neck pullover, got out.

He spotted McGarvey and went to the counter for a cup of coffee before he came over and sat down. "You're something of a surprise, laddie. Just about everyone thinks that you're dead."

"Who made up the fuse?"

"I got it from Sam Nellis." Nellis was the chief armorer at the Farm. "But one of his people probably did the work."

"Can you find out without making a fuss?"

"Sure, but fuses do go bad from time to time. One of the hazards of the occupation. The Bureau's forensics people collected some physical evidence; they might find something."

McGarvey said nothing. If there was any evasiveness or guile in Carol's expression, he couldn't see it.

"If I were in your shoes, I would be the chief suspect, so I can't blame you," Carol said. "How'd you get out of there in one piece?"

"I had a hunch that something was wrong."

Carol eyed him skeptically.

"I think there's a mole at the Farm and I'm target one because of my assignment."

"Me or someone in the armory?"

"Or someone else who would be in a position to get his hands on the fuses."

"The Bureau found blood traces, your type. Were you hurt?"

"No," McGarvey said. He told the sergeant major about the bloodmobile, and again he saw nothing but mild surprise.

"They're still dragging the river."

"Has Trotter been down to see what's going on?"

"He spent most of the morning supervising. Connelly wasn't all that happy, but there wasn't a hell of a lot he could say."

"Did he say or do anything that struck you as odd? You were there most of the morning, I suspect."

"Yes, I was. Do you mean Trotter or Connelly? Because if you mean Trotter—he's an asshole, by the way—he called your friend Janos Plonski down from Langley. They had a powwow right there at the scene, but I wasn't close enough to hear what they were saying. They were together five minutes, is all, and then Plonski got back in his car and drove off."

McGarvey's heart ached. Janos was already in deeper than he should have been, and it was far from over for him. "What did Trotter have to say to you?"

"I was with him one-on-one in the conference room for nearly three hours this afternoon. He wanted to know everything you'd ever done or said for as long as I'd known you. All the way back to when you first came to the Farm. Did we sometimes have beers together? Picnics on the beach with you and Katy and me and Barbara?"

"You told him everything?"

"Everything I could remember," Carol said. "We didn't get to the bit by the river until three, and I went over every detail of every step until I heard the explosion and came running. Then he made me go over it again, looking for discrepancies, I imagine. Trying to catch me out as a liar."

Carol wasn't the mole—McGarvey was 99.9 percent sure of it.

"He asked me if I was surprised when I realized that there'd been an accident and you were dead." Carol shook his head. "I didn't know what the hell to say except no, I wasn't surprised. Shit like that has happened on just about every battlefield I've ever been on, including training evolutions. We're in a dangerous business."

"What else?"

"He said the whole mess was 'simply stunning and terribly unfortunate.' Then he relieved me of duty, but ordered me to stick around at the Farm until further notice."

"Will you be missed tonight?"

"The guys at the gate are friends."

"I'm sorry I didn't level with you from the get-go, but afterward I didn't want you to have to lie for me. I don't think you're very good at it."

"I'll take that as a compliment, but what comes next?"

"You're not the mole."

"Thank you, but the question still stands."

"I'm going to make contact with everyone I suspect."

"Starting with me. What can I do?"

"Get me the names of everyone who could have had access to the fuse. Accidents do happen, but I'm betting someone tampered with it."

"Then you'll have a little chat with them, hoping what? That sooner or later if you strike a nerve the son of a bitch will come gunning for you again?"

"Something like that," McGarvey said.

Carol fell silent for a time, his face long, his eyes distant. "We're surrounded," he mumbled. He looked up. "On the battlefield the enemy was mostly out front, unless you were walking into an ambush. Even then you knew who was doing the shooting. But this is different. I've seen the enemy and he is us. Just like Pogo, the comic strip character."

TWENTY-NINE

□

The night was long, and McGarvey got little sleep worrying about Janos and Pat. And about Katy. Her life in the ordinary sense of the word wasn't in the same jeopardy as Janos's and Pat's, but if someone from the CIA came out to the house and told her that her husband was dead, she would be changed forever.

He got up a half hour before dawn, took a quick shower and left the hotel just as the sun was breaking over the river and the Tidal Basin on the far shore. Normally the shift change on Campus was at nine, but Janos was an early riser and usually got to his desk an hour or more before everyone else. It gave him time to order his mind, to get the cobwebs out.

"Don't tell Pat, but I don't have to put up with getting the kids off to school," he'd told McGarvey the week after Elizabeth was born. "They're primordial beasts at that hour."

He got over to Janos's house in Annandale a little past seven-thirty, parked half a block away and shut off his lights. Janos would have to come this way in order to get on I-495 up to the George Washington Parkway and to the road into the CIA's campus.

Fifteen minutes later Janos passed by in his green VW bug and got on the highway, five miles per hour under the speed limit in the right lane, traffic seriously building.

McGarvey hung back a half-dozen cars watching to see if Janos was being followed. But so far as he could tell traffic was normal for this time of the day; no one was paying attention.

It was another bit of tradecraft they had been taught at the Farm: Slow down if you want to blow a surveillance operation against you. If you're the slowest vehicle on the highway, just about everyone passing you in a rush, the car, van or even bus that matches your speed is either another nerd like you or your tail.

A couple of miles before the parkway, McGarvey pulled up and matched speed in the left lane long enough for Janos to see him, then got ahead. Almost immediately after they made the turn, McGarvey signaled for the exit to Turkey Run Park, which bordered the Potomac.

Janos got off the highway and followed McGarvey to one of the picnic areas, deserted at this hour of a workday. It would have been different in the summer, but kids were in school now, families back at work.

"All hell is breaking loose, but no one is making a noise above a whisper," Janos said, perching on the edge of one of the picnic tables, his feet up on the bench seat. He was frightened but determined, like a soldier getting ready for a gunfight.

"Has Trotter said anything to you?" McGarvey asked, a little sick to his stomach for asking. But it was another tradecraft tenet: Trust no one, especially not your friends.

"He called me down to the Farm yesterday morning, wanted to know if you had contacted me. I told him no, but that I knew you were going to Chile to kill a general, just like you told me to say."

"How'd he react?"

"He was surprised. But when I told him that you thought there was a mole at the Farm and possibly on campus, he squinted just like you said he would. He looked like he'd seen a ghost but was trying to hide it."

It was too easy for McGarvey. Sergeant Carol had been his prime suspect as the mole at the Farm, and Trotter had seemed to fit the bill for the traitor on campus, but he was certain it wasn't Carol and his gut was telling him it wasn't Trotter. He was back at square one.

"Pat wants me to stay away from this. She says that sooner or later you'll get me killed."

"She might be right."

"But I'm in it up to my neck now. So what's next?"

"I'm truly sorry, Janos."

"It's what friends do for each other. My mum told me that, in the end, friends are all we have. Now what?"

"I'm sure about Carol, and I think I'll be sure about Trotter after I talk to him."

"And if it's not him?"

McGarvey had given that possibility some thought last night. It was a long shot but he didn't have a lot of options left. "Let it slip to your secretary that I'm still alive and getting set to head off to Chile."

Janos got a puzzled look on his broad Slavic face. He shook his head. "What'll that do?"

"Secretaries take breaks together in the cafeteria. They talk."

"I see," Janos said. What he left unsaid was that the rumor would come back to him, and it was clear he was worried, and McGarvey understood both.

It was noon when McGarvey walked into the Hay-Adams and used a pay phone to call Trotter in Langley. His secretary answered and McGarvey told her his name and asked to be put through.

"That wasn't so smart, using your real name," Trotter said evenly. "Where are you?"

"Not far. We need to talk."

"You can come here, or we can meet somewhere off campus. Turkey Run Park should be fairly empty."

McGarvey nearly dropped the phone. It was possible Janos had been followed, though McGarvey hadn't detected any surveillance cars or aircraft. And the picnic area was fairly open. Could have been a homing beacon in the car, and the monitoring team might have wondered what the hell Jonos had been doing stopping at the park on the way to work. Or Trotter's suggestion could have been a coincidence.

"Union Station at four-thirty."

"The height of rush hour," Trotter said. "Someone tried to kill you outside the Capitol Hill Club and again at the Farm. Janos said you thought there were moles, so I understand your caution. But moles working for who, the Russians?"

"It would fit with what your Chilean friends told us."

"No friends of mine, believe me. And once your op is either completed or scrapped—your call—they'll be turned over to the Bureau."

"Or shot trying to escape."

"Good heavens, what do you mean by that, Kirk? What do you think is going on?"

"We both know what's going on, and why, but not who. Union Station at four-thirty. Through the front doors. Leave your minders behind, but bring Munoz and Campos. I have a couple of questions for them."

McGarvey hung up before Trotter could reply.

He was fairly certain that the call had not been traced; nevertheless, he went into the bar and had a beer and a ham and cheese sandwich in the corner, almost willing a couple of minders to show up and try to arrest him. It would solve a number of questions, if not the key ones: What the hell was really going on and what was his part in it?

The room was filled mostly with businessmen, but the service was good, and after a full hour when no one showed up, he paid his bill with cash and drove back to the Marriott. At one point he almost switched directions and headed home to see Katy. He wanted to tell her everything so that she would understand what he was doing and why.

But she hadn't understood the story about how he'd stopped the jocks from raping the girl in high school.

"It wasn't your problem," she'd said.

"I couldn't just let it happen."

"Of course not. You should have called the police."

"By the time they would have got there it would have been a done deal."

"Perhaps, but it would have been a matter for law enforcement, not some macho kid who thought he was a Sir Galahad."

He'd dropped it. A long time ago his sister had screeched at him that he would never have a clue about women. He couldn't remember what they were arguing about, but her accusation stuck with him. She was right.

His pistol was clean, but in his room he unloaded and disassembled it and wiped it down with an oily rag from his kit. He reloaded the six bullets into the magazine and the seventh into the firing chamber, then holstered it at the small of his back.

Chile, he decided, would be the easy part.

THIRTY

□

McGarvey got to Union Station at three-thirty, rush hour traffic just beginning to build. He hung around outside for twenty minutes, smoking a couple of cigarettes, watching for any signs that Trotter had sent an advance guard.

But there were no unmarked vans or trucks. No one loitering. The roofs, with clear sight lines to the station's main entrance, were clear.

A police helicopter flew over, but it continued to the south without turning back. A few minutes later a Gray Line bus pulled up and a dozen school-aged kids and two chaperones got off and headed into the station. It made him think of his own daughter, and he hoped that he would remain in her life to see her take field trips like this.

Tossing his cigarette away, he went inside and made a complete circuit of the main hall, sticking mostly to the perimeter, watching for anyone out of the ordinary. Someone other than the tourists and the people coming or going on the trains, the Metro or the Greyhound buses.

At one point he went into the Smithsonian store and pretended to look at a book while he watched out the window to see if he had been followed.

But there was no one whose tradecraft he could pick out, and after a couple of minutes he put the book down and walked to the Thunder Grill restaurant just to the left of the main entrances. The place was fairly full, commuters catching a bite or a drink before their trains left, but the maitre d' got him a booth at the windows.

"I may have three people joining me," he told the young woman.

The waiter came over and laid out four menus. McGarvey ordered a

Bud draft and lit another cigarette. He had to keep reminding himself that it was a bad habit. Sooner or later he knew it would start to affect his wind. Maybe even kill him, before a bullet did.

Trotter came in fifteen minutes early and did a slow circuit of the main hall much the same as McGarvey had. No one was behind him, and he hadn't brought the two Chilean DINA officers.

At four-thirty precisely he came back toward the front doors and spotted McGarvey through the window and came in and sat down.

"They refused to come with me and I wasn't about to bring the minders along."

"I need to talk to them off campus, before I leave."

The waiter came over.

"It'll be just the two of us," Trotter said and he ordered a Dewar's and water.

"In the clear, no muscle, no surveillance," McGarvey said. "Just you and them."

"What do you want to ask them?"

"I want to know more about the Russian they were supposed to burn."

"Baranov? He's an up-and-comer. Due for a promotion if he can establish his network in Chile. I can get you his file."

"You don't have what I need," McGarvey said.

Trotter's drink came.

"What do you need?" Trotter asked when they were alone.

"Who else besides Janos knows that I'm still alive?"

"Connelly might suspect something. There was the blood and your jacket but nothing else. No body parts, nothing in the river. It was he who ordered the dragging to stop."

"Anyone on campus that you know of?"

"If you mean your mole, there's no way of telling for sure. Unless you suspect me."

McGarvey looked away for a moment. At this point he didn't know what to think. The mole on campus, if there was one, had to be very good. Others in the past had done serious damage to Clandestine Services looking for Russian spies, so that now in order to survive in the super-suspicious environment any mole would have to be damned near Jesus Christ rein-carnated. Trotter just wasn't that good.

"No," McGarvey said. "You would have come in guns blazing."

A light went off in Trotter's eyes. "Which is why you called me, and why you confided in Plonski. Whoever the spy was would send someone to kill you. Who else have you told?"

"Sergeant Carol."

"Plonski, Tom Carol and now me, all suspects. But why us? What's the point? If anyone wanted to stop you from going to Chile, it would have to be the Russians. Baranov's in Santiago right now trying to gain a foothold for his CESTA network."

"I don't think it's that simple. Assassinating Varga wouldn't do much to stop the Russians."

"Not unless you were caught and your body put on display."

"Then why try to have me killed here? Twice?"

Trotter sat back. "Someone else, then? Someone with another agenda?"

"Maybe they don't want me to go to Chile—succeed or fail."

"And the blame for sending you would end up on whose doorstep? Ours?"

"Maybe the White House's."

"You do think big," Trotter said. "The president?"

"No. But someone close to him. Someone who knows about my assign-ment and believes that I would do more harm than good."

"Why not simply order your assignment canceled? It'd be a lot easier than killing a CIA officer on his home ground. The repercussions would be over the moon. Administrations have been toppled or at least hamstrung for a lot less than that."

There it was again in McGarvey's mind. What would be motivation for killing him before Chile? Who would gain by it? And gain what? Unless it was merely to impress someone. Make points. Strengthen a weak bargain-ing position.

"Maybe the fuse was defective after all. Maybe you and Kathleen were merely caught up in a random drive-by shooting or perhaps a case of mis-taken identity."

"I don't think it'll turn out to be that simple."

"You don't think so, or you don't want it to be so?" Trotter asked. "You're in the game now, Kirk, and you're loving it. Just what you volunteered for."

"No one likes getting shot at," McGarvey said. But Trotter was right.

"I've read your psych reports. 'Truth, justice and the American way.' Superman's motto, and now yours. What would you say if I canceled the assignment right now? Ordered you to stand down?"

"You don't have the authority. You're just the pit boss."

"So who owns the casino?"

"Who ordered the op?"

Totter hesitated for a beat. "I can't tell you that," he said, and held up a hand before McGarvey could object. "But I can tell you that I originated the idea. It made sense four months ago and it still makes sense. And trust me, the people—and I am talking plural here—who signed off on the operation are completely above suspicion. I mean they are bulletproof. Which leaves us where?"

"Santiago."

"The American with the East Coast accent."

"I want to ask Munoz and Campos about him and Baranov."

"You think there's a connection?"

"I'll call you first thing in the morning," McGarvey said. He got up, tossed a twenty on the table and walked out.

The station was crowded now as more people streamed in to catch commuter trains. Just outside the main doors a man in a dark suit, his tie loose, an attaché case in his left hand, stopped to look at something or someone behind him.

McGarvey passed him, alarms suddenly jangling in his head. He reached for his gun as he started to turn around, when what felt like the muzzle of a pistol was jammed into the small of his back.

"Keep walking, Mr. McGarvey, or I will shoot you," he said. He was an American, his voice East Coast. "And keep your hand away from your gun."

They took two steps when the soft burp of a silenced pistol sounded, like it was just next to McGarvey's ear. He instinctively rolled right as the man fell away, crumpling to the pavement, a small hole in the back of his head.

Trotter was right there, holstering his pistol. "Walk away—I'll take care of this."

People were starting to react.

"He had an East Coast accent."

"I know who he is. Now get the hell out of here before the cops come running. Call me in the morning. I'll have some answers by then."

THIRTY-ONE

□

Despite the supposed training accident, operations at the Farm continued as normal. The routine was never broken, not even for the death of one of the officers. Sergeant Major Carol sat at the bar nursing his third beer for the evening as he stared at his image in the mirror. Nothing that had happened in the past twenty-four hours made any sense to him, and he was having trouble coming to grips with the part he was supposed to play.

McGarvey was a good kid, and had the makings of a damned fine field officer, even if he was still a little headstrong. But he hadn't accepted the possibility that the fuse had been defective. He was convinced it was a conspiracy, just like in the spy movies, where the bad guy was always the one the hero was nearest to.

Dick Adams, a senior instructor who taught recruits how to resist interrogations of all kinds, walked in and Carol watched as he came across to the bar. He was a tall man, thin, his face all angles. He was dressed in jeans and a white button-down dress shirt, tails untucked. The recruits all agreed that he looked like an interrogator: his eyes, they said, saw right through you.

"Hi, Sarge," he said, taking the next stool.

"Off the reservation tonight?"

"Lockdown's meant to keep the kids in place, but I'm surprised to see you here."

"Stupid accident," Carol said, turning back to his beer and looking at Adams's reflection in the mirror behind the bar. "Have you heard anything new?"

"The plebes are a little shook up, but Connelly's take is: Shit happens.

How about you? You guys were close, and you were the senior training officer on his op."

"Shit happens," Carol said. He finished his beer and got up. "You weren't here tonight."

"Ditto," Adams said.

The main gate was only a few miles north of downtown Williamsburg and it was a few minutes before ten by the time Carol was waved through. He drove directly back to his quarters, where he sat brooding in the dark by a window that overlooked the rear of the armory one hundred yards away.

He'd been married only briefly when he'd been a young drill instructor at Parris Island, what seemed like a million years ago. Her name was Stephanie. They'd met in February, moved in together in March, got married in April and she moved out and filed for divorce in October.

For a long time, he regretted her. But he was who he was: wedded to the corps and to its people and to its mission.

"Me or the marines," she'd offered. He'd just shrugged. He had no choice.

Anyway, she'd already packed her bags and put them in the trunk of their big old clunky Olds Delta 88, and she just drove away without looking back. The divorce papers came a few days afterward, dated a month earlier.

A couple of years later he was called to the White House, where the president clasped the Medal of Honor around his neck at a ceremony in the Oval Office. For his heroism during the Tet Offensive, when, despite his serious wounds, he managed to kill at least twenty-five VC regulars, thus saving the lives of twelve of his fellow marines. Everyone had mostly forgotten about the medal, which of course he never wore on his battle dress uniforms. But a couple of days after the televised ceremony at the White House he got a note from his ex-wife, congratulating him. *He did himself and his country very proud.* Her maiden name had been Bullock, but the note was signed Stephanie Mullen. He kept it and the medal in a box in a drawer. He figured they belonged together.

Someone wearing jeans and a dark jacket came out of the armory, hesitated just a moment then walked away, around the corner toward Admin. The distance was far too great for Carol to make out any details except that he got the impression that it was a man. Tall and thin. And moved like he owned the place.

He put on a camo blouse, grabbed a flashlight, slipped out the door and headed down the dirt road to the armory, only open fields on either side. The evening was silent, no night mission training evolutions until two days from now, when the sounds of automatic weapons fire and small explosions would drift over from the urban-incursion area three-quarters of a mile to the north.

Most doors at the Farm were not equipped with locks. They would be useless for the most part, because among other disciplines, the recruits were taught how to defeat just about any lock in existence.

Besides, these were CIA officers in training. No thieves here, Carol thought. Or murderers. At least not killers of each other.

The armory was housed in a squat, hardened-concrete building about the size of a three-car garage. There were no windows, and the large service door through which bigger weapons systems, like chain guns, could pass was constructed in such a fashion that in the event of an explosion the aluminum would absorb much of the energy, channeling it outside to reduce the damage to people and equipment inside.

Carol hesitated at the door the figure had come out of, wishing that he had thought to bring his 9mm Beretta pistol. But he was being foolish. He was a hand-to-hand-combat instructor, just about the best in any service. If a situation were to arise, he was capable of taking care of himself.

He went in, the door closing softly behind him. He stood in the nearly absolute darkness for a full minute, all of his senses straining to catch any sign that someone was in here with him. But there was nothing. It was too cool for the air conditioner to be running and too warm for the heat to come on. The building was absolutely silent.

Switching on his flashlight he played the beam slowly from right to left. Steel cabinets lined one wall, while along the other side heavy wire shelves held a variety of metal boxes and cases. A worktable fifteen feet long and six feet wide, topped by a thick butcher block and equipped with a variety of vices and clamps, stretched across the room just eight feet or so from the front door. A drill press, metal lathe and a half-dozen different ammunition-loading devices were set up in a ring around the worktable. In front were a dozen lockers that held a broad variety of weapons—from the Russian-made 5.45mm PSM to just about every variety of Glock, SIG Sauer and Beretta pistols, plus Heckler & Koch's complete line of automatic weapons, along with dozens of other short and long guns, including the .50-caliber Barrett sniper rifle.

Two lockers were packed with bricks of Semtex of various sizes. Another cabinet, across the room, was filled with a variety of detonators, including those that were lit; those that were crushed with needle nose pliers at various timing points; others that were preset, many of them to fire in five seconds or more; and still others that were radio controlled, or pressure controlled, some barometric for use in bringing down aircraft.

Some of the newer recruits called the place the Madhouse, while the older hands, especially those who had come in out of the field to teach here, thought of this place almost as church. A gigantic lifesaver.

"When someone's shooting at you, it's a comfort to have a reliable weapon to shoot back," a drill instructor said. And like General Patton once told his troops: "I don't want you to die for your country; I want the other bastards to die for theirs."

Something that had come from here had either been defective or had been meant to kill McGarvey, and Carol suspected that whoever had been here in the middle of the night knew something and perhaps was trying to cover it up. He had switched off the lights inside before he had opened the door.

Not really knowing what he was looking, except maybe something out of the ordinary, something that didn't fit, he went around the worktable to the cabinet that held the detonators, and opened it.

For the first few moments he saw only marked boxes of fuses, each with a type and military ID number. But all at once he realized that a two-kilo brick of Semtex was sitting to the right on a shelf about chest high. A fuse was attached to the door.

McGarvey had been right.

Carol took a step backward and suddenly there was nothing.

THIRTY-TWO

□

First thing in the morning Baranov telephoned the Vargas' compound and got Karina on the phone. "I have to go into Santiago on business, but how about getting together tonight? I'd like to see another film, and I understand that you've become quite an artist."

"Mati's in Valparaíso and he promised to bring a new batch with him. I know that he'd like to have you come over for an early dinner. In fact, you could come now for a private tour of my studio."

"I'd love to, but I'm wanted at my embassy," Baranov said. He wouldn't have minded accepting her invitation. Her paintings on human skin would be as disgusting as her husband's home movies, but she had a lovely body and an inventive technique in bed.

"Another day, then?" Karina asked.

"I can hardly wait, but I'll see you tonight. Six o'clock?"

"Sí."

He had come to think of the Vargas, especially Karina, as a key to his mission, and possibly even to his survival. Pinochet was a man of short temper and long memory. He'd been offended by Baranov's brashness on the golf course the other day, and people in Chile had a tendency to disappear. Some of them to Valparaíso. Mati was close to el Presidente and Karina was obviously in his eye.

Anatoli Kaplin, the KGB's number one at the Santiago station, had called first thing in the morning and asked Baranov to come in, but he wouldn't say why on an open line. As a station chief he outranked Baranov, but he was also a practical man who had respect for an up-and-coming officer.

Baranov understood this, but as a realist he knew that something was up. He'd heard it in the slight catch in Kaplin's voice. The man was either impressed or frightened or both.

He'd gotten dressed in a suit but no tie and as he drove into the city, he went over the possibilities. He had stuck his neck out to make his CESTA del Sur network—the best ongoing KGB operation anywhere in the world—even better. But it was at the risk of destruction if the delegation from Moscow never came here, or it did and was snubbed by Pinochet.

For the moment Chile belonged to Washington. If Pinochet switched his allegiance to Moscow, it would be a feather in Baranov's cap. If not, it could be a disaster for him personally. CESTA del Sur would be taken away from him.

He was admitted through the gate of the embassy, drove around back and parked his car. He had a fully loaded Makarov pistol with a suppressor in the glove compartment, and he debated for just a moment taking it inside, but then got out of the car and after passing through security went directly up to Kaplin's office on the third floor. No one would have questioned a senior officer coming in armed, though it would have been noted. But he was being foolish thinking that if something was wrong he might have to shoot his way out and go to ground.

Kaplin, his jacket off, his tie loose, got up from behind his desk when Baranov came in. "You took your time." His voice was sharp, the brows of his broad Slavic face creased with worry.

"You never mentioned an urgency. But here I am. What do you want?"

"It's not me, it's General Leonov. He's waiting for your call."

As director of the KGB, Maxim Leonov was an exceedingly tough-minded man who was well connected in the Kremlin. For the first time Baranov felt the beginning of real fear. "Did he say why he wants to talk to me?"

"It has something to do with Beckett. Apparently the CIA has taken notice of you and sat up."

"Of course they know of our operations here, as we do theirs."

"The general is waiting for your call from the *referentura*."

"Are you coming up?"

"No. My instructions were that the call was to be private."

.   .   .

It was coming up on five-thirty in the afternoon in Moscow when the call went through. A communications technician had set up the encrypted connection and had left, closing the soundproof door and switching on the anti-surveillance measures.

Normally the call would have been picked up by an aide, but Leonov himself answered. "I'm told that the CIA has taken a special interest in you."

"We're making good progress here, General."

"I'm talking about you personally. The Santiago Station chief has made inquiries here in Moscow about your background, and especially about your network in Mexico—which I was led to believe was secure."

"There are not many secrets in Mexico City, sir. The place is an open book. CESTA del Sur has always been suspected, but its real objective is not Mexico; it's Cuba, of course. It's the same with the Americans' network OXCART. We know about it, and they know we know."

"And what is their real objective?"

"We think it's Cuba."

"Then why aren't you in Mexico City finding out? Because at this point Cuba is more important to us than Chile. Pinochet belongs to Washington, something you knew before you left your post."

"I'm hoping to change that, General."

Leonov was silent for a long moment or two, and Baranov thought that perhaps the connection had been broken. But it came to him that the director was getting his legendary temper in check, and Baranov now almost wished he had taken the gun. He could be placed under arrest here. It was something he would not let happen.

"Our chief of Washington Station has reported that two attempts were made on the life of a young CIA officer named Kirk McGarvey. Do you have any involvement?"

"In the first attempt, yes, sir. But it was never meant to succeed, only to prove to the DINA that I was trying to save the life of one of their generals the CIA officer is being sent here to assassinate."

"Continue."

"I want the CIA officer to come here, because we will have set a trap to capture or kill him. Either way it will be a great embarrassment to the White House."

☐

his time driving over to a breakfast bar in Georgetown, the Key Bridge, doubling back, running red lights, slowing ing U-turns, until he felt that he was reasonably safe. He called a secure line in the OHB. The number rang five times and he ut to hang up when Trotter finally answered.

s."

t's me. Who was the shooter at Union Station? There's been nothing out it in the newspapers or on television."

"And there won't be. His name is Jim Dobbs. He was a contractor for us until two years ago, when we had to dump him. He and a friend gunned down eight Iraqi civilians, all of them heavily armed. Thing is the eight of them worked for us, so it was nothing more than a case of mistaken identity. But our hands were absolutely tied—we had to get rid of both of them."

"So who the hell sent him to take me out?" McGarvey asked.

"I don't know. I swear to God. We lost track of him; no one bothered to see what he did next. We didn't care. It was just good riddance."

"A mistake. But thanks for saving my life."

"As it turns out a big mistake. But we're working to find out whose payroll he was on. We'll find out—I can promise you at least that much."

McGarvey was at a pay phone at the back of the restaurant. The pretty waitress came and refilled his coffee.

"In the meantime you might want to rethink your op—although I sincerely hope you don't back out," Trotter said. He sounded out of breath, harried. "Something else has come up."

"What?"

"You are a field offic...
a very capable one. Bu...
cians. You are simp...

"Yes, sir."

"Is McGarv...

"I'm told...

"His r...

"Ye...

"V...

"I'm ne...
But there is a ...
CIA—one at Langle...

"The one at headqua...
man?"

"No, sir, he works for the DIN...

"You are a devious man," Leonov s...

Baranov thought he heard a slight adn...
"What are my orders, sir?"

"Don't try to hide from the CIA. In fact, make y...
pletely open. Make them believe that you have become e...
with General Varga and especially his wife. In turn they'll in...
efforts to stop you, because they understand that your real reason...
ing there is to bring your network out of Mexico. But what you don't ...
derstand is that CESTA's success in Mexico has nothing to do with Mexico's
alignment with the U.S. There is no need to bring Chile into our sphere
although we'll continue to make Washington think so."

"What are my orders, sir?" Baranov repeated.

"Carry on, but with care. If you make a mistake, it could cost you more
than your life."

"There was another accident at the Farm. In the armory. Your friend Tom Carol was killed."

McGarvey's hand shook, but he forced himself to steady, thinking about Katy and Liz and about Janos and Pat. It was starting to look like anyone close to him was in danger. "Was it another sabotaged fuse?"

"It looks like it. Apparently he was standing in front of the fuse cabinet when there was an explosion."

"Anyone else get hurt?"

"It was in the middle of the night. No one else was there."

"Goddamnit, explosives are never kept in the same place as fuses. Somebody set him up."

"There's another possibility that's being tossed around. Just speculation for now, but worth looking into. There was no reason for Carol to be there at that hour. Not unless he was booby-trapping another explosive and he did something wrong so that it blew up in his face."

"I can't believe it," McGarvey said, at the same time wondering if he didn't *want* to believe it.

"Neither do I, but it's on the table now and we can't let it go," Trotter said. "The question is, are you going ahead with the op? Or maybe it should be: Is it such a hot idea after all? The world won't end if Varga is not taken out. And even if he does go down, someone else would take his place."

"I thought we were making a statement."

"That was the idea."

"But someone wants to stop me," MacGarvey replied.

"We don't know who yet."

"Let's find the *why* first, and the *who* should become evident. But I'm going to need your help."

"Good heavens, Kirk, of course I'll do everything I can for you. I want to be your friend. Just name it. Anything. Anything at all."

From the start Trotter had struck McGarvey as a man with way too much nervous energy. It came across loud and clear now. "Three things. I want you to keep a watch on my wife and daughter, and on Janos and his family. But they can't know about it."

"Can do," Trotter said. "And the third?"

"You said Jim Dobbs had a partner in the Iraqi shooting. Who was he?"

"Russell Williams. And before you ask, after we cut him loose we never kept tabs on him either."

"Were they from the same part of the country?"

"Massachusetts; they met at Berkshire Community College and joined the Army Rangers after two years. And yes, they both had New England accents, but if you're suggesting that one of them was in Chile ordering the foreign minister around for the benefit of Munoz, you're way off base. They were worker bees, nothing more than hired guns. Neither of them had the stature to get that close to any government official."

"No, but maybe someone at Berkshire recruited them even before the Rangers. Someone who became their control officer. Perhaps he was the man Campos and Munoz were supposed to overhear."

"It's a community college. He'd also be nothing more than a hired gun."

"Like me?"

Trotter hesitated. "Like you," he admitted. "And by that token you wouldn't be giving orders to a foreign minister."

"Who would be, and why?"

"We don't know who yet, nor the why."

"Maybe it was to counter the Russian advances. There's the CESTA captain running around down there."

"Just a captain, nothing more."

"The two Chilean DINA officers were ordered to go after Baranov, and the conversation in the minister's office was for their benefit."

"Yes, Kirk, but we've been driving ourselves nuts trying to figure out why."

"We?" McGarvey said.

"The mission team," Trotter said. "There're eight of us. You didn't think I was handling this on my own, did you? Good heavens, that's not how this business works. You always minimize the risk by spreading out the analysis. More eyes on the subject, more brains working the issues, means more of the unk-unks will get predicted. If we can figure out what could go wrong, we might be able to head off the inevitable glitches that can sink a mission in a New York minute."

Unk-unks was a term borrowed from the engineers at Boeing. In any complex project, like designing and building a new airplane, problems that no one ever saw coming always showed up. They were called unknown unknowns, unk-unks for short. And it was the same for CIA mission planning.

"They know my name. Read my file. Know my timetable."

"Yes on the first two, but no on the last. I don't know your timetable, and I don't think you do either."

McGarvey turned away from the phone for a moment. It was past the breakfast hour and the restaurant was mostly empty. Nothing seemed out of the ordinary; nevertheless, he lowered his voice.

"Goddamnit, my ass is hanging out here. Someone has tried to kill me two times, and I haven't even left the country yet. And now all I can think about is Katy and Liz and Janos."

"Surveillance units will be in place within the hour. I'll have a satellite retasked to monitor their movements and their houses—your house—twenty-four/seven. And for now you're going in by sea. That's according to the mock-up you had constructed on the river at the Farm."

"But first I need to find the mole."

"Which one?"

"Not at the Farm—I'm not going back there anytime soon."

"What's your plan, if you can share it with me?"

"I want you to tell your mission team that I'm mole hunting. In the meantime I want to talk to Campos and Munoz."

"About what?"

"Arrange it, John. For some time tonight. Midnight."

THIRTY-FOUR

It was just past eleven when McGarvey doused his headlights and pulled up at the end of the short block. The windows in some of the houses showed lights, but many were dark, including his. It was odd. Liz was with his sister, but Katy usually stayed up reading until well after midnight, and the upstairs hall light was always on.

Worse yet, no car was parked on the street or in the driveway. But Trotter had promised there would be a surveillance team here by now.

Making a tight U-turn Mac flipped on his headlights and raced to the other end of the block, turning left toward the long curving drive, lined with trees, that led to the country club. It was a weekday night and the clubhouse closed at ten unless there was a special party. But except for the maintenance lights, and the lights illuminating the trees, the place was in darkness.

Struggling to control himself, he drove around to the pro shop, past at least one hundred golf carts lined up in rows, then down the narrow cart path past the driving range and out to the first tee. Dousing his headlights again he turned left through yet another line of trees, some low hedges and flowerbeds, to the gravel road leading from the groundskeeper's building. There he cut directly across the fifth fairway through the rough and onto the thirteenth fairway, just missing a pair of very large, very steep sand traps.

The back of his house was on the left, halfway down the fairway, just before a creek guarding the green.

He angled toward the line of trees just off the fairway, shut off the engine and got out of the car. Drawing his pistol he started on foot toward his house but stopped short. Two sets of footprints in the dew tracked directly across the fairway from the stone bridge toward his house.

He headed in a run through the trees and held up just at the clearing that opened onto his large backyard. None of the rear windows were lit, and he had a very bad feeling. Trotter had promised to have Katy covered. If anything had happened to her, the son of a bitch was a dead man.

Keeping low he ran in a zigzag path across the lawn and held up at the sliding door from the kitchen onto the patio. It was half open, but it wasn't damaged. They had not forced an entry; they had picked the lock. And they must have deactivated the alarm system.

He listened for a sound, any sound, but the house was quiet.

Slipping inside he swung his pistol left to right, sweeping the room, the open door to the walk-in pantry, and the corridor that led past the dining room to the front stair hall.

He tried the telephone on the wall next to the counter with the coffeemaker and blender. There was a dial tone, so the line had not been cut.

Keeping close to the wall, he moved down the corridor, pausing long enough to sweep the dining room, before continuing to the stair hall, stopping in the shadows just out of sight from anyone on the upstairs landing.

In the light filtering in from the lamppost at the end of the driveway, he spotted two sets of still-wet footprints, one set at the open alarm pad. As far as he could tell it was undamaged. The intruders knew the security code.

The footprints crossed the stair hall and went up.

Everything within him wanted to race upstairs and kill the bastards, but he dreaded what he was going to find.

A man upstairs said something that McGarvey couldn't quite make out, but then another at the head of the stairs answered, "They're not here."

"Are you sure?" the first one demanded.

"Goddamnit, clothes in the kid's closet and drawers were missing, just like in the broad's. They're gone, so let's get the fuck outta here."

McGarvey eased back down the corridor and slipped just inside the dining room. His relief was sweet, only tempered by an almost blinding anger that someone had come gunning for his wife and child. Had actually entered his home.

The two men came down the corridor. The first one passed the dining room door, and McGarvey grabbed him by the jacket and yanked him inside at the same moment he reached around the doorframe with his pistol and fired two shots center mass at the other man, who went down hard.

McGarvey swung back as the first man was reaching inside his jacket. He stopped when the muzzle of McGarvey's gun steadied on his face.

"You broke into my house to kill my wife and daughter. Who sent you?"

"I swear to God we didn't come here to kill anyone; our orders were to kidnap them."

"Why?"

"I don't know."

McGarvey took two steps forward and jammed the muzzle of his Walther into the man's forehead. "Who sent you?"

"It'd mean my life."

McGarvey laughed but there was no humor in it, and the intruder knew exactly what was going to happen.

"Russell Williams."

McGarvey was shaken, but not really surprised. First it was Dobbs at Union Station and now Dobbs's partner had sent these two guys here. It was possible that Williams was the one calling the shots, but the man had been nothing more than a contractor, according to Trotter. There was someone else higher up the food chain.

"Do you know the name Dobbs?"

The man's eyes tightened. "He's disappeared."

"I want to talk to Williams. How do I get in touch with him?"

"I don't know."

McGarvey jammed the gun harder, shoving the man's head backward and breaking the skin.

"I think he was a contractor like us, and there's an old-boys network of guys who do some work on the side for anyone with a little money. It's like an employment agency, called Madison Travel, over in Georgetown by the university."

"What makes you think he was a contractor?"

"He knows the jargon, and he knows about Madison. He left the information and a credit of five thousand on completion for each of us."

"Where were you going to take my wife and daughter?"

The man was confused. "I don't understand."

McGarvey's anger spiked and he almost pulled the trigger. "You son of a bitch. You didn't come here to kidnap them; you were ordered to kill them. Did you think it would stop me?"

"Christ."

McGarvey pulled the trigger. The man crumpled to the floor.

For several long seconds McGarvey just stared at the body but then emptied his pistol into the man's chest.

Reloading he went back into the kitchen and phoned Trotter at home.

"I was waiting for your call. Where do you want to meet with them? I think coming here might not be such a good idea."

"Where did my wife go?"

"It was obvious that she wasn't home when my team showed up. We checked with the airlines. Kathleen took a flight to Salt Lake City this morning."

McGarvey's sister and her husband and two kids lived just outside Salt Lake. Katy had gone there for support because she was so frightened about her husband being a spy, and to be with Liz. For the moment it was the best place for her.

"How about Janos and Pat and the kids?"

"They're just fine."

"I'm at my house. Two men were here looking for my wife and daughter, and their orders were to kill them."

"Good Lord in heaven."

"Send a cleanup crew for the bodies, John. And bring Campos and Munoz over to Georgetown in a surveillance van. Make it one o'clock. I'll call with the address."

THIRTY-FIVE

☐

Baranov came instantly awake, aware of Spanish classical guitar music, soft and mournful, coming from the stereo in the living room. Karina lay nestled against his side, naked like him. But Mati was gone.

He listened to the music for a long time, in part because it was sad and beautiful—reminding him in some ways of Russian folk music—but in larger measure because it was in stark contrast to the reality of the Vargas' lives here. The butchery at Valparaíso, the home movies, her artwork—all were points of immense pride for both of them.

The sex was interesting and at times even surprising and exciting, but now in the aftermath, the bedroom had a funky, fishy smell, and an unpleasant odor came from Karina's body.

Coming here around six in the evening he had stopped on the gravel road at the crest of the hill that overlooked the compound and got out of his car with a pair of Russian military binoculars. He glassed the walls, especially the coils of razor wire on top, starting at the far west corner and working slowly east to the gate, and then to the far corner beyond it. Spotlights were placed every fifteen or twenty meters along the perimeter. They would automatically come on at night when the intrusion detectors sensed movement out here.

It was irritating at first, Mati had explained. "There were so damned many animals, goats, and sheep and even the occasional wild horse wandering by, that the lights came on a half-dozen times every night."

"What did you do about it?" Baranov had asked, even though he figured he knew the answer.

"I had my guards slaughter every animal that came near enough to set off the detectors. After a month or so nothing came near."

Baranov had been about to ask if the animals they'd killed had been processed into roasts and steaks or other cuts for the local peasants out in the country, but he hadn't bothered, because he knew the answer to that question as well.

The gate opened and an American-made jeep came out of the compound, two men in army fatigues in front, and a third standing up in back at a mounted machine gun. It headed up the hill directly toward Baranov.

He stepped aside, laid the binoculars on the hood of his car and held his hands out in plain sight.

They pulled up a couple of meters away, the machine gun trained on him, and the driver got out and walked over. He was a young man with slick hair, lieutenant's bars on his uniform. He sketched a salute.

"Señor Baranov. We were expecting you, but why did you stop here?"

"I wanted to take a look at your security measures. You know, of course, that the Americans are sending an assassin to kill General Varga."

"He will not get within one hundred meters of the compound, and certainly not over the wall."

"I believe that you are right, Lieutenant. I just wanted to take a look for myself from the outside. But my compliments, your people are doing a fine job."

What he hadn't discussed with the lieutenant or the general was the American cleverness with gadgets. Every surveillance system had its weakness. Every invention had a counterinvention, just like matter and anti-matter—one could defeat the other.

His real concern was the laser detection equipment that Henry said had been requested by the Santiago station chief. His people in Moscow had told him that such a device would shoot out a beam of coherent light, invisible to the naked eye. The beam could be trained on the glass in a window, or on a door or even a wall, and it was theoretically possible that minute vibrations caused by human voices could be detected and deciphered.

The question in Baranov's mind was who the device would be aimed at.

Baranov disengaged himself from Karina and got out of bed. The suite was in semidarkness, illuminated only by the lights from the bathroom. Mati wanted to see what was happening. He liked looking at his wife's body, and he especially liked to watch when she was having sex with other men.

He pulled on his trousers and went out to the pool deck where Varga, dressed in a silk kimono, sat at a table drinking brandy. He drank every day, he'd explained, but never to excess. Becoming mellow and staying there was fine with el Presidente, but drunkenness was not. The keys to his rise within the regime were his work at Valparaíso, his golf game—he always let Pinochet win, of course—and Karina.

Baranov did not ask if she shared her bed with the president, but he suspected that she did.

Varga looked up. "Would you like a drink?"

"Vodka."

"It's on the sideboard. Karina got it for you."

At the drink cart Baranov poured a stiff measure of vodka, drank it down, then poured another and joined Varga.

"This evening was enjoyable," he said. "The movies were an eye-opener. The capacity for human pain never ceases to amaze me."

"The Nazis quantified it for us. They did the pioneering work. Without them we'd be groping in the dark."

"I understand."

Varga looked at him. "Do you, Captain? Do you really? Because as a Russian with your bloody history I would think that your comment was unnecessary."

"It was a pleasantry, General, nothing more. A thank-you for this evening's . . . activities."

"We'll wake my wife in a little bit. There'll be more. In fact, she would be disappointed if we didn't wake her."

Wanting to shift the subject Baranov said, "Our efforts to have the assassin taken down have been unsuccessful so far."

Varga shrugged. "Is he still in Washington, or is he on his way?"

"He's looking for a mole at Langley."

Varga's eyebrows rose. "Will he find him?"

"I don't think so. He's young with a lot of energy, but he hasn't learned patience yet, nor has he developed any finesse or panache."

"You admire this man."

Baranov looked away for a moment to wonder if it was a valid question.

He nodded. "I think I do. His wife and daughter were to be killed, but the contractors missed them, and when he showed up, he killed both of the men."

"Did you send them?" Varga asked sharply.

"No."

"Good. A man's wife and especially his children, if he has any—Karina unfortunately cannot conceive—should be sacrosanct."

The comment was so insane Baranov almost laughed out loud, but he kept himself in check. "I couldn't agree more."

For a long time they sat in silence. Varga poured another brandy and Baranov went to the drink cart for another vodka.

The night was soft, ten billion stars filled the sky, and in the distance the whistle of a large ship echoed off the hills from the harbor below.

"It would be easy for him to get here aboard a cargo ship," Varga said.

"It's a strong possibility," Baranov said, and he explained about the mock-up at the Farm.

"Then I'll order security measures to be reinforced. Perhaps when he sees what he's facing, he'll run away."

"We want him to come here, General. In fact, we want him to at least reach the walls of this compound and perhaps even come over them."

"You want to make a political statement out of his attack on me and, finally, his death."

"Exactly."

"With my life as your bargaining chip." Varga laughed. "You have cojones, Valentin."

"So do you, Mati."

Karina, still naked, came to the sliding door. "Good, now would you gentlemen like to share them with me?"

THIRTY-SIX

Madison Travel was on the ground floor of a three-story brownstone on Dent Place NW just east of the Georgetown University campus. Mc-Garvey parked his car across the street down the block, powered down the window, and switched off the engine and lights a couple of minutes before one. He was directly under a streetlight. If there was any surveillance in place, he wanted to make it perfectly clear that he was here.

Trotter agreed to the meeting place, and if there was any hesitation, Mc-Garvey hadn't heard it, except that Trotter had insisted on bringing a minder along, just to keep things tidy.

"I'm not one hundred percent about them yet, and I don't want to have a pair of runners on my hand. It'd be hard to explain it to Danielle."

Driving back to the Marriott, McGarvey had thought about phoning Katy at his sister's in Utah, but he decided against it. That she was well away from Washington for now was something of a comfort. And yet the opposition would have little or no trouble finding her.

He'd considered taking the time to fly out there himself and stash her and Liz in a safe house somewhere. But he knew damned well that Katy would never sit still for it. It was brittle between them now, and whatever he tried to do would go against her grain.

A plain gray windowless Chevy van pulled up and parked just down the street. The headlights went out, but the engine remained running.

After a minute Trotter got out and walked back to McGarvey's car. He was dressed in a three-piece suit, even at this late hour, the tie still correctly knotted.

McGarvey reached over and opened the passenger-side door.

"This is a damned odd place for a meeting," Trotter said, getting in. "And I thought you wanted to talk to Campos and Munoz."

"First you," McGarvey said. "Do you know what that place is down the street?"

"From here I'd guess a travel agency, just like the sign in the window says. Closed now."

"Do you remember the Mossad operation to kidnap Eichmann and bring him back to Israel for trial? They had to move agents in and out of Rio without bringing any attention to themselves."

"So they opened a series of travel agencies in Europe to mask their movements from Tel Aviv. I know my history too. Are you saying this place is something like that?"

"It's an employment agency for contractors," McGarvey said. He let it sink in for a beat. "The two guys who came to my house to kill my wife and child were hired from here."

"The mess is being dealt with, Kirk. And I have to say that I feel personally responsible for the near miss. And absolutely no one will blame you for their deaths, though it would have been a real bonus if we could have interrogated at least one of them."

McGarvey let Trotter work it out.

"My people say the body in the corridor was first, the one in the dining room with the close-range shot to the forehead was second," Trotter said. He looked down the street toward the travel agency. "You got something from him. He was hired from here."

"By Russell Williams."

"Good Lord almighty. That's nothing short of fantastic. But did you believe him, Kirk? Did you see the truth of it in his eyes before you pulled the trigger?"

"There wasn't any need. He came up with the right name."

Trotter saw the logic of it. "So what are we doing here?"

"Do you have a television monitor in the van?"

"The full suite."

"Did either of them have any reaction when they saw the travel agency?"

"Not that I could see. In any event the connection, if there is one, would have to be very thin. Certainly artificial. Their job was to keep track of Baranov."

"Bullshit, John, and you know it," McGarvey said. "They were set up to overhear the American in the foreign minister's office, just as they were ordered to make their way to us with their story. The questions are: Why, and who's calling the shots?"

"The Russians?" Trotter asked. "It's a typical KGB op."

"By someone here in Washington, at Langley."

"Your mole," Trotter said. "Which still leads back to the Russians. They'd have the most to gain in Chile, and Baranov is their point man."

McGarvey looked away. It didn't seem that simple to him, but he didn't know the why of it—why he was leaning toward some deeper conspiracy.

"What are you thinking?" Trotter prompted.

"Why not simply let me go to San Antonio—apparently everyone knows I'm coming—set a trap and either kill me or capture me, and put me on trial as an American assassin?"

"A trial wouldn't happen, because questions would be raised about General Varga and why we wanted him dead."

"What would killing me accomplish?"

"It'd be Pinochet's way of telling us that he understood that we wanted Varga out of the way, but that we should have left it up to him to take care of the situation."

"Then why not cancel the op? I'd just as soon stay here and find out who's the mole at Langley."

"Your orders don't come from me. And looking for a supposed mole inside the Company is not in your brief."

"It's become mine ever since they tried to kill my wife and daughter," McGarvey said, hot under the collar. "Whether I go to Chile or not, I'll find out what's going on here. Starting with Williams."

"I thought you wanted to talk to Munoz and Campos."

"I wanted to find out if they had any reaction to this place."

"I'm telling you as a friend, you need to back off from anything that doesn't involve your primary operation."

That made no sense to McGarvey. None of it did. Why send someone like him into what everyone agreed was a trap, and on the other side of the coin, why try to stop him? Two opposing factions were at work here. His worry was that both of them lived under the same roof, but with separate goals. And it was possible neither of them knew about the other.

. . .

Paul Reubens sat at the rear of the van, while Munoz and Campos were seated behind a surveillance technician who was working the equipment. Everyone's attention was focused on the travel agency.

Climbing in with Trotter from the front, McGarvey was struck by the fact that they were looking at the agency. He'd only given Trotter an address where to meet him.

"I was curious about the specific address you gave me," Trotter said as if he were a mind reader. "On paper it's a legitimate business that, so far as I could find, has never been on our radar."

"What is this place?" Munoz asked, looking up. He was wary, but neither he nor Campos seemed overly nervous, as if they were hiding something.

"I'd hoped that you could tell me," McGarvey said.

"It's a travel agency; are you sending us somewhere?"

"Does the name Jim Dobbs mean anything to either of you?"

Munoz and Campos exchanged a look. "No," Munoz said.

"Russell Williams?"

Munoz's eyes tightened slightly, but he shook his head. "Is this where they work?"

"I don't know," McGarvey said. He motioned for Trotter to get out.

They walked back toward McGarvey's car.

"They're lying," Trotter said. "They know Williams."

"You're right."

"I'll keep them isolated until it's all over."

"No," McGarvey said. "Give them access to a phone, but make it look as if you've made a mistake."

"What good will that do?"

"Tell Paul and the other minder that I'm staying at the Marriott out by the Pentagon, but that the op is a go."

THIRTY-SEVEN

□

McGarvey phoned Janos from a booth outside a McDonald's in Tysons Corner. Only a few cars were in the parking lot. Janos answered on the fourth ring.

"Yes?"

"It's me. I'm on my way over; I need to talk to you and Pat."

"I don't think that's such a good idea."

"Neither do I, but it's necessary," McGarvey said. "And Janos? Have Pat pack a bag for you and the kids. You're leaving for vacation."

"Christ."

It took twenty minutes to drive down to Annandale, Mac working his tradecraft to make sure that no one was on his six. But the light traffic on the Beltway made it relatively easy. When he got there, all the lights were on in the house, which he knew was Pat's doing, and exactly what he wanted. They had listened. But there were no minders outside.

Janos met him at the door, and he did not look happy. "You'll have to explain it to Pat. She doesn't want to listen to me."

Dressed in sweatpants and a T-shirt, she was in the kitchen tossing ice into a Styrofoam cooler filled with bottles of Coke. She stopped. "This better be fucking good, Kirk," she said through clenched teeth.

"Two men came to my house tonight to kill Katy and Liz."

"Oh my God. Are they okay?"

"They were out of town."

"What about the shooters?" Janos asked.

"They're dead," McGarvey said. "But I've stirred up a hornets' nest, and

I think that once the two don't report in, someone will be coming here. Maybe a couple of hours, but no more than that. You'll have to be out of here before then."

Pat's mouth dropped open and she shook her head. "Goddamn you both. Playing your games."

"This is not a game," McGarvey said. "There's a spy, maybe two of them, inside the Company, who are probably working for the Russians. They've tried to kill me two times already and my family once, and they'll do whatever it takes to stop me."

"From doing what?"

"I can't tell you."

She laughed, a note of hysteria in it. "You can't tell me? That's rich. You've practically opened every door in the barn, and now you don't want me to take a look at the horses inside?"

"I'm being sent to Chile to assassinate a general."

"I don't care, except that you've dragged my husband into it, and now me and my children. Just go and do it. Or, better yet, refuse the job. Go home and take care of your own family instead. From what Katy tells me you need to do something before it's too late."

McGarvey wasn't overly surprised that Katy had talked to Pat, but it hurt hearing it. His pride was banged up. He was taking care of the Company's business, but not his own. "I can't walk away from it now. Katy and Liz are out of the way and safe. I want you and Janos and the kids to do the same."

"Kirk, are you listening to yourself? Some tin pot general in South America is more important than your own family? Is that what you're saying?"

"He's a bad man."

"The world is filled with bad men."

"He's tortured and murdered hundreds, maybe thousands of innocent people."

"No one is innocent."

"Women and children?"

She turned away, looked at the freezer door, still open, and softly closed it. "This is nothing but politics and you know it. I read the *Post*, I know about Pinochet's regime and how we've been propping up the economy for years. The bastard's a dictator, and he's our pal. And let me guess: this general has become an embarrassment to us. Pinochet refuses to do anything about him, so you've been ordered to go down there and do the job. Am I close?"

"The Russians want to stop me."

"So they can become Pinochet's new friends? They'll kick us out, and maybe make a trade agreement. Chile has copper, which we need. Can it be that simple? Not just politics, but money too? Is that fucking it, Kirk? Because if it is, I have to agree with your wife: you need to get a new job before you get yourself and the rest of us killed!"

Sometimes in the middle of the night over the past couple of years, McGarvey would wake up in a cold sweat, his heart racing. It was the same nightmare that had started just after he'd finished training at the Farm. He was on a tall, sheer cliff that looked down on a ragged jumble of boulders. Huge waves were coming in, one after the other, crashing against the base of the cliff. He could feel their power shaking the ground he was standing on.

At one point when he was about to turn away and go inland, he spotted Katy and their new infant walking out of the shadows. The footing was terrible and Katy was having a nearly impossible time making her way with Liz in her arms toward where the waves were breaking.

McGarvey screamed at her to turn back, but she looked up at him and shook her head. It was then he saw a dark figure behind her, prodding her forward to her certain death, and there wasn't a thing he could do about it.

"Katy!" he would scream over and over, until finally Katy woke him up from his dream.

Pat and Janos were looking at him.

"Kirk?" Janos asked. "Are you okay?"

"Get the kids and go," he said. "Now, please."

"Take the cooler to the car," Pat said. "The suitcases are at the head of the stairs—put them in the trunk. I'll get the kids."

"Should I take my gun?" Janos asked when she was gone.

"Yes," McGarvey said. "Where are you going?"

"Key West. An old friend of my mother's lives there."

"Drive straight through, and don't contact anyone until I get word to you, or until you find out I'm dead."

"How will you know how to find me?"

"I'll know," McGarvey said. "Go."

THIRTY-EIGHT

□

McGarvey had pulled a chair next to the living room window, where from a spot in the shadows he had a clear sight line to the street. He was sipping a can of Bud, his pistol on the small lamp table beside him.

It was nearly dawn now, the sky to the east beginning to lighten. It had been four hours since Janos and Pat and the kids had left. They would be at least two hundred miles, probably more, south by now. Outside Raleigh at least.

Janos was tough—he would be good to drive until at least noon, when Pat would take over so that he could get a few hours of sleep. They would stop to use the bathroom and get something to eat only when they got gas.

"What are you going to do tonight, Kirk?" Pat had asked.

"I'm going to stay here to see if anyone shows up."

She'd given him an odd look. "And heaven help the bastards if they do show up," she'd said.

"Take care of Janos," McGarvey had told her. "He needs you."

"We do love you, you know," she'd said at the front door. "God bless you."

A VW bus painted in psychedelic colors rattled around the corner and came slowly up the block. McGarvey reached for his pistol as someone in the passenger seat tossed a newspaper out the window a few doors down across the street. At the end of the block, the van made a U-turn and came back, the woman passenger tossing newspapers onto the driveways of several houses, including the Plonskis', and at the far corner disappeared.

It was possible that the phone line here was tapped, and the opposition knew that Pat and Janos were gone. As soon as they had left he'd made a thorough sweep of every room in the house looking for bugs, but found nothing.

It was also possible that no one had thought of using the Plonskis to put pressure on him. Or their timing had been off, and they had not gotten organized to get here soon enough.

There was no question why someone—either the DINA or the KGB—wanted him dead to protect the general's life. They were being fed information from inside the Company. But they would have to understand that if he failed or was killed even before he left for Chile, the CIA would almost certainly send someone else. Maybe a string of someone elses, until sooner or later one of them got lucky.

Holstering his pistol at the small of his back he went into the kitchen and called Information for the number of Madison Travel in Georgetown. He phoned and got an answering machine that gave normal office hours from nine to five Monday through Saturday.

"For special requests or information, please dial the private number at any time. Or after the beep leave a message and a callback number."

McGarvey called Information again and asked for the company's private number, but there was no listing.

He called the agency again and at the end of the recording left his name. "I'd like to meet with a representative to discuss some important travel arrangements for a special assignment I've been given. I think we could discuss terms. Leave a message for me at the Arlington Marriott."

He'd just unzipped his fly with the Chilean intel officers through Trotter, and now with whoever was behind the contractor employment agency.

It was time to up the ante another notch and see who might come out of the woodwork. Katy and Liz and Janos and Pat and their kids were out of harm's way. It was just him and the opposition now.

It was a couple of minutes before eight by the time McGarvey made it back to Georgetown and found a place to park a half block and across the street from the travel agency. There was quite a bit of traffic now; people were on their way to work. No one paid him much attention as he picked the lock on the front door, screening his actions from view. He was just a man trying to get to work himself and having difficulty with the key.

He was inside in under a minute.

The place was laid out like an ordinary travel agency, a receptionist's desk in front and two desks for agents in each corner. Blinds covered the front window, though from outside the travel posters taped to the glass were clearly visible. More posters covered the walls. Brochures, magazines and other travel-agency-type literature were arranged on a couple of low tables. A door led to what was likely a back room.

McGarvey drew his pistol and, keeping out of a possible line of fire, turned the knob and eased the door open with his foot.

The room was carpeted and furnished with a small conference table, around which were six leather chairs. Nice posters of the Eiffel Tower, the Colosseum, the Taj Mahal and Machu Picchu hung on two walls, while three tall cabinets sat side by side along the rear windowless wall. Two of the cabinets were unlocked, the shelves of each filled with travel brochures.

Holstering his gun, he went back to the front room and made a quick search of the desks, and especially the Rolodexes, for any names that might stick out. But if there was any information to be found connecting this office with the work of a contractor service, it wasn't obvious to him at first glance. Nor did anything else seem out of the ordinary.

He turned to leave when something odd suddenly struck him. The file cabinets and all the desk drawers in the front room were not locked. Nor were two of the three tall cabinets in the rear room locked. All but one.

It took him less than a minute to pick the lock and open the third cabinet. Two eight-track recorders on the top shelves were on and recording. Small video monitors showed images from cameras in the front room and this one, in stop action, one frame every ten seconds.

He rewound the front recorder to the point where he came through the door, and then the second one, which showed him coming in this room, his pistol drawn.

The bottom three shelves were filled with eight-track tapes, dates printed on them. He pulled out tapes for the past four days, leaving the one showing him.

For a moment he considered setting fire to the office, but dismissed it because of the likely collateral damage to the upstairs business and to adjacent buildings. He also considered putting a bullet into each of the recorders, but also dismissed that idea. He wanted whoever was in charge here to know who had come here and why.

Back in the front office he hesitated a moment longer, considering staying until the staff showed up. But confronting them, some if not most of whom might be totally innocent of any involvement with the contracting service, wouldn't accomplish much either.

Taking the tapes with him, he let himself out, not relocking the door to send another message: *I was here. You've seen my image, you know that I took some of your tapes and you know to contact me at the Marriott. Send your hired guns.*

THIRTY-NINE

□

Driving to Santiago from San Antonio just before lunch, Baranov sincerely wished to get this business over and done with as soon as possible. At the moment it seemed that killing McGarvey before he left Washington would be the best of all possible worlds. Yet leading the man here into a trap and then killing him so that a clear message could be sent to Washington would carry the most political weight.

At that point it wouldn't really matter if Varga was dead or not. CESTA del Sur would benefit, because at the very least, he figured that Pinochet would give his tacit assent to let the KGB have a relatively free rein here. It would be a nearly ideal outcome for everyone—Pinochet would still have Washington's support, Moscow would have a foot in the door and Baranov would get his promotion.

But something was not right in Washington. Something else was going on. Someone other than the sources Baranov knew about was stirring the pot. Not only did he not know who it was, he had no earthly idea what they were trying to accomplish. The situation was starting to spin out of control and he didn't know what to do about it.

And on top of everything Kaplin had called first thing this morning and actually ordered him to come to the embassy. It was a matter of some urgency, he'd said. Which was purely shit, of course. The station chief was tired of having someone meddling on his playing field. This morning would be nothing more than an exercise in establishing who was boss.

He was passed through the gate and parked in back as before. This time he'd brought his Makarov holstered under his left armpit.

The young plainclothes security officer looked up. "Good morning, sir. Please sign in."

"Something new?" Baranov asked.

"Yes, sir."

Baranov signed his name in the log.

"Are you carrying a weapon, Captain?"

"*Da.*"

"I must ask you to surrender it."

"*Nyet.*"

The officer picked up the phone and made a call. "Captain Baranov is here, sir. He is armed and refuses to surrender his weapon."

Baranov wasn't alarmed, but he was more than curious now. His instinct to arm himself wasn't so far off after all.

The officer handed him the phone. "It's Mr. Kaplin, sir."

Baranov took the phone. "What the hell is going on?"

"There is no reason for anyone other than security to come into this building carrying a weapon," Kaplin said harshly. "The ambassador's orders, not mine."

"No."

"Then unfortunately I will have to order security to place you under arrest."

"*Pizdec,*" Baranov swore.

Almost immediately two large security officers, one of them with his sidearm drawn, but pointing down and to the side, came out of a room on the other side of the corridor. They stopped a few feet away.

Baranov nodded. "This better be good, Anatoli," he said. He handed the phone back to the security officer at the desk, then unbuttoned his jacket and eased his pistol out of its holster by the handle and laid it on the desk.

The young officer came around the desk with a security wand, which he ran over Baranov's body. "I'm sorry, sir. Just orders."

"May I go up now?"

"Of course."

The KGB station chief was waiting at the open door to his inner office. "We're not to be disturbed," he told his secretary and he stepped aside to let Baranov through, then closed the door.

"You know what I'm doing in Chile, so what the fuck is going on?" Baranov demanded. A worry nagged at him.

"We may be in some serious trouble."

"You or we?"

"All of us. This embassy, especially this station. We have reason to believe there may be a spy here. Someone in a position to handle sensitive materials."

"Am I a suspect? Is that why you wanted me unarmed?"

"Not you. Someone inside the building. Someone with daily access to the *referentura*."

"The list has to be small."

Kaplin was worried. "Too small," he said.

All of a sudden Baranov got it, or thought he did. Something about the laser his source at Langley had told him about. At the time it was too esoteric, almost pie in the sky. A bit of information to be passed along to the technicians in the First Chief Directorate's Scientific and Technical Division.

But now it was making some sense.

"Do we have the ability to monitor the CIA station's traffic to Langley?" Baranov asked.

"Yes, of course. But at the moment we have only partial decryptions of their new equipment."

"But you can decrypt some of it?"

"Yes."

"Let's go to the *referentura*. Clear it of everyone but us."

"I don't understand."

"I think I know where your leak is."

They sat at the conference table in the securest room within the *referentura's* four-room suite. It was here that the most secret of meetings were held. The latest Russian anti-surveillance equipment was on, including white noise generators that produced a signal that dampened any type of listening device, and a Faraday cage, surrounding the floor, ceiling and walls, which would defeat any type of electronic eavesdropping.

"My work here is nearly finished," Baranov said.

"I don't understand."

"I was told to keep this as compartmentalized as possible, Anatoli. Need-to-know and all that." Baranov nodded, and Kaplin got it.

"As it should be."

"But you need to keep the pressure on to find your spy here in the embassy. I'm sure he—or she—is passing damned near everything they hear or read over to Beckett. Thank the skies they can't know what goes on here when it's just the two of us."

"So what's next, Vasha?"

"I'm returning to Mexico City within twenty-four hours. As I said, my work is just about finished here. I have friends inside the DINA who are willing and even eager to help my little project. But I have to get back to my office now, for obvious reasons."

Kaplin didn't understand. He spread his hands.

"The answer is in Mexico City, my friend," Baranov said. "Not here." He got up and gestured for Kaplin to leave with him.

Downstairs in Kaplin's office, Baranov wrote a brief note on a piece of stationery.

Referentura may not be secure. Consider possible CIA laser surveillance. Call me on secure line if you decrypt any reference to me and especially to Mexico City. Just leave the message: YES. The CIA must not suspect that we know about their new capabilities.

Kaplin was thunderstruck, but he nodded his understanding.

Less than four hours later, Baranov got a phone call from Kaplin.

"*Da.*"

The game was on.

FORTY

☐

McGarvey kept loose for the rest of the morning, driving past his house once—the housekeepers had come and gone—and then past the Plonskis', where the neighborhood was quiet. He bought a six-pack of beer from a small liquor store just off Dupont Circle and then drove over to West Potomac Park, where outside the entrance he bought a couple of hot dogs from a vendor.

Parking in the lot behind the Lincoln Memorial he had his lunch as he watched the tourists piling in. The weather was still good, but as soon as it changed to cold and rainy most of the park would be empty except for a few diehards, mostly old men remembering World War II and Korea.

Someone was trying to stop him so that he would not go to Chile—first by trying to kill him and then by trying to kill the people closest to him so that he would back off. But instead of making him crazy with anger, so that he would be prone to mistakes, he felt a sense of loneliness, as if he had no one close in his life. No one with whom he could have a conversation and not have to explain himself.

He could see his entire life stretching in front of him, assignment after assignment, he supposed. Seemingly never ending. Some field officers did come in from the cold to act as instructors at the Farm or as senior officers at Langley. But some of them ended up merely as unidentified stars on the wall of the lobby in the OHB. Their names and triumphs would never be made public, at least not in this lifetime. And in many cases not even their families would know of the circumstances under which they were killed. Often there wasn't even a body to bury. Just a citation for an unknown deed or deeds in the service of a grateful nation.

Small comfort, McGarvey thought. And for a moment he understood how Katy must feel, and it was a wonder that she hadn't learned to hate him yet.

He drank just one of the beers and ate only one of the hot dogs, then drove back to Georgetown, parking on Dent Place just down from the travel agency. He called the Marriott from a booth on the corner.

"Are there any messages for Larson, three-oh-three?"

"No, sir."

Next he called Trotter's private number, and after one ring it rolled over to a message system, asking that a callback number be left. He gave the phone booth number. Trotter called almost immediately.

"Where are you?"

"At a phone booth. Have our guys had a chance to make a phone call?"

"Yes, but so far they're just sitting there, talking mostly about sports and wondering when they'll be released. Good heavens, hope does spring eternal."

"They know they're being monitored."

"Of course they do. But listen, Kirk, Janos hasn't shown up for work. Do you know anything about it?"

"After what happened at my house I sent him and Pat and the kids away."

"Where?"

"Out of harm's way."

"Goddamnit, I need him."

"Not dead, you don't," McGarvey said.

Trotter was silent for a beat. "There's been a development. Beckett's already getting laser product from inside the Russian embassy. Specifically the referentura. We don't think it'll last long, though. We have a source in Moscow who says that their Scientific and Technical Directorate has been on it for the past year. They'll almost certainly come up with a countermeasure very soon."

"But for now we've had a breakthrough in Santiago. Anywhere else?"

Again Trotter was silent for a moment. "No."

McGarvey wanted to ask Trotter if he knew how to spell coincidence. "What has Dick learned?"

"Captain Baranov met with the KGB chief of station a couple hours ago. He said that his work in Santiago was just about done, and that he was heading back to Mexico City."

It was too over-the-top obvious for McGarvey. If Baranov knew about the laser surveillance equipment, he'd sent a message that he was returning to his Mexican network, and maybe if McGarvey was listening, he might care to come along.

"Who knows about this?"

"Beckett and his intercept team, our signals people here and, of course, the seventh floor."

"Campos and Munoz?"

Trotter was startled. "No."

"Tell them."

"Are you sure?"

"Everyone else knows; they might as well be on board," McGarvey said. "I want as many people coming out of the woodwork after me as possible without making it totally obvious it's what I want. Maybe they'll start to stumble over each other, like a bunch of clowns in a three-ring circus."

"Except that the one who doesn't stumble will be your man."

"Something like that."

"Are you going to take up Baranov's challenge?"

"Of course."

"Why?"

"There's more going on than General Varga, and I think that Baranov might have some of the answers."

"When do you leave?"

"Soon."

"And Varga?"

"That depends on what happens next."

"In Mexico?"

"Here."

"Keep in touch, Kirk. And watch your back."

"Will do," McGarvey said and he rang off.

He went back to his car and got in. A moment later a woman dressed in a man's suit came out of the travel agency and walked up the street directly to him. She got in the passenger seat.

"Mr. McGarvey," she said. "A pleasure to finally meet you." She was slender, with fine high cheekbones and startlingly black eyes. Her hair was cut very short in the back, a flip over her right eye. She wore almost no makeup and small gold hoop earrings. She smelled of Chanel, but it was subtle. Her voice was French.

"I'm at the disadvantage."

"Marlene will do for now," the woman said. She stuck out her hand and McGarvey took it. "We were surprised to see you come into our shop earlier today. We believe that you took something that belongs to us."

"Just a couple of surveillance tapes."

"We have security. No crime there. Certainly not like breaking or entering."

"Or attempted murder," McGarvey said. "Have you called the police?"

She smiled and shook her head. "It's not necessary. In any event you came to us, asking about our private number. It's for contractor services, as you know by now. So what can we do for you? Do you seek employment?"

"Who do you work for?"

"Dr. Chad Morris. Used to work for the UN's security service in New York. Good man."

"Do the names Jim Dobbs or Russ Williams mean anything to you?"

"Of course."

McGarvey reached over and ran his hands over her sides, up to her armpits beneath her jacket, then between her small breasts and, when she spread her legs, her thighs.

She smiled faintly. "I'm not armed, though I suspect that you are," she said. "You came to us—what do you want?"

"Stay away from my family and friends."

"Are you threatening me?"

"Yes. I'll begin by killing you."

She shrugged. "And in the meantime?"

McGarvey reached past her and opened the door. "Send your best next time."

"We will," she said, and she got out.

FORTY-ONE

☐

Torres agreed to meet with Baranov, this time at another busy sidewalk café downtown. As before security was tight: two black surveillance vans, one parked just across the street and the other a few meters down the block. In addition Baranov spotted at least one sniper on an adjacent rooftop.

They ordered coffee and empanadas. Baranov also ordered a de Jerez.

Torres smiled faintly. "Chile is rubbing off on you a little."

"I like vodka, but the people are friendly here, the food is good and I think that I'll miss this," Baranov said, raising the glass.

"Your job is not done here yet, I think."

"I won't be gone long, but I've been recalled to Mexico City. There's been a development."

"Involving Señor McGarvey?"

"Yes."

"Tell me."

"I think you must already know."

"Don't overestimate our capabilities. We haven't penetrated your security."

"Yet."

Torres gave no answer.

"But your source in Washington must be giving you regular reports on McGarvey's doings," Baranov said.

"We know that someone tried to kill his wife and child, which is a very bad business."

"It wasn't us."

"No, but it's believed in some circles that it was your doing."

Baranov thought for a moment. "If we trust each other—and I can see no other reasonable choice for now—we have to agree that someone else must have an agenda. One separate from ours."

"We've come to the same conclusion," Torres said after a beat. "But for the life of me I can't think of who or why. For that I think we'd need to know more about Señor McGarvey's background, beyond his banking trip to Moscow—which is why we assumed it was you again."

"I would share more of his file with you if there was any. But he's relatively new to the CIA, and before that he was in the Air Force Office of Special Investigations."

"What were his duties? Perhaps knowing that might help."

"In school he specialized in abnormal psychology and the French philosopher Voltaire."

Torres laughed out loud. "Not so farfetched for an intelligence officer, I suppose. Motives are everything, after all. What to believe: the ravings of a lunatic, or the writings of an atheist who had faith in God? But maybe he's young before his years. Brash, perhaps. Naive. A sentimentalist."

"A fool?" Baranov suggested.

Torres nodded.

Baranov looked across the street at the van and along the roof line but he couldn't spot the sniper. "I'd like that to be true. But I think we're wrong."

Torres suddenly got it. "You're returning to Mexico City not because you've been recalled. You've somehow lured McGarvey to come to you, and you mean to test him, to see just how good he is."

"Yes, before he comes here."

"You think that if he came here, he would have a chance of success? That he might kill Mati after all?"

"That's what I intend to find out."

"How?"

"I'm going to try to kill him myself," Baranov said. "But first I have a couple of things to finish here."

Dick Beckett hadn't seemed all that surprised when Baranov telephoned him at the embassy and asked for a meeting.

"I thought that perhaps we could talk in private," Baranov had said after he'd introduced himself.

"I know who you are, and I was wondering if we might meet face-to-face at some point. Might be to our mutual advantage. No need to waste resources and all that."

"Agreed. How about four o'clock on the San Cristobal cable car? I won't bring a minder, and I suggest you don't either."

"I'll have someone on top."

"I won't be armed."

"No, I don't think a shootout in public would do either of us much good," Beckett said. "Four."

The chief of the CIA's Santiago Station was a short, somewhat overweight, anonymous-looking man—as many chiefs of station tended to be. He looked more like a midlevel manager, or perhaps an executive at a small commercial bank. He was dressed in a herringbone sport coat and open-collar shirt, glasses perched on his nose, and at that moment, with his short cropped hair, he could never have been mistaken for anyone but a norteamericano.

They shook hands before they boarded the car for the short ride to the top of the twelve-hundred-foot hill. A statue of the Virgin Mary was there, a gift from France, along with a small café on a terrace, some gardens and walkways. The view across the city was popular, especially at sunset when the lights below began to come on.

Only a few other people rode up with them.

"A pretty city," Beckett said. "Nice people. Friendly. Always laughing."

"But then there's General Varga."

"An anomaly. The mood is mostly upbeat here. You must have felt it already."

"It'd be a shame if all that changed," Baranov said.

"Not so much like Moscow."

"Give us a chance—we'll change. It's an economic necessity. The people are demanding it."

"That's surprising, coming from a man such as yourself."

They passed not too far from the zoo.

"Sooner or later there'll have to be a decent peace between us."

Beckett laughed. "Bullshit, Valentin. We know about CESTA del Sur, and we know that you've come down here to negotiate with the DINA—you're speaking directly with Felipe Torres, who, if you haven't already learned yet, is a dangerous man. You want to expand your network, which you think will help contain Cuba from the south. Keep Castro isolated. But if you mean to keep us out of the picture, it's a wasted effort. Our embargo will last until the island goes democratic."

"Which has the same chance as a snowball in hell."

"So what are you doing here?" Beckett asked.

"Orders."

"No, I mean here and now with me."

"To warn you."

"Against what?"

"An officer of yours has been assigned to come here and assassinate General Varga for crimes against humanity. But that mustn't be allowed to happen, though I personally agree with you that Varga is a monster who has to be stopped. But not that way."

If Beckett was surprised, he didn't show it. "Assuming your information about an assassin is correct—which it isn't—what do you propose?"

"Varga has to be stopped."

"Everybody agrees," Beckett said.

"But it's delicate for both of us. For Washington because you need Chile to make sure South America remains as stable as possible for as long as possible. And Moscow needs Chile for the very reason you suspect."

"I'm listening," Beckett said.

"I'll kill him and his wife myself, make it look like a love triangle gone bad."

FORTY-TWO

□

McGarvey drove over to Arlington Cemetery to kill some time before he called Trotter again and put all the pieces he had set in place into motion. He wanted the cover of darkness, and perhaps even the bustle of the last of the workday traffic to mask some of the commotion that was likely.

Beyond the maudlin reasons for coming here—President Kennedy and American war heroes and all that—he was drawn to this place. It was the peace, he supposed. Everything bad for the people buried here had already happened to them. They were immune now, unlike himself, his family and his friends.

He parked on Memorial Drive just down from the amphitheater and Tomb of the Unknowns, and sat for a long time, the windows down, watching the occasional car pass, and a few visitors on foot wandering by.

Around five an older couple parked behind him and walked hand in hand up to the amphitheater, where they sat looking straight ahead toward the tomb. Maybe they had lost a son or brother or friend whose body had never been found, and this was the best they could do to preserve the memory, to pay their respects.

He guessed that he needed a place like this before all hell broke loose. He supposed that if he stuck it out long enough with the Company, he'd learn how to pace himself. But for now he'd forced himself to come here—to slow down, to think things out, to put everything in perspective.

He understood killing General Varga. That op was clear in his head. He had no question or doubt that it was the right thing to do. But it was everything else that was confusing to him.

After a half hour the couple came back to their car and drove off. Shortly after that the last few people at the tomb left, and fifteen minutes later several older men in blue blazers, white shirts and bow ties got out of a van. They carried small American flags on short wooden sticks and began distributing them on the graves, down the hill in the general direction of the Confederate Memorial.

What a waste, the dead in that war, he thought. The dead in just about every war.

He left the cemetery and headed toward the George Washington Memorial Parkway, pulling off at Kirby Road outside Arlington to call Trotter's office from a phone booth at a gas station.

"Good heavens, what are you doing calling here?"

"Meet me just inside Turkey Run Park in ten minutes. I have something for you," McGarvey said and he hung up.

He drove to the park, turning in at the first entrance just down from the highway, got out of the car and walked over with the tapes from the travel agency as Trotter pulled up in a blue BMW.

"Have a look at these, see if there's anyone we know. And show them to Campos and Munoz. I want to know how they react."

"Surveillance tapes from Georgetown?"

"Yes, and I'm on one of them."

"Okay, then what?"

"Send your guys over to me at the Marriott. Three-oh-three."

"Alone?"

"Have one of their minders drop them off out front, then back off."

"Until what happens, Kirk? What are you playing at?"

McGarvey told him about the encounter with the woman from the travel agency, and her admission that she knew Dobbs and Williams. "She said that she'd be sending her best next time."

"I'll have the Bureau arrest her and everyone else over there."

"Not yet. She gave me a name, but he'll just be a front. We still don't know who she's really working for. Maybe we'll find out tonight."

Trotter shook his head as if he were at a loss for words. "You're going to get yourself killed, you know."

"Nature of the game, isn't it, John?"

. . .

He parked his car in plain sight of the Marriott's lobby entrance and went inside, where he checked at the desk for messages. But there were none.

It was six-thirty, still early for anyone to show up. He went into the bar, where he ordered a Jack Daniel's up, but the young bartender made a mistake and poured him a Korbel Brandy instead.

"Sorry, sir," he said, realizing his error.

McGarvey held his hand over the glass. "This'll be fine, thanks."

He'd seen the mistake. Details, he thought. He had become hyperaware of his surroundings without even trying to force it. Something his instructors at the Farm said would either come or not come to the field officer. The best—meaning the ones who survived the longest—developed the talent early, because without it you were practically blind.

Finishing his drink, he signed for it and went into the dining room, where he ordered a rib eye and fries, and a bottle of Heineken. The place was more than half filled, at least forty people, most of them businessmen. Without making a show of it, he noticed and remembered each of them: the one with the blue tie, the two talking as if they were hatching a plot, the woman with large breasts, the man with the thin mustache, the four men just as obviously drunk as they were obviously ex-military. Ordinary. No one suspicious. Background noise through which he could pick out someone who did not fit. The one here to kill him.

He took his time with his dinner, cataloging those who came and those who left. Still no one suspicious. Yet.

Except for the drunks. Something about them tickled at the edge of his consciousness for just a brief moment and then was gone.

Signing for his check he asked at the desk again for any messages. There was one from Trotter.

They'll be there at ten. Nothing interesting on the surveillance tapes.

Three-oh-three was across the corridor from the stairs, and had a tiny balcony that looked across the water to the city, coming aglow with the darkness.

Without turning on the lights, he pulled the sheer drapes and opaque liners aside and opened the sliders. The sound of traffic was steady, and just to the south a jet took off from National Airport, turning west and then south almost immediately. He could almost smell the burned Kerojet. Somewhere in the distance a siren raced off to some emergency.

He took the lamp off a small table, then pulled the table and the easy chair over to a spot beside the slider, from where he couldn't be seen from the outside but had a clear sight line on the door.

Taking off his jacket and laying it on the bed, he checked the load on his Walther and set the pistol along with a spare magazine of ammunition on the table.

For a half minute or so he stood in the shadows next to the open slider and looked at the city in the distance and then the parking lot directly below.

Waiting, a CIA field operations instructor had told the class, was often the most difficult part of any op: "Wait patiently and you survive; wait badly and you have a chance of dying for your country."

McGarvey unlocked the door, then sat down next to the slider to wait.

FORTY-THREE

□

Baranov showed up unannounced just before 9:00 P.M. at the main entrance of La Moneda Palace. He powered down his car's window as two armed guards came out. One of them stood back and to the side as Baranov handed out his passport and KGB identity wallet.

The Plaza de la Constitución to the north and Plaza Libertad to the south were already crowded with traffic and pedestrians. Santiago and other major cities in South America generally came alive in the evening, dinner sometimes not happening until ten, eleven or even twelve o'clock.

Many offices and commercial establishments stayed open late. And work in the Presidential Palace often went on late as well.

"What is your business here, sir?" the guard examining his papers asked politely. His name tag read RUIZ.

"I would like a brief meeting with el Presidente."

"Do you have an appointment?"

"No, but it's important that he's told I'm here," Baranov said. He was already on shaky ground with Pinochet, but he needed the president's understanding and approval of what was coming next.

Ruiz handed Baranov's papers to the other guard, then stepped back. "I'll require that you step out of your automobile, señor, while keeping your hands in plain sight at all times."

"Pizdec," Baranov swore.

Ruiz raised his weapon, an American M16, while the second guard spoke into a lapel mic.

Baranov eased the door open and, keeping his hands away from his body, got out of the car.

"Turn around, spread your legs and place your hands on the roof of your car, please," Ruiz said.

Baranov did as he was told.

Ruiz slung his weapon over his shoulder and quickly frisked Baranov, who was glad that he'd left his pistol in the glove compartment.

"As you can see I'm not armed. If you want to verify my identity, call Señor Felipe Torres at the DINA. I'm working with him. But it is essential that I speak with the president this evening."

The second guard was finished on the radio. "Is this an official visit, sir?" he asked.

"Yes."

"May we know the nature of your business with el Presidente?"

"It's classified."

The guard spoke on the radio again, and at length he nodded. "An escort is on her way," he told Baranov. "But the president's chief of staff requests that you be very brief."

"Of course," Baranov said. He turned to get back into his car but Ruiz stopped him. "You will be going the rest of the way on foot. Your car will be waiting for you when you come out."

An attractive woman with long, sleek black hair, wearing a long-sleeved gray dress cut to her knees with a modest bodice, came out of the palace and walked directly across to where Baranov stood with the guards.

"The president has been expecting you. He'll meet with you in his private conference room if you'll follow me."

There was nothing pleasant about her demeanor or attitude. She had been ordered to fetch someone to a meeting inside the palace, and following her Baranov got the impression that her attitude would have been no different if she were fetching him to a firing squad.

"The willingness to make bold moves is the mark of a man who will either rise greatly or fall greatly," his father, the general, told him more than once. "No worthwhile reward is without risk. Never."

His father had eventually been sent to Siberia to count the birches. He had dared greatly enough to work in a senior Kremlin position, and his fall had been just as great.

With care and imagination, he'd wanted to tell the old man, but he'd never got the chance.

Inside they took an elevator up to the third floor, still busy with people coming and going from various rooms, where the woman led him to a suite of offices at the northeast corner of the building, looking toward the Church of the Agustinas.

A door off the anteroom opened to a small, artfully decorated conference room with a hand-carved mahogany table and chairs for ten. No one was there yet.

"The president will be with you momentarily," the guide said and she left.

The tall windows were heavily curtained, the drapes pulled back and tied in the middle. Baranov went over and looked outside at the people and traffic on the street.

A door on the opposite side of the room opened and Pinochet, along with Torres, came in. The DINA deputy chief closed the door.

"I'm not surprised that you're here, just a little curious so soon after your meeting with the CIA's chief of station," Torres said.

"You've had me followed," Baranov said.

"Of course."

"Shall we sit down?"

"No," Pinochet said. "You've met with Mr. Beckett without informing us. Tell me why I should not order your arrest and return to Moscow for trial."

"I'm sorry, Mr. President, charged with what?"

"The CIA is no friend of yours, especially considering what you came to warn us about," Torres said.

"Nor ultimately a friend of Chile's," Baranov said. He almost felt as if he were already standing in front of that firing squad.

"Don't toy with us, Captain," Pinochet said, his anger obviously in check for the moment. "Why did you meet with Beckett?"

"To tell him that I was going to assassinate General Varga."

Even Torres was taken by surprise. "Did you tell him that you suspected the CIA was sending someone to do it?"

"Yes, and he denied it, of course. In effect I told him that I was willing to save them the trouble, because General Varga was as much a disappointment and potential embarrassment to Moscow as he was to Washington."

"Is that why you're fucking his wife, just to get close to them?" Pinochet demanded.

"Yes, and him too," Baranov said.

His admission that he was having sex with both wife and husband hung in the air for several long beats.

A look passed between the DINA director and el Presidente. Torres went to a phone on a side table and called someone. "Hold the president's meeting, please," he said.

"Why?" Pinochet asked Baranov.

"The reasons are complicated."

"Don't try our patience," Torres said angrily.

"I have a source within the CIA's headquarters, and Señor Torres has his inside the CIA's training facility." Baranov spoke directly to Pinochet. "We have spent the last several days comparing notes about the assassin they are sending here. We've each tried to engineer this man's elimination without success. He is resourceful, and lucky. But we've discovered the possibility that someone else is also trying to stop him. At first I thought that Felipe was lying to me, and I expect that he thought the same of me. But now I'm sure it's a third party, though I have no idea of their agenda."

"I agree," Torres said.

"If I assassinate Varga and his wife, and if Felipe and I tell our sources, all that will be left is the third party. Their next action will not only reveal who they are but what their purpose is."

Torres understood but Pinochet was puzzled. "You won't actually kill them," he said. "I don't care about Karina, but I do need his services."

"No, Señor Presidente, but it will have to be convincing."

"A state funeral could be arranged," Torres said. "After all, Mati was a hero of the nation."

FORTY-FOUR

□

The telephone on the nightstand in McGarvey's room rang shortly after ten. He picked up his pistol, and checking out the slider to the parking lot below for anything or anyone out of the ordinary, he got to it on the second ring. It was Trotter.

"Paul just radioed. He's turning into the hotel's driveway right now. Where do you want him to park?"

"In front but away from the lights."

"Stand by," Totter said. He was gone briefly. "He's parking. What next?"

"Have him wait five minutes. If anything looks bad, tell him to get the hell out of here."

"Do you think someone from the travel agency is going to show up?"

"I have a feeling they're already here," McGarvey said, thinking about the four ex-military drunks in the dining room. "They'll probably be expecting me to call for help so they'll be on the lookout. Have Paul keep a sharp eye."

"Do you want me to send some backup?"

"No. I don't want to scare these guys off. With any luck I'm going to take one of them alive and ask him a few questions."

"What do you want Paul to do with our guests if no one shows up?"

"Bring them up to me."

"Why, in heaven's name?"

"I want to see how they react when they come face to face with me."

"What the hell would that tell you?" Trotter blurted.

"Who they were working for. Or at least a hint."

"Paul's in place," Trotter said.

"Five minutes," McGarvey told him and he hung up.

He went to the door and listened but the corridor was quiet, though he thought he could hear music in the distance. Probably from the bar downstairs.

Back at the slider he cautiously looked down at the parking lot. From his vantage point he spotted a windowless gray Chevy van of the type the Agency used for any number of jobs—including surveillance. Its lights were out, and he could just make out the figure of someone behind the wheel. Paul Reubens, the minder.

A Mustang came into the entrance but turned left toward the other end of the parking lot. He watched it until the driver pulled into a spot and doused the lights.

The music was clearer here at the open slider, and for a moment or two it held his attention.

A couple got out of the Mustang and walked to the front entrance.

A flash of light off to the left, so dim against the parking lot lights that it nearly escaped McGarvey's notice, was followed by five other flashes in rapid succession.

He turned in time to see what looked at this distance to be a woman dressed in dark clothes—possibly the large-breasted woman from the dining room—walk away from the Company van.

The flashes had been pistol shots.

McGarvey raced to the door, opening it just far enough so that he could make sure that the corridor was clear.

He stepped across to the stairwell door, checked through its window to make sure the stairs were clear as well, then headed down in a dead run, but on the balls of his feet so he made as little noise as possible.

On the ground floor the door to the outside was fifteen feet to the right. He burst out into the corridor and started to turn right, when a big man in a dark sport coat came out of the men's room, his right hand inside his jacket.

McGarvey swiveled left, keeping his profile as narrow as possible, and brought up his pistol in both hands, aiming at center mass.

For a long moment the man was stunned, rooted to the spot. But then his mouth opened, he staggered back a step and his hand came out of his jacket, a pocket comb dropping to the floor.

McGarvey almost shot him on instinct, but then he backed off and lowered his pistol. "Get out of here," he said.

The man didn't move until McGarvey flicked his pistol at him, and then he turned and hurried toward the lobby.

Before the guy was out of sight McGarvey was outside, in a crouch, sweeping the parking lot left to right. Nothing moved.

Keeping to the shadows as much as possible he hurried to the west end of the building and took a quick look around the corner. Whoever had been at the van, a woman or one of the drunks—though he thought it was the woman from the dining room—was nowhere in sight.

A car started up, backed out of its parking spot and headed his way.

He ducked back out of sight, holding the pistol just behind his right leg, the muzzle pointing outward, until the car came around the corner. As it passed him, he got the impression of a young woman with long blond hair driving, and then it was gone, exiting toward the parkway.

Stepping away from the building he checked the open slider at his room for any sign that someone was up there waiting for him to take the bait and show himself. But if anyone was there, they were hidden just inside the room, like he'd done.

He sprinted directly across the parking lot to an old Ford Fairlane, and keeping low, using it for cover, he made his way the last fifteen yards to where the van was parked.

All the lights were out, but its engine was running. He worked his way up to the driver's side and rose up to take a quick look inside.

Paul Reubens, blood pooled on the center console from a wound in the side of his head, lay slumped over, his eyes open. He was obviously dead.

Making sure again that no one was at the window to his room, he worked his way around to the open sliding door on the opposite side of the van. Campos and Munoz had both been shot in the face at close range. Both of them were dead.

Reubens and the two Chilean DINA offices had been lured into a trap. But by whom—someone from the travel agency or the mole at Langley?

The latter pointed toward Trotter—so obviously toward Trotter that he couldn't accept it. The obvious wasn't always a lie, neither were coincidences. But in this case he'd bet just about everything that Trotter was not the mole.

McGarvey walked back to the main entrance, sticking mostly to the shadows, and holstered his pistol under his shirt at the small of his back before he went inside.

Checking at the desk for messages—there were none—he walked into the bar. A woman had just finished a set at the piano. The four drunks had moved there from the dining room, but the woman and many of the others who'd been having dinner earlier had not. If anything the four guys were drunker than before, and loud, but maybe it was an act.

McGarvey made sure that they had spotted him, then walked out into the lobby as a police car pulled up. The man he'd confronted in the corridor was outside to meet it.

Angling around the corner to the elevators he went up to his room, again checking the corridors and easing his door open before he went inside to make sure no one was waiting for him. He phoned Trotter.

"Paul and your two guests are dead. Someone shot them at close range."

"He was better than that. He knew that he was coming into a likely hot zone."

"Was he a chauvinist?"

Trotter was at a loss. "What?"

"Was he divorced?"

"I don't understand."

"Was he divorced?"

"Yes, I think so."

"He got himself killed because he couldn't believe that a woman could be a hit man. And you'd better pass that along to the instructors at the Farm. The CIA is no longer just an old-boys club."

"I'm still not following you."

McGarvey explained what he'd seen and guessed from the time he'd had dinner in the restaurant until he'd found Reubens and the two Chileans shot dead, and the cops showing up.

"Are you going to wait for the travel agency to send someone?"

"It may have been the woman. Maybe they're less worried about me than they are about the people around me."

"Points back to the mole here at Langley," Trotter said. "To me."

FORTY-FIVE

□

It was well after midnight when Baranov got to the Vargas' compound. He'd called ahead to let them know that he was on the way.

"We were retiring for the evening," the general said.

"I've just come from meeting with the president and with Torres. This is important, Mati. And delicate."

"Now I'm curious."

"I'll explain everything when I get there. But at some point I'll need to meet with all the officers on your security detail as well as your house staff."

Varga had hesitated for just a moment. "Will this be strictly business? I have a couple of new films."

Baranov had laughed. "We'll have the whole night—I promise."

The gate swung open as he reached the bottom of the hill, and he was passed inside without having to stop for an ID check. Karina, wearing a sheer nightshirt, was waiting at the door for him, an amused look on her face.

"You have Mati all excited. Can you give me a hint?"

"I'm going to kill him. And I have the blessing of el Presidente."

For just an instant her eyes widened and her mouth dropped open, but then she realized that he was joking. "That's not a very nice way to start the evening."

"There'll be a state funeral with all the trappings for a fallen hero."

Karina turned and headed back to the bedroom suite. "We'll sit at the pool," she said over her shoulder. "I could use a drink."

Baranov went outside to the pool deck, where he poured a de Jerez for himself and sat at the table. The evening was cool, not like Moscow or even Mexico City at this time of the year, but pleasant. For the past few days he'd felt that the Chilean part of his assignment was nearly at an end. If McGarvey showed up, he would be shot before he got to the compound wall. In a way Baranov supposed he would be returning to Mexico with his op here considered a failure.

But he wasn't so sure. Maybe McGarvey would come to Mexico City after all, and they could have their little pas de deux, which would be delicious.

He tossed back his drink and was about to get up for another when Karina, now dressed in a pair of jeans and a T-shirt, came out with Mati, wearing khaki slacks and a Chile national football team shirt. Neither of them was smiling.

"You came as a man of surprises, and this evening you're back with still another," Varga said.

Karina brought the brandy bottle and a couple of glasses to the table, and she and her husband sat down facing Baranov. She poured them drinks.

"I'm going to assassinate you. Torres, with the approval of the president, suggested that there be a state funeral. It'll mean that you'll have to remain here out of sight for several days, maybe even a bit longer."

"Why?" the general asked.

"Because you'll be dead."

"I meant why such an elaborate plot? I have a lot of work to do, and I don't want to be interrupted. El Presidente has to understand this. Or does this have something to do with the assassin who you say is on his way here?"

"It has something to do with him, of course, but there is more."

"Tell me."

"I have a contact inside Langley, and Torres has his own inside the CIA's training facility outside of Washington."

"The Farm."

"Da. It's how we both knew that an assassin was being sent. As you know, I sent men to kill him, but they missed. But now someone else is trying to stop him, and neither Torres nor I know who it is. Or what their reasons might be."

Varga exchanged a look with his wife.

"Stand back and let them do it," she said. "Solves our problem."

"The real problem is why they're doing it. Why they're trying to stop McGarvey before he comes here."

The general was silent for a moment. "When you say that someone is trying to stop him, do you mean trying to kill him?"

"After they tried to kill his wife and daughter, he sent his friend and the man's family away in case whoever it was tried the same thing on them. In the meantime two field officers who Torres sent to Washington to find out more about McGarvey's plans were shot and killed outside the motel where he was staying."

"That doesn't make any sense," Karina said. "Whoever this third party is, do they want McGarvey to come here and try to assassinate Mati, or do they want him to fail?"

Baranov had thought long and hard about that very thing. "It could be that they're trying to distract him. Make him angry."

"What good would that do?" she asked, and her husband answered it for her.

"Angry men tend to make mistakes."

"Which has to mean that they want McGarvey to come here," Karina said. "But they want him to screw up. To fail. It's political."

In the end everything was political, Baranov wanted to tell her. But he held his tongue.

It was obvious that the general understood. "When do you want this to happen?"

"I'm leaving for Mexico City in the morning, so let's do it now."

"I have some things to take care of in Valparaíso first."

"Your assassin wouldn't miss an opportunity for the sake of your schedule."

It took a full fifteen minutes for Captain Luis Riquelme, the officer in charge of the security detail, to get out of bed, get dressed and make it over to the main house. The buttons on his uniform blouse were misaligned, and his eyes were still heavy with sleep.

"I'm sorry for the delay, but I wasn't expecting to be called into the general's presence on such short notice," he said, bringing his boot heels sharply together. He was a slightly built man, clean-shaven. A standout in his class at the academy, according to Varga.

"Something extraordinary is going to happen here this morning, and you'll have to keep your wits about you all week, perhaps even longer."

"Sir?"

"I'm going to assassinate the general and Mrs. Varga as soon as you go back to your quarters," Baranov said.

Riquelme was not armed but he instinctively reached for his pistol.

"Of course I'm not actually going to do it, but you will be the only one in the compound who knows differently. We'll depend on you to help pull off the deception."

"I don't understand."

"You don't have to understand, Luis," Varga said. "But I need your help. Tell us what you need."

The captain was at a loss for a moment.

Baranov motioned for him to sit down.

"You'll have to stage the murder without noise—perhaps in the bedroom—and then leave as normal," Riquelme started. "I assume that you'll also be leaving Chile. There will be a manhunt, of course."

"My flight leaves at ten."

"Cook will call me when you do not rise and ask for breakfast," the captain told Varga. "I will discover your bodies."

"You'll have to keep everyone else away," Baranov said. "Including the police at first."

"This is strictly a matter for the DINA. I'll put a guard on the room, with instructions that no one be allowed inside without my orders."

"What about the doctor?" Karina asked.

"I'm sorry, señora, but this will have to be kept quiet until the captain is aboard his flight and well outside Chilean airspace."

"Why?" Varga asked.

"Because at first your deaths will be made to look like a murder-suicide," Riquelme said. "The incident will have to be hushed up."

FORTY-SIX

□

Forty-five minutes later another windowless van pulled up next to the one Reubens had been driving. Two men jumped out of the back, and McGarvey watched from the window in his room as they moved Reubens's body to the rear and covered the bloody front seat with a piece of plastic.

They were careful with their movements, making sure that they didn't seem to be in a hurry. Someone in the van that had brought them out from Langley would be monitoring their surroundings as well as the police bands to make sure no one was watching or reporting anything suspicious going on in the hotel parking lot.

In less than sixty seconds they were done, and both vans headed away.

A couple of minutes later the police cruiser from out front made a slow pass through the parking lot, and finally turned around and left. Incidents of men running around with pistols in hand weren't all that uncommon in the Washington area. No shots had been reported, and there were no bodies or blood to be found. Besides, the man McGarvey had encountered in the downstairs corridor had been drinking.

The music from downstairs finally stopped, and the bar closed at two. Within twenty minutes the hotel had settled down for the night.

McGarvey waited another half hour before he slipped out of his room and took the fire stairs down to the rear exit across from where he'd moved his rental car. Instead of going that way he went down the corridor to the lobby, where a maintenance man was cleaning the floor. Another was on a tall stepladder changing a fluorescent light tube in a ceiling fixture, but no one was behind the front desk.

Outside he stepped away from the automatic doors and walked out from under the portico to a spot where he was partially in shadows and some-what, but not completely, concealed by a tall flowering bush.

The only noise was the hum of traffic on the nearby parkway, and from somewhere across the river another siren. Like any big city there were al-ways sirens at night.

But someone was here. He could feel them, and the hairs at the nape of his neck rose.

"Trust your instincts," he and the others had been told in class. "Very often they're all you have to go on. Hunches, anomalies, the out-of-place thing just at the edge of your peripheral vision or almost below your thresh-old of hearing."

Their instructor was a former British intelligence officer. "Keep a sharp eye, ladies and gentlemen, or one day something you should have paid attention to is likely to jump up and bite you in the arse."

Taking out his pistol, McGarvey darted directly away from the hotel to the first row of cars in the lot, where he pulled up and crouched be-side a Caddy. He looked over his shoulder at the second- and third-floor balconies, but if anyone was there he couldn't make them out in the dark-ness. Televisions were on in a few of the rooms, but mostly the hotel was asleep.

But someone was watching.

Keeping low, his movements broken, he made his way between the cars to the far corner of the lot from where he could see his rental car. He'd parked it as far away from the overhead lights as possible to keep it in rela-tive shadow, but he couldn't miss seeing a slightly built figure dressed in dark clothes suddenly appear on the driver's side of the car as if they had suddenly stood.

He was about twenty yards away, and crouching low again he made his way to the rear of his car as the person, their back to him, was looking toward the hotel. They were dressed in black trousers, probably sweatpants, a black T-shirt and a black watch cap.

McGarvey stood. "Did the travel agency send you?"

The figure turned around and McGarvey raised his pistol. It was Mar-lene.

"We thought you might be watching from your room, but you weren't there," she said calmly.

"You came to kill me. Why?"

"For interfering in our business. Though if you'd care to join us, the money is better than anything the Company could ever pay you."

"Dr. Morris doesn't exist."

She shrugged. "Just a work name. You know the value of those sorts of *choses.*"

"DGSE?" McGarvey asked. It was the French intelligence service.

"That was a long time ago." She smiled.

McGarvey glanced beyond her to the hotel. "You've come to kill me, as you promised you would, and you've brought help. So it might be for the best if we got out of here." He pulled his car keys from his pocket and tossed them to her. "You drive." It was another of the little homely lessons he'd learned: Never put your car keys in the same pocket as your gun hand.

"I don't think so."

"Either that or I shoot you before your friends show up."

She started to look over her shoulder.

McGarvey raised his pistol. "Now, please," he said.

"I placed two kilos of Semtex under the driver's seat."

"How does it detonate?"

"An accelerometer. First bump you hit."

McGarvey knew the trigger mechanism. "Or if I slam the door hard. Or something hits the rear fender." He bumped his hip against the side of the car.

Marlene shrank back. "Jesus."

"Disarm it."

"I can't."

"Ease out one of the detonator wires."

"You son of a bitch."

"You came here to kill me, sweetheart. If you remember what they taught you in tradecraft school at Orléans, you'll do fine. But take your pistol out, butt first, and lay it on the hood."

She pulled out her pistol, which looked like a compact Glock, and placed it on the hood. "You won't leave this place alive."

"Let's take that one step at a time. The Semtex first."

She dropped down out of sight, and McGarvey took a knee so that he could see her under the car.

"What then?" she asked, their eyes meeting.

"We find your friends. I want to know who's coming after me and why."

"They'll never tell you."

"We'll see," McGarvey said. "Do it."

She wiggled her way farther under the car, and McGarvey looked up. Someone was coming.

He scrambled around the back and made it two cars down, when his rental went up with an impressive bang and a fireball, sending debris fifty feet into the air. Most of the windows on the hotel's ground floor were shattered, as were half on the second floor and some on the third. Fire alarms shrieked and even from here McGarvey could see that the sprinkler systems inside the hotel had popped off.

Unless she was incredibly inept and had done something stupid, the explosives had probably been booby-trapped without her knowledge, in case McGarvey had either discovered the package or had gotten the drop on her.

A bullet slammed into the body of the car just inches from his head.

He moved back toward the burning wreckage, rather than away, and once he was past it, another two shots hit the windshield of the car he'd been hiding behind.

The shooter was using an infrared targeting system, which was defeated by the heat from the explosion.

Someone was at the open slider of his room. He could just make out the glint of the fire's reflection from the lens of a scope.

Holding his right wrist with his left hand, and steadying his elbow on the rear fender of the Ford he stood behind, he fired four shots in measured succession—one at the scope, one to the right and the last two to the left.

The glint of firelight from the scope's lens disappeared.

McGarvey holstered his pistol and went back to the front of the hotel, where people were beginning to come into the lobby, to help with the evacuation. He was pissed off with himself for missing the obvious fact that the woman would have a backup willing to take her out if the need arose, and for missing the opportunity of taking the shooter alive.

He was making too many mistakes and they were beginning to pile up on him.

□

FORTY-SEVEN

Baranov's flight on Lan Chile Airlines direct to Mexico City was scheduled for takeoff at ten. He'd already packed a few necessities at his compound, just the right amount to make it look as if he had been in a hurry to leave. Yesterday he'd done the same at his quarters in the embassy, packing only a few things, except for a different reason. He was coming back to Chile if in fact McGarvey actually made it that far.

Driving into the city from San Antonio he couldn't get the thought out of his head that a third party or parties in Washington also wanted McGarvey to fail. In itself it wasn't a bad thing. He'd lose some standing with Pinochet for not having stopped McGarvey himself. But the final objective of the still-unknown third party was bothersome. It was a loose end, something Baranov had never been comfortable with.

"The dangling threads will in almost every case be the final determinant of an operation's success or failure," one of their strategy instructors at School One had lectured.

"Why bother with minor shit?" one of the students had asked. "I say just go for the fucking kill."

That evening, the student's locker was empty and he was gone. There were no explanations given and none asked for. School One wasn't for *pizdecs*.

Kaplin had risen early at Baranov's request and he was waiting in his office. Only the overnight staff was here, but the shift change was due in an hour. The chief of station wasn't happy.

"What is it this time?" he asked.

"I'm returning to Mexico today. My flight leaves this morning."

"Your work isn't done here. Or have the Americans decided not to send an assassin after all?"

"The bodies of General Varga and his wife will be found in their bed later this morning. Initially it'll be treated as a double-suicide, at least until I'm safely outside of Chilean airspace. Or very possibly until I'm on the ground in Mexico City."

"Initially?"

"I don't know how long that fiction will last, until my name comes up as a suspect. But it won't hold for long. Pinochet doesn't like his heroes tarnished."

"You're out of your mind."

"They're not dead, but they'll stay out of sight at their compound for a few days, until after their state funeral."

"That makes absolutely no sense to me," Kaplin said. "I thought the idea was for McGarvey to come here and run into a trap you'd set up. Either kill him or maybe even put him on trial. Teach the Americans a lesson, make a point with Pinochet."

"There was never a chance of a trial, and certainly not a public one at that. I was going to kill him with my own hand, and then either make his body disappear somewhere or possibly send it in a coffin back to Washington."

"But?"

"You're aware that I have a source in Washington who told me that the CIA was sending an assassin. Felipe Torres has his own source up there who told him the same thing."

"I'd hate to trade places with Beckett. The poor man wouldn't know who to trust at Langley."

Baranov stifled a laugh. "No service is without its informants."

Kaplin waved him off. "You could end up like a dog chasing its own tail. I'll let the mole hunters in Moscow cover that end of the business. I have Santiago to mind."

"The same job Dick Beckett has," Baranov said. "Actually he's a pleasant man. We had a chat the other day about McGarvey."

Kaplin took a moment to respond. His face was a study in disbelief and resignation. "That could be construed as an act of treason."

"It served a purpose."

"The same as faking the murder of Varga and his wife? And as long as you evidently discussed it with Beckett, why not share your thoughts with me?"

"Something else is going on in Washington that neither my source nor Torres knows about. Someone has been putting a lot of pressure on Mc-Garvey. They've threatened his family, they've tried to kill him."

"They want to stop him from coming here."

"I don't think it's going to turn out to be that simple."

"And?"

"It'll be made known to McGarvey that I killed the Vargas, but not why. He'll also be told that I've quit Chile and gone back to my network in Mexico City. I think he'll come to me."

"Why?"

"To have the same sort of chat I had with Beckett. By all accounts the man is as curious as he is driven. His wife and daughter were threatened, and he'll want to know if I had a hand in it."

"And then?"

"He'll want to know who's been trying to kill him, or at the very least distract him from coming here and assassinating Varga. And he'll want to know why I killed the general and his wife."

"Again—and then?"

"Perhaps Mr. McGarvey and I will work together to solve the mystery in Washington."

"You are out of your fucking mind."

"Perhaps I'll kill McGarvey myself, bring his body back here, and then blame the Vargas' deaths on him after all."

"But they'll be alive."

"I'll kill them for real."

Kaplin looked toward the open door to the anteroom where his secretary usually sat. She wasn't here yet. "I'll have to report this conversation, of course. If for nothing else than to cover my own ass. From where I sit you're on some rogue operation that could go flying off on a tangent at any second and get us—this station—in some sort of an international shit-storm."

"Fine," Baranov said. It was about what he expected from Kaplin, who was basically a decent person and a good administrator, but not much of a spy and especially not much of a spymaster. "In the meantime I need to use a secure phone in the *referentura*."

"It's not completely secure."

"That's not a problem."

Kaplin got it. "Disinformation," he said.

One of General Leonov's aides at headquarters outside of Moscow answered Baranov's call. "*Da.*"

"Everything is going according to plan. Do you understand?"

"I'll pass your message along. Do you need any further assistance?"

"Not at this time."

"Very well. Good hunting."

"*Spasiba,*" Baranov said, but the aide had already hung up.

Baranov spent most of the early morning out of sight at the embassy, only bringing his bags down to the car at the last minute. He slipped away without saying goodbye to anyone just after eight-thirty for the drive to the airport.

Traffic was reasonable at this hour. When he arrived, he parked in the long-term lot and took his two bags into the terminal, where he checked in at the desk, got his ticket and boarding pass, and headed across to a bar at the international gates.

He bought a beer and took it to a pay phone between the men's and ladies' across the corridor. Using a phone card he called Henry at the secure Washington number and left the callback.

Henry called three minutes later. "Are you on your way?"

"I'm at the airport now. Do you have any updates?"

"I don't have everything yet, but someone from Madison tried again."

"And failed?" Baranov asked.

"From what I understand, yes."

"Does he know I'm returning to Mexico?"

"I doubt it," Henry said. "But if he finds out, he'll come for you before Santiago. Wild horses couldn't stop him."

"Make sure he finds out," Baranov said.

"Be careful what you wish for, my friend. You might just get it."

"Oh, I sincerely hope so."

FORTY-EIGHT

□

It seemed strange to McGarvey to be sitting alone in his own house, a hunted man. But for the moment he figured it was a relatively safe haven until it was time to leave Washington.

In the chaos immediately after the explosion, he'd managed to slip upstairs to his hotel room. The shooter's body lay on its side, next to a Winchester deer rifle and powerful scope. He'd taken one shot to his left eye. An infrared scope was set up on a tripod just left of the open balcony door, and lying next to it on the floor was a miniaturized walkie-talkie that had probably been used to detonate the Semtex.

The coldness of the premeditation against the woman got to him the most.

The man, who appeared to be in his mid to late twenties, was dressed in dark slacks and a dark polo shirt. He carried a Maryland driver's license, which identified him as Ronald Dahl, and a matching American Express credit card. Tucked in a back compartment of his wallet was a dining hall pass for Ft. Hood Army Base in Texas dating back five years.

He carried a standard-issue Colt .45 pistol in a shoulder holster, and a couple hundred dollars in cash in his left trouser pocket. But no pictures of a family, a girlfriend, a favorite car or boat. None of the ordinary keepsakes that just about everybody carried around with them.

The mistake had been the dining hall card, which identified the shooter as Specialist First Class Roger Digby. The name card was genuine; the name on the driver's license and credit card was fake.

Pocketing the dining hall card, McGarvey got his two spare sets of IDs—passports, credit cards and family photos, including of three children—along with a few thousand dollars in cash. He left his bag, clothes and Larson passport, and within five minutes was out the back door.

The next twenty minutes had been dicey. Police were everywhere, along with fire trucks and several ambulances. But he'd managed to slip away in the chaos and phone for a cab from a gas station a half block away.

"I don't know what the hell just happened over there, and I don't want to know," he told the cabbie.

"Fucking city is getting worse every year," the driver said. "Where to?"

"The Greyhound bus depot."

"Getting out of town?"

"Just to Baltimore," Mac said. From there he would take another cab home. Just a minor bit of tradecraft, but it wouldn't hurt.

The yard lights were on a timer and had gone out just at dawn. The newspaper delivery people showed up, and an hour later neighbors were out and about heading off to work. Watching for another half hour from an upstairs window, he'd spotted nothing out of the ordinary.

He finished packing some clothes and another pair of shoes. He would pick up shaving gear and everything else he needed later at one of the airport shops at Dulles, and just before he checked his bag he would pack his pistol, holster and two spare magazines of ammunition for the first two legs of his trip. After that he would never go anywhere unarmed.

Downstairs he tossed the bag in the trunk of Katy's powder-blue Mercedes convertible. Back inside he stared at the kitchen telephone for a long moment.

Trotter promised that Katy would not be told of his supposed death at the Farm, and yet he wanted to call her at his sister's, just to hear her voice, to tell her that he was fine. But she would catch the lie. She would be able to tell that he wasn't fine. He was on a mission, so why had he stopped to call her? It wouldn't make any sense to her, so she would know he was lying. And she would put pressure on him again to quit the Agency.

On top of that he was fairly sure that a tap had been put on his phone. He'd checked the house first thing, but he'd found no bugs. Tapping the line at a nearby distribution box, however, would be simple.

He left a note on the counter for her that he was okay, that he missed her and Liz, that he loved them and that he'd be back in one piece soon. And a P.S. that he was sorry about her car, but that it would probably be in the police impound yard nearest to Dulles.

Katy was forever nearly running out of gas. It was one of those details that didn't register on her radar. With just fumes in the tank McGarvey stopped at a gas station six blocks from the house, filled up, and then used the pay phone to call American Airlines. He booked a round-trip first-class to Atlanta, returning in two days, using an American Express Gold credit card in the name of Stewart Bentley.

Finished there he drove to an IHOP down in Somerset and had breakfast, after which he phoned Trotter's direct number at the OHB.

"Yes?"

"I'm leaving Dodge in the morning," McGarvey said. He had no idea why he lied—it simply came out. ("Survival is a learnable skill, ladies and gentlemen," the instructors at the Farm drummed into their heads. "Trust your training, but also trust your instincts.")

"Santiago?"

"Yes."

"Was it you they were after?"

"You might want to check on a shooter who was a grunt at Fort Hood a few years ago. Name of Roger Digby. Mid to late twenties."

"They found the body of Ronald Dahl in three-oh-three. But the room was registered to Michael Larson, same as on the rental car agreement, which the locals managed to find from the tag in the burned-out wreckage. You?"

"Yeah. The same woman from the travel agency who said 'the best' was coming for me showed up too. Only the guy in three-oh-three pushed the trigger on the Semtex while she was crawling around under my car."

"God in heaven."

"They're not screwing around, John. Put someone on the travel agency."

"First thing I thought of. But the place was empty when our guys got there. Moved out in the middle of the night. No traces, not even a decent set of prints."

"First-class," McGarvey said.

"I don't think we could have done any better," Trotter said. "What are you going to do for the rest of today and tonight?"

"I have a couple of things to check out."

"We can get you in the back gate, put you up. You'll be safe for the night."

"It didn't help Campos and Munoz."

"They were a lost cause from the day they showed up at our embassy. Their job was to misdirect us, which they did, and then they became expendable."

"Same as us?" McGarvey asked.

"Same as every intelligence agent. It's what we all agreed to when we signed up. No different than any GI who swears to defend the Constitution with his life against all enemies, domestic or foreign."

"Yeah, but in this case who are the enemies?" McGarvey said. "Are they foreign or are they domestic? Are they us?"

Trotter was silent for a beat. When he replied, he sounded subdued. "I don't know, Kirk," he said. "But whoever they are, they have an agenda. One that has to make sense at least to them, if not us. Anyway, keep in touch in case something comes up."

A depression came over McGarvey, all at once, like a black cloud. It made him wonder if what he was doing was worthwhile. And maybe Katy was right. Maybe he was tilting at windmills, after all.

"I guess we'll have to find out," he said.

PART

THREE

First Kill

FORTY-NINE

□

The flight down to Atlanta went smoothly and they pulled up to the gate ten minutes early. The plane had been little more than half full, and first-class only had a handful of passengers so the stewardess had a lot of time for them, but McGarvey had been mostly lost in thought.

Trotter's last words kept coming back to him. They'd been unnecessary, even dangerous. He was on his way into badland and his control officer wanted him to check in for updates?

It was almost axiomatic that once an officer was fully engaged in the field, he cut all ties with Langley.

"Once you drop under the radar stay there until it's time to come back to the barn," the senior tradecraft instructor told them. He'd been NOC, a field officer who worked under a nonofficial cover. They were so deep none of them ever came close to Langley, or to any U.S. embassy until they retired. Most of the time they didn't have direct contact with their control officer. Only in case of an extreme emergency would they phone home, and then the standard assumption was that they had been blown, and they would try to make it to safety. Most of the stars on the wall in the lobby of the OHB represented NOCs whose cover had been blown and who had been killed trying to make it out.

McGarvey's original plan was to reach Atlanta, retrieve his bag, and then make reservations for a round-trip flight to Miami, and from there a day later to La Paz, Bolivia, where he would rent a car for the final leg to the border with Chile.

His passports, credit cards and other IDs were clean. He'd gotten them on his own on the black market shortly after graduating from the Farm. On his two previous trips he'd used the documents that the Company provided him, but he'd also carried one of his own sets. Papers he'd not reported to anyone at Langley.

If you want to survive, you will develop your own go-to-hell kit. Papers, money, anything else you might need to stay ahead of the bogeyman.

Nevertheless, walking through the terminal at Hartsfield International toward baggage claim he took time with his tradecraft to make sure that no one was paying any particular attention to him. He hadn't left the country yet, and already he felt as if he were in badland.

But if someone were here, and tried to make a hit, it would mean that not only was his Larson identity blown, but that his other IDs were possibly no good as well.

Paranoia may not be such a bad trait for a field officer to develop.

He passed a tavern, and twenty feet later, he suddenly turned around and walked back to it. No one turned around or even gave him a double take.

He took a seat at the end of the nearly half-empty bar from where he could watch the people passing and ordered a Bud draft.

"Anything to eat?" the bartender asked.

"The beer's fine for now. Do you have a phone I could use?"

"Pay phones are just across from gate sixteen-A."

"Pretty noisy out there."

The bartender shrugged and brought the phone from the back bar. "No long-distance."

"Thanks," McGarvey said. He got the operator and asked for a collect call to Trotter's direct line.

When it went through, Trotter accepted the charge. He seemed out of breath, as if he had just run up a flight of stairs, or had heard some disturbing news. "Where are you calling from?"

"Atlanta."

"Are you in a secure spot?"

"It's not likely this phone has a bug on it, and no one is paying much attention to me."

"I just got the overnights twenty minutes ago. Beckett's laser product out of the *referentura* is already falling off, but he's made two extraordinary reports, both about Baranov. Apparently he's on his way back to Mexico City to tend to his network."

"What'd he leave behind in Santiago?"

"I don't know for sure yet, but Dick said he and Baranov met face-to-face. Apparently he's working on an in-depth report, which he intends on hand-carrying up here within the next twenty-four hours."

"Did he give any hints?"

"No. And your name and your op were not mentioned. But if he's bringing whatever it is up here in person, it has to be big. I know Dick personally, and he never goes off half cocked. Before he gets here he will have already worked out just about every possibility."

"What's your take on the timing?" McGarvey asked. But he was already three steps ahead. "One day Baranov meets with our COS and the next he bugs out back to Mexico."

"I'm not sure. But it's a real possibility that he's set something up in Santiago, and he has to get out of the country before it goes down."

It was about what McGarvey figured. But something else that Trotter had said suddenly made sense, at least from an angle.

"You said that the laser product from the Russian embassy has fallen off; what did you mean?"

"They probably figured out that the *referentura* was no longer secure, so they stopped work until they got it figured out. SOP."

"But not before Baranov announced that he was returning to Mexico."

Trotter took a moment to respond, and when he did he seemed cautious. "Could be an innocent coincidence. Might not be such a good idea to jump to conclusions. The bastard could have set up any number of nasty little surprises. It's his style."

"You're right."

"Maybe you should sit tight for a bit until Dick gets up here with his report."

"I'll stay the night here, talk to you tomorrow afternoon. Maybe by then you'll know what Dick's bringing."

"Where're you bunking?"

"Hold on," McGarvey said. He motioned the bartender over and then covered the phone's mouthpiece. "What's a decent hotel here at the airport?"

"The Windsor's okay. The shuttle will get you there."

"Anywhere else?"

"The Clarion."

"The Windsor," McGarvey told Trotter.

"Watch your back."

McGarvey got his bag and took the escalator back up to the ticketing counters, where he found that American Airlines flew to Acapulco on Mexico's Pacific coast, about 170 miles from Mexico City. It was an eighteen-hour trip leaving in just an hour, going to Dallas first, then ironically Mexico City for a nearly seven-hour layover before arriving at the resort town a little after eight in the morning.

He booked a first-class round-trip under the name Kenneth Whiteside, paying with a Gold American Express and presenting his matching passport.

After he surrendered his bag, he went to a pay phone and, using his Larson identification, booked rooms for two nights first at the Windsor and next at the Clarion. Then he went back to the international terminal, where he got another beer and waited for his flight.

The flight wasn't long, and dinner wasn't served until the Dallas-to–Mexico City leg, but McGarvey managed to snooze off and on, so by the time they touched down at Benito Juárez International Airport a little after midnight he was in reasonable shape.

He went back up to the nearly deserted American Airlines ticketing counters, where after nearly one hour he managed to talk to a supervisor and explain that his company wanted him to stay here in Mexico City, and not continue on to Acapulco until the day after tomorrow.

He was willing to pay the stiff rebooking fee, as well as any other handling charges, but he would need his bag before it was loaded aboard the AeroMéxico flight to Acapulco, which left at seven in the morning.

And it was nearly an hour later before the bag showed up at customs, and he was passed through by a sleepy agent without questions. Afterward he took a taxi into the city to the Four Seasons in midtown, where he registered under his Whiteside work name.

Baranov's people would be expecting him to come here, not under his own name of course. So they would be looking for anyone coming in from the U.S. whose itinerary was out of the ordinary. Anomalous.

He had just unzipped his fly and told the Russian he had come to town.

FIFTY

□

First thing in the morning Baranov was in his office at the Russian embassy in Mexico City watching the Chilean government news television state *Canal 24 Horas*. The newsreader was recapping the story of the murdersuicide of General Varga and his wife at their compound outside of San Antonio.

A special unit of the Investigations Police refused to make any comment or even name the chief officer in the case, but questions were already being asked if something more ominous had occurred.

A spokesman for President Pinochet had promised that every possible effort would be made to find out what really happened to the general and his wife, who were close personal friends of el Presidente.

Baranov turned down the volume. In effect Pinochet had just admitted that the problem that bothered the White House no longer existed, while at the same time thumbing his nose at the Americans—especially the CIA.

He went up to the *referentura* and made an encrypted call to Felipe Torres.

"Switching over," he said when Torres answered.

"Si."

"I've just watched el Presidente stick it to the Americans on television. Has he gotten any reaction from Washington?"

"None that's been reported to me," Torres said.

"There's been no mention of my name."

"And there won't be. We thought it would be for the best to leave it as is for the time being, until the issue of Señor McGarvey is taken care of. The state funeral is in two days. Closed coffin."

"The fiction won't last long, at least it won't if your president wants Mati to continue his work at Valparaíso."

"We understand this, but it will be enough to delay or even recall McGarvey. Our ambassador in Washington has been called to the White House for lunch with the president and some of his advisors. President Pinochet has ordered him to place all of our cards on the table."

Baranov was intrigued, despite himself. The business had taken a turn for the surreal. "What cards would those be?"

"That we are aware of Señor McGarvey and his mission to interfere in our affairs. And demand that he be ordered to stand down."

"There'd be no need for a recall unless your ambassador admits that the murder-suicide was faked."

"I'm told that he has been authorized to go in that direction, yes."

"In return for what?" Baranov asked. "Mati's work at Valparaíso will still be on the table. The Americans will want President Pinochet to end the program."

"Which he will not do."

"Then what is he willing to offer?"

"I don't know."

"And if you did, you wouldn't share it with me."

"That's correct," Torres said. "Now, if you have nothing further."

"We think that McGarvey, almost certainly traveling under false documents, was in Atlanta yesterday. It likely means that he is on his way to you."

"He'll be recalled."

"Don't be so sure you don't have a leak somewhere. Possibly at the compound. Maybe the cook or maintenance man, or someone on the security detail."

"We've taken steps."

"As you wish," Baranov said. "If my name is to stay out of it, I'll be returning in a day or two."

"No."

"What's going to happen?"

"That'll depend on what our ambassador brings back from the White House."

Shit, Baranov said under his breath.

"We knew that you would make this call, and I was told to assure you that your delegation from Moscow will be welcomed."

"After the funeral."

"Si," Torres said, and he hung up.

Petr Yezhov, the chief of intelligence operations for Mexico, came in. He was an old hand in the game, coming up through the ranks in the KGB at the height of the Cold War with the West. He'd spent a fair amount of time in East Germany, and almost as much working out of the UN in New York. He was tall, slender and blond, with the looks and manner of a Western movie star. At each new posting he acquired a mistress, sometimes two, even before he brought his wife to join him.

He was urbane and knew just about everyone in the Kremlin. It was expected that one day he would become director of the KGB. He thought the world of Baranov and was behind him 100 percent.

They were in one of the small, windowless offices in the center of the third floor that were used for encrypted phone calls and top-level private meetings. Unlike the referentura at the embassy in Santiago and a few others around the world, this place was absolutely secure. Yezhov had the best technicians in the entire service completely sweep the place every thirty days.

"So, Vasha, I suspect that you left Chile in better shape than you found it," he said, perching on the edge of an adjacent desk.

"I left it a different place. Our Moscow delegation will be welcome next week. And Pinochet seemed receptive."

"After the funeral."

"You heard."

"Was it your doing?"

"It was my suggestion. In fact, I was going to be accused of murdering both of them. Not publicly, of course. But openly enough so that the CIA would learn of it and back off."

"And you would take the credit."

"We would."

"But Valparaíso wouldn't come to an end for them."

"The general would be allowed to go back to work in due time. It would send a clear message to Washington."

"And what about your CESTA del Sur?"

"That's not so clear," Baranov said. And he told the chief of intelligence operations about his suspicion that something else was going on in Washington, something just outside his ken. "My resource at Langley is just as puzzled as I am."

"Kaplin tells me that you met with Dick Beckett."

"Yes. I warned Beckett that we knew about the assassin, and I told him that I would kill General Varga myself."

Yezhov chuckled. "Do you think he believed you?"

"The television has reported their deaths." Baranov said. "But it doesn't matter what Beckett believes; it only matters what the other party in D.C. believes."

"And if they do, what then?"

"I don't know, but they'll have to react somehow. Throw a pebble into a pond and you'll see the ripples."

Yezhov stood up, smiling. "Or, toss a stick into a pack of dogs and the one that yelps is the one that got hit."

"Something like that," Baranov said.

Yezhov patted him on the shoulder. "Keep me posted, Vasha." At the door he turned back. "By the way, we think that your Kirk McGarvey is here. He was spotted at the airport last night, and he has a suite at the Four Seasons."

FIFTY-ONE

Trotter always had the ability to compartmentalize his thinking. When he was a child, he could lie to his parents, who always believed him for the simple fact that he believed the lie himself.

It wasn't a skill he had to work on to perfect—it had always been there. When he got his first job in law enforcement with the FBI, he defeated every lie detector test ever given to him. And he proved it by answering some of the questions with such outrageous lies that even the examiner had to laugh.

"You'd make the perfect criminal," the FBI director had told him after the swearing-in ceremony for new agents.

Or a spy with the CIA, he'd thought at the time. And three years later he'd applied to and was accepted by the Agency. That was more than ten years ago, and his rise through the ranks had been nothing short of stellar.

Walking into the director's suite on the seventh floor he put on his serious face. "Am I late?" he asked the DCI's secretary.

"No, but you may go right in; they're waiting for you," she said.

Hollis Morton, director of the CIA, was seated on one of the brown leather Queen Anne couches, across from Lawrence Danielle, who was about to go back to run the Clandestine Services Directorate after having served for a year as the assistant deputy director of the CIA. Everyone at Langley was hoping that the president would appoint him as the new DCI. It would be refreshing to have a career intelligence officer once again at the helm.

"Good morning, John. We assume that you've already heard the news out of Chile," Danielle said.

"Yes, nothing short of stunning."

Morton, a short, rotund little man whose career as a neurosurgeon had made him a multimillionaire, motioned for Trotter to take a seat. "You're McGarvey's control officer; what's your take on this?"

"There's no confirmation that it's real," Trotter said.

"Dick Beckett is on his way in," Danielle said. "Should be here later this afternoon. I talked to him by phone before he left, and he told me that he and Valentin Baranov had met. You're familiar with this name?"

"CESTA del Sur, Mexico City," Trotter said.

"He spent a couple of weeks in Santiago stirring the pot," Danielle said. Physically he was a study in contrasts: small hands, long legs, hooded eyes, but almost always with a ready smile. He looked ordinary, but mentally he was sharp, even brilliant.

"Unusual that they would meet."

"The Russians know McGarvey's name and his assignment."

"We've got a goddamned mole," Morton said.

"Baranov told Dick that he was going to assassinate General Varga and his wife, save us the trouble."

"Good heavens, that's wrong on just about every level," Trotter blurted. "The Russians want to engage Pinochet, get a foot in the door; killing the general would be the last thing they'd want."

"You think it's a lie?" Danielle asked.

"It has to be."

"Why?"

"At the very least they'd want McGarvey to get there and ambush him. Either kill him and ship his body back here, or better yet capture him and put him on trial. It'd be simply terrible for us."

A look passed between Morton and Danielle.

"The president is meeting with Aguilera right now," Morton said. Tomas Aguilera was the Chilean ambassador to the U.S. "It was the president's call, but I wasn't told what the substance of their meeting would be. Almost certainly it'll have to do with General Varga and the genocide in Valparaíso."

"With Varga supposedly dead, it becomes a moot point," Danielle said. "Which was why we wanted to talk to you. Is he dead or is this a sham?"

"I suspect the latter."

"Why the hoax?"

"I want to say in the hope that we would swallow it and McGarvey would be called off."

"But?"

"There'd be no need for the president to meet with Aguilera, except to demand that Valparaíso come to an end. Something I don't think Pinochet would want to do. Maybe the president will offer them something."

"Such as?" the DCI asked.

Trotter's thoughts were racing in a dozen different directions. "I don't know. Maybe we'd agree to take their dissidents, like we've been doing with the Cubans."

"None of us think that'll happen."

"Economic sanctions, then."

"The Russians would love that. They'd be down there in a flash with open checkbooks."

"Maybe go public with what's happening in Valparaíso."

"It'd be another cause for strained relations between us," Morton said.

"Baranov wants to expand his CESTA del Sur network beyond Mexico all the way down to Chile," Danielle said. "What do you think about that possibility?"

"It'd give them a back door to Cuba," Trotter said.

"We'd leave and the Russians would take over?"

"No more than they seriously expect us to leave Mexico. They'd want us to stay there so that they could spy on our people as well as the DINA. At least initially." Trotter spread his hands. "They have missiles along their western borders to cover Europe, in Siberia to cover us, and we've built defenses to counter those threats. But how about putting nuclear-tipped missiles in Chile? Attack us from the south where we're least protected."

"Hell, why bother with Chile?" Morton asked. "Why not Mexico, or even Cuba?"

"Because we'd go to war if they moved that close to home," Trotter said.

"But?"

"What about Chile?" Trotter asked, and the question hung in the air for a moment. "If there's nothing else, sir."

"I've read your DKDISTANTMOONLIGHT summaries," Danielle said. "Starting with the accident at the Farm, or incident, if you prefer. All the way through the body outside Union Station, to the bodies at McGarvey's house, the disappearance of Janos Plonski and his family, and the mess at the Marriott. Where has he got himself to this time?"

"He called me yesterday from Atlanta. I told him that there were some developments up here, and he promised to stay the night there and call me this afternoon for an update."

"But he didn't call?" Danielle said.

"No."

"Where is he?"

"Not at the hotel where he said he'd be staying, nor do we think he continued to Miami, where we think he'd fly to Bolivia or someplace close and cross into Chile by rental car or bus."

"Then you don't know where he is," Morton asked.

"No, sir."

"Give us your best guess, John," Danielle prompted.

"Mexico City or en route."

"Why?"

"By now he knows about General Varga, and he knows about Baranov, and he might make the leap that the Russian was somehow involved in the deaths and would return to running his network, at least until after the funeral."

"How did he know about Baranov?" Danielle asked.

"I told him, of course. He'd have to know everything happening in or around the capital, as operational-necessary considerations."

"You believe it's possible that he's going after Baranov?"

"He'd want to find out if General Varga was actually dead."

"I'll call Justin and have him keep an eye out for McGarvey," Danielle told the DCI. Justin Watson was the chief of station in Mexico City.

FIFTY-TWO

☐

Baranov stood on the sidewalk just a few meters from the driveway into the Four Seasons. He wore a long coat, dark glasses and carried a white cane. Pinned to the front of his coat were a string of Mexico's national lottery tickets.

In the ten minutes since he had taken up position to watch the hotel's entrance he'd sold five 60,000-peso tickets—each worth around two U.S. dollars. Blind people, *ciegos*, standing on street corners sold lottery tickets. They were so common they seemed to be on every street corner. And they were never cheated.

He was too early to meet McGarvey face-to-face, but he wanted to see the man. To take his measure. One of the female clerks at the Russian embassy whose English was perfect left a message at the hotel for McGarvey that Justin Watson wanted a meeting in his office as soon as possible after lunch. It was around that time now.

A cab pulled up, and a man slightly under six feet with the build of an athlete came out of the hotel. He wore a dark blue blazer, khakis and an open-collar white shirt. And even at this distance, through tinted glasses, Baranov could see the aura of self-confidence radiating off the man, like heat from glowing coals. And he could also see the obvious tradecraft, the searching of passing traffic, the roof lines across the street, the pedestrians. His gaze lingered for a moment on Baranov and then he crossed to the cab and got in.

There was absolutely no doubt in Baranov's mind that the man was Kirk McGarvey. He could have recognized him from the end of the block, in part from the couple of photos he'd seen, but mostly from the stories Henry had told him. What stuck out at this moment, though, was the measure of the man. He was a force—he'd already proved that at the Farm, at his home when the two men had come for his wife and child, and again at the Marriott—that wouldn't be as easy to stop as Baranov had first suspected.

McGarvey was young and, in the way he moved coming out of the hotel, and then climbing into the cab, was like a ballet dancer going through his steps. Light on his feet, his movements seemingly effortless. Henry said that his scores on the firing range, at close-quarters combat drills, on the Farm's difficult confidence courses and in the various tradecraft disciplines— explosives, weapons and weapons systems—had been consistently at the top of his class.

Formidable. The term crossed Baranov's mind, and he had to smile. Mc-Garvey was going to be an interesting opponent.

He sold another two tickets before he left his spot and, taking off his dark glasses, collapsing the cane, and removing his long coat, walked around the corner to where he'd had a man park his four-door BMW.

Parking was another quirk peculiar to Mexico City, where traffic down-town was almost always impossibly heavy. Older guys would stake out four or five parking spots at the curb, and rent them out for petty change by the hour. It was entrepreneurship, and the cops never bothered with them.

He paid his parker, giving the man a little extra, and drove off to a small bar and dance club on Avenida Moreles across from the Plaza de la Consti-tución y Parroquia de San Agustín de las Cuevas in the area of Tlalpan on the city's south side. Called the Ateno Español, the somewhat seedy place occupied the ground floor of an old three-story apartment building. For a long time, even before the Cuban revolution, it had served as an informal gathering place for Mexican dissidents, communists, Cubans, even the emerging Russians who came to Mexico to make a lot of money, almost always by extortion schemes, kidnapping, murder-for-hire and, lately, drug running.

Luis Alvarez ran the place from behind the old bar. He was an arranger, for a fee, who knew everybody and could connect you with whatever sort of muscle-for-hire you needed. No questions ever asked, and guarantees that nothing would ever splash back to the man with the cash. And no one screwed with him. In his younger days he'd been a professional boxer, and when he put on too many pounds, he became a professional wrestler, known as the Killer.

When Baranov came in, Luis poured him a stiff measure of a good Polish vodka. "Ah, Vasha, I heard you were out of town for a while."

They spoke English, which had always been the lingua franca of the place, even when Castro and the others came here in the fifties.

"Someday you might hear too much."

Luis laughed, his big frame shaking. "People talk. What am I supposed to do, turn a deaf ear?"

"I've a little job for you," Baranov said. "Maybe not so little, but it's important to me."

"How important?"

"Five thousand U.S. for two men."

Luis was interested. "Wet work?"

It was the old KGB term for *mokrie dela,* the spilling of blood. Assassination.

"Yes. He's a CIA operator and good, from what I've been led to believe."

"Not Watson?"

"No, no one local. But he's someone who's come here to stick his nose into my business."

"How soon?"

"Now. Tonight. He's staying at the Four Seasons."

"Only the poor gringos are bums. Drunks, running from jealous wives, jealous husbands, jealous prosecutors. But not this one?"

"No."

"Will he be armed?"

"Almost certainly. But he's the sort of man who might not need a pistol or a knife. It'll warrant your best."

Luis went to the other end of the bar to pull beers for a pair of Mexicans in business suits who just came in. When he returned he nodded. "Difficult business killing a CIA officer. What's he doing here?"

"He came to kill me."

Luis laughed again, but this time without humor. "Kill him yourself. Save the money."

"There're reasons that wouldn't be such a good idea."

"What has he against you?"

"You'll never know," Baranov said, a hard note in his voice. "Will you take the job?"

"Of course. Fifteen thousand Swiss francs." It was steep—at the current exchange rate a bit over ten thousand U.S.

"Agreed."

"For each man, plus me."

"Thirty thousand dollars is a lot of money. It'll take me a few days to arrange it."

"But you want the job done immediately."

"Yes, it's important," Baranov said.

Luis reached across the bar and they shook hands. "Then it will be a matter of trust between us. And you know what that means, tovarich." His grip was like steel, as was the look in his eyes. *I'll do the job, but if you don't pay, you'll be next.*

"His name is Kirk McGarvey, but we believe that he's traveling under the name Kenneth Whiteside," Baranov said. He gave Luis the two photos that Henry had sent him in Santiago. "I saw him leave the hotel a little while ago. He took a cab to the U.S. Embassy."

"Does he travel with bodyguards?"

"He feels there is no need for it."

"The ones believing they are invincible usually fall the hardest and the easiest."

"Do you want a down payment now? I have dollars."

"I'll wait. The Swiss are to be trusted more than the Americans or the Russians when it comes to managing their money."

The rumor was that Luis had money in stocks and bonds in several exchanges around the world, except for London, New York and Moscow. It was said he was rich enough to retire, but that he stayed here to play the game.

"I'll be back tomorrow with some of the money—in Swiss francs."

"It should be an interesting evening," Luis said, grinning.

Baranov tossed back his drink. "There will be no payment for failure."

"The ones I am sending do not fail."

FIFTY-THREE

□

The cabbie dropped McGarvey off in front of the U.S. embassy on the Paseo de la Reforma a little before two in the afternoon. Traffic was horrible as usual, and the air stank of car exhaust and something else not pleasant. The embassy building itself was a five-story fairly modern structure, just blocks from the Zona Rosa section, which was essentially the downtown of the city, and only a few blocks from his hotel. But the front desk had recommended that he take a cab, which would be air conditioned, because of the air inversion and horrible smog today.

He showed his passport at the reception desk, and told the young woman that he had been called to a meeting with Justin Waston.

She called upstairs and gave McGarvey's Whiteside name on the passport. She looked up. "I'm sorry, Mr. Whiteside, but Mr. Watson's secretary says that you are not on this afternoon's appointments list."

"Tell them that I'm a friend of Larry Danielle's."

She relayed the message.

"Someone will be down to escort you," she said, handing McGarvey's passport back and giving him a visitor's pass.

A young man in a white shirt and loose tie but no jacket showed up a minute later and they took the elevator up to the fifth floor. "You must be Kirk McGarvey. We were told you might be showing up."

"Who told you?"

"Mr. Danielle, of course."

Watson's office was on the east corner of the building, the last in a suite of offices and cubicles the CIA occupied that took up nearly half the entire floor. They were shown straight in, and the young man turned and left, closing the door behind him.

The chief of station was a gruff-looking bear of a man, with a crew cut, a sloping forehead and hair on the backs of his hands. His jacket was off, his tie loose, and sweat stained the armpits of his shirt. He did not seem friendly.

"What are you doing here, McGarvey?"

"I'm looking for someone. And when he and I have a little chat, I'll get out of your hair."

"Back to Langley?"

"No."

"You're on an op?"

"Just beginning."

"But not here, not in Mexico, or at least I wasn't told any details. Larry said that you'd fill me in."

Watson had not gotten up from behind his desk, nor had he motioned for McGarvey to take a seat.

"There's not much I can tell you, except that I'll be out of your hair by tomorrow morning."

"Exactly who is this person you came here to chat with?"

"A Russian by the name of Valentin Baranov."

Watson reacted as if he had been shot. "No."

"He already knows that I'm here and he told me so. He had someone leave a message at my hotel that you wanted to meet with me."

"That's not surprising, but no, you're not going to have so much as one minute of eyeball time with him. Not today, not any day. I want you out of Mexico on the first flight that leaves for anywhere."

"Do you read the daily summaries that the DI sends you?" McGarvey asked. He'd expected that Baranov would find out that he was here, but just not so fast. It had to mean that this source in Washington was highly enough placed that they knew what was going on in Chile, and what his role was to be.

"Of course."

"The murder-suicide of General Varga and his wife?"

Watson's eyes narrowed slightly. "Go on."

"Baranov was in Chile until just yesterday. There's a very real possibility that he was somehow involved. I want to ask him about it."

"We wondered where the bastard had gotten himself to. We figured he'd come home. But the answer is still no. I want you out of here now."

"We think he wants to expand CESTA del Sur to Chile. He courted Pinochet, and the general. This latest event might have something to do with it."

"Christ, do you have any idea what the fuck you're talking about?" Watson demanded angrily. "Whoever the fuck told you about that operation will be hung by the balls." He phoned someone. "Have you got a minute, sir? I have a gentleman from Washington here you might want to listen to." He looked at McGarvey. "No, sir. Langley."

Watson tightened his tie, put on his jacket and they took the elevator up to the top floor. The engraved nameplate on the door at the end of the broad corridor read HON. ROBERT B. MASLAK. The U.S. ambassador to Mexico. They were shown directly inside to the ambassador's palatial office, which looked to the west toward the mountains.

Maslak was a tall, somewhat patrician-looking man who'd played basketball at Northwestern for all four years, and at one time had even considered going pro. Instead he moved on to Harvard for his law degree, and made a name for himself in New York City defending multinational corporations and their CEOs and CFOs, mostly against anti-trust disputes.

"This the gentleman?" Maslak asked.

"Yes, sir. Let's take this into your conference room."

They went into the adjacent windowless conference room, which, unlike the ambassador's office, was safe from surveillance.

Watson introduced McGarvey and they sat down at a small table, where he recounted their conversation. The ambassador didn't seem overly surprised.

"I was briefed on the situation in Valparaíso about six months ago," he said. "I had dealings there with the financial team working with President Pinochet, and I was asked for my opinion. Which was that General Varga's program had to go at whatever the cost to us. Has that something to do with your assignment, Mr. McGarvey?"

"I'm sorry, sir, but I'm not at liberty to discuss it with anyone," McGarvey said. If Baranov had meant him to be tied up like this and maybe even be sent home, his plan was working.

"You were not sent here yet you came to talk with Justin, which, as you say, was Valentin Baranov's doing. And now you want to talk to the Russian about his spy network? Is that correct?"

"Yes, sir. I think he'll have some answers that could be a help."

The ambassador was a little surprised. "And you think that he would cooperate with you?"

"I can be persuasive, sir."

"What do you know about CESTA del Sur?"

"Only that it's a Russian spy network in this hemisphere and that it's possible Baranov has been ordered to expand it into Chile."

"It makes sense from their standpoint. But I still don't see why—as you say you were not assigned here—you came to talk to him."

"It has something to do with the deaths of Pinochet's chief executioner and his wife," Watson said.

"If there's a connection, we'll find that out. We have someone working from the State Department on the issue. Actually, until recently one of yours. And quite good."

"May I be told who he is?"

Watson shook his head. "You're not cleared for that. You have to understand that the issue is very sensitive for us at the moment."

"The Russians are offering the Mexican government the sun and the moon for concessions," Maslak said. "Exactly what they are, we're trying to find out."

"Which is why you can't go running around crowding Baranov," Watson said. "It'd screw up everything we've worked on for the past year and a half. I want you gone."

"I'm sorry, Mr. McGarvey, but I'll have to insist," the ambassador said.

FIFTY-FOUR

□

Meeting with Watson and the ambassador meant almost nothing to McGarvey except for the fact that Baranov had maneuvered it. What was interesting, however, was that Baranov had made the call knowing that McGarvey might be ordered out of Mexico.

The next step, then, was to make a show of going nowhere, at least for the time being, until either Watson sent a couple of minders from his shop to take him to the airport, or Baranov sent someone for him.

He was betting on the latter.

The same escort who'd brought him upstairs to Watson's office took him back to the lobby. "Have a nice day," he said with no sincerity and walked away.

"You too," McGarvey said.

He took a cab back to the Four Seasons, and when he got out under the portico, he looked over to where the blind lottery vendor had been standing, but the man was no longer there. At the time the guy had seemed out of place to him.

The uniformed valet who'd opened the cab's door for McGarvey stepped back and raised a salute to the brim of his cap.

"Did you happen to notice the blind man who was selling lottery tickets earlier?" McGarvey asked him.

"Indeed I did, sir. He was new."

"You were here when I came out of the hotel less than an hour ago?"

"Yes, sir."

"How long after I left did the lottery vendor leave?"

"Actually I thought it was odd, sir. As soon as you were around the corner, the *ciego* left."

"That is odd," McGarvey said, and he went inside. The blind man was Baranov come to watch for him—he was almost certain of it.

He went up to his suite, where he loaded his pistol, screwed a compact silencer on the muzzle, and holstered it at the small of his back, under his jacket. Pocketing a spare magazine of bullets, he went back to the lobby bar, where he drank a Heineken. It was just a little after three in the afternoon but the bar was already half full, mostly with foreign businessmen meeting with their Mexican counterparts.

No one paid any particular attention to him. He signed for his beer and left the hotel.

"A cab, sir?" the same valet as before asked.

"I'll walk."

Broad swaths of trees lined sections of both sides of the broad avenue, providing some shade. But the day was hot and the air so polluted that the mountains were not visible, nor were the clouds straight overhead. Within a block of the hotel McGarvey was already feeling the effects of the terrible air and the elevation—Mexico City was over seven thousand feet above sea level.

Traffic was extremely heavy, and it took him one light to make it to the big fountain in the center of the roundabout with a dozen other people, and a second before he could get all the way across with several others. Many people stayed in the middle, to sit downwind and enjoy the occasional spray of water that drifted across.

On the Paseo de la Reforma he headed back toward the U.S. embassy, stopping every fifty feet or so to cross through openings in the trees and look into a shop window. Once, he snapped his fingers as if he had forgotten something, and he suddenly turned around and walked back to the last shop he'd stopped at, from where he had a sight line on the street.

An old Mercedes diesel sedan pulled out of traffic and double parked. McGarvey didn't turn around but he could see the reflection in the window of the car and three men inside. It wasn't a taxi but the two passengers sat in the backseat, leaving the driver alone in front.

The light at the corner changed and traffic surged through the intersection. As a bus belching black smoke lumbered past, McGarvey turned and walked away.

The next time he caught a glimpse of the Mercedes the backseat was empty. He crossed in front of several food vendors, and climbed into the backseat of the car before the driver could react.

He pulled out his pistol and pointed it at the man's head. "Drive," he said.

The man hesitated.

"I will kill you."

The driver pulled out into traffic. "You are making a very large mistake, Señor McGarvey."

"So are you. Drop me off at Chapultepec Park then go back for your friends and bring them to me. I have a few questions I'd like to ask."

The entrance to the park was near the U.S. embassy. The driver headed in and McGarvey directed him to pull up just off a path lined with park benches. A lot of people were out and about, some of them jogging or bicycling despite the poor air, others seated on blankets, lovers embracing under a tree. Fifty yards through the trees and down a long sward, people were sitting on blankets along the shore of a small lake.

"I'll be waiting," McGarvey said. Holstering his pistol he got out of the car and went to one of the concrete benches and sat down.

The driver, an older man with a deeply lined dark face, stared at him for a moment or two before he drove off.

It was a little cooler here, but not much, though a slight breeze off the lake helped. A police car, a cop behind the wheel and another riding shotgun, cruised slowly by, but neither of them paid him any attention.

Baranov had spotted him coming out of the hotel, and had hired the three guys in the Mercedes to watch for him. The driver had been older and slightly built, but the impression McGarvey had got of the two in the backseat was of much younger, much larger men.

Several minutes later the car came around a long curve in the distance. McGarvey got up and walked to one of the trees behind the bench and leaned against it so that he was still visible from the road but mostly protected. A simple drive-by shooting would be next to impossible.

Moments later the Mercedes pulled up, with the same two men, one in the backseat, one in the front passenger seat, the windows rolled down so they could take the shot. They were about twenty feet away.

McGarvey pulled out his gun and held it out of sight at his side. "I just want to talk for a couple of minutes, and then you guys can go crawl back into the hole you came out of," he called to them.

The man in the back turned to the driver and apparently said something. Then he and the man in the front seat got out and came over. They were both Hispanic and very large, bursting out of their suit jackets. McGarvey got the impression they might have been rugby players, though he had no idea if the sport was even played in Mexico.

At that moment no one else was in the near vicinity. As they passed the bench, one of them held back while the other one started to pull a pistol.

McGarvey raised his gun and shot the man in the chest, just above his sternum, the shot barely audible beyond ten feet.

The man seemed surprised, one hand rising to the wound, and his other reaching for the edge of the park bench so he could steady himself.

"If you reach for your gun, I will kill you," McGarvey warned the other man.

The wounded man's legs were wobbly. He said something in Spanish.

"Get out of here," McGarvey said. "And take your friend to a doctor before he bleeds out."

"How do I know you won't shoot me too?"

"No reason to, if you don't try to pull out your gun, and if you tell me who sent you."

The first man said something else in Spanish, more urgent now. Blood covered the front of his shirt.

"Luis hired us, and it was nothing personal. Just a job."

"Where do I find Luis?"

"Anteno Español. I think he would very much like to meet you."

McGarvey motioned with his pistol. "Get the fuck out of here."

FIFTY-FIVE

☐

Before returning to his hotel McGarvey stopped at a bar a couple of blocks away, where he ordered another Heineken and went to the pay phone at the rear. The place was nearly three-quarters full, mostly couples, but the noise level wasn't too bad.

He got the number for Aerolíneas Argentinas and booked a business-class flight to Buenos Aires using his Larson identity. He had to give his passport and credit card, but he'd memorized all the numbers from all the documents for his work names. It was another bit of tradecraft drummed into the head of every field officer in training.

The flight left at quarter to twelve this evening, stopping for six hours at Bogotá, Colombia, and didn't get to Buenos Aires until eleven in the morning. But it was perfect. After what he was planning to do later today, he would need to drop out of sight for a few days, maybe longer. Give the opposition the thought that perhaps he'd backed off from the op.

Next he called American Airlines and booked a direct flight to Miami for first thing in the morning, using his Whiteside passport and credit card.

He went back to the front and sat at the end of the long L-shaped bar where he could watch the window and the front door. It was possible that he had been followed here. Despite what had gone down at the park, he didn't think whoever Baranov had hired through a man named Luis at someplace called the Ateno Español were the kind to give up easily. For every operator who got shot up, there would be dozens more ready to take his place.

Guys like them, especially the young ones—many from the police or military special forces—thought that they were invincible. The ones who got themselves taken down were the dumb ones, and deserved to die.

He nursed a second beer and after a half hour, he paid his tab and walked back to his hotel, where he stopped at the bell captain's desk. A sharply uniformed man in his mid to late thirties looked up. His gold name tag read ALBERTO.

"How may I help you, sir?"

"I need some information, but confidentially, do you understand?" McGarvey said. He took out a hundred-dollar bill and handed it to the man. "I need to know about a place called the Ateno Español."

The bellman hesitated for a moment before pocketing the money. "It is a club, but a very bad place, señor. Very dangerous. Even the police don't go there."

"Who does?"

"Criminals. Communists. Whores."

"And?"

"Sometimes a businessman needing a certain type of service."

It was about what McGarvey thought. Mexico City was a wide-open place for lots of endeavors. Murders-for-hire, drugs, information. "Where is it located?"

"On the Avenida Moreles, near the Plaza de la Constitución y Parroquia de San Agustín de las Cuevas. Any cab driver will know it. But they will want to charge you extra. Pay it."

"Thanks," McGarvey said and he started to turn away, but the bellman stopped him.

"Go now, señor. Do not wait until after dark. And when you are finish walk over to the plaza. There will be people there."

Outside he had the doorman hail him a cab, and when it came a told the driver the place, he had to give the man a hundred-dollar b

"I will not wait for you, sir," the driver said.

"No," McGarvey said.

Rush hour was just getting into full swing so it took a full half get down to the south side of the city. Baranov had pushed an going to push back. But the bellman was right: showing up at the dark wasn't such a good idea. Or even waiting for another day v so smart. The muscle who had tried to kill him at the park just ago would be backing off for now. But if the one he'd shot di two would want their revenge. He wasn't going to give them

The club was about what he'd expected, tucked away out of the main stream of traffic. The front door of the place was open, and getting out of the cab McGarvey could hear guitar music coming from inside.

Before he could cross the sidewalk the cab was already around the corner.

A couple of men were at one end of the bar, and a few couples—men with their whores—sat at tables drinking champagne and listening to the guitar player seated up on a small stage. The place stank of stale booze, cigarette and cigar smoke, cheap perfume and something else that smelled like an overflowing toilet.

An older, muscle-bound woman behind the bar came over when he sat down. Her makeup was thick, her hair bright red and her large breasts practically spilled out of a man's white shirt, the first three buttons undone.

"What're you drinkin', sweetheart?"

"A Heineken."

She got one for him from a cooler and smiled. "Glass?"

"This'll do," McGarvey said.

"Would have taken you for a Kentucky bourbon man—that's what most of the Americans who come here drink."

"Has Luis come in yet?"

"Who wants to know?"

"Tell him Kirk McGarvey came down to say thanks."

Her smile died. "For what?"

"He'll know."

She hesitated for just a beat. "I'll leave him the message," she said. She walked down to the other end of the bar and used the phone.

The guitar player ended his set and left the stage. One of the couples at the tables went upstairs, arm in arm.

Luis Alvarez came through a door from the back at the other side of the club's main floor. He spotted McGarvey and walked over. Despite his size he was very light on his feet. McGarvey figured that he had been an athlete at some point in the past. Most likely a boxer. His face was banged up and lumpy, his nose obviously broken more than once.

The woman said something to him as he stepped behind the bar, and he came the rest of the way to where McGarvey was sitting.

"Thank me for what, Señor McGarvey?" he asked, his manner pleasant, his English very good.

"For sending amateurs to kill me. Did the one I shot survive? I hope so, because if he died it would mean that my aim was off."

Luis said nothing for a long second or two. Still, the pleasant expression on his face didn't change. "How did you hear about my place?"

"The one I didn't shoot because he was at least smart enough not to try to pull his gun told me about the club and gave me your name as well. I had to give the cabbie who brought me down here a big tip. He was apparently afraid of your reputation. Apparently, so are the cops."

"Didn't you think that coming here would put you in danger?"

"I don't think you do that kind of work here. This is a place for drinking, and whoring, and making plans for revolution, or drug drops, and hiring murderers. Pretty much all the same sort of business, wouldn't you say?"

"As you say, señor, even the cops don't come here. So if I were to kill you, no one would take any notice."

"But before you could do that I would have taken out my pistol and shot you in the middle of your forehead," McGarvey said. "And believe me, Luis, I am a very good shot."

Luis's control was perfect. He smiled slightly. "Then your business is finished here for the day? Or do you have other insults for me?"

"Not for you. You're just an expediter, a businessman. But the next time you talk to Comrade Baranov, tell him if he wants me dead to come do it himself. If he has the balls for it."

McGarvey finished his beer and started to lay a ten-dollar bill on the bar, but Luis shook his head.

"The beer is on me."

"Thanks," McGarvey said. He got up and, keeping an eye toward Luis, sidled out of the bar and headed up to the plaza.

FIFTY-SIX

□

It was around six in the evening and Trotter still hadn't been able to reach McGarvey, though he did talk to Watson in Mexico City two hours ago, who told him to try the Four Seasons.

He'd tried but the hotel refused to give out any information on its guest. Anyway, Mac would have registered under a work name.

"He came here to talk to a Russian who is of great interest to us. I told him that it was out of the question and ordered him out of the country on the first available flight. The son of a bitch all but laughed in my face, so I took him upstairs to have a chat with the ambassador, who told him the same thing."

"I can just imagine how he reacted to that."

"Right. In the meantime your man showed up at a club on the south side that caters to the Russians and just about every revolutionary, drug runner and gun-for-hire in the city."

"The Ateno Español," Trotter said. "Did he actually come face-to-face with Baranov?"

"He had a beer at the bar and talked with the manager for a couple of minutes, then left. How the hell do you know about the place?"

"I'm on the CESTA del Sur product committee. It's my job to know about it."

"Did you send him down here to interfere in my operation?" Watson demanded. "Because if you did, I'll personally take it up with Mr. Danielle."

"He's on an operation, but not anywhere inside Mexico, and most definitely not Mexico City. His showing up there was not in the game plan."

"Does your op have anything to do with Baranov?"

"Only insofar as Baranov is trying to expand the network into Chile," Trotter said. "Is McGarvey still in the city?"

"I don't know. I had a tail on him, but he ditched them. They said that he didn't even seem to be trying. One minute he was there and the next he was gone. But he'd damned well better be out of the city, if not already, then soon. There was an incident in one of the city parks. A man was apparently wounded in a gun battle. Witnesses said that a man more or less fitting McGarvey's description was the shooter. But by the time the police showed up, the shooter and the victim were gone. All they found was some blood."

"Did they ask for your help?"

"No reason for it," Watson said. "None of the men were identified as American. But if you can contact your man, tell him to get out of here right now."

"I suspect that he got what he came for and is already gone or on his way."

"And what did he come here for, exactly?"

"To get word to Baranov."

After the call Trotter sat at his desk for a full fifteen minutes, trying to work out all of the ramifications of McGarvey's showing up in Mexico City. It was very possible that the shooter in the park was McGarvey defending himself against someone Baranov had sent.

Beyond that he had no earthly idea where Mac had gotten himself off to, but there was no doubt he would show up in Chile sooner or later, and Baranov would come after him to protect his network.

He snugged up his tie, got his jacket and was turning out his office lights when Danielle phoned him.

"I'm glad I got you before you left," Trotter said.

"Just on my way out the door. Do you have something for me?"

"Come up to the director's office; there've been a couple of developments."

It was just Morton and Danielle when Trotter got up to the DCI's seventh-floor office.

"Care for a drink?" the director asked. Neither he nor Danielle was smiling.

"I'll wait till I get home, sir. I have a feeling I'm going to need one by then."

They sat across from each other.

"I got a call from Shirley Hamilton," Morton said. Hamilton was the president's adviser on national security affairs. A Harvard PhD graduate in international affairs, she was about the sharpest person in the White House. "She sat in on the meeting with Ambassador Aguilera."

Trotter held his silence.

"It was good news, not so good news," the DCI said. "The ambassador said that with the death of General Varga the enhanced interrogation techniques used at Valparaíso—his exact words, according to Shirley—would come to an immediate halt."

"*Halt* as in shut down permanently, or *halt* as in for the moment?"

"That part was left unsaid. But the president felt it gave us some wiggle room."

"And the not-so-good news?" Trotter asked.

"Two parts, actually. They know McGarvey's name and knew he had been sent to Chile to assassinate the general."

"How can that be possible?"

"The ambassador didn't say, but one likelihood is a leak somewhere here in the building, or possibly at the Farm. Someone tried to kill him out there."

"The operational need-to-know list is pretty short," Trotter said. "I know all of those people personally. But I agree with you, sir. It's my op, and they're my people, so I'll get on it immediately. But I'm at the head of that list."

"We've checked your bank and credit card statements for the past three years, along with your travel itineraries going back five," Danielle said. "Sorry, but we had to make sure our lead investigator was clean."

Trotter nodded. "I would have done the same thing if I had been in your shoes. But I think you've discovered that I'm an unrepentant clothes horse. Can't help myself."

Danielle grinned. "Everyone in this building who's ever had any contact with you knows that much."

"Your primary job at this point is to find the mole or moles," the DCI said.

"But with a delicate touch," Trotter said. "We may be able either to turn them, or at the very least use them as conduits for disinformation."

"Does any name come to mind?" Danielle asked. "Something that pops out at you, or at least has been a niggling suspicion at the back of your head? Just the slightest of notions that a thing or two haven't added up?"

"Sergeant Carol at the Farm. He was very close to McGarvey. He knew most of the operational details, because he was the chief mission instructor."

"Could his death have been an accident? The detonators they use sometimes can be tricky."

"If it was anyone but Carol, I would have agreed with you. But he was the best. I think the odds that he killed himself making a mistake are miniscule." Trotter shook his head. "No, I think he was murdered."

"Why?"

"Because he was protecting McGarvey."

Danielle was startled. "Someone working for the DINA?"

"That'll be my starting point."

"Any idea where to begin looking?"

"Spanish translators," Trotter said.

"Makes sense, though the DINA's people, at least the ones working here out of their embassy, are fluent in English," Danielle said.

"But you said two bits of not-so-good news. What's the second?"

"McGarvey has to know by now that General Varga is dead and there is no reason for his oparation."

"He doesn't believe the general is dead. He thinks it's an elaborate scam to buy Pinochet some time."

"Time for what?" the DCI asked.

"To negotiate with the Russians for a better deal than they're getting with us."

"That's diplomacy. For now McGarvey needs to be recalled, and that comes from the White House."

"Even if I could reach him, which I think at this point might be impossible, he wouldn't back down. He's still going after Varga, but he's also gunning for Baranov."

"They know he's coming; they have his description," Danielle said.

"Even if he got across the border, every cop, intel officer and soldier in the country would be gunning for him. And that's the bad news."

Trotter nodded. "I'm just now beginning to get a true measure of the man. He won't stop. But I'll do what I can."

FIFTY-SEVEN

Forty-five minutes out of Buenos Aires's Ezeiza International Airport, Mc-Garvey woke from a fitful slumber. Forward in the head he splashed some cold water on his face then in the galley snagged a Heineken from one of the stews and took it back to his aisle seat in the empty row.

He'd done a lot of thinking since Mexico City. Baranov had been expecting him, and he had cracked the Whiteside work name at the Four Seasons. Which wasn't terribly surprising to McGarvey; it only proved what he'd suspected, that the Russian had a source inside Langley. Someone who knew enough about McGarvey's movements, if not his actual work names, to put Baranov on alert.

McGarvey is coming to you, and his usual style is first-class. He has money, and he's not afraid of using it.

A number of people inside the CIA knew those things about him, so narrowing down the identity of the mole or moles would not be easy. In fact, it would be impossible, made so because he had decided against keeping in touch with Trotter.

He'd come to another understanding because of Baranov's contract on him—that General Varga was not dead. Someone, probably Baranov's contact inside the DINA, had arranged for the fake murder-suicide in an effort to have McGarvey recalled until some sort of a diplomatic solution to Washington's problem with Valparaíso could be arranged.

It would be a nifty bit of geopolitics for the Russians, courtesy of Baranov, that could put Moscow on the inside with Pinochet, while handing Washington its marching orders. It would be a paradigm shift in the southern hemisphere, or at least the start of one.

Baranov, because of his contact inside Langley, and therefore the DINA because of the Russian's connection, not only knew that McGarvey was coming to kill the general, but what he looked like.

But they'd failed to take him out in Mexico City, and as long as he didn't phone home, they couldn't know if he'd backed off and gone to ground somewhere, or was on his way to Santiago and then San Antonio. And the longer it took him to get there, the harder it would become for the general to stay out of sight.

After he got through passport control and then customs, he got a cab and asked the driver to take him to a reasonably priced hotel nearby, which turned out to be the Hotel Plaza Central Canning.

It was an odd name but it turned out to be pleasant enough. He checked in under his Larson work name. Once he was upstairs in his small, plainly furnished room with a view of the parking lot, he got his gun and a magazine of ammunition from under the lining in his suitcase.

Downstairs again he had the bellman call him another cab, which he took into the city center, where he had the driver take him on a mini-tour. The streets were as busy with cars and people as downtown Manhattan on a weekday. And except for the cathedrals with their Spanish flair, Buenos Aires could have been a cosmopolitan city in any country.

They worked their way in widening circles from the Río de la Plata to the east, and out to the Avenida Callao to the west and the Congressional Plaza. The driver, whose English was excellent, pointed out all the important landmarks. In under an hour McGarvey had found what he wanted, and had the driver drop him off near the north end of the tree-lined Avenida 9 de Julio.

He walked a few blocks up the Avenida Santa Fe, to the sporting goods store he'd spotted earlier. Using cash he bought a couple of pairs of jeans, two work shirts, a dark zip-up jacket and a pair of ankle-high hiking boots and two pairs of wool socks, a couple changes of underwear, along with a hunting knife and a pair of compact binoculars. He also bought a nylon rucksack into which he stuffed everything.

A block and a half away he went into a drugstore, where he bought some shaving gear, a toothbrush and toothpaste, putting them in the rucksack.

In a liquor store he picked up three bottles of de Jerez brandy, then walked all the way over to the Retiro, which was one of the city's largest barrios, and where the huge Retiro railway station and bus terminals sat just across from the Torre Monumental in the Plaza Fuerza Aérea. This was the major ground transportation hub for the entire city as well as all of Argentina and most of the South American continent.

The district was also home to a lot of high-end stores, shops and restaurants, along with upper-class houses and apartments along tree-lined streets, where Mercedes, Jaguars and even the occasional Ferrari, Bentley and Rolls were parked. By contrast more than twenty thousand illegal immigrants lived in a shantytown called Villa 31, and pickpockets were everywhere around the train and bus terminal, which was crammed with departing and arriving passengers.

In the Terminal de Ómnibus he went into a stall in the men's restroom, where he changed into the clothes he bought at the sporting goods store. Then, following the signs to the second floor for west-bound buses, he found an English-speaking ticket agent and bought a round-trip ticket to Santiago on CATA Internacional, which left every afternoon at five and got to the Chilean capital around noon the next day.

He opted for the cheapest seat with no service—rather than the more expensive Pullman coaches—paying with cash.

Back outside he was practically mobbed by a dozen or more children, some of them probably as young as five. He pulled out a wad of notes and change and tossed the money over his shoulder. The kids scattered long enough for him to get clear before more came to see what was going on.

Earlier he'd spotted what looked to be an older, inexpensive hotel on Avenida Paraguay just a half dozen blocks from the train station. Housed in a ten-story building, the Gran Hotel Orly fronted on the narrow, unpretentious street, which, like just about every other street in the city, was busy with traffic.

It took him less than ten minutes to reach it, but it took nearly twenty for the sour desk clerk to rent him a room without reservations. It was the Argentine attitude.

On the eighth floor the shoebox of a room looked over the street through dirty windows. The bed was made up, but the small bathroom, though not filthy, hadn't been cleaned very well.

He'd used cash, but he didn't think anyone would look for him in a place like this. And tomorrow by five he would have dropped completely out of sight.

Baranov knew that he was probably coming and would have told his contact at the DINA. But they would be watching for him at the airport, not at the bus terminal. And, if the information about the loading dock mock-up at the Farm had been passed to Baranov, or the DINA, they might be expecting him to reach San Antonio by sea.

No one would be expecting him to come to Santiago from Buenos Aires, by bus. And workman's-class at that.

FIFTY-EIGHT

□

Baranov went upstairs to the *referentura* a few minutes before one in the after-noon to call Henry on a secure line. He'd spent a day and a half trying to figure out where McGarvey had gotten himself to, but to this point he'd come up empty-handed.

He was almost certain that the American would turn up in San Anto-nio to make sure that Mati was not dead, and that the funeral was a sham. But he wasn't willing to bet the dacha on it, at least not yet.

Henry answered on the first ring as if he was expecting the call. "Yes."

"I've lost him," Baranov said. "We traced his Whiteside ID to a flight for Miami, but our people didn't actually see him getting on the plane, nor was he spotted getting off in Miami."

"His tradecraft included some pretty good disguises."

"The passport photo wouldn't match."

"It's likely that he's carrying more than one."

"Under the same name?"

"It's been done before. But he hasn't shown up here."

"My bet is that he's on his way to Chile, or he could be there already."

"Aguilera met with the president yesterday. Now, I don't know all the details, only what I heard from a couple of my sources, but apparently Pi-nochet has agreed to shut down operations in Valparaíso. And supposedly McGarvey has been recalled."

"I don't think so," Baranov said.

"You don't think what?"

"Valparaíso won't stop any time soon, and even if McGarvey gets word that he's to back off, I don't think he'll do it. I sent two contractors to take him out; he shot one of them and the other stupid bastard gave him the name of the Ateno. And he actually showed up there and had a little chat with Luis Alvarez. Said that if I wanted him dead to come do it myself."

"He mentioned you by name?"

"Yes."

"When did you hear about it?"

"I was there, in a back room meeting with someone."

"Anyone I would know?"

"No."

"Then why didn't you take McGarvey out right then and there?"

"The authorities don't bother us there, and Luis means to keep it that way. There's never any trouble of any kind in the club. Never."

"I'll see what I can find out on this end. But McGarvey's started to build a legend for himself as a dangerous bastard."

"I thought that this was his first mission."

"His first wet mission, but the body count is already rising. What about those guys you sent after him in Mexico City? Were they any good?"

"Professionals. Former GAFE operators, and from what I was told very good, but overzealous. Their body counts were high, too high, so they were kicked out." GAFE was the Mexican army's Special Forces Airmobile Group. "They were veterans."

"You tipped your hand, my friend. Sending them told McGarvey that the general was still alive. Why else would you have done it? And what about the contractors—will they talk to anyone?"

"Nyet. They're dead."

"Good," Henry said. "What about you? What's next?"

"I'm going back to my compound outside San Antonio to wait for him."

"What will Moscow say?"

"This time I'm not asking permission. But if you hear anything about McGarvey, contact me at the usual number," Baranov said. It was a highly secure forwarding service in Luxembourg. When he was on mission, messages could be left for him at the number. He had to use a special ten-digit alpha-numeric code to retrieve them.

"Good hunting, then. I think that this man, unless dealt with very soon, will become a serious threat to both of us."

. . .

Baranov went downstairs to Petr Yezhov's office. The KGB chief of station was perched on the edge of his secretary's desk. She was young and attractive, as was every secretary he'd ever hired.

"Ah, Vasha, you have the look," he said. They went into his inner office and he closed the door. "I assume it's the thing with the American. He left for Miami and now he's disappeared. Is that about right?"

"My guess is San Antonio."

"You don't think he bought the fiction about General Varga?"

No. I think he's going to show up in Chile and I'm going to be there when he does."

Yezhov frowned. "Have you passed this by control?"

"No, and I won't unless you include it in your daily to Moscow."

"It's become a vendetta, Vasha? For what?"

"The man is an insult to me," Baranov said, and he felt hot just thinking about the American, and about Henry's warning.

"If you win, you'll be a hero. But if you fail, you'll be sent back here with your tail between your legs, and the Russian delegation will be forced to cancel its trip to Santiago."

"Unless you stop me."

Yezhov smiled and waved the suggestion off. "I admire initiative, always have. And I think you have balls down to your knees. No, I won't report our conversation today, because we never had one."

"Thank you. I fly out first thing in the morning."

Yezhov smiled again. "I know," he said. "Good hunting."

Baranov went back to his quarters in the embassy's residential section and packed a small bag with a few personal items—he already had most of what he needed at his place in San Antonio. He also packed his Russian-made Makarov 9mm pistol and a loaded eighteen-round magazine of ammunition in a diplomatic bag. He had personal weapons at his compound, but first he would have to reach it from the airport in Santiago, after a quick chat with Torres.

McGarvey was becoming a serious problem, and he wouldn't put it past the man to show up at the least opportune time and place.

FIFTY-NINE

Trotter was not invited to the private meeting among Morton, Larry Danielle and Dick Beckett, which he found a little odd since he was McGarvey's control officer on the Varga operation. But the Santiago chief of station agreed to have dinner at the Hay-Adams. He was returning to Chile first thing in the morning.

It was just seven when Trotter showed up at the elegant Lafayette Restaurant right behind Beckett, who was being seated. It was a weekday, but the restaurant was more than half filled with well-dressed people including a few congressmen and several upper-level White House staffers from across the street. This was one of the premier power lunch and dinner meeting spots.

The maître d' looked up in disapproval as Trotter walked over instead of waiting to be escorted. "We're together," he said and sat down.

"Nice place, Mr. Trotter," Beckett said. He wore a striped sport coat and a tie that was loose, the top button of his white shirt undone. He looked like he'd been working all day, which he had over in the Directorate of Operations' territory. And to Trotter it seemed as if he'd rather be somewhere less formal.

"Please, it's John. And this is just the sort of place I wanted to meet with you. Everybody here is usually so busy making their own little deals that they never listen to anyone else. Almost as good as one of our safe rooms."

Beckett was dubious. "If you say so."

The waiter came with menus, and Trotter ordered a cognac and Beckett a Budweiser.

"I'm sorry that I couldn't attend your meeting with the director and Larry, but I wanted to have a few words with you before you left. It's about

Valentin Baranov, the head of the Russian CESTA del Sur network. From what I understand he wants to set up shop in Santiago."

Beckett glanced over at the four men seated at the next table, six or seven feet away. "Maybe we should take this back to Langley."

Trotter nodded to one of the men. "Nice seeing you again, Don."

"Discussing secrets, John?" the man asked, smiling.

"Same as you," Trotter said. He turned back to Beckett. "Don Parker is an assistant to the president's national security adviser, and the three men with him are from the Hill. Appropriations. The president is fishing for votes for the new aircraft carrier the navy wants, and the White House would just as soon keep it a secret for now."

"I know how this town works," Beckett said.

Their drinks came.

"Are you gentlemen ready to order?" the waiter asked.

"Give us a few minutes," Trotter said. "We'll signal."

"Very good, sir," the waiter said and left.

"You and Baranov had a meeting, which is quite extraordinary considering all that's happening down there. Apparently he's trying to expand his intelligence network to include Chile."

Beckett pursed his lips. "Frankly I wasn't aware that you were on the list."

"I'm one of the project managers, and until now we've more or less kept to our own shop in Mexico City."

"I'll have to include this conversation in my daily report."

"As will I, Dick. But good heavens, we're all on the same team here. Both of us are keenly interested in keeping CESTA del Sur bottled up in Mexico. But I'm told that you and Baranov discussed the Valparaíso issue. General Varga's work. And that it was possible he knew that an assassin was being sent."

"Are you telling me that it's true?"

"Is it true that Varga and his wife are dead? A murder-suicide, from what the media is reporting?"

Beckett hesitated for a long moment. "No one has seen them, and operations at the stadium have stopped."

"The funeral is for tomorrow?"

Beckett nodded. "Surely to God we're not sending anyone."

"What else did you and Baranov discuss?"

"Two things, actually, and I'll be damned if I know which is the more startling, or even if I should believe anything the man said to me." He glanced again at the four men seated at the next table. They were deep in conversation. "He hinted at economic changes coming in Moscow. Said the people were starting to demand it. Said that sooner or later there'll have to be a decent peace between us."

"There's been talk about Gorbachev making some dramatic move, though what that might be is anyone's guess," Trotter said. "What was the second thing?"

"He said that Varga had to be stopped, but not by an American assassin. He said the situation was delicate for Washington because the U.S. needed to keep Chile stable, and all of South America, for that matter, stable for as long as possible. And that Moscow needed Chile for the reason we suspected—CESTA del Sur."

"No surprise there."

"He said that to keep the peace he'd kill Varga and the wife and make it look like a love triangle gone bad."

Trotter was surprised that Baranov would admit such a thing to the head of CIA operations in Chile. "He said a love triangle. Who's the third person?"

"He didn't say."

"And you didn't ask?"

"I don't much care for pawing through people's dirty laundry."

"Maybe you should have made an exception in this case."

"I know a little something about Baranov. He has a compound not far from the Vargas' outside San Antonio, and it's my guess that he's the third. But what I can't fathom is his relationship with the DINA."

"He met with you, why not their intel people?"

"Because he also met with Pinochet, whose golfing partner is General Varga. And the rumor on the street is that Pinochet has an eye for Varga's wife."

"How about that," Trotter said. "Is it possible that el Presidente is the third?"

"No, we keep close tabs on his movements. The point I'm trying to make is that Baranov's relationship with the DINA is something of a mystery. To me there's more there than Baranov trying to work on setting up his net-work."

"Why?"

"Baranov has never gone to the DINA's headquarters. It's another place we watch around the clock. And he always meets with the same officer, Felipe Torres."

"The agency's number-two man. A tough bastard, from what I read."

"Torres and his wife are also friends with Pinochet. So if Baranov had actually assassinated Varga and his wife, it would put him in an untenable position."

Trotter took a drink of his cognac. "We're apparently back to square one is what you're telling me?"

"As I said, the funeral is tomorrow."

"Then you'll see the bodies."

"Closed caskets," Beckett said. "And we really are at square one. It's why I came up here to speak with the director and my boss."

"Why'd you agree to talk to me?" Trotter asked, although he knew the answer.

"I was told that you'd want to see me, and I was ordered to be open with you. Which I have been. Can you do the same for me?"

"Why not?"

"Were we sending someone to assassinate the general?"

"Yes."

"But it's still not on yet?"

"Frankly I don't know," Trotter said, but before Beckett could object he raised a hand. "We've lost contact with our man."

"Varga and his wife are dead?"

"No one knows that for sure. But it's a safe bet that because of Baranov's relationship with Pinochet and Torres he won't do it. But it's something the White House wanted to happen."

Beckett caught it. "Wanted, as in they changed their mind?"

"Yes, he's been recalled."

"Then do it."

"Easier said than done."

SIXTY

□

McGarvey awoke from a fitful sleep a little after two in the morning. It was pitch-black outside, no signs of any habitation in any direction. The front door of the bus was open and the driver was gone.

From his window near the rear of the bus Mac could make out the driver talking with two men just off the side of the road. It looked as if they were arguing. One of them was holding a Kalashnikov rifle.

The bus, which was about three-quarters full, of mostly working-class people, including two pregnant women, had been noisy and filled with laughter through the late afternoon and into the night, especially after McGarvey had passed around one of the bottles of brandy. But now no one made a sound.

Four American girls in their late teens were huddled in the back, holding each other.

The man in the aisle seat next to McGarvey was wringing his hands. He was old, his sun-weathered face cracked, his hair white, his clothes rough. McGarvey had shared his brandy with the man, whose name was Pedro, who in turn shared his supper of empanadas. The old man's English was fairly good.

"Have we been stopped by the police?" McGarvey asked.

"No, they are highwaymen."

"We're being robbed," the pregnant woman across from them whispered. Like the others she was very frightened. "They sometimes shoot people."

"Where are the police?"

The old man shook his head. "They almost never come this far east from Villa Mercedes. Not east of the new tunnel."

McGarvey had bought a route map at the Retiro and had studied it, especially the instructions for the border crossing, which Pedro had translated for him. The old man was only going as far as Mendoza, but he knew people who had gone all the way to Santiago.

There wasn't much out here, the flatlands of the interior beginning to give way to the foothills that in turn led to the Andes, passing very close to Aconcagua, the highest mountain in South and North America.

"I want to see my sister in Santiago," one of the pregnant women said. Tears streamed down her cheeks. "Now I'll never see her again."

McGarvey checked out the window again. The driver was still arguing with the two men. "You will," he said.

He got up and made his way into the aisle, where he pulled out his Walther, unscrewed the silencer and put it in his jacket pocket. "Tell everyone not to make a sound, no matter what happens."

The woman's eyes were wide, but Pedro nodded. "Go with God, my son," he said.

"Everything's going to be okay," he told the American girls.

They nodded but said nothing.

McGarvey checked out the rear window to make sure other bandits weren't within sight. Seeing no one, he unlatched the door and jumped lightly down to the road. He edged to the corner of the bus and took a quick glance. It was very cold. About fifty feet in front of the bus an old American pickup truck was parked. No traffic moved in either direction.

The one with the rifle was the farthest away, his body blocked by the bus driver's. There was no viable shot, especially not at this distance.

Holding his pistol just behind his right leg, he stepped out into plain sight and started walking toward the three men. "Hey, what the hell is going on out here?" he shouted.

All three of them turned in surprise.

"I said, what's going on? *Qué pasa?*"

The driver stepped back in reflex and one of the gunmen, in the clear now, started to bring his rifle around.

McGarvey raised his pistol and fired three shots, all of them hitting the man center mass. The other bandit was reaching into his jacket pocket, and Mac, still moving forward, shot him in the head. He fell to the pavement just a couple of feet from his partner. Both of them were dead.

"Are you okay?" McGarvey asked the driver.

The man was in his forties and wore a uniform. He was impressed. "They would have killed us all."

McGarvey holstered his pistol. "That's what they told me in the bus."

"You're norteamericano. Are you a policeman?"

"No. Drive their truck back here; we need to get these bodies off the road."

The driver hesitated for just a moment. People, including the American girls and the pregnant women, were at the windows looking out.

"Now, before someone comes."

The driver ran back to the pickup truck, as McGarvey went through the bandits' pockets. But there was nothing to be found except for several spare magazines of ammunition for the rifle, and an American-made Colt .45 pistol with a couple of spare mags. No money, no wallets, but enough bullets to kill everyone on the bus. They were young and very skinny. McGarvey figured them to be in their late teens or early twenties. And they looked like rough trade.

The driver came back with the pickup truck and lowered the tailgate. A couple of passengers came out of the bus and helped lift the bodies into the truck.

"We need to get them off the road, where someone driving by in the morning won't spot them," McGarvey said.

"I've been on this road many times," one of the men said. "There are some trees and a narrow arroyo forty or fifty meters away." He was thin, his face narrow, and he spoke English with a drawl.

"You're American?"

"Houston. I married an Argentine woman, and I teach high school in Mendoza."

"Be as quick as you can," McGarvey said.

The man was gone in a flash, pulling off the road and bumping down the hill. Within a minute or so the pickup's lights disappeared.

"Tell everyone it's over now," McGarvey told the driver.

The man went back inside, and McGarvey, working by the illumination from the headlights, kicked dirt from the roadside to cover the blood.

The truck and the bodies would be discovered sooner or later, and the local cops, if they were sharp, would figure out what traffic passed this way overnight, and notify the customs authorities at the border crossing. But because the two boys were bandits, the cops might take their time about it.

A few minutes later the schoolteacher from Houston came up the hill. "Could take days, maybe even longer for someone to discover the bodies. Give you time to disappear. Out of the country."

McGarvey looked at him.

When the man reached the top step of the bus, he looked back. "But the banditos around here sometimes pay off the cops."

"Thanks, I'll keep that in mind," McGarvey said, and he got into the bus.

All the passengers began applauding, and as he made his way back to his seat, those he passed reached out to touch him, some of them patting him on the back, others his arms, and some of the women kissing the tiny crosses that hung on silver chains around their necks.

Pedro shook his hand and moved over for him. "Thank you," he said.

The driver closed the door and they headed away, people chattering and happy, some of them singing, others praying.

McGarvey passed the other bottle of brandy around to more laughing and cheers. He was their savior.

"You are crossing the border into Chile," the pregnant woman across the aisle said.

"Yes."

"You will not be able to bring your gun across the border," Pedro said.

"I'll hide it somewhere on the bus."

"They search the bus," the woman said. "And in the terminal they have a new X-ray machine. They miss nothing."

"She's right," someone else said.

"But it's okay, señor. I'll take your gun across. They never search a pregnant woman."

SIXTY-ONE

The bus stopped at a combination gas station and restaurant on the out-skirts of Mendoza around four in the morning to refuel and allow the passengers to get off and stretch their legs, and get something to eat. It was eight hours from here to Santiago depending on how much time they were held up at the border crossing. Most of the delays happened during peak traffic hours in the late morning.

The schoolteacher from Houston came back to McGarvey. "I suggest you stay on the bus. The less people who see another gringo the better off you'll be. I'll get you something."

"Thanks," McGarvey said. He hadn't eaten since the empanadas, and there was no telling what the situation would be like once he got to San-tiago. He reached for some money.

"That won't be necessary. My wife and I own this place. Anyway, it's payback time."

A lot of the people had gotten off earlier at Villa Mercedes, San Luis, La Paz and a few other towns. And some others had gotten on. Eight or ten people with their bags came out of the restaurant and queued up to have their tickets stamped by the bus driver, but they had to wait until the bus was fully refueled.

Pedro was gone, and the pregnant woman had slid over to sit next to McGarvey. "Before they come aboard give me your pistol and anything else you need to hide."

"I don't want you to get into trouble."

"All of us were in trouble on the highway. And we'd probably be dead by now except for you."

McGarvey took out his pistol and fast-draw holster from the small of his back under his jacket and handed them, the suppressor and two spare magazines of ammunition to her.

Without hesitation she hiked her dress up over the top of her panties, mostly concealed by her large belly under a camisole, and stuffed the weapon and other items in the waistband.

"I'm sorry, but that can't be comfortable," McGarvey said.

She straightened her dress and smiled. "A lot more comfortable than being shot."

Ten minutes later the passengers came aboard, and the schoolteacher brought McGarvey a bacon and egg sandwich and a couple bottles of Quilmes lager, one of the most popular beers in Argentina.

"Save some of the brandy, if you have any left, or at least one of the beers just before you get to the border crossing. They pretty much expect that every guy on the bus will smell of booze. If you don't, they might get suspicious and wonder who the hell you are. The same as I do."

"Thanks for this, and for your advice, but you don't want to know who I am," McGarvey said.

The teacher smiled and nodded. "Then go with God, and watch your step in Santiago. There's a lot of turmoil going on over there just now."

"I hear you."

Mendoza and the surrounding suburbs and smaller towns had a population approaching one million people. But as the bus rolled through the city there was almost no traffic, and very little to see. To McGarvey it looked like a large modern city in just about any Western country. Tall buildings, broad avenues, a lot of parks and trees.

In a half hour the pregnant woman next to him was sleeping, and they were out of the city and starting to climb up to the Andes, which they had to cross in order to get into Chile.

The newcomers were mostly quiet, half asleep. But many of the passengers from the shooting were keyed up. Every now and then McGarvey caught some of them looking at him, and it made him a little uncomfortable. Not for himself, but for them. Customs at the border crossing where they would have to get out of the bus would be an ordeal. In addition it would be very cold at that altitude.

But there had been no way around taking this journey. He would have been nailed before he ever got clear of the Santiago airport. And it was almost certain that the mock-up of the dock at the Farm would have been reported, which meant they would also be expecting him to come to San Antonio by sea.

Those two avenues would definitely be covered. The bus station might not be.

The pregnant woman woke up just as they were pulling into the parking area for the border crossing. One bus was just leaving the large terminal building, and theirs was allowed inside.

"Everybody must get out now," the driver told them. "Make sure that you have your papers." He looked directly at McGarvey. "Everybody must have their papers and their baggage."

"My name is Maria," the pregnant woman said, getting to her feet with some difficulty. She was young, and not very pretty, except for her smile, which was wide and genuine. It was clear that she was frightened.

"You don't have to do this for me," McGarvey said. It was very dark away from the customs area, and they were deep in the mountains. It would be within the realm of possibility to slip away, and later commandeer a car. He'd trained for more difficult scenarios.

"Yes, I do," she said and followed the others, who were slowly shuffling up the aisle.

McGarvey took a deep draft of the brandy. He waited until a few others had passed, then got up and headed toward the door. He felt naked without his Walther. Without it he was vulnerable. Lost before he even reached Chilean soil.

The people were directed inside to customs, where they stood in three lines in front of a counter where officers, their assistants and bomb-sniffing dogs were waiting. A few bored-looking Argentine soldiers stood by, their sidearms holstered.

When Maria got to the front of the line, one of the officers came around from behind the counter and said something to her. She shook her head, but didn't back off.

He raised his arms out to either side and motioned that he was going to pat her down.

"No," she shouted, and she held out her passport. Her small cardboard suitcase was already being sent through the X-ray machine.

The officer looked over his shoulder at a man in civilian clothes who stood back a ways. The man shrugged.

"No," Maria screeched. She stepped back, spread her legs and lifted her dress all the way up to the bottom of her panties. She shouted something in Spanish.

A couple of other women passengers went to her, and all of them shouted at the customs agent. One of them pulled Maria's dress down, and she shouted something even more loudly at the man.

Some of the other passengers were protesting as well.

Finally the customs officer went back behind the counter. He checked Maria's papers, and when her suitcase came out of the machine, he put it and her passport on the counter and waved her off.

Maria snatched her things and stalked back outside, giving McGarvey a slight smile as she passed.

The passengers who'd been on the bus at the time of the shooting applauded, and the customs officer continued his inspection.

When it was McGarvey's turn, the same customs officer who had dealt with Maria looked at his Larson passport, comparing the photo to McGarvey's face, then sent the backpack through the X-ray machine.

The customs officer who'd stood back was probably a supervisor. When Mac's bag came out of the machine, he brought it over to the counter, and the first officer handed over the passport.

"Señor Larson, all of these items are new," he said. "Are you carrying nothing else?"

"No. I decided on the spur of the moment to take a look at some of the ski areas around Santiago, for later in the year. I have friends in Colorado who are interested in a holiday."

"You flew all the way from Colorado to Buenos Aires and then decided to take a bus to Santiago?"

"I wanted to get a feel for the mountains."

"Why not fly to Mendoza and then take the bus across?"

McGarvey shrugged. "It never occurred to me. I'll do it that way the next time. Or better yet, fly direct to Santiago."

For a longish moment the supervisor looked at McGarvey, then nodded and handed the passport back to the customs officer at the counter.

"In the morning you'll have a very good look at our mountains. They are spectacular. Welcome to Chile."

Bag in hand, McGarvey went back outside to wait with the other passengers until their bus was inspected and brought back out of the big garage.

Maria stood with some other women. He went up to her.

"Are you okay?" he asked.

She smiled. "It was nothing."

But it was something. And what he'd seen nagged at the back of his head. "You're a brave girl," he said.

"That was the tough part," she said. "Everything else from here is downhill. You'll see."

SIXTY-TWO

□

Baranov reached Santiago just before noon aboard a Yak-40D VIP jet that Yezhov had arranged for him. He was the only passenger and the KGB chief of Mexico City Station had warned him that there would be some resistance from Moscow over the expense.

"I understand your hurry, Vasha, but you have to ask yourself, Is it worth risking your career for?" Yezhov had asked before Baranov had left for the airport late yesterday afternoon.

"If we're going to make any real progress, I have to keep expanding the network. Chile is ripe now."

Yezhov dismissed the statement. "Save that for your dailies. It's McGarvey you want. Like I said before, it's become a personal vendetta for some reason."

"My source in Langley warned me that we either deal with McGarvey now, or he'll turn out to be the most dangerous adversary that the service has faced in a very long time."

"You're not convinced that McGarvey bought the lie about General Varga's death?"

"He's disappeared. Apparently even his control officer can't make contact."

"You think that he's on his way to Chile?"

"I'm certain of it."

"Then, like I've also said before, good hunting, Vasha. And I hope in the end that you keep your head firmly attached to your shoulders. They don't ring the bells in Moscow just for dinner."

They'd landed in Quito in the middle of the night to refuel and continued south, the sun tingeing the Andes with red and yellow by the time they were well into Peru's airspace.

He'd slept only in brief snatches because he was keyed up over the operation to stop McGarvey and pave the way for the delegation from Moscow. But also in part because he was beginning to come to the understanding that the American was no ordinary CIA field officer. He was young and brash, but he was showing some skills and abilities that were well beyond an operator so new to the Agency.

And with that understanding, he'd realized in the middle of the night, came a healthy respect and maybe even a little fear.

He'd brought his gun along with the suppressor and three eighteen-round magazines of ammunition in a sealed diplomatic bag. He'd always liked the pistol because it was reliable and was the preferred sidearm of the KGB.

If he got into a shootout with McGarvey—which he sincerely hoped he would—he wanted an old friend in his hand.

After landing they were directed to a hangar across the field from the main terminal that accommodated VIP and special diplomatic flights. A customs agent in uniform and a man in a suit and tie, almost certainly an officer of the DINA, were there to meet the plane when the male flight attendant opened the door and lowered the stairs.

The cockpit door was open, and Major Oleg Dyukov, a veteran MIG pilot, turned in his seat. "Do you require us to wait, Captain?"

"I don't know how long I'll be staying, and Yezhov would have a hemorrhage if I made you wait."

The major chuckled. "We'll refuel and get some sleep. Probably until morning. If you're done by then, leave word at flight ops."

Baranov hefted his overnight bag and the leather diplomatic pouch and headed down the stairs.

"Good hunting, sir," the attendant whispered.

At the bottom Baranov handed over his diplomatic passport to the customs agent, who in turned handed it to the officer.

"Welcome back to Chile, Señor Baranov. But we may have to ask you to wait here until I receive clearance."

"What's the holdup?"

"The funeral for General Varga and his wife. It will begin within the half hour, and there has been some opposition. Demonstrations, even shootings and fires. The city just now is not safe."

"I need to speak to General Torres."

"I'm sorry, sir, but that's not immediately possible. The general is on his way to the reviewing stand with el Presidente and other dignitaries."

"Have operators been stationed at the airport?"

"I don't understand."

Baranov was frustrated. "This is a state emergency, you idiot!" he shouted. "I have to speak with General Torres now, before it's too late."

"Come with me," the officer said, handing Baranov's passport back. He turned and marched into the operations center, which occupied several glassed-in offices on the second floor at the rear of the hangar.

Three men were there, two checking on other incoming VIP flights, and one just hanging up from a telephone call.

The officer grabbed the phone and called someone. "Yanez, this is Carlos; I have the Russian with me. He insists that he speak with General Torres. It's a matter of state. What do you want me to do?"

"Let me talk to him," Baranov said.

The officer relayed the message and handed over the phone.

"Do you know who I am?" Baranov demanded.

"Yes, sir."

"The American assassin coming here to kill General Varga may already be in the city. I need to speak to General Torres to make sure that all arriving flights are being watched."

"But General Varga is already dead, sir."

"That doesn't matter. Right now only catching the American is important because he may have another target. El Presidente."

"Dios mío," the man said. "Give the phone back to Carlos."

Baranov did it.

The conversation didn't last long. The officer slammed down the phone. "Come with me," he said.

Baranov followed him on the run back down on the floor of the hangar to a black Ford Bronco, and they took off, peeling rubber across the back side of the airport toward the rear gate.

"General Torres is being notified of the danger to the president and that we are on our way. He'll radio us as soon as possible. In the meantime I'm to get you downtown to the reviewing stand in front of the Moneda."

Once clear of the airport, on the main highway, traffic, though heavy, moved smoothly, and they made good time.

Baranov was getting the almost overwhelming feeling that McGarvey was very close, maybe even arriving at the main terminal behind them, and that if they didn't hurry he would manage to get into the city and lose himself. At that point the entire operation would devolve on the Vargas' compound that was supposed to be empty.

Torres called on the car's communications radio. "Unit seven, Eagle Two, are you en route with the passenger?"

"Eagle Two, unit seven, about fifteen minutes out."

"Let me talk to him."

Baranov took the mic. "Do you have people at the airport?"

"Of course we do. But what's this about the other possible target?"

"That was just to get your attention. Listen, his control officer may not be able to reach him, and I'm almost certain that he's here already or will be soon. Have you heard anything from your airport units?"

"Nothing yet."

"What about trains or buses? He could be coming from anywhere."

"I've had people on every train and bus coming into the city or to San Antonio for the past two days. And I've had officers on the platforms and in the stations watching for him. Trust me, señor, he will not get into the country unless he knows magic."

SIXTY-THREE

☐

Shifting her body so that what she was doing was kept out of sight from the other passengers, Maria reached under her dress and pulled out McGarvey's holster and pistol, the two mags and the suppressor, and handed them to him.

They were coming down out of the foothills, the city of Santiago laid out below them, the upper peaks of the mountains they'd crossed dusted with snow despite the fact it was late spring.

"That must have been uncomfortable," McGarvey said. "I don't know how I'll ever thank you. Although if I tell my friends that I was saved by a pregnant women, they'll have a laugh."

"We're good for more than just the one thing, you know," she said. Her English was much better than it had been last night. And it had a harder edge.

His pistol was too light. Obviously she had removed the bullets from the mag and the one in the breach sometime during the night, or possibly even outside the bus barn as he was going through customs at the border.

He popped the empty magazine from the pistol and put in a loaded one, pulling a round into the firing chamber.

She started to get up, but he took her arm and held her back.

"How did you know?" she asked after the first shock of fear passed.

"You lifted your dress too high, and it wasn't your belly sticking out; it was padding. You work for the DINA?"

She nodded.

"There'll be armed men waiting at the bus station where you'll point me out?"

"So far as we were told you have done nothing illegal except bring a firearm into the country. At the appropriate moment you will be handed over to your embassy and then deported."

"We?"

"The arrivals hall at the airport is being watched, and we've had agents on every bus and train coming into the country for the past three days."

"What about the bandits on the highway? Were they your people too?"

She looked away, embarrassment on her face. "No, they were for real. And it's possible they would have killed us all."

"Did you know beforehand that I was the one you were watching for?"

"You fit the general description, but I wasn't sure until you killed those guys."

"Is that what they taught you at your academy? Arrest the man who saved your lives?"

She was almost in tears now, real or not. "Nothing will happen to you, except that you'll be kicked out of Chile."

"You know enough English to understand the word bullshit," McGarvey said. "The question now is, How do we get past your people at the bus depot?"

"You won't, trust me. If you run, you'll be shot."

"And I'll shoot back. I just want to get the hell out of Chile in one piece."

"Then give me back your gun, and I'll let them know it's you. You'll be sent home."

"They'll just turn me over to General Varga."

"He's dead. In fact, his funeral is about to start right now."

"Then whoever takes over from him," McGarvey said, letting a note of desperation come into his voice.

She touched his arm, the expression of sadness seemingly real. "I have no anger for you, especially not after last night. I want you to go in peace. Just leave Chile."

"I would if I could."

She thought about it for a moment. "Are you CIA?"

"Yes. Just here to observe."

"Observe what?"

"The funeral. We want to know if there are any riots or protests. General Varga was a very bad man. Because of him a lot of Chileans are dead."

"How do you plan on getting out of the country?"

"A bus to Mendoza and then fly probably back to B.A. Worst comes to worst, I'll try to make it to my embassy."

"But first you have been ordered to witness the funeral," she said. "Nothing more than observe?"

"That's the plan."

"Then why did you bring a gun?"

"If I hadn't, we wouldn't be having this conversation."

The route to the bus terminal in Santiago followed the metro line, passing within a couple of blocks of the Moneda, but the driver had to take a detour because the roads were clogged with people. The crowd seemed to be headed north toward the Presidential Palace and the Plaza de la Constitución.

McGarvey holstered his pistol at the small of his back under his jacket and pocketed the spare mags.

Maria watched him. "I don't want to start a shootout in the middle of the terminal. I don't want innocent people to get hurt."

"Neither do I."

"You came to witness the parade. Does it have to be in person, or can you watch it on television? I can take you to my apartment. I live alone. And tonight I can take you to the Terminal Alameda. No one will be suspecting you to be leaving so soon."

McGarvey decided she was an amateur, sent because her DINA boss thought that McGarvey would more easily spot an experienced officer. "Do the spotters know you by sight?"

"Yes," she said. She got up and went forward to the bus driver and had a few words with him. When she came back, she was excited. "He's going to let us off here."

"The other passengers—especially the new ones who came on at Mendoza—might report it."

She shook her head. "We tend to mind our own business these days. Besides, it's not unusual for people to get off early."

The bus driver pulled over and opened the door. They were just south of the city center, in a neighborhood of tall office and apartment buildings, boutiques, restaurants and outdoor cafés. But there was almost no traffic on the broad avenue or on the sidewalks.

McGarvey went with Maria to the front of the bus. No one said a word, most of them looking out the windows. He was an American who had brought a gun into the country. But he had saved lives.

"*Gracias, señor*," the bus driver said softly. "*Vaya con Dios.*"

They watched the bus drive away, and when it was gone, McGarvey could hear the mélange of voices and shouts of a very large crowd not too far in the distance. A siren came from that general direction, followed by a short volley of gunshots.

"It sounds like it's getting bad," Maria said. "We need to get off the streets; my apartment's not far from here."

"How far are we from the bus terminal?"

Maria shrugged.

"How far?"

"Three blocks. But why?"

"Because that's where we're going."

SIXTY—FOUR

□

Terminal Santiago was a large place, bustling with buses to and from just about every point on the South American continent, and with shuttles and taxis and even a nearby metro station. In Las Condes Plazas, it wasn't far from the Mondea, where the funeral procession would soon be passing, and people on foot were streaming toward it.

A half block away Maria stopped in her tracks. She was frightened. "Are you trying to get yourself killed?" she demanded.

They were on a broad sidewalk, and the people walking or running past paid no attention to them.

"I thought you said that I would be peacefully arrested, no shooting unless I opened fire first?"

"That was coming out of the terminal, not trying to get back in, or trying to sneak up on them."

"How many are there?"

"I don't know."

He grabbed her arm. "It was a setup. I wasn't going to be arrested—they were going to shoot me on sight, and the hell with collateral damage."

"No."

"Then let's go. You can point them out to me."

She shook her head and started to pull away, but he held her close. "How many more like you are in this country?"

"I don't know what you mean."

"Willing to lead someone to their death. But right now I just want to get the hell out of Chile."

"I thought you wanted to observe the funeral. See if there was any vio-lence."

"I heard the gunfire—that's enough," McGarvey said. "But you gave yourself away on the bus after the border. You had my gun; why didn't you just arrest me, or shoot me?"

"The other passengers wouldn't have allowed it. Anyway, those weren't my orders."

"Right," McGarvey said.

"But why did you want to come here? You might be seen." She was worried, because she would have to explain why she'd gotten off the bus early with him. It was written all over her round face. In the light of day she didn't look so much like a peasant.

"To find a cab."

There were dozens waiting to pick up passengers from their buses and several others that had just arrived. The terminal was mobbed.

"My apartment isn't far," Maria said.

McGarvey hustled her over to a cab and ordered the driver to take them to the airport. American Airlines.

Maria relaxed a little. "You're really leaving?" she asked as the driver pulled away.

"No reason for me to be here," McGarvey said. The surveillance officers would be watching the arrivals gates, and not those passengers coming to catch flights. Just as it wasn't so risky for him to show up outside the bus terminal. The DINA officers were watching the buses, not people on the streets.

Maria said nothing further on the ride out to the airport, which was west of the city. Traffic was heavy—cars, trucks, buses and shuttles plus taxis. The spring morning was fresh, the air clear enough to see the Andes behind them in crisp relief.

There was no smog here, like in Mexico City. Almost everything was different, but if Baranov and his Russian masters had their way, everything would start to turn toward the Mexican model, with drugs, crime, spy networks. And he had to wonder if at least some things might get better if they got rid of Pinochet and his regime.

A Boeing 727 was coming in for a landing from the east when the driver dropped them off in front of American Airlines. McGarvey paid the fare and he and Maria went inside. The modern glass and steel terminal was busy with long lines at the ticket counters.

He stepped to one side and for a full two minutes he watched the comings and goings, looking for men in suit coats and ties not standing in any of the lines, obviously not businessmen on their way somewhere, but surveillance officers, with nothing to do other than look for someone.

"What is it?" Maria asked. "Do you already have a ticket?"

"No," McGarvey said. And holding her arm by the elbow he turned and headed to the terminal's main concourse, where they took an escalator up two levels to a skyway bridge across the busy eight-lane arrivals driveway, then back down where signs in Spanish and English directed them to Parking.

"Where are you taking me?"

A lot of people were coming from the parking area to ticketing, while others, having arrived by air, were heading to where they'd left their cars.

"I need to find a car, and you're coming with me."

Maria tried to break free but his grip on her upper arm was too strong.

"You got me past security at the bus depot—how the hell would you explain to your boss why you brought me out here? Are you a traitor?"

She backed down. *"Cabrón!"* she practically spat at him. *Bastard.*

"I'll let you loose as soon as we get clear of the city. You can tell them that I forced you at gunpoint. You fought back but I was too strong."

They had stopped in the middle of the corridor, but except for a few mild glances by passersby, no one paid much attention to them. A couple arguing, nothing unusual.

"I won't hurt you if you cooperate. You have my word. I'm just going to make a run for the border."

"Even if you make it that far, you won't get across."

"That'll be my problem."

She shrugged. "For that alone they'll not hesitate to shoot you."

"My problem, not yours."

"As you wish," she said.

They followed the signs for under-roof parking to the elevators, which they took up to the third level. The floor was not completely full, so they went down to the second, where a sign directed drivers up one level because this floor was at capacity. Any cars coming into the garage would not look for a parking space here.

In five minutes McGarvey found what he was looking for—a car with the parking ticket on the dash showing it had been brought in last night. It was a white BMW 535i four-door, maybe five years old or older, but in reasonable condition.

Two people were loading their luggage into a car several rows away, and McGarvey waited until they left before he picked the lock on the driver's door with his thin-bladed knife.

Maria had backed off a couple of paces.

"I'm not going with you," she said.

No one else was on the floor, but someone could come off the elevator at any moment.

McGarvey pocketed his knife and went to her, but she produced a switchblade from inside her shirt between her breasts, and popped the blade.

"You're not going anywhere either!" she screeched and she attacked him, swinging the knife in an underhand thrust toward his stomach.

McGarvey easily sidestepped the thrust and grabbed her wrist, but not before she had switched hands and swung the blade directly at his throat.

In that instant he knew exactly what would happen next, and he regretted it, though he had no other option.

He grabbed her wrist as he moved the other way. Her body was pulled in toward him, turning slightly to the left, and the arc of her thrust, directed down now, buried the blade to the hilt between the ribs to the left side of her sternum, piercing her heart. She slumped to the floor.

"Goddamnit," he said. It wasn't what he'd wanted. Not this.

He pulled her body out of sight between the BMW and the next car. Finding the trunk release he popped it and, making sure that no one was coming, manhandled her body into the trunk.

There was a fair amount of blood on the front of her dress, but none was flowing now. Before he closed the lid he found a rag and wiped the small amount of blood from the concrete floor and then his hands.

They knew he was coming and they had sent a girl to out him.

Bastards.

□

SIXTY-FIVE

Baranov reached the Russian embassy shortly after three-thirty, where he was stopped by armed security guards at the back service entrance and made to show his credentials. Even then he had to wait until Kaplin personally vetted him.

The COS met him at the rear door. The man's hair was mussed, his eyes bloodshot and he had a deep five o'clock shadow. "All hell has broken loose in the past twenty-four hours," he said on the way upstairs. "I assume Pinochet got back into the palace in one piece."

"There was a riot and some deaths, but this was never about him," Baranov said.

They got off the elevator on the fourth floor. "You told them that the American was coming to assassinate the president! You did! *Pizdec*."

"I needed to get their attention."

"Which you did!"

"McGarvey's actually made it this far, and I had to get Torres to believe me and do something."

"The Americans don't believe Varga is dead—is that what you're telling me?"

"The Americans might, but McGarvey doesn't. I think he'll try to make the hit tonight."

"Impossible," Kaplin said.

"I think that we need to help him actually do it."

They had reached Kaplin's office, and the COS was stopped in his tracks. A lot of functionaries were coming and going and there was a constant buzz of telephones ringing, news broadcasts on radio and television, conversations, typewriters and teletypes. But Baranov had spoken in low tones so that only Kaplin could have heard him.

"We're taking this conversation down the hall."

They went into the *referentura*. Once the door was closed and the anti-surveillance system was switched on, the COS turned on him.

"We're in the middle of what looks like to me a mounting shitstorm, Captain. Would you mind sharing your thoughts with me for a fucking change?"

"McGarvey's better than I thought he was. Varga is a problem for Washington—no one really believes the general is dead. So we let McGarvey kill him, and then capture him after the fact."

"If he's as good as you think he is, might he not make it back to Langley?"

"Then we kill him in Washington. Maybe we take out his wife. And child."

"Christ."

"We'd be killing two birds with one stone. Eliminating Varga, thus keeping Washington happy. And eliminating McGarvey, keeping Santiago and Moscow happy. The point is a delicate one. Varga will be replaced—there is absolutely no doubt of it. Pinochet will keep his purges going while getting rid of his lightning rod, and we will be rid of someone who has the potential of becoming a serious threat to our operations here, but especially in Mexico."

"Do you have any comprehension what you're saying, Captain? Every day you change your mind about McGarvey, and about the situation here. How do you know that you're right this time? Or the last time, or any time?"

"Washington will know all about it as soon as Beckett can send a twixt to Langley about this conversation."

"We've defeated their laser."

"How?"

"It's a state secret."

Baranov hadn't expected Kaplin's change of attitude, though he supposed he should have. The most important game when dealing with Moscow was covering your own ass. At all costs.

"I need to make a phone call," Baranov said.

"I spoke to General Leonov this morning. He said that I was to handle the situation from this point on."

"I'll call him anyway."

"He won't be in."

Baranov picked up the phone at the end of the small conference table and called Henry's contact number. "I'm back in Santiago in the *referentura*." He hung up.

"Who did you call?"

"My Langley contact."

Kaplin was incredulous. "He has this number?"

The phone rang and Baranov picked it up. "Where is McGarvey?" he said.

"We still haven't made contact. He could be anywhere, but I'm betting he's there."

"The op has been canceled. No change?"

"No change. If you find him, kill him. But don't take any chances you might regret."

Something wasn't right. He could hear it in Henry's voice. "Is your position secure?"

"The possibility that we have a leak on campus has reached the seventh floor."

"It has to be a small list. Are you on it?"

"I imagine that I am."

"Then take care, my friend," Baranov said. He had a feeling that it was only a matter of time now before he lost his resource, and that would be too bad. DKHENRY had been a longtime gold seam. The information that he'd provided important enough on which to build a career.

Finding an equal replacement would be nearly impossible. Which left CESTA del Sur and all that was going to happen in Mexico in the next few years. Startling things. World-shattering things.

Kaplin was leaning against the opposite side of the conference table. When Baranov hung up, the COS shook his head. "I want you out of here as soon as possible. You've meddled in my business far too long already. You've made relationships with Torres and with President Pinochet. You've actually met with Beckett. And from what I've been able to piece together you may have gotten yourself into some sort of a twisted relationship with General Varga and his wife."

"Charming couple," Baranov said. "I've fucked them both."

"You sick bastard," Kaplin said. "Get out of here."

"Two more calls, Anatoli, and then I promise I'll be gone from Chile first thing in the morning."

Kaplin was married and had brought his wife and two children with him to this posting. His was the perfect Russian family. "There's no room in the service for people like you."

Baranov had to laugh. "Where were you on the day at School One when the instructor talked about the effectiveness of honey traps? Oldest ploy in the business."

"Fuck you," Kaplin said and he walked out.

Baranov left word at flight ops for Major Dyukov that he would be flying back to Mexico City first thing in the morning after all. Then he got through to Torres at DINA headquarters.

"I'm at the embassy," Baranov said. "Any word yet?"

"He's here as you said he would be. He came on a bus from Mendoza that got in just as the funeral was starting. One of my people was on the bus as a spotter and now both of them are missing."

"Are you sure it's him?"

"We finished interrogating the imbecile of a bus driver about a half hour ago. He said the man got on in Buenos Aires, and on the highway west of Mendoza he shot and killed a pair of heavily armed highwaymen who were about to rob the passengers and most likely kill them. Everyone was so grateful no one wanted to say a word."

"I thought you said you had people watching all the terminals."

"They got off three blocks early. We've checked her apartment but she and McGarvey have vanished."

"He probably killed her and hid her body somewhere. He'll need a way to get out to San Antonio so check with the car rental places, and check for reports of stolen cars."

"There are more than a hundred cars reported missing every day."

"Try the parking lots and garages at the airport and anywhere else in the city where people leave their cars for extended periods," Baranov said. "He's on his way to the Vargas' compound, and I'll tell you what we need to do."

SIXTY-SIX

☐

The main highway southwest from Santiago was modern and divided for the first twenty-five miles. At the town of Talagante it split to the west to San Antonio. From that point the relatively narrow highway was filled with all manner of trucks going to and from the port.

For now the car McGarvey had stolen from the airport was anonymous. But there was a fair amount of police traffic and the anonymity wouldn't last. If his luck ran out, the owner would return at any minute, find his car missing and report it stolen to the police.

Combined with the missing DINA agent, they would put it together and San Antonio would be the bull's-eye.

The afternoon was too flawless for Mac's taste. The sky was a crystal-clear blue with no hints of any clouds. And even when he topped the rise of the hills that led down into the city of eighty thousand, there were only a few clouds low on the horizon out to sea.

Last night there'd been a nearly full moon. Conditions couldn't have been worse.

Munoz had drawn a rough sketch of Baranov's compound above the city, and just four or five kilometers from the Vargas' place. McGarvey had only glanced at it, but he could have made a perfect copy from memory. It was another bit of tradecraft that had been drummed into their heads at the Farm.

You need to speed read upside down, right to left. You need to glance at a row of figures and write them down two days later. You need to take a quick look at a map, or chart, or aerial photograph, or a building's layout, the plan for a town center, and instantly recognize your escape routes. Your memory could be the only thing that saves your life. Trust me, people, perfect it.

Just beyond the suburbs in the hills above the city, McGarvey took a gravel road that led south, paralleling the coast. He checked the rearview mirror for traffic on the highway, watching for someone to pull off behind him; no one came.

Nor was there anything in the sky: no light planes, no helicopters, no military traffic with aerial spotters or cameras on board. In fact, the sky was empty, which was bothersome.

The DINA would have to suspect that he was here. When Maria hadn't shown up at the terminal, the bus driver and passengers would have been questioned. She and McGarvey had gotten off a few blocks before the terminal.

I'm sorry, señor, but he saved our lives last night, and there is nothing illegal about letting someone off early, the driver might have explained. *And the streets were in confusion because of the parade. It would have been easier to let everybody off early.*

How he and the passengers had been treated afterward was anyone's guess, but it was a fair possibility that at least some of them would eventually wind up at the soccer stadium in Valparaíso.

The highwaymen he'd taken out were scum, but people on the bus—all but Maria—were innocent of everything except being grateful for a man with a gun who'd saved their lives in the middle of the night.

Around a sloping curve the road dipped down into a long, narrow ravine, and a mile farther, a long driveway cut off to the left, up and over the next rise and down into the next narrow valley, where he stopped.

Below was Baranov's walled compound just as Munoz had described it. Two hundred feet on a side, spotlights were perched at each corner of the ten-foot-tall stuccoed walls.

McGarvey got out of the car and took the binoculars from his pack. The front gate was open, and the place looked deserted. No car was parked at the house, nor were there any signs of movement at either of the small outbuildings, one of which he took to be the generator shed. It had an air intake vent on one side, a propane tank below it and an exhaust pipe on the roof. The weather flap on the pipe was motionless; the generator wasn't running.

Baranov wasn't in residence, and it appeared as if his house staff were gone as well. It was possible that the Russian was still in Mexico City tending to his network.

McGarvey lowered the binoculars, and listened with all of his senses for something, anything, but the afternoon was quiet. Too quiet.

From the get-go he'd had the option of turning down the assignment, or making a one-eighty whenever it started to go bad for him. But Trotter had shown him General Varga's file, and the two Chilean defectors had made it clear what the man had been doing at Valparaíso. All of Chile feared they could be next.

But he'd never really had the option of backing down. He was in all the way. He'd tried to explain to Katy that it was what he was. *I am what I am. I can't change.*

Or won't? he asked himself.

Back in the car he laid his pistol on the passenger seat and trundled slowly down the uneven rocky driveway. He looked for the chance gleam of reflected sunlight off the lenses of a surveillance officer's binoculars, or from the forward lens of a sniper rifle scope. Someone along the top of the wall.

But there was nothing, and his hackles rose the closer he got.

If they thought it was likely that it was him on the bus today, they might suspect that he would make his way to San Antonio, but they might also suspect that he wouldn't just march blindly into the Vargas' compound and take them out. He would have to first scout the lay of the land. Observe. Plan.

Coming through the open gate into Baranov's compound, he parked in front of the main building. Taking his pistol, he left the car's engine running as he went into the house. Checking corners, sweeping left to right, moving low and fast, he went room to room through the place.

No one was at home: not Baranov, not the staff, not any KGB security people left behind in case the American CIA officer showed up.

It only made sense to him if Baranov had elected to stay in Mexico. Yet everything in his gut told him that the Russian was here.

Holstering his pistol he went outside and drove the car over to the garage. Parked inside was a gray Fiat Regata station wagon. The keys were in the sun visor. He backed it outside, then pulled the BMW in.

For a moment he stood at the trunk lid, feeling an almost overwhelming sense of regret for the girl Maria. *Collateral damage* had almost always been a war term. Dresden, Hiroshima, Nagasaki. The list wasn't endless but it was long.

But this now was up close and personal, and he had the almost pre-scient feeling that shit like this was just the beginning for him.

Transferring his backpack to the Fiat he drove the car back to the east side of the compound, where the sun wouldn't be on it until morning, casting a reflection, then went inside to the kitchen.

Laying his pack on the table, he tried the phone. It had a dial tone. He considered for just a moment calling Trotter, but he decided against it. He didn't want to know whatever orders had been issued in Washington. He was on a mission. Nothing else mattered now.

He found a Dos Equis lager in one of the refrigerators, and he sat down at the table with the beer and his gun-cleaning kit and prepped his weapon and the magazines for tonight's work.

In his head he studied the map of San Antonio and the region all the way down to Pichilemu and up to Valparaíso, and especially the Maipo River and the Arevalo estuary to the north.

Because of the mock-up of the dock at the Farm they might expect him to make his escape via the sea. It was only a small edge, but it was better than nothing.

□

SIXTY-SEVEN

Baranov followed the maître d' to a seat by a window in the restaurant at the newly opened Plaza San Francisco hotel downtown. It was only a few minutes after seven and the dining room was nearly empty, most of the others foreigners, by their appearance, not used to dining much later.

When the waiter came, he ordered a de Jerez, which immediately made him think of the Vargas, especially Karina with her lovely legs and great ass. His mood darkened. He would be leaving Chile in the morning, a failure.

His mission here was to open a dialogue with the DINA to pave the way for expansion of CESTA del Sur. But earlier Torres had made it clear that such a proposal, though not totally out of the question, wouldn't be up for discussion until sometime in the future.

And General Leonov had refused to take his call.

His drink came and he opened the menu but didn't really look at it. He had lost his taste for Chile and things Chilean. Especially arrogant attitudes that were, in his estimation, completely unwarranted.

"Mr. McGarvey is our problem, not yours," Torres had told him just an hour ago after they'd talked for the second time today. "But we will take your suggestions under advisement."

"General Varga needs to be eliminated—we can agree on at least that much. And if McGarvey is here, let him do the work. It will give you the political advantage over Washington. But it's afterward that could be more important. A coup if you kill him, but a gold seam if you capture him alive and question him. Maybe even put him on trial."

"We're not even sure that he's here after all. The descriptions that the passengers and bus driver gave us don't match McGarvey's description," Torres replied.

"They probably don't even match each other's. They're lying to protect him."

"That's a possibility. But the general has been advised what may be coming his way, and he's set a trap."

"His security detail has been notified as well?" Baranov asked.

"All but two of his lieutenants are gone."

Baranov could scarcely believe what he was hearing. It was madness. "Tell me that you have people standing by."

"The two men with him are highly decorated naval officers, with the Rapid Intervention Team. Much the same as your Spetsnaz. And both the general and his wife are excellent marksmen. Four highly trained and well-equipped shooters against one American."

"But he's good."

"Not that good," Torres said.

Baranov had packed a few things from his quarters in the embassy and had them sent out to the airport. He'd considered driving down to his compound and picking up his uniform and a couple of books he'd been reading, but he'd decided that it wasn't worth the trip.

Now he wasn't so sure.

"I'm going back to Mexico City first thing in the morning."

"Yes, I know."

"My place in San Antonio has been shut down, but there are a few things I'd like to get."

"No," Torres said. "I want you to confine yourself to Santiago tonight. Whatever happens in Chile is a Chilean problem, not a Russian one. Is that clear?"

"You're making a mistake."

"We all make them from time to time."

The waiter came back. Baranov ordered another de Jerez, and then a small salad, a steak with fried potatoes, and a bottle of local Malbec. "You choose the label and the vintage. I want the steak rare."

"Very good, sir."

A minute later the waiter brought his second drink and when he was gone, Dick Beckett showed up.

"Mind if I join you, Captain?"

Baranov was irritated but he didn't let it show. He motioned for the CIA's chief of station to have a seat. "You come as a surprise," he said, and he looked toward the entrance to see if any minders were there.

"I'm alone. Just came to say goodbye before you flew out in the morning."

Baranov had to smile. "That was good of you, but I'm beginning to wonder if anyone here knows how to keep a secret."

"Works both ways, comrade."

The waiter returned and Beckett ordered a Budweiser.

"When in Rome?" Baranov said.

"The local beer? Tastes like crap if you ask me. But you were right about one thing: some idiot in Langley actually did concoct a scheme to send an assassin down here to take out Varga."

"The general's dead."

Beckett dismissed it. "No one believes it. He'll surface fairly soon and make a statement that rumors of his passing were greatly exaggerated, but necessary for some reason or another of state. The point is that the operation has been scrubbed."

"It's always bad when politics gets in the way of need, because in the end you'll still have to deal with the issue of the general and his little hobby in Valparaíso."

"Can't say that I'm sorry to see you leave with your tail between your legs, but it has been sporty around here ever since you showed up. Hopefully you've learned your lesson."

"Which lesson would that be?" Baranov asked. He was armed, and he had the almost overwhelming urge to pull out his pistol and shoot the smug bastard right between the eyes.

"Chile is on our side of the pond. It belongs to us, not you."

"You should take a look at the globe in your office. It's a rather nice one. You might notice that my country actually spans eleven time zones in all. We own both sides of both ponds."

Beckett took his time answering, the expression on his face neutral. "Changes are coming, Captain. You and I both know that's it's only a matter of time before your entire stupid system falls apart. Leaving you with what?"

"Ten thousand nuclear-tipped missiles and the means to deliver them."

"We too have an arsenal," Beckett said, getting up. "And the means of deliverance."

The American walked away, leaving Baranov to wonder exactly what he meant by *deliverance*.

Baranov took his time with his dinner, even though he was anxious to be off, not leaving the hotel and retrieving his Mercedes until just before nine. Twenty minutes later he was on the highway to San Antonio, the Makarov in his shoulder holster.

SIXTY-EIGHT

☐

McGarvey was ready a few minutes before eleven. He'd found one of Baranov's uniforms, which he put on. The fit was a little snug, and the shoes weren't even close, but all he needed was an entry.

He stood at the front door, which was slightly ajar, and watched where the driveway disappeared over the low hill about four hundred yards away. There were no headlights passing on the main gravel road, nor were there any lights visible in any direction.

The night was soft, the slight breeze redolent of the sea, the moon still below the horizon until around two in the morning.

Coming here first he'd half hoped to find Baranov in residence. It was a good possibility that the Russian had engineered the attack on him and Katy, and probably ordered the mole to set up the accidents at the Farm.

The mole wasn't Trotter, but it made him sick thinking that Trotter knew the person, probably worked with them every day; maybe they even had drinks and dinner from time to time.

He'd wanted to ask Baranov who it was, and then before he went to the Vargas' he would kill the man. Payback time for the most part because Katy had been put in harm's way.

Settling the uniform cap on his head, the bill pulled down just above his eyes, he went out to the car, laying his pistol within easy reach on the passenger seat, and took off up the hill.

The fact that he was on his way to kill a man had weighed heavily on him since he'd accepted the assignment from Trotter. But during his training at the Farm, and everything that had happened afterward, right up to this moment, he had been able to put the idea of the thing in a back corner of his head. Every now and then it would come out like a shooting star, but then fade to background noise—always there, but in the distance.

Within days after he'd volunteered for black ops, he'd had his first serious psych eval, which had lasted for twelve hours straight. The Company shrink was fascinated and he made no bones about admitting it.

"Guys like you are a rare breed," Dr. Sachs told him. Morris Sachs could have played as a linebacker for the Packers—he had the size—but he was a mild-spoken man, filled with awe at what he called the ever-fascinating business of the human psyche.

At first Mac had been hooked up to a lie detector machine, but he'd been taught at the Farm how to defeat it, which only made Sachs even more interested.

"Neat technique that might fool an ordinary operator. But when I tried to provoke you, talking about your wife, and asking if you'd ever witnessed her having sex with another man, or perhaps a woman, or even an animal, your respiration and pulse actually slowed down. Anything but a normal reaction."

"To answer your question, no," McGarvey had said.

"Apparently there's either no rage inside of you, or else you've buried it deeply, maybe trained yourself to think around it. And yet you want to become an assassin. You want to kill people."

"Not innocent people."

"Just the bad guys?"

"Something like that."

"Or the bad girls? Maybe teenagers?"

That was the only bad moment of that or any of the other evals over the next month or so. "I hadn't thought about it."

"Maybe you should. There're a couple of places in the Middle East where young women are being trained as assassins, some of them even as suicide bombers," Sachs said. "Think about it, Mr. McGarvey. They're coming, and the point may arrive where you'll have to make a decision, kill or be killed."

"I've thought about it."

"And?"

"It's a decision I'll make if and when the time comes."

"Are you sure about that?" the doctor had pressed.

"Yes."

Sachs disconnected the lie detector. "There'll be other psychiatrists who'll try to prove that you're nuts."

McGarvey had laughed. "Is that the technical term?"

"Close enough for government work," Sachs said and they shook hands. "Think long and hard about what you want to do. Because once you're in, it'll be very hard to get back out. You'll develop a lot of enemies, maybe even among your family and friends, because you'll never be able to explain to them what you are. But you'll have to be able to explain it to yourself. And accept it, without nightmares destroying you."

At the door the doctor turned back. "I don't think America should be using people like you. Just like I don't believe in torture or drugs to find out things. But the hell of it is that I can see the need." He shook his head, a sadness coming into his eyes. "God help you, son."

Just below the top of the next rise a couple of miles past Baranov's driveway, McGarvey doused the headlights and stopped.

Holstering his pistol and taking his binoculars he went the last twenty yards to the top of the rise, where he got on his hands and knees.

The Vargas' compound was about three hundred yards down in the valley, the front gate closed. Razor wire topped the tall walls, and even at this distance McGarvey could hear the diesel generator.

He took off the hat and glassed the walls and what he could see of the inside of the compound, including the front and east side of the main house. No lights showed in any of the windows, nor was there any movement in or around the place. To the right what appeared to be a barracks building was also dark as were a couple of other outbuildings.

Except for the spotlights on the walls and the noise of the generator, the place could have been deserted as had Baranov's. Perhaps Varga had been warned, and perhaps a trap had been set below. Like a sap he would drive down there and the fifty soldiers hiding would come out, guns blazing. It would be game over before he even got started.

McGarvey eased back below the crest of the hill before he got up and went to the car.

Everything was against him. Baranov was gone—probably in Mexico City, though there were no guarantees. General Varga knew that he was coming. The DINA had set up a trap with no way out for him.

SIXTY-NINE

□

From the outside of his compound nothing looked as if it had been disturbed, except that the front gate had been left open. Probably by cook and the maintenance man. Baranov hadn't treated them especially badly; nevertheless, he was sure that they resented him because he was a foreigner. They'd left the house open hoping that someone would come up from the city and steal things.

Baranov parked in front of the house and went inside. He stopped short just inside the entry hall. Someone had tracked dirt in from the gravel driveway. He took out his pistol and thumbed off the safety catch, and held his breath to listen for something, anything.

McGarvey had come here looking for him, and maybe he hadn't left yet. But the American would have heard the car.

"Mr. McGarvey, have you come here to kill me or just to talk before you do the general?" Baranov said.

He flattened against the wall and eased to the end of the short corridor where it opened to the expansive living room, beyond which was the lanai and big swimming pool. He swept his pistol left to right. Nothing moved.

"Let's talk, then, about the mole at Langley."

He darted across the room and slowly opened one of the sliding doors to the lanai and stepped outside. He covered the pool area with his pistol, but still nothing moved. The night was silent.

Gliding on the balls of his feet to the left, he came to the sliding glass door into the kitchen. It was open. Again he held up just out of the line of fire.

"I promise not to shoot first."

He smelled the faint but distinct odor of gun oil.

Reaching around the corner with his pistol he took a quick peek inside. A bottle of beer sat on the small table.

The son of a bitch was gone—Baranov was sure of it. But he had sat there drinking a beer as he cleaned his gun. The clever bastard had come this far, but he had stopped here first. For what? A confrontation?

Or something else? Something that would gain him easy entry into the Vargas' compound?

Baranov went back to his bedroom suite, where the closet door was open. His uniform, including the hat, was missing. But his shoes must not have fit, and McGarvey had left them in the middle of the room.

Gun in hand he hurried down the corridor and outside to the garage, where he threw open the door. His Fiat was missing, replaced by a white BMW.

He had to laugh. The bastard had balls. McGarvey came here first, then had dressed in the uniform and had taken the Fiat. But the American had made a mistake, or his intel had been faulty. The Vargas never went to sleep until well after one or two in the morning. It was too early. They'd still be up, and both of them were supposedly good shots. Torres was right; it would be four to one.

But McGarvey was good. Much better than most of them had thought.

He turned around when he was illuminated by two strong flashlights.

"Put down the gun and place your hands together on the back of your neck," someone shouted in English with a Spanish accent.

Baranov hesitated. If McGarvey had reached the Vargas, he would either be dead by now, or the Vargas and the two special lieutenants would be. Either way the outcome would essentially be the same. McGarvey was going to end up an embarrassment to the White House.

"Drop your weapon now, or we will open fire."

Baranov thumbed the safety on, dropped the pistol and put his hands on the back of his neck. "Who the hell are you people, and what are you doing at my home?"

A uniformed soldier, his sidearm holstered on his chest, came into the light and turned Baranov around, then frisked him.

He stepped back and said something in Spanish.

"The question is what are you doing here, Señor Baranov?" someone else asked. "I believe that you were warned to remain in Santiago."

"May I turn around?"

"Yes."

Baranov turned to face the lights. "I'm leaving Chile in the morning. I had some personal belongings I wanted to get."

"Have you had contact with General Varga this evening?"

For just an instant the question made no sense to Baranov, but all at once he understood everything. As el Presidente and Torres had both explained to him, Chile belonged to Chileans, not to Americans and not to Russians. "No," he said.

However it happened, tonight both General Varga and McGarvey would be dead, Varga to end Pinochet's embarrassment to the White House and McGarvey to shift the embarrassment north.

The beauty of it was that the entire scenario had been worked out in advance, probably even before McGarvey had been given the assignment. It was too bad, because Baranov had come to admire the man. The only question left was who had tried to kill him in Washington and again at the Farm? And why? Unless it was merely to test the man's abilities and his resolve. It was something Russians would do, but not Americans—they were too soft. And if Henry were involved, it would mean that he had lied from the beginning.

"What's next, gentlemen? Have you come to arrest me?"

"Go back to Santiago and leave in the morning as you have planned."

"Will I be allowed to return to Chile?"

"I don't know."

"Will I be driven back?"

"No."

"What about my cars?"

"Take whichever one you want."

"I'll take the Mercedes. It belongs to the embassy," Baranov said. "May I take my pistol?"

"No. Leave now, señor."

"As you wish," Baranov said. He had a good idea what was in the trunk of the BMW. And sooner or later someone would figure it out and come looking.

On the way out, he almost regretted McGarvey's death. He wanted to come up against the man, one on one. Be that as it may, his work here was done.

SEVENTY

McGarvey waited a full five minutes to see if he'd been spotted by one of the security people and someone was coming up to investigate. But the night remained quiet, and the only lights were the glow from the valley.

He screwed the suppressor on the Walther's muzzle, then put the cap back on, the bill low, and with the headlights on drove up the hill and turned at the Vargas' driveway.

The uniform would get him through the gate, and possibly as far as the house. With any luck there wouldn't be a trap, and he could get inside. Baranov had partied here, so he was well known to the staff. The ruse only had to work long enough to kill the general and then get back to the car. Two minutes, maybe three, tops.

Varga's wife was the only problem. So far as he knew she'd done nothing wrong other than marrying the Butcher of Valparaíso. If she screamed before he could subdue her, it would be game over.

"Pay attention to details," they'd been taught at the Farm. "And never forget it could be the smallest thing you overlook that could jump up and bite you on the ass. A dog. A child, or worse yet a baby crying. Do your homework."

But there'd been no time at the Farm or in town. He'd been too busy protecting Katy, getting the Plonskis safely away and defending his own life.

Next time, he told himself. If there was a next time.

Thirty feet from the gate a spotlight atop the wall suddenly came on, illuminating the inside of the car. Momentarily blinded, he stopped but did not avert his face.

Moments later the light went out, the gate powered open and he drove inside.

The compound seemed deserted. Nothing moved in any direction. No lights shined from any window in the house or from any of the outbuildings.

He parked directly in front of the house and got out of the car. Holding the pistol out of sight, low and to the right, he walked up to the door, which opened.

A man in jeans and a black T-shirt was there in the dark entry hall. He was bulky but obviously fit, and Mac got the instant impression that he was an athlete. He had a pistol in a shoulder holster and a small walkie-talkie clipped to his belt.

"Captain Baranov, we weren't expecting you, sir," the bodyguard said, but he suddenly realized his mistake and reached for his gun.

McGarvey shot him once in the heart, and he fell back without a sound on the terrazzo floor.

Inside, McGarvey closed the door and stepped over the body.

He breathed through his mouth. At this point he felt no anticipation or fear, only a sort of detachment. He was on mission, and the only direction was forward.

According to the sketch of the house that Munoz had drawn, the master bedroom suite was straight back past the kitchen and to the right of the living room, the layout almost exactly the same as Baranov's place.

Taking off the hat and laying it on the hall table, McGarvey made his way through the house and pulled up just around the corner from the short corridor that led off the living room to the master suite.

The house was deathly still until a woman cried out from the bedroom.

"Mati, Madre de Dios!"

A man said something indistinct.

The door to the bedroom was open and as McGarvey reached it he understood that the general and his wife were in the middle of making love. Or at least it sounded like it.

For a longish moment he hesitated. If he killed the general, he would have to also kill the wife. At this point there was no other way around it. Varga had earned the title of Butcher. Mac had read the reports. The man was a monster and he wouldn't stop.

McGarvey stepped around the corner, and in the dim light coming from outside he could make out the figures of the general and his wife, both naked. She was on her knees, her legs spread, her back to her husband, who was having intercourse with her, his hands on her hips.

"Dios!" she cried out again.

McGarvey stepped closer to the bed and hesitated for just an instant longer. His stomach settled. He raised the Walther and fired one shot at a range of less than ten feet into the back of the general's head.

Varga was dead almost instantly and his body went slack, slumping to the left.

Karina looked over her shoulder. "Vasha?" she whispered. She was stunned.

McGarvey stared at her.

She shoved her husband's body aside and reached for something on the nightstand.

McGarvey shot her once, hitting her in the right shoulder.

She started to cry out, when he fired a second shot, this one catching her in the side of her head just above her right ear. She convulsed once then fell forward, her head on the pillow, still on her knees, her legs spread.

"Goddamnit," McGarvey said.

He walked closer and put another bullet into the general's head, and another in Karina's.

"Never forget the insurance shot," he had been taught. "It might seem cruel, but it's necessary."

At that moment, in Mac's mind, cruel didn't come close.

He turned and went back to the front hall as he changed out magazines. He stepped over the body and opened the door a crack just as someone in jeans and a black T-shirt came around the Fiat in a dead run, a pistol in his right hand, a walkie-talkie in his left.

McGarvey fired three shots in rapid succession at center mass. The bodyguard stumbled, tried to raise his pistol, but then fell forward on his face.

For several long beats McGarvey remained inside the house, waiting for more bodyguards to come on the run, for an alarm to sound. But the night remained quiet, the front gate still open.

He turned back, fired one shot into the bodyguard's head, and outside fired a shot into the back of the second bodyguard's head.

He'd forgotten Baranov's uniform hat in the hall, but maybe it would slow the investigators down if they suspected the Russian had done the assassinations.

He'd done his first official kill, and now it was time to get the hell out of Chile before escape became impossible.

The only real issue now was the probability that this had been an elaborate setup. But not Baranov's doing, or even at the orders of someone in the DINA. Which left Langley, though he could not guess at the purpose.

SEVENTY-ONE

A driver from the embassy took Baranov out to the airport, dropping him off at the VIP terminal without a word just before five in the morning. He carried only a small briefcase with a few papers. Inside, a customs and immigration officer checked his diplomatic passport.

"Do you have anything to declare, Captain Baranov?"

"It's a diplomatic passport."

"Yes, sir, but I am obliged to ask nevertheless."

"Nothing," Baranov said. He would be glad once they'd cleared Chilean airspace. Mexico wasn't home but in his mind it was a hell of a lot more interesting than here.

"Thank you, sir. There is a gentleman waiting for you in the facility manager's office."

No one else was in the place, which had struck Baranov as odd when he walked in, but now he understood why no one was here. It was Torres, making sure he got off without a hitch. The DINA was on a heightened alert status since the disturbances yesterday during the funeral.

The deputy director, in civilian clothes, was perched on the edge of the facility manager's desk. Outside the big windows, the Yak-40D was parked, its forward hatch open, its boarding stairs down. Major Dyukov was doing his walk-around.

"I assume that you are happy to be going," Torres said.

"I don't like leaving unfinished business behind, but yes."

"The Moscow delegation has been rescheduled for next month, and as for your network, we'll just have to see. Perhaps you could send me a précis of the type of material you would be willing to exchange if such an office could be set up here. Of course it would be under the aegis of the DINA."

"I'll be happy to send something for you to look at," Baranov said. "But I was thinking about Mati and his wife."

"They're dead."

Baranov wasn't really surprised after the events of last night, but he nodded. "McGarvey?"

"Yes."

"May I assume that he's either dead or in custody?"

"He will be soon," Torres said with a straight face. "A BMW was reported stolen at the airport yesterday, but it's disappeared. We think that he's trying for the border the same way he came in."

"In the BMW?"

"Yes. Every police officer has been given the description. Trust me, he will not escape. This is Chile. He has no friends here."

"Too bad about Karina. She was a lovely girl."

Torres smirked. "Did she show you her paintings?"

Baranov shrugged. "A lovely girl, but with the one fault. And who among us is without sin?"

"One interesting point. Your uniform hat was found on the hall table at the general's house."

"I must have left it by mistake when I visited last."

Torres pushed away from the desk and shook hands with Baranov. "Do not return until you are sent word."

Baranov went outside to the jet just as Dyukov was finishing his inspection.

"Are we ready to depart?" the major said.

"Looking forward to it," Baranov said, and he meant it. He was very much wanting to get back to a couple of projects in Mexico. His only disappointment was the likelihood that he would never come face-to-face with McGarvey.

SEVENTY-TWO

□

It was a few minutes after 5:00 A.M. when McGarvey pulled over to the side of the road and doused the headlights. He'd seen the lights at the border crossing five miles ago, and he figured at this point he was half that distance away, but around a curve and out of sight from anyone watching.

Outside of Santiago he'd had a bad moment when a pair of army jeeps, their blue lights flashing, came up from behind him at a high rate of speed. All four soldiers in each vehicle glanced at him as they passed, but the officer in the lead car just nodded.

They'd spotted the Russian uniform and assumed he wasn't the man they were looking for, if in fact the Vargas' bodies had already been discovered.

Traffic was very light, mostly trucks out on the highway, delivery vans and other service vehicles.

When he'd reached the foothills, he looked back at the city, but if any massive search was under way there were no signs of it that he could spot.

Leaving the car running, McGarvey got out and changed out of the uniform and back into his own clothes. He tossed the uniform inside, and pulled out his rucksack, which he set down on the side of the road.

There were no guardrails here, and just a few feet off the gravel breakdown lane, the ground fell away into a deep chasm at least five hundred feet to boulders and scrub brush, and farther down to a mountain stream.

The early morning was cold, the moon full, and no traffic moved in either direction.

Back behind the wheel, McGarvey drove the car directly to the edge of the breakdown lane, and put it in park.

He rolled down the window, got out, reached inside and put the car in drive, then stepped back out of the way.

Baranov's Fiat slowly moved forward in idle, until the edge, when it seemed to hesitate, then went over.

Hefting the pack, he headed up the highway toward the border crossing, looking for a spot from where he could make a wide detour around the customs officers and the armed soldiers.

At this altitude the sun came up much earlier than below in the valleys and already the sky to the east was brightening. Twice in forty-five minutes oncoming trucks forced him to slip out of sight over the edge. The first time he'd hung on to a boulder, the side of the mountain dropping almost as far and as steeply as it had when he'd sent the car over.

Near the top, however, a broad section of the mountain had been carved away, leaving a level area, some of which had been paved, a couple hundred yards on a side, for the border-crossing facility.

The entire area was lit as brightly as day. Two buses were inside the customs sheds, the passengers standing around outside under the watchful eyes of the soldiers.

Keeping low at the side of the road McGarvey took out his binoculars and scanned the place. Nothing seemed out of the ordinary. Nothing looked any different than it had when he'd come across from the Argentine side less than twenty-four hours ago. If the Vargas' bodies had been discovered and the alarm raised, it apparently had not spread this far.

And that made absolutely no sense to him. They'd known he was coming. They'd known his target, and yet there'd only been the two bodyguards. By now the DINA had to know something was wrong.

He glassed the perimeter facing him. Rubble had been bulldozed over the paved area, leaving a debris field two hundred feet down into the ravine. No lights illuminated the ravine. No one expected someone to try to make it into Argentina on foot from here.

McGarvey gingerly picked his way down the steep slope into the foot of the valley, then worked his way back up to the bottom of the field of rubble just below the border-crossing post, but far enough away from the highway that it was unlikely anyone would spot him from above.

Farther down the valley, the way he had come, an army helicopter suddenly rose above the horizon. The noise of the rotors slapped against the sides of the cut, echoing and re-echoing.

It disappeared as suddenly as it had appeared, just about where Baranov's car had gone over the edge. He'd been traced this far after all.

Keeping low, and moving as fast as he possibly could over the broken terrain, he made his way to the edge of the rubble field and rounded the corner, the highway and customs facility now to his right. The border itself was in the direct middle of the paved area above. Chile and Argentina had apparently agreed that bulldozing and paving two separate areas was impractical up here.

The helicopter rose up directly to McGarvey's left, less than one hundred feet above and close enough that the rotor wash kicked up dust and sand into his face.

"Stop now!" a voice speaking English said from the chopper.

McGarvey redoubled his efforts. He was less than one hundred yards from the border.

"Stop immediately or we will open fire!"

Someone from above at the facility opened fire with an automatic weapon that sounded like a Kalashnikov. The rounds struck well below him, but the shooter began walking up the slope.

The helicopter made a swooping turn to the left and came back, low and hard into a hover, firing a door gun ten yards ahead of McGarvey and then ten behind.

"Stop now!"

McGarvey ducked under an overhanging boulder and began firing at the chopper's windshield on the left side, one measured shot after the other.

On the fourth shot the chopper veered sharply left again, and McGarvey sprinted toward the east side of the rubble field below the facility, firing shots upward as he ran. No civilians would be there, only Chilean soldiers with orders to kill him.

The helicopter came around again, and McGarvey had nowhere to take cover. He changed to his last magazine, turned and raised his pistol ready to fire, but the chopper hovered where it was, about fifty yards to the west.

He had made it to Argentina.

. . .

The sun was fully up two hours later when a bus pulled off the side of the road and stopped next to McGarvey. He didn't think the Argentines would be helping the Chilean army or the DINA, but he had no way of knowing that for sure.

He reached inside his jacket for his pistol, when the bus's door opened.

"Señor, I am driving to B.A. Would you like to take a ride?" the driver asked. It was the same man from yesterday, making the return trip. He was smiling.

McGarvey nodded. "Don't mind if I do."

SEVENTY-THREE

□

McGarvey flew Pan Am first-class under his own name direct to Miami. He had taken a shower at the bus depot when they'd arrived in B.A., but his rough clothes were dirty and he needed a shave. Nevertheless it was first-class, he carried a diplomatic passport, and he was treated the same as any man dressed in a business suit and tie.

"All the bother back there was about you, wasn't it?" the bus driver had said when they'd made it.

McGarvey nodded. "But I'm surprised that the cops in Santiago let you go."

"Even in Chile they need bus drivers more than they need prisoners."

He had his first decent meal in what seemed like weeks: a good Argentine steak, a salad and a bottle of Dom Pérignon. Afterward he'd managed to get four good hours of sleep, so that finally back in the States, and aboard an American Airlines flight to Dulles, he was feeling reasonably good, at least physically.

Except for the general's wife. She'd grabbed for a pistol on the nightstand, and he'd had no other choice. It was something he kept telling himself, but so far it hadn't stuck, nor had the thought given him any solace.

His mission was a success, the general was dead. But so were two women and his mood was dark.

"I hope you had a good flight, sir," the stewardess said at the door.

"I did, thanks. It's good to be home."

Trotter, dressed impeccably as usual, was waiting for him after passport and customs. He had an odd, almost unreadable expression on his face. "I have a car and driver to take us to Langley."

"I want to go home first."

"They want you debriefed. Everybody, including me, wants to know why you went ahead with it, despite orders to the contrary."

"What orders?"

"When I couldn't reach you, I left orders with Dick that the op had been canceled, that you were to return home immediately."

McGarvey stopped him. "I was out of the system, John. Isn't that what's taught at the Farm? SOP against disinformation?"

"This was different."

"Different how?"

"Goddamnit, Kirk, the order to stand down came from the White House. The president himself."

"I was asked to do a job, and I did it," McGarvey said. "And now I want to go home. I'll come out to the Campus in a day or two."

"Give me your passport," Trotter said when they got outside. A Caddie limo was waiting at the curb.

McGarvey handed his over. "I have others."

"We'll want those too. What about your weapon?"

"I'll keep it for now."

Trotter was frustrated. "You're not listening, Kirk. Good heavens, I'm trying to help out here, even though I've been ordered to keep my distance. I'm not supposed to be here like this."

"Keep your distance why?"

"You've been terminated. You no longer work for the Company in any capacity. They're calling you a rogue. You've gone off the reservation. There's no way to control you."

McGarvey stepped closer. "You gave me a job and I did it."

"Brilliantly," Trotter said. "No one denies it. But it's over, Kirk. You're out." He held out his hand. "Your gun."

McGarvey handed over his rucksack without a word.

"People are fighting for you. You have six months. Lawrence thinks that you can be rehabilitated. And for what it's worth, so do I."

"No."

"No what?"

"Too many loose ends. Who killed Sergeant Major Carol? Who tried to kill me? What haven't I been told, John? Because from where I'm standing it seems like the entire Bible has been held back. And what about Janos's family?"

"They're on their way back from Florida, safe and sound," Trotter said. "But I'm truly sorry about the rest."

"The mole?"

"Exactly."

"And you want me to come back for six months, giving the bastard another chance?" McGarvey said. "Goodbye, John."

He walked off to the queue for the taxis.

Kathleen came to the head of the stairs when he let himself in. "You're finally back," she said, coming down. She was dressed in jeans and a pink T-shirt and no shoes. Her hair was a mess, by her standards, and she hadn't put on makeup, even though it was after one. But she looked fabulous to Mac.

"You are back," he said. "It's over now."

"Yes, it is, Kirk. I can't take this kind of a life. I've had my fill of being worried sick while you jet off on some new adventure, like Don Quixote tilting after windmills." She said it all in a pent-up rush.

"What are you saying?"

"It's come to the point where you'll have to make a choice."

"Where's Liz?"

"Elizabeth!" Kathleen screeched. "She's still at your sister's. I needed to get this settled with you first. Do you understand what I'm saying?"

"No," McGarvey said, though he did.

"It's me and Elizabeth or the CIA. You can't have your job as a spy and still have this family. It's something even your own sister agrees with."

They didn't understand his pain. They didn't know how much he needed just the kind of helping hand that Katy was refusing to give him. And the hell of it was that he couldn't explain it to her—he didn't have the words.

On paper signing up for black ops, and even the training, did nothing to prepare a man for taking the life of another. Not to mention the lives of women. And maybe someday, it had been put to him, the lives of children. Watching the life drain out of a human body, and then taking the insurance shot, was not something that could be explained in any way that didn't sound like insanity.

"Well?" Kathleen demanded.

It was his first kill. Because of it he had lost the three things that meant the most to him: his wife, his daughter and his job.

"I'll get my things," he said.

AUTHOR'S NOTE

I always like hearing from my readers, even from the occasional disgruntled soul who wants to pick a bone with me, or point out a mistake I've made.

You may contact me, McGarvey, Pete, Otto, and the computer Lou at kirkcolloughmcgarvey@gmail.com. But please understand that because I'm extremely busy, quite often I won't be able to get back to you as soon as I'd like. But I will make every effort to answer your queries.

For a complete list of my books and reviews, please visit Barnes & Noble, Amazon, or any other fine bookseller.

If you would like me to do a book signing at your favorite store, something I have absolutely no control over, or if you would like me to attend an event as a guest speaker or panelist, please contact:

Tor/Forge Publicity
175 Fifth Avenue
New York, N.Y. 10010
Email: torpublicity@tor.com

If you wish to discuss contracts, movie or reprint rights, or e-business concerning my writing, contact my literary agent:

Susan Gleason Literary Agency
Email: sgleasonliteraryagent@gmail.com